PRAISE FOR

*The Last Time I Saw Paris*

"American money, Nazi skulduggery, British sangfroid, French passion—in *The Last Time I Saw Paris*, Lynn Sheene delivers more drama, romance and suspense than we've seen since the Paris Occupation in *Casablanca*."

—Katherine Neville, *New York Times* bestselling author of
*The Fire*

"*The Last Time I Saw Paris* is an absorbing, suspenseful and delightful debut. Lynn Sheene has delivered a fantastic romantic thriller, which perfectly balances convincing historical research with page-turning thrills. It is an absolute joy to read."

—David Liss, bestselling author of *The Devil's Company*

"Set against the backdrop of Paris during the Second World War, *The Last Time I Saw Paris* is a breathtaking tale of love, courage, intrigue and betrayal. Beautifully written and heartfelt, it is a thoroughly enjoyable and memorable read."

—Pam Jenoff, bestselling author of *The Kommandant's Girl*

"*The Last Time I Saw Paris* glows with the faded but indomitable beauty of the city herself. Sheene's research is impeccable, her writing lyrical, and in Claire Badeau she has created an unflinching heroine who haunted me long after I regretfully devoured the last page. Sheene is a powerful writer, and I cannot wait to read whatever comes next."

—Rebecca Cantrell, award-winning author of
*A Night of Long Knives*

# The Last Time I Saw Paris

## LYNN SHEENE

BERKLEY BOOKS, NEW YORK

**THE BERKLEY PUBLISHING GROUP**
**Published by the Penguin Group**
**Penguin Group (USA) Inc.**
**375 Hudson Street, New York, New York 10014, USA**
Penguin Group (Canada), 90 Eglinton Avenue East, Suite 700, Toronto, Ontario M4P 2Y3, Canada
(a division of Pearson Penguin Canada Inc.)
Penguin Books Ltd., 80 Strand, London WC2R 0RL, England
Penguin Group Ireland, 25 St. Stephen's Green, Dublin 2, Ireland (a division of Penguin Books Ltd.)
Penguin Group (Australia), 250 Camberwell Road, Camberwell, Victoria 3124, Australia
(a division of Pearson Australia Group Pty. Ltd.)
Penguin Books India Pvt. Ltd., 11 Community Centre, Panchsheel Park, New Delhi—110 017, India
Penguin Group (NZ), 67 Apollo Drive, Rosedale, Auckland 0632, New Zealand
(a division of Pearson New Zealand Ltd.)
Penguin Books (South Africa) (Pty.) Ltd., 24 Sturdee Avenue, Rosebank, Johannesburg 2196,
South Africa

Penguin Books Ltd., Registered Offices: 80 Strand, London WC2R 0RL, England

This is an original publication of The Berkley Publishing Group.

This is a work of fiction. Names, characters, places, and incidents either are the product of the author's imagination or are used fictitiously, and any resemblance to actual persons, living or dead, business establishments, events, or locales is entirely coincidental. The publisher does not have any control over and does not assume any responsibility for author or third-party websites or their content.

Copyright © 2011 by Hawkeye Sheene.
"Readers Guide" copyright © 2011 by Hawkeye Sheene.
Cover photos: Eiffel Tower © Gregor Schuster/Getty. Soldier & Girlfriend © Alfred
Eisenstaedt/Getty. Planes: Mary Evans Picture Library/Alamy.
Cover design by Annette Fiore DeFex.
Text design by Laura K. Corless.

PRINTING HISTORY
Berkley trade paperback edition / May 2011

Library of Congress Cataloging-in-Publication Data

Sheene, Lynn.
   The last time I saw Paris / Lynn Sheene.—Berkley trade pbk. ed.
     p. cm.
   ISBN 978-0-425-24084-7
1. Socialites—Fiction.   2. Americans—France—Paris—Fiction.   3. World War, 1939–1945—
France—Paris—Fiction.   4. World War, 1939–1945—Underground movements—France—
Paris—Fiction.   5. Paris (France)—Fiction.   I. Title.
   PS3619.H45128L37 2011
   813'.6—dc22

                                                                                    2010046281

PRINTED IN THE UNITED STATES OF AMERICA

10   9   8   7   6

*To my husband, Ken*

*To my parents, Jim and Joan*

*In memory of James Alfred Comstock,*
*poet and grandfather (1911–1983)*

# Acknowledgments

Thank you to my wonderful husband, Ken Spalding, for his patience, support and never-failing joie de vivre; to my parents, who passed on their love of books; to my grand-dad, who revealed the lyrical beauty of the perfect word; and to Mohican Laine, a true friend who never doubted. I must especially thank Rochelle Staab, fellow writer and dear friend, who read every word of every draft—I am a better writer for it. I am immensely grateful to my agent, Kevan Lyon, who made it all happen, and Kate Seaver at Berkley for her enthusiasm and guidance.

# Chapter 1

## THE SOCIALITE

Manhattan, New York. May 8, 1940.

Claire Harris Stone breathed in the faint scent of roses from the courtyard garden below as her yielding body swayed to the strains of "In the Mood" drifting out the open French doors. The sounds of the orchestra inside her Manhattan brownstone blended with the late-night rumble of traffic along Fifth Avenue.

Buoyed by the Veuve Clicquot champagne, she felt as though she floated above her partner as their gliding shoes whispered against the balcony floor. He held her tight, his hands warming her body through her thin silk dress. Her arms were draped around his shoulders.

He was tall. That was nice. And he knew how to dance; even better.

"You're dreaming, Claire," von Richter said.

"Of you." Claire opened her eyes.

He was nearing forty, she guessed. Slender, perfect posture, the polished manner of a European aristocrat. Dark hair slicked back, he had the tan of a denizen of ocean liners and Riviera beaches. A light trace of a scar on his chin, he said from a duel. Not what she expected, with all that she'd heard of Hitler's rants about the Aryan race.

"Say something in German," she said.

He spoke against her throat.

"What did you say?"

"I am going to remove—" His hands slid past her hips. "What is this, in English?"

"My stockings?"

"Stockings." He tasted the word. "I am going to remove your stockings with my teeth."

"But what would Russell say if you ripped them?"

"He can afford another pair."

"Mmm." She breathed into his shoulder, wishing for another drink. "Tell me about Berlin." Anywhere but here, she thought.

"Berlin has its charms. Merkel longs to return. But Paris, that is the place. The clubs . . . Josephine Baker dancing, the Moulin Rouge, Pigalle, the women . . . Well, I won't say what they do. Only the French take the pleasure of a woman's body so seriously."

Claire felt his fingers slide closer to her thigh. At least this one was a charmer. She rarely was so lucky with Russell's clients. She flirted and tempted, and then her husband came in for the business kill.

With one sure hand, von Richter guided her across the floor to the rhythm of the music. The other hand discreetly explored her, gliding across exposed skin from the nape of her neck to the leg revealed by the side slit in her gown.

"When is your husband going to join us?" He gestured

toward the doors with his head. "Poor Merkel grows tired and impatient inside."

She composed a pout and threaded gloved fingers through his hair. "You're not having a good time?"

"I would prefer your husband never return, lovely. You are a sublime hostess, entertaining your guests until he arrives."

"Yes, I am." She pulled free, leisurely swatted at the hand reaching for the curve of her behind. She blew him a kiss. "I am going to check my stockings. Sharpen those teeth."

As she stepped inside, Claire squinted at the glare from the glittering chandeliers. The thirty-two-piece orchestra dueled against chattering voices and clinking crystal. Men in tuxedoes and women in sparkling gowns chatted in clusters across the ballroom floor.

Arranging a polished smile, Claire advanced from the shadows. With an imperceptible flick of her hips, the glittering cream folds of her dress swept around her legs like a curtain of stars poured onto the white marble. All eyes in the room swiveled toward her. A sharp voice cut through the din.

"Claire, darling! You're missing your own party. Where have you been?" Surviving exclusively on cigarettes and gossip, Margo Townsend's rail-thin body was adorned in couture and dripping with jewels. She planted a dramatic kiss on Claire's cheek, then leaned in to whisper. "Did you see Flora Foster? She brought a photographer with her. Drop Hitler a thank-you card for this one. Everyone is in Manhattan tonight."

Margo was right. With Germany's invasion of Poland last fall, State Department travel restrictions meant that only diplomats and journalists could travel to Europe. Everyone was in town this spring—and at the Stone mansion tonight. Claire scanned the room for Foster, the matriarch of the *New York*

*Times* society pages. She'd written up Claire in her column a number of times in the past year, but a photo spread was a significant accomplishment. Russell ought to be pleased that his wife was the toast of Manhattan. Whenever the bastard showed.

A white-coated server glided by with drinks on a silver tray. Claire downed a glass of champagne and pressed through the dancing couples, smiling, kissing and maneuvering her way across the floor.

Flora was holding court in the corner, a lean brunette surrounded by admiring socialites gunning for a mention in the coveted first paragraph. "Ah, there's our hostess." Flora stabbed a long cigarette toward Claire's necklace. "That piece is devastating! Cartier?"

Claire stroked the jewels with the tip of her finger. She loved their feel against her skin. Intricate spiderwebs of diamonds spun toward a glittering pendant that hung between her breasts. In the center, an enormous faceted diamond reflected dancing lights.

"What was the occasion for that sparkler, darling? Spill for our readers."

The necklace had been a present from Russell for her twenty-ninth birthday this spring. A reward, and damn well earned, for her social climbing on his behalf.

"Kiss and tell? Never," Claire said to twitters of laughter.

A gloved hand tapped her elbow. Her butler, Davis, caught her eyes, his lips pressed into a thin line. Irritation flashed through her. Had her ass of a husband finally called? She forced a smile, excused herself, and followed Davis into the hall.

"Did Mr. Stone telephone? How late is he going to be?" Claire didn't know what she was going to do about von Richter if Russell didn't show soon.

"No, Mrs. Stone. There is someone at the servants' entrance."

"Let him in."

"He's not invited, Mrs. Stone."

"Well, have him tossed out, then."

"I don't know if that would be a good idea." Davis leaned in, his voice dropping to a low murmur. "He purports to know you. Know you well."

Her mind churned at all the possible ghosts outside that door. "Are you the only one he's spoken to?"

Davis nodded.

"Keep it that way," she said.

Claire stepped outside the kitchen door, Davis at her shoulder. A large dark figure stumbled up, smelling of bad whiskey and sweat. Broad shoulders strained at the tattered fabric of his jacket, spotted with food and drink and road.

Her own personal nightmare, in the flesh. The champagne fuzz in her head burned away. She forced the words past the dread gripping her throat. "Davis, please go inside and attend to our guests."

He frowned, his gaze on the man.

"Now, Davis."

"Yes, Mrs. Stone. Ring the bell should you require anything." He pulled the door shut behind him.

The visitor's sour mouth turned down as he examined Claire. "My, my Clara May. Don't you look fancy."

"Bernard. What do you want?"

"I saw you in the paper, read about your fancy sham pedigree and your rich husband." He sneered at her thin dress, the creamy skin that glimmered in the moonlight. "I got a little something for you."

Her jaw clenched. She'd had plenty from him and his sweaty obsessions years ago. She reached for the door.

"It's a letter from your family. Your real family."

Claire crossed her arms in front of her. It wasn't possible. Not after eleven years.

Bernard pulled out a tattered envelope and flashed rotted teeth in a caricature of the smile he plied on her father's doorstep years ago. "I've carried it a long way. Maybe you could spare a little something for my effort?"

She examined him. A bum, but there were vultures inside who would pick his story apart. And a goddamn reporter and photographer. "Fine. I'll be right back. Don't speak to anyone." She turned toward the door.

He grabbed her arm. "I don't believe you, Clara May. You have a habit of leaving me behind. I remember where you keep your money." His gaze fell to her breasts.

Claire yanked her arm free. The bastard was right. Old insecurities died hard. She fished out the folded bills tucked in her cleavage. Bernard snatched the money, his face greedy. Claire slipped the letter inside her dress.

He leered at her and rubbed a dirty hand against his crotch. "I still got my Studebaker. I'll give you a ride anywhere you like."

"Get out."

He crowded her against the door, his bulk blocking out the night. The stench nearly overwhelmed her. "That's a pretty necklace you got. You wouldn't want anyone in there to find out what you really are, Clara May Wagner. I might just go tell them where you come from."

A latch clicked behind them.

Russell Stone towered in the doorway, cigar clenched in his mouth. Going on fifty, his powerful physical presence made him look younger. His silk tuxedo didn't disguise the hardness won from the street. "Who's this, Claire?" Russell's eyes were on Bernard.

"You the husband? I got something to tell you about this one."

Russell took a deep pull on his cigar as he stepped between them. In one movement, he flicked the cigar into the darkness and swung a meaty fist at Bernard's jaw. The man crumpled onto the sidewalk, blood pouring from his face. With the toe of a polished shoe, Russell flicked him off the bricks and into the grass.

A gasp came from the doorway where Davis stood wide-eyed.

"Clean up this mess, Davis." Russell reached for Claire.

His grip dug into her arm as he led her toward the party. She struggled to build a lie. A friend of her eccentric uncle's. A charity case. A crazy drunk.

"Take the Germans to my study. I want them softened, understand? I'll give you an hour." He straightened her necklace and prodded the diamond pendant with a thick finger; the force pushed Claire back a step. "Take better care of that."

Claire hid a wince as he jerked her through the doorway.

Flora met them just inside the ballroom. "Oh, how wonderful. Mr. Stone has arrived. We must have a photo of the darling couple." A smile and a flash.

Russell's hand enveloped Flora's thin fingers in greeting. "Mrs. Foster, we are so pleased you joined our little soiree tonight, hosted by my talented and beautiful wife."

Claire offered her cheek for a perfunctory kiss from the adoring husband.

As Flora walked away, Russell faced Claire. He stroked her lips with skinned knuckles. "That grifter called you Clara May

Wagner. Funny you responded, isn't it, Claire Harris? Or maybe I should call you Clara too?" His hand moved down her arm, stopping to dig a thumbnail into the soft skin inside her elbow. She flinched. "Maybe you need to join him in the gutter, huh?"

Her throat constricted as she watched him stride into the crowd at the center of the ballroom. Russell didn't tolerate disloyalty from any of his crew. Not at all. She picked a glass from the silver tray of a passing waiter and took a long drink, allowing the cold bubbles to wash the knot down her throat. His dealings with the Germans would take a few hours. She'd find a way to cover this up. She had to.

Von Richter and his business partner, Heimler Merkel, stood together near the fireplace, heads bent together in conversation. If von Richter was the playboy, Merkel was the accountant. A grey little man in his sixties, silently noting every gay laugh, kiss and toast. Claire imagined a tally sheet in his breast pocket. *Bottles of champagne, twenty four.*

A partygoer in a tuxedo wobbled over to the fireplace to face von Richter. Holding himself up with an arm slung across the mantel, he swung an empty glass in his free hand.

Claire cringed as she overheard the man mutter *Nazis*. She straightened the seams of her Schiaparelli gown, traced fingers over her necklace and sauntered toward them.

His voice dropped to a piercing whisper. "They say they're going to invade France or England next."

Claire slid in next to von Richter, hooked her arm in his. "Alby, darling, are you going to attack those Parisian clubs you were telling me about?"

The thin scar on his chin curled as he smirked and slid his

hand out of view down her backside. "I already have, *Fraulein*, many times."

"Russell sends his regrets for his tardiness. He'll meet you in his study shortly. May I pull you gentlemen away from our festivities?"


The dim light of the study revealed heavy chairs gathered around a fireplace and leather-bound books in mahogany shelves from ceiling to floor. Russell's immense desk faced the door.

"Your husband must be quite a scholar," von Richter said as Claire shut the door behind them, bottle of scotch and three glasses in her hand.

"So it seems." Claire waved Merkel and von Richter into chairs as she poured. She sat on the arm of von Richter's chair, curving against his side. "Alby, darling, tell me about Paris."


The bottle was empty and the last revelers were being poured into waiting cars when Russell materialized. Von Richter clumsily disentangled Claire from his lap. Merkel swayed as he stood. Russell appeared not to notice and apologized for the delay. Claire bid the men good night and blew von Richter a kiss as she closed the door behind her. With that performance, those Germans should buy Russell's steel at top dollar. Not that the success would pay for Russell's mercy. But it would give her more time.


The upper floor was quiet; gold-leaf sconces radiated ovals of light through the hallway. Claire shut her bedroom door and slumped onto a velvet stool facing her mirrored vanity. She frowned at her pale reflection and smoothed the dark honey curl over her right brow. A fresh coat of lipstick was drawn over her full lips and mascara combed onto thick lashes, but her deep blue eyes were hard as images careened through her mind.

She was sixteen when she met Bernard R. Morris. That was how he introduced himself as he stood on her porch in a pressed shirt and tie, his hair slicked back with pomade. She stepped out to get a better look; no one had come to their Oklahoma farm in so long.

Clara May, as she was called then, had been up for days, soothing Mama's gaunt face with a wet cloth, washing her wasted body, cooking anything she could scrounge up into a broth in hopes Mama would eat. Clara begged her to accept even a sip of water, but her mother's cracked mouth stayed closed. *Tired, so tired,* was all Mama would say. Tired of living, Clara thought she meant, or what passed for living on that dried-up land. And so Mama starved and withered in Clara's weary arms while Pa and her brothers worked the farm, only coming inside at night to sleep and be fed.

Seeing another soul that morning made Clara come alive. Bernard was clean-shaven with a thin moustache and smelled like warm wood. He looked her up and down and stepped close. Selling Bibles all the way from New York City.

Three days later the musty scent of death settled over the dusty farmhouse, and Mama's rough-hewn casket was laid out across the worn table in the middle of the room. Her brothers, Hank and Willy, stood heads down, their meaty hands folded in front of them. Pa seethed silently behind Clara's shoulder. To him, Mama's death was a personal insult, just like the drought. Clara stepped forward and fingered the jagged edge of the coffin rim, breathing in the sharp tang of freshly cut pine.

She felt Pa's hard gaze digging into her back. "If you can't stand here like a proper daughter and honor your Ma, Clara May, you get back in that kitchen."

There was no need for Clara to look inside the casket. She'd dressed Mama in that sky-blue dress she favored, combed her thin hair into a bun, tucked a faded yellow flower into her top buttonhole. Though Clara felt a piece had been torn from inside her, from her aching stomach to her burning eyes, she knew there wasn't even any need to cry. Her mother wasn't really in there anymore. Mama had escaped Pa's temper and the farm the only way she could.

A burst of heat burned away the pain in Clara's heart. There *had* to be more to look forward to than dying. She needed more.

It had only been two long steps to the screen door. Three short miles to town and Mrs. Johnson's boardinghouse, where that handsome Bible salesman was loading up to head back to New York City. Clara left town that night in the front seat of a Studebaker with Bernard's hand on her knee.

The sting of the long-buried pain pulled Claire back to the present. She took a deep breath and fished inside her gown for the letter. Thick fingers had painstakingly printed *Clara May Wagner, New York City.*

Claire could recognize Willy's heavy-handed print anywhere. She had worked on it with him, their heads bent close over a flickering candle the winter after he quit school to help Pa. She felt a familiar pang as she remembered the soft smile lighting his sweet eyes when she'd praised his careful lettering in front of Mama. But by the following winter, when he had time to practice again, he had given up the idea of learning.

She carefully smoothed the letter open against the vanity's lacquered surface.

*Dear Clara May,*

*I hope this letter finds you well in New York City. Bernard Morris is back in town today. He says you are rich now. He has seen you in the newspaper and will pass this letter to you.*

*Pa died last winter. The drought here got real bad. Worse every year. Finally, last summer we lost the farm. There wasn't much left of it, anyway. We live in town now, next to Mr. Nelson. I drive a truck for Morris. Hank works in the slaughterhouse. We don't need anything. I just wanted to let you know about things. I hope New York City is as pretty as you wanted.*

*Willy*

Claire stared into the mirror's reflection, the letter gripped in numb hands.

Gone. The past she had worked so hard to escape had disintegrated on its own. She couldn't scrape together any sympathy for Pa. Any strained bond they might have shared died long ago with Mama. The farm—well, it was just a dirt hellhole that swallowed up lives. Maybe Willy and Hank could have a life now. She'd send money to help.

*I hope New York City is as pretty as you wanted.* Claire examined the room surrounding her. The glitter of the Venetian chandelier reflected off the white Italian marble floors and lacquered furniture. The best money could buy, a room of her own, designed for a woman of her standing. But also a crypt, a mausoleum filled with finery. As cold and empty as her insides.

Heavy footsteps lumbered down the hall. Claire listened, breath held. A high-pitched giggle, the steps continued, a door opened and closed. Air drained from her chest. Russell had once again found himself one of the serving girls they'd hired for the night. Good. A few hours reprieve, then.

*Clara May Wagner.* Still, with his connections, Russell would uncover everything tomorrow. The blue-blooded wife he'd married to claim a glimmer of respectability was a fraud. A destitute farmer's daughter.

Bernard received just the tip of Russell's anger. Claire had made a fool out of him for the past five years. He wouldn't let her stay, not now. But his reputation was on the line. He couldn't afford to drag her through the mud; he'd be exposed too.

He'd make her disappear.

She fought to breathe. The walls were cracking around her. Claire Harris Stone was exposed. Lost.

Her eyes focused on a black-and-white photo tucked in the corner of the mirror. A quiet garden scene, artfully captured, no larger than a snapshot. A gift from Laurent during their final afternoon together, months ago. Before her lover returned to Paris. Alone.

The beating of her heart sparked a warmth in her chest that spread through her body. She pulled the photo from the frame, caressed the crisp paper with her fingers.

Lost, or could this mean free?

The word fluttered inside her. She glided to the painting hanging next to her bed. In a massive portrait, nearly life-size,

Russell leaned against a fireplace, a bulky elbow resting on a stone mantelpiece.

Claire smirked up at his glaring face. "Have you enjoyed guarding your wife's bed and her so very valuable jewels, Russell darling?"

She tugged on the right edge of the carved frame. The painting swung away from the wall, revealing a locked safe. The walls might be cracking, but she was going to kick them down.

A single phone call, a flurry of packing, and Claire slipped downstairs. Emptied of guests and staff hired for the night, the house was dark and still. She crept into the shadowed kitchen, padding toward the door.

"Mrs. Stone."

The voice stopped her in her tracks. Davis leaned against the counter, a glass of scotch in his hand. He took in the red traveling suit, hat and sable, the hatbox and leather-bound train case clenched in her hands.

"Best of luck to you, Claire."

Claire grinned and let out a breath. "Thank you. Same to you, Davis."

LaGuardia Airport Marine Terminal,
New York. May 9, 1940.

Sunrise gilded the East River as Claire descended from the airport terminal onto the metal gangway. The docked Yankee Clipper floated like an immense metal seabird at the end of the passage below. Bullet-shaped engines rumbled from beneath the massive wingspan. Whirling propellers buffeted the line of passengers advancing into the airship's belly. Claire welcomed the cool bite of the prop's wash against her face.

A young officer stepped up to her side, his white Clipper uniform glinting in the morning light. "She's something to see, isn't she?" He meant the Clipper, but his eyes were on Claire and her suit, cut to show an hourglass figure.

She offered him a smile but her thoughts focused on the throbbing in her chest. It had been so long since she felt this mix of freedom and—no, not regret. Never that. Today the scents were a cocktail of gasoline and the river's briny flotsam. Not choking dust or death's cloying musk.

"Ready to fly over the ocean?" Pride resonated in his voice.

She made a last searching look back at the early morning crowd inside the round terminal building. Russell didn't know she'd gone. Not yet. Her smile brightened as she slipped her arm through the officer's and adjusted the sable that threatened to blow off her shoulders. "You have no idea how ready I am, flyboy."

"Yes, ma'am." A blush darkened his tan as he reached for the hatbox at her feet.

Claire gripped the silver handle of her train case and sauntered down the gangway. Her gloved hand slid along the Clipper's cool metal hide. Inside, she chose an empty seat next to the window and set her case on the floor beneath her feet. A breathy kiss brushed the officer's cheek as she retrieved her hatbox and then settled into silk cushions.

The plane was occupied mostly with State Department types. Dark wool suits, long coats, briefcases tucked discreetly beneath their seats. Except for a few military officers in dress uniforms, they were a sea of charcoal. She could feel their stares as she shrugged off her sable. She was used to the looks, but today, the only woman on board, it felt like a bull's-eye was painted on her back.

She adjusted her hat and smoothed the skirt against her legs. Andrew, darling Andrew, shook his head this morning when he met her in front of the marine terminal with her papers, but the red Schiaparelli suit was the most conservative thing she owned.

As close to a friend as she'd met in New York, Andrew and Claire made good sport of the city's nightlife the first year after she left Bernard. She taught the buttoned-up college boy the finer points of speakeasies. He spoke five languages and taught her one. Upper-crust American English. When she phoned him last night after seven years, he refused to help at first. *The risk is too great,* he told her. *The risk to you, you mean,* she replied. Then she wondered aloud what the State Department's Chief of Protocol ambassador would say to the kinks his son-in-law enjoyed in bed. The ones his wife didn't have the stomach for. The phone line went quiet for a moment then Andrew came up with a plan.

He met her at sunrise and handed her a thick envelope. *Your ticket, a passport validated for Europe by the State Department, and Portuguese and French tourist visas,* he said, *made out to Claire Harris. But, you realize that after you land in Lisbon, you are on your own. This is not an official operation. These are only papers with stamps. If something goes wrong, not only have I never heard of you, Claire, no one else will have either.*

The roar of the engine and churning propellers filled the compartment as the plane skimmed across the water's surface, then, with a lurch, took to the sky. Claire pressed back in her seat as she watched the airport then the skyline drop away. The last time she'd run, the very day Mama died, there had been a broken-down farmhouse behind her. She swore she'd never end up like that, worn down with nothing left but despair. Staring

down at the Atlantic, Claire could still feel the packed dirt road
beneath her bare feet.

The plane straightened out and the noise dimmed to a roar.
Claire pulled the diamond wedding ring off her finger and
squeezed it in her palm. The bite of the stone against her skin
didn't diminish the ache growing in her diaphragm.

It wasn't the end of her marriage that hurt, she realized, but
the waste of effort, of years. She slipped the band on the ring
finger of her right hand and smiled grimly. It was the first diamond she'd been given as Claire Harris Stone. Too conventional
for her taste and not the biggest rock, by far, but damn well
paid for. Her marriage, after all, had always been one of conve-
nience. Convenient for him to own a pretty, high-society wife he
could cheat on; convenient for her to have the wealth and position she needed. She breathed in and welcomed the throbbing in
her chest. It meant she was still alive. It meant another chance.

She flipped open her new passport. A blurry photograph of
a dark blonde, eyes shadowed, expression formal, passable for
Claire caught on a rough morning. The adjacent page was filled
with official looking stamps permitting travel to Europe. She
looked out the window as the plane shifted its flight. Twenty-six
hours to Lisbon. There she would drop off the end of the world.
A train to Paris. Then Laurent and a new life.

She'd met Laurent Olivier last summer at a gallery in Manhattan. Half-drunk and bored as hell, she was wasting the afternoon
with a friend looking at photos of Paris: Old men with gnarled
faces leaned against worn brick buildings in narrow streets.
Children smoked cigarettes on street corners. Lovers kissed in
shadowed doorways. Darkly romantic, yes, but not something to
hang over the mantel. She beelined for the alcohol.

Three cocktails later, Claire lost her friend to a married

Texas oilman and found a quiet corner. She was about to hail a cab home when she saw it. All by itself, a small photo in a thick black frame.

"This one is so different, it doesn't fit with the others." A delicious accent, the words formed deep in the mouth.

She was so absorbed by the picture, it was a moment before she turned. Still, her body flushed when she saw him. Tall and lean; his lips, directly in front of her gaze, were full and brought to mind how they might feel on her skin. His features were angular, an artist's sharp stroke for a cheekbone, a jaw, the nose. A half-empty glass was gripped in one hand, a burning Gauloises in the other. He squinted through the curling smoke.

"You like it, no?" His warm brown eyes stared intently into hers. "Then I am glad I brought it. I am Laurent Olivier. This is my show."

She forgot the taxi.

In the summer that followed, Claire hadn't learned a lick of French, but she knew the bitter tar smell of a Gauloises and why her society friends had insisted for years she take a lover on the side. More importantly, she was reminded that, after five cold years of being another of her husband's acquisitions, there was a living, feeling woman underneath all that polish. Of course, her friends hadn't meant for Claire to chase off after anyone, no matter how talented he was in the sheets.

Neither had Claire.

Claire shifted in her seat as she remembered her last afternoon with Laurent. A hotel room like countless others in Greenwich Village. The furniture a little more sophisticated, the art a bit more deco, maybe, for Washington Square. Leather-bound trunks were pushed up against the wall, lids open. He'd been packing when she'd interrupted him.

A long afternoon was spent gorged on stolen pleasure, and they lay cupped together in his small bed. They faced the dim room's one small window, drowsy bodies tangled, his leg flung over her rounded hip. Half-asleep, he traced a pattern on her bare shoulder. She rolled onto her hip at the edge of the bed; the cotton sheets slipped down below her thighs. She felt Laurent stir next to her, heard the flick of a lighter as he lit a cigarette.

"I am leaving on the ship tonight, *ma chérie*. To Paris," he said.

His few unsold photographs were piled up against an open trunk, frames leaning front to back, ready to be packed. She slipped off the bed and pulled out the smallest photo, cradling in it with one hand. A faint stream of light filtering through the curtains illuminated the picture, enhancing the quiet dreaminess of the scene.

"So soon?" She devoured the image with her eyes to fight the emptiness rising in her belly.

"*Oui.*" He snuffed out his cigarette as he climbed from the bed. "Why do you always look at that one, Claire? It is so naive, no? Done on a lark, for a friend. I don't know why I even brought it." He wrapped his arms around her.

His naked warmth softened her back as she studied the photo. She shook her head. A simple garden scene. Worth less than the price of the silk slip he'd torn from her shoulders. It was impossible to describe what made this small image so arresting. It drew her in, that's all.

He tapped the photo's glass and spoke into her hair. "I can take you to this place. I will undress you in the grass and—"

"What color are the roses?"

Laurent tossed the photo onto the floor. He turned her to face him; his gaze consumed her. "This beauty deserves Paris. Come with me."

"Laurent—"

"I don't have riches, Claire, but I know people. I live like a king. Dinner at the Ritz, parties at Le Meurice. Champagne, fashion, art. The beauty of it all. You are unhappy here, but in Paris you would shine. My muse."

She allowed herself to be tempted until the long breath was gone. She led him toward the bed. "No."

He pushed her back onto the sheets. He kissed her knees and began moving his way toward her waist. "No? Why?"

Because, she could have said, I am Claire Harris Stone and I worked too damn hard for this life to just walk away. Instead, she opened her legs and pulled him to her.

The Clipper's engines droned. Claire allowed herself one more glance down at the wisp of continent disappearing like a mirage. And this morning, nine months later, that glittering life was gone. And she wasn't just walking, she was flying away.

Lisbon, Portugal. May 10, 1940.

The Yankee Clipper touched down in the waters of the Tagus River in the early afternoon and glided to Lisbon's marine terminal gangplank. Claire handed her papers to the official waiting inside the terminal building, her attention drawn to the eerily quiet crowd of travelers that pressed toward the plane.

Picking up her luggage, she pushed past somber faces toward the door and the lot outside.

Outside the terminal, a woman sobbed into a lacy white kerchief next to a mound of luggage piled on the sidewalk. Her sweating taxi driver battled with a steamer case wedged in the car's open trunk.

"Could you direct me to the train station?" Claire said.

The woman only shook her head, face buried in her kerchief.

"What is it? What's happening?" Claire asked.

A loud crack and the case gave, thudding onto the street. The woman wailed.

Grimacing, the driver straightened. "The Nazis. They attack."

Claire caught her breath. "Attacked who?"

"The north. Far north. Not here." He shrugged then motioned Claire toward his open taxi door. "I take you to the train. Estação de Santa Apolónia."


French/Spanish Border. May 11, 1940.

The Sud Express rolled through the countryside, steel wheels stroking a rhythm against the track. Her second endless day on the train, Claire dozed as the sun sank behind the dense shadowed forest outside her window, her case gripped against her stomach.

"*Vive la France,*" the man across from her muttered. She opened her eyes to a view of the darkening Atlantic. The train slowed as they descended into a small harbor town. Hendaye. A change of trains at this French border town, then Paris by morning.

She pressed her hands against the glass, letting the evening chill seep into her palms as she gazed out. A mass of people crowded the platform and surged toward the train as it rolled into the station. A man in a dusty suit shouted and shoved at a French policeman who struggled to hold him back. Claire's skin prickled as she exited the train and followed the line of passengers crossing over to the platform to the next waiting train.

An official sat behind a table at the head of the line, his jacket unbuttoned, shirt collar loose. "Passport." He stamped it without a glance. "Visa." He paled as shouts grew behind her. He scribbled her name on the form, took her fingerprint, smudged, too fast, then waved her on. *"Allez, Madame, allez!"*

Claire hurried onboard. She found a window seat in a crowded compartment and watched, mesmerized, as the police pushed the frantic crowd off the platform. The train jerked forward and accelerated away from the station. Shivering, Claire pulled her case close and flipped open the latch. Her fingers slid over a soft silk bundle to the cool celluloid of a photograph. She held the image up to the moonlight pouring through her window.

A marble statue of a woman stood in razor-sharp focus. Covered in a patina of centuries, her serene stone face looked down at the threads of ivy that swathed her legs. An unseen sun traced sparkling patterns of light through heavy branches onto her stone skin and danced on the grass at her feet. Trellised roses tumbled down a stone wall behind her. The roses captured in film were light shades of grey but, but in her mind, Claire painted them palest pink. The curved arm of a stone bench in the edge of the photo invited rest.

Claire felt the tightness flow out of her. The scene felt so familiar and yet so different from her life. The garden's beauty filled up a person. It added something that wasn't there before. She flipped the photo over, ran her fingers over Laurent's address, written in curving print across the back. Clouds obscured the moon and the compartment faded to darkness. When you wake, you'll be in Paris, Claire told herself, slipping the photo inside the case. She closed her eyes and let her body sag against the cushions.

I t was pitch dark when the train lurched into a station, wheels grinding to a stop. Claire woke confused, her arms asleep. The sign read *Biarritz*. The conductor hurried down the passageway shouting into each compartment. A man across from Claire protested toward the conductor's disappearing back.

"What is it?" Claire said.

The man scowled and reached for his suitcase. "*La guerre*. War. We stop here."

The passengers around Claire grumbled, voices fearful, as they pulled their bags together and filed out of the compartment. Her body tensed as she joined the line emptying out onto an already full platform. The train pulled away, smoke boiling. She turned at the sound of a thud. A heavy wooden frame slammed shut over the ticket seller's window.

A gruff English voice shouted over the din. A white-haired man clambered up the steps to the platform, his stomach straining against the wood buttons on his rumpled white linen suit. He waved a ticket over his head. "Dear God, was that the Lisbon train?"

"No. We were going to Paris," Claire said.

"I started in Paris two days ago. Got as far as Bayonne on the Sud Express. Then the damn frog army turned us off and left with our train. They said to catch the Lisbon-bound train again here. I rode a blasted bicycle. I can't go any farther," he said.

It felt like she'd been kicked in the stomach. She'd spent her last dollar on the train. "How am I supposed to get to Paris?"

"You won't be getting another chance from here. Try Bayonne. And hold tight to your ticket, miss, it's worth gold."

The shutter rattled in the ticket seller's window. Claire elbowed her way over and pounded on the wood. The shutters opened a crack, revealing squinting eyes.

"How much to rent an automobile?" Claire asked.

Bared teeth reflected in the moonlight. The man cackled, and the window slammed shut.


Claire tried a large hotel facing the beach, with a grand portcullis and rows of balconies overlooking the water. The line at the front desk extended out the door. The place was full. Everywhere, she found, was full.

She wandered aimlessly in the faint moonlight along the beach boardwalk. Exhausted, she finally dropped her bags and slumped against a low iron railing. Her eyes were on the white lines of waves nipping at light sand, but her tired thoughts whirled. How the hell was she going to get to Bayonne to catch the train?

"*Bonsoir*, Madame." A man approached, his thin neck jutting from the open collar of a dark suit. He faced her and asked a quiet question.

Claire caught the last two words, *le train*.

She jerked to her feet, smoothing her skirt. "The train to Paris? Yes. Is it coming?"

His eyes flicked over her, his mouth tensed into a hard line. He jerked a knife from his coat pocket and held the point to her neck.

*"Votre billet, s'il vous plait."*

Claire froze. Now that she did understand. *Billet* meant ticket. Her train ticket.

Her heart skittered in her chest. She forced in a breath. "I'm sorry, I don't speak French," she said, stalling.

Surely someone was going to walk by, there were people camped out all over this town. But the sidewalk remained empty.

*"Votre billet de train!"* he hissed.

The moonlight sparked off the blade hovering inches from her throat. Desperation burned in his eyes, his gaunt stubbled cheeks were sharp shadows.

Claire fumbled at the purse draped casually on the railing. Her trembling fingers were clumsy as she flicked open the clasp. Cursing, he jerked the bag from her hands. The knife point fell away from her neck as he clawed inside.

*"Fuyez, Américaine. Fuyez maintenant!"* Ticket clenched in his hand, he flung her purse into the surf and rushed into the darkness.

"My papers!" Claire swore, her eyes on the bag disappearing beneath an incoming wave. She slipped off her fur and ran into the surf. Stumbling in the wash, she spotted a light shape floating in the darkness. She snatched the dripping purse and staggered, drenched, toward the boardwalk.

She collapsed onto an empty bench, her legs weak. Her body began to shake, more from emotion than the cold. Her throat throbbed as though the blade had cut it. She doubled over and vomited in the sand.

Claire wiped her face with a salty wet hand and sucked in a deep breath. The knife had frightened her, but it was the despair in the thief's eyes that chilled her. She remembered well the look from her first hungry days in New York among the bread lines.

The man might once have been important. But tonight he had nothing to lose. And Claire did.

She peeled the wet papers from her purse and used her skirt to press them dry. It was all here, except for the ticket. *Worth gold,* she thought with a sharp pang. There wasn't money to buy another. She shivered as she stared at the waves. She'd been worried about getting to Bayonne. Now how the hell was she going to get to Paris?

Claire spent the rest of the night curled up on a bench with her fur coat pulled tight around her. She slept fitfully, waking at every sound, her train case and purse clenched to her chest. She woke the next morning to the shrieking of gulls, chilled from the sea mist.

A train passed her going north. Soldiers hung out of windows and leaned over the railings between cars. War, a cold voice whispered. She found the main road and pointed her face toward the rising sun. *Bayonne,* the sign read. What choice was there? She began to walk.

At midday Claire rested on a low brick wall along the roadside, in the shadows of a line of elms. Her feet were raw from hours of walking, her stomach queasy from nerves and hunger. She watched a string of heavily loaded cars rumble past her toward the coast as she rubbed her cramping calves. She frowned at the new scuff along a grey heel. Sighing, she slipped the shoes into her hatbox. Skin grows back, but she didn't know when she'd get another pair of custom crocodile pumps.

She limped back onto the road and pointed her bare toes east, her eyes on the dirty pavement at her feet. She heard a curse and glanced up to see a man lumbering straight at her on a sagging bicycle. He cursed as the handlebar clipped the hatbox in her hand and the bike wobbled. The large suitcase strapped behind the bike seat hit her square in the stomach and knocked her off balance. Her luggage flying, Claire fell hard and rolled across the asphalt into the flow of traffic. Her eyes shut and her body tensed at the squeal of tires.

She sneezed. Her eyes opened to see dust wafting around a tire vibrating inches from her face. She sat up and peered over the hood of a green convertible. A man in a rumpled blue suit clenched the steering wheel, his face white. The woman sitting next to him stared, her eyes wide. He leapt from the car. A torrent of words Claire couldn't understand; the concern in his voice was clear. He pulled her to her feet and retrieved her bags and sable, dusting them off with shaking hands. The woman joined him. She phrased a question, speaking slowly, her soft face worried.

Claire's straining ears caught a single word. "Paris?" Her heart leapt. "Yes!"

"*Bon.*" The man set her luggage into the backseat of the car, wedging them in between their large bags.

"Pardon?" Claire warily eyed the distance between her and her bags.

"You may join us to Paris. Our apology for *le petit accident*," the woman said, her gaze on Claire's scraped legs. "I am Adele Oberon. This is my husband, Martin."

"Oh. Well, then. I am Claire Harris. And thank you."

Accepting Martin's guiding hand, Claire wedged her body into the small cushioned backseat in the slight gap between the luggage and the door. Her sore muscles relaxed as the little car accelerated on the rolling asphalt road. With one hand firmly securing her hat in the gusty backseat breeze, she let out a deep breath.

Adele turned back to Claire. *"Américaine?"* Her forehead wrinkled at Claire's nod. "Not a good time to find Paris, *vraiment?"*

"Well," Claire said. "A good time to find an old friend."

Adele's bright eyes were mystified. "But you know about the fighting, no?"

Claire's mouth dried up. "What do you mean?"

"The Germans have broken through. In Belgium, in Holland, in Luxembourg. In the Ardennes in France. They push south toward Paris."

Claire bit back a curse. Damned Laurent and everyone claimed the Nazis couldn't get past the French army. Not with the British backing them up. It was silly to try. That's why this was called *La drôle de guerre.* The phony war.

"But what about the French army?" Claire said.

It took a moment for Adele to muster an answer. "Our soldiers are wounded, prisoners, scattered to the winds." The woman pulled a photo from her purse. A father, mother and son grinned in front of a beach umbrella. She pointed at the boy and broke into rapid-fire French.

Claire heard the warmth in Adele's voice, saw her eyes mist over. The woman in the photo had a deep brunette bob, not Adele's salt-and-pepper bun, but the same wide, dark eyes, the soft face, the slender frame. It had to be her. Martin, she realized, didn't look much different. His hair was darker, but he wore the same thin mustache even then. The boy was about seven, Claire thought. His blazing smile highlighted a missing tooth.

"Your son?"

"Michele." Her face twisted and she glanced at Martin.

He didn't take his eyes from the road but lightly stroked Adele's shoulder.

"A soldier. He was called in a month ago. To protect the border in the Ardennes." Adele stared out at the passing road. "These people flee to the south. But Michele will come to Paris. He will come home. And we will be there waiting."

Martin gripped the wheel tighter.

They traveled in silence for the next few hours. Progress slowed as the car maneuvered through clumps of weary people walking, bicycling and pulling carts. They finally pulled over and parked under the shade of tall elms out of sight from the road. Claire stretched as Adele rummaged through a wicker basket and Martin pulled the gasoline can from the trunk. A blanket was spread over a carpet of leaves. Adele put out plates, glasses, a bottle of wine. She unrolled a sandwich wrapped in white paper and deftly cut small finger-sized pieces.

"Madame Harris?" Adele patted the blanket next to her and held out a plate.

Legs folded beneath her on the blanket, Claire gratefully took a bite. Her teeth crunched through the bread's thick crust. Inside a thick slice of soft cheese, a cut of herbed chicken, a slice of tomato. A sip of red wine to wash it down. The earthy flavors melted against her tongue. She breathed deep and smiled. Better than every spoonful of Russian caviar she'd served at her party three nights ago.

Martin closed the hood and joined them. A quick meal and the little car pulled back onto the road, fighting its way upstream. Night descended and still they drove. Claire pulled her fur close, leaned back and stared at the stars until her eyes closed.

The rising sun woke her. Claire squinted, rubbing at the

stiffness in her neck. Martin had driven all night. The road had grown more crowded, rustic farmland gave way to great expanses of cultivated fields. A large château towered in the distance. They rested a moment next to a wooded stream and took quick walks into the trees before splashing water on their tired faces and climbing back in the car.

"How much farther to Paris?" Claire said.

Adele looked at Martin then shrugged. "Not far, but . . ."

They passed through a city. Orleans. The car slowed to a crawl, nudging through families with carts, pulling goats and horses, then urban travelers, stumbling along in wool suits and dragging suitcases or bursting out of cars filled to the roof with trunks.

They crested a knoll. Beyond the rolling hills, tiny villages and steeples; in the far distance, a grey line of buildings interrupted the horizon. Claire knew instinctively it was Paris. Her breath caught in her throat.

By midday they entered the outskirts. Heavy traffic in all directions snarled the small convertible. Martin slowed, then stopped. A concrete barrier had been erected across the road. Dust carts were locked together on each side. A line of policemen in blue uniforms stood behind the makeshift barricade, smoking cigarettes. Claire watched as Adele and Martin shared a look. This was Paris's line of defense? Martin reversed the car; they turned off onto a side street.

Claire's attention was drawn to the Parisians themselves. Men in fine wool suits and ties, women in gloves and felt hats pulled, just so, over one eye. They had a certain walk; it reminded Claire of the models in New York. But their expressions were too hard, their pace too fast.

The car scraped behind a newspaper stand and turned into

an alley. Martin pulled the brake and switched off the ignition. They sat for a moment then slid out of the car.

"Can you find your way from here?" Adele asked.

"Of course." Claire examined her suit, tried to smooth her rumpled skirt, wiped futilely at smudges of road dust and grime. Not the entrance she'd planned. She tried a smile. "I'll be fine."

Adele pulled out a white starched kerchief from her purse. She slipped it to Claire, her expression kind. "You are a beautiful woman. He will be happy to see you."

Claire's eyes misted over as she took the kerchief; her fingers traced the elegant *AO* embroidered in one corner. Nothing had been said, but somehow Adele knew a man had brought Claire to Paris. The woman handed her a slip of paper as she planted a light kiss on each cheek.

"*Merci beaucoup,*" Claire said carefully, with great conviction, and accepted her case and hatbox from Martin. She glanced down at the paper as she stepped out into the street, an address was written in firm script by Adele's careful hand. Claire felt markedly alone on the busy cobble street. Not for long, she told herself.

# Chapter 2

## THE ADVANCE

22, rue d'Artois, Paris. May 13, 1940.

Claire didn't mind the walk through Paris streets. The brick sidewalks lined with precise-shaped trees. Elaborate stonework on grey buildings created an older, more fanciful world. Patisseries and newspaper stands. Cafés with small tables pulled out on the sidewalk. Even in her crumpled suit, men's heads followed as she walked by. Crossing the river Seine on the pont de l'Alma, Claire was struck by the sight of the Eiffel Tower above a line of leafy green treetops. The graceful curve of metal lace stitched into the fabric of pale blue sky. She couldn't help but think of how much Mama would have loved to see this, just once.

It was late afternoon when she turned onto rue d'Artois and sat on a bench in the shadows of Laurent's building. She wiped down bare skin with Adele's kerchief as she stared up at the windows and tried to ignore the anxiety tightening her throat.

Laurent had made plenty of promises in New York, his face buried in her breasts, in her soft stomach, in the heat between her thighs. It was amusing then because she recognized something in him she knew very well. A price tag.

After all, it was well established in the society pages that the Harrises were old money. A now rare but still distinguished lineage. What little matter would it be for a Harris to leave her industrialist husband's vulgar new money? Laurent offered so much pleasure for a taste of dusty old treasure. How wrong he was.

Claire stared up at the building's stonework, worn with the years but still showing the artistry of its birth, the depth of its history. Black iron railings curved out from balconies overflowing with plants. Beautiful, as Laurent promised, in a city drenched in beauty.

She shivered in the sunlight. It wasn't the Germans that concerned her. In fact, the confusion from the invasion might buy her a few more weeks. The truth was the problem. Soon enough Laurent would guess the truth. Or a shade of it.

Harris was a name, read from a dusty obituary in the recessed stacks of the New York Library on Fifth Avenue. Just a name, as her husband had learned three nights previous, picked out years ago by the runaway daughter of an Oklahoma dirt farmer.

A wave of weariness swept over her. Eleven years ago, she'd gone to New York and stood in the breadlines like all the rest. But she didn't stay with them. After she'd married Russell, she thought she was done with the struggle. Damn, but she thought she'd won. A shadow moved against the glass in the fifth-floor window. Claire caught her breath and straightened. Laurent.

That simple county girl was dead. She never really was alive, was she?

Claire smoothed her jacket and straightened her skirt. Head held high, she marched up the shallow brick steps to the carved wooden door. Past the lobby, a small metal stairwell curved enough to make her hold fast to the railing. Five flights of stairs then a heavy door with the snarling mouth of a tired-looking bronze lion as a knocker. She rapped twice, pulled back her shoulders and cocked her hip to offer her best introductory silhouette.

Painful seconds ticked by but the door remained closed. Her smile faded and she pressed her ear against the door. Voices rumbled in the background. The words, unintelligible, were heated.

She recognized Laurent's voice, but he wasn't alone. She tamped down her rising sense of foreboding and listened close. Heated, yes, but both male. Claire didn't bother with the lion and pounded on the door with a closed fist. The thuds echoed through the empty hall.

Claire put her ear to the door again. Silence. She waited, back arched, an elegant ankle extended nonchalantly in front of her.

The door swung open. Laurent stood before her, a frown marring his aristocratic face. He could be standing in this same doorway in any century, dark hair, sculpted cheekbones, strong nose and brown eyes.

"Well, darling, aren't you going to invite a girl in?" Claire let her gloved hand skim across her chest.

His frown melted. He stared, his mouth hung open.

"Laurent? *Qui est-ce?*" a voice shouted from the background.

"*Zut alors*, Claire!" Laurent swept her into his arms and inside the door in one motion. His hands cupped each shoulder; his gaze drank her in from her feet to her hat. "What in the world are you doing here?"

Claire smiled. This was the reception she'd hoped for.

"What the hell is it, Laurent?" a gravelly English voice demanded from the next room.

Over Laurent's shoulder, Claire watched a man stomp through the arched doorway. In his late thirties, perhaps, muscled where Laurent was slender. His hair was dirty blond and cut short, strong cheekbones softened by stubble. Razor-sharp, blue grey eyes narrowed as he strode toward them. His lips compressed into a scowl, arms folded in front of his chest. "A woman. Of course. Bloody hell."

Laurent turned to him, smiling as though he had been awarded a hard-earned prize. "Claire Harris Stone, this is Grey. Thomas Harding Grey. Please, forgive his rudeness, *ma chérie*. He is English."

Claire ran her fingers over Laurent's lips. "It's Claire Harris now, Laurent darling. There is no Stone involved." She turned then to smile at Grey, her expression sweet as she sized him up. "Grey? How very appropriate," Claire purred, staring at his rough grey trousers and worn sweater, pulled snug across his chest.

Grey's frown deepened as he stared at her.

Laurent broke in. "Claire, *ma chérie*, you must join us in the salon."

Ornate bureaus and tables, curved chairs and chaise lounges were grouped for conversation around an immense stone fireplace. Stacked groups of photographs leaned against a corner wall. The room was lit from the outside through oversized windows that looked out over a quiet courtyard, invisible from the street.

Laurent poured a glass of Bordeaux from a half-empty bottle then slid into a high-backed chair next to her. Grey stationed himself by the windows, just out of range of conversation.

"How did you get here?" Laurent asked Claire.

"Yankee Clipper. It was breathtaking." Claire opened her eyes wide and took a sip, shifting her sable on her shoulders. "The plane took off right out of the East River, Laurent."

"But . . . the Germans. Surely someone told you . . ." Laurent said.

"Well, first of all, we left New York before things got so interesting." She adjusted the hem of her skirt, covering a bare knee while managing to show more skin.

Grey glowered at the curve of her knee and the glimpse of cream thigh. "You must not count travel restrictions among your interests."

"Second of all . . . " She spoke as if she didn't hear. "We landed in Lisbon, well, let's see, three days ago. I didn't really talk to anyone there, just boarded the train for Paris. You know I don't speak French or Portuguese. How could I know what others were doing?"

Laurent leaned in to stroke her fingers, splayed across the armrest. "I am so relieved you made it safely. Traveling is too dangerous right now for a woman alone."

"Americans are lining up to leave. She must get out and quickly," Grey said.

"Pardon?" Claire's tone was sugary, her eyes hard.

"Nazi armored units are pushing through France. There's nothing left between them and Paris. Nothing. You can't take on a woman like this, Laurent, not now." Grey faced them. "I know a man who can get her on a ship tomorrow."

"Tomorrow?" Laurent said doubtfully.

"It must be tomorrow."

Claire looked back and forth between them. Who the hell is this bastard and why was Laurent listening to him? She kicked off her shoes and swung her feet up, tucking them beneath her knees and showing more skin. "I just arrived. I haven't been any-where yet. I'm certainly not leaving tomorrow."

Grey looked to Laurent for agreement. Laurent, however, was admiring her thigh. She leaned back into the chair cushions, body curving to reveal every feminine bend. She caught Lau-rent's eyes, feigned shock to find him staring.

"I am so surprised you decided to join me, *ma chérie*." Lau-rent stroked her hand with a soft finger.

"I couldn't spend another day away. Are you only surprised? Not at all pleased?"

Claire tilted toward Laurent, lips in a pout. He leaned in to kiss her, but she turned her face and offered him a cheek. She shot a glance at Grey, baring her teeth in a smile.

A few terse words in French to Laurent, then Grey looked back at Claire. "Good day to you, *Mrs. Stone*." He slammed the door behind him.

"I am pleased." Laurent kissed her.

A half hour later, Claire stretched languidly as she climbed out of the deep porcelain tub. Body dripping, she retrieved a soft towel from a hook placed at head height on the bath-room wall. She leaned against the cool porcelain of the sink as she dried herself, methodically scrubbing stray memories of the past few days from her skin and mind. Slipping on a thick robe, she stared into a full-length mirror. Not bad, even without her marabou-trimmed sheer silk robe.

Laurent stared as she entered the salon. "You are even more ravishing than in my dreams." He took her in his arms, his mouth probing hers.

Claire felt her body respond in spite of her fatigue. She pressed against him, allowing the robe to slip open. He ran his hands over her waist and stroked her hips with his fingertips.

"Forgive me." Laurent pulled back from Claire. "I offered lunch and then I attack you. You must be hungry."

She could eat a horse. "A bit." She shrugged her robe off one shoulder.

They sat on a chaise lounge in front of the windows. Between them, a silver tray held a spread of cut fruit. A bottle of champagne chilled in a silver bucket on the parquet floor.

"I'm afraid I can't offer anything more extravagant. My grocer was ordered to report to his unit yesterday and . . ." Laurent popped the cork free with a crack and poured.

Claire rearranged her robe and bit into a pear. A long swallow of champagne and she smiled. After the warm bath, the wine and food hit her system like a good bottle of scotch. A wave of goodwill rolled over her.

"Who's Grey?"

"He's an old friend." Laurent smiled, his eyes turning back years. "We were in school together. At École des Beaux-Arts."

"But, he's English," Claire said.

"I know." Laurent nodded with a sigh. "He's very English. But, please forgive his rudeness. It is the fighting, the German advance. Grey hears his own call to arms. He can be very passionate in his own way." He paused as he refilled her glass. "He's a good man, a good friend. But, I hope you didn't come all this way to think about another man."

Claire took a sip of champagne and deposited the glass on a marble-topped table. She felt almost giddy. *Paris.* She slid across the chaise to Laurent, her robe slipped from her shoulders. "I was thinking about this." Her lips tasted his. "And this." She pressed his hands against her hips.

Laurent pulled her against him and kissed the soft hollow of her neck. "Tonight, I will make your journey worthwhile."

Claire barely registered his words over the pounding of her blood. His lips were like caressing fingers. *Make your journey worthwhile.* A sliver of doubt wedged itself in her mind. "What do you mean, exactly, Laurent?"

He smiled. "Do you want me to spell it out for you? I will, if you like."

Claire covered a frown. "You said tonight. What will happen tomorrow?"

"This is war. Who can say?" He leaned in to kiss her shoulder.

His lips traced the line of her collarbone, but Claire hardly noticed. She understood what he wasn't saying. He was going along with that damn Englishman.

"Laurent, darling, you wouldn't send me away tomorrow, would you?"

In response, his kisses moved lower.

Claire felt her face flush. She fought to keep the anger hidden. *All this and he offers one sorry night?* She let the robe flutter to the floor, pushed him back against the cushions and straddled his legs. "Over and over, you told me of the pleasures, the beauty, of your Paris."

He watched her, his expression hungry.

She pressed her lips against the pulse thrumming in his neck. "I want your Paris."

He pulled her onto him as he fumbled with his shirt buttons with one hand. Peeling open his shirt, she ran her hands down his stomach, her fingers sliding beneath his waistband.

Keeping her tone low and sweet she spoke again. "I'm not leaving. You understand, don't you, darling?"

He reached for the buttons on his pants. She blocked his hands. "Don't you, Laurent?"

A low groan as he sat up. "I want you, *naturellement*, with me. But these are not good days. Grey's people can get you back to New York. Go back to your life, until . . ." He shrugged and reached for her.

Until it's convenient for you, Claire thought, silently cursing. Her fresh start was about to dry up if she didn't somehow raise the stakes. She forced a smile. "*Naturellement*, I've enjoyed our time together, Laurent darling. But what makes you think I would stay with you?"

He said nothing, eyes drinking in her exposed body. Lips pursed, he raised his hands, palm up, in an exaggerated shrug. "You know nothing of Paris. Where else would you go, *ma chérie*?"

Her face flushed. A helpless American woman, he assumed, to be kept, pleasured and, yes, bled of some of her fictitious money. She pushed off him to her feet. "You underestimate me, *Monsieur*. I will stay in Paris. But not with you."

Doubt marked his face.

She pressed her fingers against his lips. "A shame. We would have enjoyed each other." She turned on her heel and marched from the room. Jerking on her clothes, she scooped her things in a jumble against her chest.

Laurent caught her at the front door. "You cannot go alone. It's too dangerous."

Claire glared straight into his eyes. "Laurent, step aside."

"No. I won't let you."

"Very well." She kicked him in the shin.

"*Merde.*" He gasped and grabbed his leg with both hands.

Laurent didn't move as she stomped around him, down the stairs and out into the afternoon sun. Randomly picking right over left, she strode down the street, blood pounding.

As she turned onto the next block, a cool current of thought trickled through her anger, stopping her in her tracks. *Alive.* The word bubbled up in her head. She felt so damn alive.

Two women walked their bikes along the sidewalk behind her. Their laughter echoed off the bricks and fluttered like birds. Laurent said there was something about this city. She was starting to think that in this regard, he hadn't lied. She felt alive for the first time she could remember. The barest smile. And she'd left him wondering. She left him wanting.

Give it a week, maybe two. A surprise meeting on the street, at the Ritz, she'd be in a new dress, a man on her arm. *Yes, Jean-Luc has been so kind introducing me to all the delights of Paris,* she'd say in a way that meant so much more. Laurent would beg her to come back. And damn that Englishman—she just might.

She pulled back her shoulders and, chin up, continued down the sidewalk.

Claire wandered for hours through the streets until her stomach growled and her body ached. She paused as she stepped onto a grand avenue. The last sliver of sun outlined a giant stone arch, squared at the top, streets radiating from all sides.

The Arc de Triomphe. Claire trudged toward the arch, her gaze on the buildings around her. This was the Champs-Elysées. The only Parisian avenue she knew of, home of the most luxurious stores in the world. But tonight, the wide sidewalks were empty, windows dim.

She turned onto a small street, a slender channel between tall brick buildings on each side. A quaint neighborhood, as if from a postcard, picturesque shops amidst apartment buildings. A tailor, a grocer, a baker, a café, all closed, and an elegant little flower shop.

Claire paused in front of the flower shop. *La Vie en Fleurs* was printed in white flowing script on a large blue canvas awning stretched over the front door. The building was small, two stories pressed in between larger buildings. Potted plants cascaded off a second-story balcony, pouring red, pink and white blossoms through the iron railing. Masses of flowers overflowing from tin buckets crowded the wide sidewalk around the door and beneath the front window. A small white bistro table and two chairs were nestled between the blooms.

One bucket of roses in particular caught Claire's attention. Each stem featured a crush of pale blush-colored petals packed tightly inside its blossom. She kneeled, cupping a bloom in her hand. The petals felt of silk, the scent delicate and sweet, a hint of honey and tea, warm breezes and sunshine.

These must be the roses from the photo, the roses cascading down the garden wall, Claire decided as she buried her face into the bloom. Exactly what she pictured all along. Without thinking she reached for a potted ivy and snugged it up against the bucket of roses, arranging the green tendrils to curve around the blooms. She smiled. Perfect.

"*Bonsoir.*"

Claire pushed to her feet and turned. The proprietor of the flower shop stood in the doorway. She looked to be in her sixties, petite, with angled cheeks and a firm jaw sweeping back to silver hair held firmly in a bun. Her posture was erect like a dancer's, slender arms crossed in front of her chest.

"I don't speak French. But your flowers are beautiful."

"*Américaine*, eh? Strange time to be out alone arranging my flowers, no?"

Claire blushed. "I'm sorry, I didn't mean to offend. I just . . ."

"There is no need to apologize. You have an eye, a touch for beauty." The woman smiled gently, her large brown eyes taking in Claire's bags and travel-worn clothing.

Claire looked down at herself, achingly aware of the dust and creases. This woman, in a simple white shirt and charcoal-colored skirt, midnight blue scarf draping from her slender neck, projected an unmistakable quiet chic. Claire felt more self-conscious than she had in years. She swatted futilely at a spot of road oil staining her skirt and attempted to stand a little straighter.

"But truly, on a day like this, one can do nothing better than enjoy a thing of beauty." With a practiced eye, she pulled the freshest flower from the bucket and handed it to Claire. "*C'est mon plaisir.*"

"Thank you." Claire cupped the rose to her face and breathed in deeply.

A teenage boy carrying an overloaded box stepped from the darkened grocer's doorway across the street. His face was friendly, his smile open and simple, and a dark mop of hair framed his head. Though his arms flexed at the weight of the box, he carried it with ease. A loaf of bread and the neck of a wine bottle peeked out the open top. He offered Claire a shy "*Bonjour*" then whispered to the woman. She replied quietly.

The boy picked his way through the masses of plants over to the table set amongst flower pails. He plucked out a loaf of bread, a bottle of wine, a hunk of cheese and two ripe golden pears he set gently on a brown paper wrapper. Nodding shyly to both women, he mumbled, *"Au revoir,"* and hurried down the street.

The woman watched him go. "Georges. He is a good boy. He is a touch slow in his mind or his father would have already lost him to this *catastrophe*." She nodded toward the table. "It is the time of evening when I take a *petit* dinner. You will join me?"

The florist hurried inside, rattled around behind the counter and returned with a pair of white porcelain plates, stemmed glasses, silverware and linen napkins on a worn silver tray. She placed a single white lily in a small silver vase in the center of the table. *"C'est acceptable?* I am Madame Palain. This is my establishment. Please. We will eat and speak of good things before I retire this evening."

Claire clasped the florist's hand. Her grip was warm and strong, but softer than Claire had imagined. "I am Claire Harris. Thank you. I would love to join you."

Madame motioned Claire to a seat, then took her own. "Claire is a French name. Did you know? It means clear, like clarity."

Claire gratefully sank into the proffered chair then smoothed the napkin over her lap. "Clarity. Well, that's fresh."

Madame cast an eye in her direction but said nothing as she expertly cut slices of cheese and fruit, and deposited them onto each plate.

In spite of her hunger, Claire forced herself to tear off a piece of bread and yield it as daintily as the woman across from her. As her teeth sank into the soft center, she suppressed a moan. She realized she had closed her eyes, blinked open and found Madame watching her as she sipped at her wine. Claire blushed and turned her gaze to the flowers surrounding them.

The florist surveyed the tin pails that nearly covered the brick walkway. "You look at the flowers. They are quite beautiful. Which are your favorites?"

"How could I possibly choose?" Claire shrugged, her attention on the food hitting her stomach. Another glance at Madame and she realized it wasn't a rhetorical question. The florist leaned forward in her seat, expression as serious as Claire could imagine on that pleasant face.

Claire took a sip of wine and sat back in her chair. She thought back to the countless arrangements she had ordered or made for her parties in Manhattan. Flowers were what she was known for. Among other things. She grinned.

Claire pointed to a pail of apricot-colored ranunculus, their tissue-thin petals packed tight on a slender green curving stem. "Those would look amazing in a golden vase, among golden candlesticks for a semiformal dinner party. For an all-white spring dinner among ladies, I would choose green wire baskets with white narcissus, purple pansies, hyacinth and green viburnum."

Madame nodded with pursed lips. "And?"

Claire picked up the single rose she had sat on the table. "For a very special event, or just for me, this would be my choice."

"Accompanied by what else?"

"Nothing else. I would mass them by the dozens in crystal vases."

Madame smiled approvingly. "Very restrained. Tasteful." She nudged the remainder of the loaf toward Claire as an offering. "Though I would rethink the wire basket. That would be a disaster." She took a sip of wine as if to wash away the disturbing thought.

The simple dinner was what Claire needed, in nourishment as well as company. No personal words were exchanged, but it was clear Madame Palain had a level of sophistication that made

Claire's New York crowd seem like little girls playing dress up. It wasn't any single thing, like the manner in which she held her fork or sipped her wine. The florist enchanted with her ease and polish. Being the center of her attention felt an honor. She challenged Claire to be clever in her thoughts, to pick through the jumble of words in her head to find the one that expressed perfectly what she meant to say.

Night crept in without their assent. The women murmured over the crumbs of their dinner in near darkness, their only illumination the dim half-eaten moon. The light of the streetlamp above was covered in deep blue paint. "The war," Madame explained with a frown.

Sheer weariness finally forced Claire back to the reality of her situation. With real regret, she reached for her things. "Thank you for the lovely dinner, Madame. I'm afraid I must go."

"Of course," Madame said, her tone unconvinced. She deftly emptied the table onto the silver tray and stood.

Claire pushed herself to her feet and stared into the darkness. She was tired but couldn't make herself walk away. "I've made you late. Perhaps I can help you clean up?"

Madame nodded, the flicker of a warm smile. She turned to face the shop and instantly converted into a general. "All the flowers must be pulled in. Then we must cull them and freshen the water. I lost my delivery boy as well as my assistant to this ridiculous war, so I have many flowers left tonight. Then everything must be cleaned and swept for a fresh start in the morning."

A silent groan as Claire realized she was going to work off her dinner tab. She bent down to grab a bucket. The sweet scent of peonies brushed delightfully against her nose. She had nowhere else to go, after all.

* * *

The women pulled, pushed and cleaned until the shop was in perfect order. Claire went through the motions in a daze, moving from one task to the next at Madame's brisk request. Buckets of flowers were lined up in the back room, chilled by heavy brick walls and ice. The counters were wiped, the floors swept. Finally, Claire settled a stack of zinc pots against a wall. She straightened stiffly, her skirt displaying wet splotches and a smattering of shredded leaves.

"Very good." Madame pulled a key from under the counter. Her appearance remained spotless, her clothes still crisp and bun smoothly pinned. She flicked off the dim lamp. "You must remember, Madame Harris, elegance is in the details."

"Yes, Madame. I'll remember." Claire was so tired, she was nearly wobbling, but this was a woman who knew of what she spoke. Claire picked up her cases and followed her to the door.

Madame waved Claire out and locked the shop behind them. Dropping the key in her small black purse, she gazed through the window at the flowers. "I can only offer you 150 francs a week. There is war coming, after all, and we must be practical."

Claire stared at the florist, her mouth open. A job offer to be a flower girl? Her snort turned into a sigh as she looked down at her clothes. She couldn't very well sweep into Parisian high society in this state.

"It is harder work than you may imagine," Madame continued. "And I demand my employees work full days and they give complete attention to their tasks, whether creating grand arrangements for a ball at the Ritz or sweeping up the petals from the sidewalk."

"The Paris Ritz?"

"*Oui.* And Le Meurice, Hôtel Emeraude, Hôtel de Crillon and the others. We *are* La Vie en Fleurs." She extended a delicate finger toward the balcony over their heads. "The wage includes the use of the apartment upstairs. It is small, a sink but no real kitchen, and you must use the bathroom downstairs in the shop."

Claire stared up at the cheeky little balcony in the dim moonlight; ivy and blossoms threaded through iron railings. Her body ached to tuck in there for the night, to close her eyes to the scent of flowers wafting in through an open window.

"It is not required you take the room. It is used for storage now." The florist smoothed a stray hair back into her bun. "Fresh paint, scrubbing, and it could be quite *agréable.*"

Claire turned to examine Madame. The woman obviously knew a few things about taste and seemed more than willing to impart them. What would it hurt to play with flowers for a few weeks? Get her Parisian feet wet. Get inside the Ritz. It was perfect—in a sense. "But what happens if the Germans do make it to Paris?"

Madame Palain stiffened. "Will we have any less need for flowers? Any less need for beauty?" Her face and tone were icy. "I know what war does. I know its cost. But this is still Paris. This shop will survive. It always survives."

The florist's indignation startled Claire. "Madame Palain, I didn't—"

"My assistant Natalie left when her father and brothers were called up from Lyon. Jon Pierre, my delivery boy, was called away to fight this week." Madame pointed up at the sign. "You must understand, La Vie en Fleurs is one of the finest, most trusted flower shops in all of Paris. We have a duty to Paris, to France."

A breath was expelled from pursed lips and she shrugged. Madame had made her offer and wanted Claire to see it was all the same to her. "*Eh bien*, it's late. I need to get home. If you're not up to the task, then it would not benefit either of us."

"I would be truly grateful if I could work here," Claire said, surprised at the genuine enthusiasm in her voice.

"*Bon*." The merest curve of a smile as Madame buttoned her coat.

Gazing through the window at the tidy little shop, at the stone floor, the worn plaster walls, the rows upon rows of tin buckets that held cheery blossoms, Claire realized she actually did want to be a part of this place. She listened to Madame's shoes click away down the dark sidewalk. The steps paused.

"That will be your first task in the morning, after you help me prepare the shop to open. You must clear out the storage from your new room and find a place for it. Come along. You'll stay with me tonight." Without a further word or glance, the older woman started off down the sidewalk at a rapid clip.

Claire didn't trust herself to speak. She hurried to Madame's side, struggling to keep pace. She looked back at the shop as they turned the corner. The curving lines of the awning and balcony were barely visible in the moonlight. The brass plaque on the wall read *rue du Colisée*. The whole damn shop would have fit in her ballroom on Fifth Avenue. But, somehow, it looked strangely like home.

Over the next few days, following careful directions from Madame, Claire emptied out the bulk of the items stored in her new bedroom. It was small, as Madame promised, not much wider than the balcony itself and about twice as long. Just enough space for a single bed, which Claire uncovered from under a layer of boxes. A dresser Georges carried up the stairs balanced on his shoulder now stood against the wall by the door. A mirror, clouded with age, leaned against the wall. Beyond that, the room was empty, waiting.

Claire had next to nothing, which was why it took her so long to unpack. Twenty pairs of shoes can exist in a jumbled pile. One pair must be thoughtfully placed. The cream-colored evening gown and silver heels from her hatbox and the sable were hung in the back of the closet.

She pulled the silk bundle from her train case and laid it on the bed in front of her. Propped up on an elbow, she untied the ribbon and unrolled a thick jewelry roll. Diamonds sparkled in the faint light. With a finger, she nudged apart the Cartier necklace, matching earrings, and the few other baubles she'd taken from the safe. "Armies march, but diamonds conquer all," she whispered with a grin. After some searching, her jewelry roll was tucked in an old newspaper and wedged behind the dresser's top drawer.

Finally, Claire pulled the garden photo from her case and slipped it into the edge of the mirror. Now that she was here, the image felt more real. As if she would turn a corner down the next street and this garden would be awaiting her.

A clatter of tin buckets from below startled her from her reverie. The florist called up the stairs. "Madame Harris, êtes-vous prête?"

Claire smiled and shook her head. Such a crazy world. But this was just for a few weeks and then Paris would be hers. The Nazis couldn't have it. "Coming, Madame," she said with an unexpected lightness as she hurried down the steps.

## 52, rue du Colisée, Paris. June 3, 1940.

Claire jerked awake as the darkness flared to bright white. A deafening boom shook the room. She wrenched free of her tangled sheets and fell from the small bed. She crawled to the window and peered into the darkness. Another flash, the balcony windows glowed scarlet, and rumbling thunder threw her to the floor. Now two red suns glowed in the distance.

A string of explosions ripped the sky apart. Far off, crimson towers flared into the night sky, lighting the graceful lines of the blacked-out city like a fiery sunset. The stars were veiled by a murky grey blanket of dense smoke.

The Germans were bombing Paris.

She pulled herself to her feet and swung open the windows, arms hugged against her chest. An acrid breeze that smelled of cinders tugged at her thin cotton slip. Stepping outside on the small balcony, her gaze was trapped, unblinking, on the destruction in the distance. She listened for the Nazi planes that must be responsible, the dreaded Luftwaffe, but couldn't make out the buzzing engines over the blood pounding in her ears.

Another barrage and the balcony shuddered. Now several different parts of the city were ablaze. Claire cursed under her breath. Paris was for expiring, like Greta Garbo in *Camille*, in silk sheets, amongst flowers and despairing lovers. Damn well not for dying alone, blown to bits. Her knees buckled and she sank to the balcony floor.

A blast, too large, too close, rattled her teeth. She leaned her head against the wrought-iron railing; the cool metal bit into her cheek. Figures crowded the street below, only their outlines visible. Their shouts sounded thin amid the baritone explosions as they scurried in all directions. Who did they run to?

Laurent . . . She grabbed his name like a lifeline and scrambled to her feet. Running for the door, she grabbed a coat and slipped on her shoes. She half fell through the bedroom door and charged down the stairs, one hand in her coat sleeve, the other hugging the curved stone stairwell. Another explosion and the building shuddered. Claire caught her heel, landed hard and bumped down another two steps before she wedged sideways in the small passage.

The walls reverberated around her. Her back was jammed against the cold stone wall, her coat bunched up against one shoulder and her feet pressed awkwardly against the opposite wall. A curse tore from her throat as she slammed the wall behind her with a fist. The world might be ending, but she couldn't—wouldn't—crawl to Laurent. Not this way.

Claire tasted blood and her lip stung fiercely. She glared into the darkness, wiping a hand over her mouth, the image of her mother's cracked lips, clenched tight against food or water, burning in her mind. "You think I'm scared of you? You don't know what bad dying looks like." She pulled herself up the stairs and limped back to the balcony. She sat amongst the flowers and watched fires burn until the sun rose.

There was a certain look. A tight half smile, a nearly imperceptible tilt of the shoulder. Sometimes words. C'est la vie. That's life. More often nothing was said. The weary eyes said it all. Claire recognized the look now. It was purely French. The way she read it, it meant, "Well, we survived that, so we may as well hold on. This is Paris, after all." There had been many thats to be survived.

She first saw that look the morning after the bombing. She

learned from Madame the Nazis targeted the Renault and Citroën factories in the darkness and dropped thousands of bombs in southwest neighborhoods in Paris. Nearly a thousand dead. And yet at ten in the morning, a man came in to buy flowers for his wedding anniversary. Thirty years married, a day worth celebrating. He was almost apologetic as he picked out the bouquets. But the look, a shrug. This was Paris. Life goes on.

A week later, June 11, and the air was thick with a heavy smoke that hung over the city like a shroud. The dingy sky smelled of dirty fires. No one wanted to think about what burned. Some said it marked the end of the world. Claire and Madame spent the day indoors reorganizing the back room, a wet rag stuffed into the crack between the front door and the floor.

The next morning dawned and they found they still lived. A mother came in for a large order of flowers for a fête that night for her daughter's fifteenth birthday. The harried woman rushed to pull together all the details, making up for lost time after shops closed the day before. The greatest inconvenience, however—the government had abandoned Paris two days previous. Many invitees were bureaucrats and their families—the departure played havoc with the party's seating arrangements. *"C'est vraiment terrible."* The look again. Her daughter was only this age once. What could one do? This was Paris.

News got worse. The German army plowed through the last of the French troops to the north. The Nazis would be here any second. The Luftwaffe had bombed the heart of Rotterdam into the ground less than a month ago to guarantee a Dutch surrender. What might they do to Paris?

Claire took her first paycheck and bought a thin summer dress. It was the deep blue of a clear evening sky and swished playfully around her hips. She sprang for a little felt pillbox hat, dark grey with a ribbon in matching blue. She wore it that Sunday when she walked alone around the Left Bank. The city was nearly deserted but enchanting still. She rested on a park bench near the foot of the Eiffel Tower, craning her head back to see the rise of the massive spires. A handsome Frenchman sat beside her, smoking a Gauloises and unabashedly drinking her with his eyes. He tried in vain to make conversation *en français*. Claire finally said *au revoir* and left him, as well as his implied offer for company of an intimate nature. She moved on to see the jardin des Tuileries then watched what must be all the city's remaining children ride the painted ponies at the jardin du Carrousel. It was a beautiful Sunday. And this was Paris after all.

By the next Friday, June 14, the radio said units of the German Sixth Army marched from the north into Paris. It was a quiet morning in the shop, and Madame and Claire froze when they heard a low rumble. They watched people stream toward avenue des Champs-Elysées.

"What is it?" Claire said, her chest tight.

Madame Palain just shook her head.

"I'll see." Claire hurried along behind the crowd.

The sidewalks lining the avenue were filled with people. Claire pushed her way forward into the mass as far as she could. She heard, or more felt, a rhythmic pounding. A collective gasp; a silver-haired man ahead of her cried out. Straining to see, Claire scrambled up on the base of a streetlight. She turned her head toward the Arc de Triomphe.

A line of Nazi soldiers, as far back as she could see. Led by a horseman, their grey uniforms impeccable, rifles slung over their soldiers. Marching like machines, their hobnailed boots rang out like a massive hammer battering the asphalt street.

As she watched, a bloodred flag was unfurled from the top

of the Arc. At its center, a massive black swastika flapped in the breeze. The man standing near Claire's feet turned away from the parade, tears streaming down his face. Feeling sick, Claire jumped from the base and headed toward the store.

"They are here," Claire said as she entered the shop.

Madame turned back to her roses. "Bring me the dried greenery from the back. Supplies will be a challenge. You will need to learn how to use more fill to accentuate fresh blossoms."

Paris still stood, Claire thought the florist meant. They would outlast this.

She worked a full day then crawled into bed and cracked open a tattered children's grammar book Madame had scrounged from Georges. Claire tried out the new words—they all sounded like poetry—until early morning when she slept.

The French tricolor flag was lowered and the swastika rose all over the city. That Sunday, Claire sat on a high stool in the flower shop, her elbows resting on the long zinc counter as she stared at the large print in the children's book. Around her, the tin pails that brimmed with flowers the day she arrived were stacked empty against the walls. Only the hardiest blooms now graced the shop. Music crackled from the radio beneath the counter. "Mood Indigo" then "Fleur de Paris."

Madame flitted about the shop, busy as ever. Claire knew nothing actually needed to be done. The florist only paused when asked a question or to correct pronunciation.

"*Mon père est un homme d'affaires,*" Claire said, face buried in the book. My father is a businessman.

"No. No." Madame looked over Claire's shoulder at the pages. "*Mon père.* It sounds like you are choking. *Encore.* Try again."

The radio scratched loudly, then went silent. Both women

froze, eyes wide. A man broke in, his somber voice old and tinny over the airwaves. Claire could only pick out two words. *Coeur,* meaning heart, and *France.*

The broadcast ended. A tune started up, something solemn. Madame flicked the knob off. She turned away; her slender shoulders trembled.

Georges barged through the door, his young face a mask of fear and hurt. He rushed around the edge of the counter. *"Madame, la France s'est rendu. Maréchal Pétain—"*

The florist gently cupped his shoulders and pulled him in to her. His head rested on her shoulder, great shuddering sobs exploded from his chest.

"What is *rendu*?" Claire asked.

"Surrender. Marshal Pétain has surrendered us."

France had fallen.

Claire shifted on her stool and took Georges' free hand. His grip was strong, the skin hot. He burned with the emotion they tried not to feel. Madame stroked his hair, her eyes on Claire.

Claire looked back to the pages of the book. *"Mon père est un homme d'affaires."* She carefully butchered the sentence.

The florist tilted Georges' face up with a thumb under his chin. She spoke a few emphatic words then shook her head and sighed dramatically, rolling her eyes toward Claire. Understanding dawned on Georges' face as he stared at the book, then at Claire. His sobs softened to sharp gasps as he gulped air. A trace of smile tracked across his red face.

"Georges will help you learn to speak, Claire," Madame said. "I cannot. You are impossible."

# Chapter 3

## THE CANE

Avenue Montaigne, Paris. November 27, 1940.

The wind clawed at Claire's face as she trudged through the frozen slush coating the sidewalk. The sky was murky, the faint sun shrouded by writhing pewter clouds. A storm brewed sullenly overhead, but it was too cold for snow. Claire felt the bite despite the long wool overcoat, two sweaters, and yesterday's issue of *Le Temps* stuffed between each layer of fabric.

Winter had come early and with malice. It was as if Paris closed the door and shut off the lights. Go home, the city told the occupiers. But Nazis weren't the ones freezing in their beds.

A woman passed by, her breath fogging the cold air in front of her. In her arms, a heavy bundle of fabric. The lump startled Claire when it chortled, baby laughter. Claire sighed and tugged up her coat collar around her ears. Somehow life moved on.

Her shoulder ached from the weight of the cart behind her, clenched fingers numb on the handle. The intersection ahead was avenue Montaigne. Another block to the delivery entrance at Hôtel Emeraude. And warmth. Claire moved faster, taking short strides on the balls of her feet to keep from sliding on the ice-covered cobbles. Instinctively, one hand reached back to test the blanket stretched over the cart's top. The arrangements she had worked on all morning. Yes, still wrapped up tight like her own newborn babes.

A man rushed around the corner and smacked full-body into Claire. She fell hard to a knee, wind knocked from her. From the cart, the loud clink of jolted vases. The man scrambled to his feet and scurried away.

"*Merde!*" Claire hissed as she stood and steadied the cart before it tipped. She didn't even want to imagine the flowers, twisted and broken on the cobbles. They would be impossible to replace. She glared back down the street, looking for the rushing man. From her quick impression of a tailored wool coat and the faint scent of woodsy cologne, he didn't seem like the type to trample a woman and leave. But he was gone. This was not the Paris she had found six months ago.

Claire glanced down at her faded green coat, a kindness from Madame Palain. Heavy black stockings swathed her legs beneath her long skirt. But then again, maybe it wasn't the times that kept him from stopping. Perhaps it was her. Sighing, she tucked her scarf carefully into her coat collar and reached for the cart. Too bad she couldn't have dressed a little more interestingly for Leluc. She would have had a better chance of getting something extra, perhaps a chunk of coal for the stove at home from the hotel's special supply.

The wind was stronger on avenue Montaigne, channeled down the wide linear boulevard. Claire pulled her hat lower and squinted against the chill. She blinked and then froze.

A half block ahead, a black sedan idled at the curb, its muffler smoking. Her heart skipped. Only the Germans had cars. Her gaze swung to the sidewalk next to the car. Soldiers in *feldgrau*, field grey. The color buried Paris and made the harsh winter even colder.

Two soldiers stood in front of a man in a worn suit. He was talking earnestly, gesturing with a clenched hand that flashed white. Papers. The Nazis were examining identification papers.

A sweep.

A third soldier stepped into view from a doorway. He returned to the car, cigarette in his mouth. His eyes caught hers. An irritated frown and he gestured her toward him, his gloved hand flashing impatiently.

Her mind raced. She forced herself to start walking, but slowly, a limp forming on one leg. She thought of the passport and visa tucked in the lining of her coat. Useless. After six months in France, the stamps expired two weeks ago. Excuses bubbled into her thoughts. She'd been hurt. The limp, didn't they notice? But how to explain why she'd never gotten her *carte d'identité*, the identification card required by the Nazis since October?

The soldier scowled at her progress, he turned and spoke to the others.

The truth—she couldn't get the damn card. As Andrew had said long ago, all she had were stamps, she wasn't on the lists. If she went in to the police, the best she could hope for was to be sent back to the States. Welcomed home with jail time for illegal travel or worse—Russell or one of his goons with a knife. No, she wasn't going back.

Hôtel Emeraude loomed on her left, across the wide avenue. Soldiers stood guard at the front entrance beneath a monumental archway, rifles at attention. Her throat tight, she stared at the stone columns that glimmered like a mirage. She raised a shaking hand, forced a cheerful wave at the staring soldier then pointed to the hotel entrance. She stepped onto the street, her ears straining for the thud of boots pounding behind her.

A shout, but she didn't dare look back as she tugged the cart onto the sidewalk. She tried a smile for the hotel guards eyeing her approach, but it felt like a grimace. *"Blumen,"* she said to the nearest guard, displaying the hotel pass made out for La Vie en Fleurs for flower delivery. Picking up a corner of a blanket, she waved at the greenery peeking out as though it were a gift made just for them.

He flicked his eyes over her then back to the street. A long moment then he nodded, jerking his head toward the door. Claire stole a glance behind her as she climbed the limestone stairs. The soldiers across the street were stuffing the man into the backseat of the car.

Her legs went weak as she entered the lobby. She gripped the cart and forced herself to examine the hotel's interior as she pulled herself together. Swags of golden silk hung from windows. Intricate rugs nearly covered the oak parquet floor. Silk upholstered chairs clustered around a glowing marble fireplace. Not bad, but the German officers gathered by the fire ruined the ambience.

"Madame?" A voice, consternation evident in the tone.

Claire forced a smile. *"Bonjour,* Monsieur Leluc."

A small man with large glasses peered over the front desk. Leluc's face was owlish, with wide-open eyes and a surprised expression that never quite went away. He was manager of the hotel, a distinguished position before the war. The precariousness of his position looked to be wearing on him. "The front entrance, Madame?" He shook his head and scurried toward a long hallway. "Come with me, please."

Claire peeled off her scarf as she followed him down the corridor. Hôtel Emeraude was balmy compared to most buildings in the city. The German officer residents made sure Leluc had plenty of coal to keep their little pink asses warm. She tried not to notice the men she saw through open doors, bent over desks or staring out at her, cigarettes smoldering in their hands.

Leluc turned into a cramped room at the corridor's end. He squeezed past boxes overflowing with papers and behind a large desk wedged into a corner. The room's one small window was covered with fabric and newspaper to keep out the cold.

"Yes." He glanced about his new office, answering Claire's unspoken question. "But I am lucky." He sat back in his chair and nodded toward her cart. *"Madame Palain sait se débrouiller."* She gets things done. A high compliment. "I don't know how you have anything in your shop. No one else does."

Claire just smiled as she eased wrapped bundles from the cart and set them on his desk one by one. Georges once explained *Débrioullard. Le system D.* It meant, he told her, to manage the system. And Madame Palain did. For the starved in the occupied zone, every spare patch of dirt was used for raising vegetables, for scratching out any kind of food at all. Flowers couldn't be eaten. But the petite florist made phone calls, wrote letters. And the flowers came.

"The service you offer is a reminder of civilization in these dark days. You do not see and hear what I do in this place."

Claire unwrapped the arrangements as he spoke, each a study of a few cheery blooms adorned with dried flowers, shining polished twigs and ribbons. All showcased a different color: pink, white, crimson and gold. *"Voilà.* What do you think, Monsieur?"

His eyes brightened and a small smile skittered across his face. He hurried around the desk to inspect each one, his face inches from the blooms. "Ah, exquisite. Very elegant." He straightened; momentary pleasure animated his pudgy cheeks. "Madame Palain has outdone herself. Such liveliness, such joy. I will need a dozen more."

Claire smiled with pride.

He caught her expression. "Was it you? Did you make these?"

Warmth crept up her neck. These were the first important arrangements Claire created alone. Her own design. She nodded.

"You have a talent, Madame. A real talent. To create beauty to share in times such as this. It is a gift."

The thing of it was—the damned thing—Claire knew he was right. She'd realized it her first week at La Vie en Fleurs. It wasn't just that each flower's beauty was amplified in her compositions; it wasn't only that architectural forms built themselves under her hands. Under Madame's tutelage in the little flower shop, Claire somehow become inspired—driven. The labor was a challenge, the product ephemeral. But this simple art had become her barricade against the growing darkness.

She swallowed the lump in her throat. Of all the flattery laid on her over the years, this odd little man touched her. "Oh, please, Monsieur, your praise is too much."

Leluc blushed and busied himself with unlocking a metal box on his desk. He popped the lid open and counted out bills. With the smallest grin, he added several more to the pile. "For your talent."

"*Merci.*" She kissed his cheek and slipped the money into her coat pocket, smiling as he escorted her out the back entrance.

The empty cart bounced behind Claire as she nearly skipped along the alley behind the hotel. She squeezed the francs in her pocket. Her mouth watered. Without proper identification, she couldn't get a ration card. Without a card, she couldn't legally buy food. Georges was sweet and slipped her what he could from the store. Madame Palain brought breakfast and sometimes dinner too, but Claire knew Madame was making a great sacrifice. She doubted either ate much when they weren't sharing a meal. They both had lost more weight than they could spare, and the worst of winter lay ahead. This would buy food for them both. A demi-kilo of black-market butter. A chicken, perhaps. If she had enough, potatoes. She would need cooking fuel, as well.

She paused, a careful glance on avenue Montaigne. No cars, no sweeps, but a line had formed in front of the Théâtre des Champs-Elysées for an early show. An afternoon's warm diversion for a lucky few. Claire turned onto the sidewalk, adding up the dinner's costs in her head for an evening's diversion for herself and Madame.

The strong whiff of chocolate and warm pastries stopped her in her tracks. A café, Claire saw as she turned, displaying dessert in a large window. She paused next to the doorway, letting her gaze wander over the tables inside while she knocked the icy muck off her shoes. There were white tablecloths, real china. Rows of pastries, fruit. Judging by the location, maybe even real coffee. It was warmer next to the door; a couple of men bundled in worn coats leaned against the wall nearby, pilfering the faint heat. Claire riffled the bills in her pocket.

Just inside the café's doorway, an elderly Frenchman tugged a heavy wool coat over bent shoulders. He noted Claire's desiring expression through the window and glanced down at the chocolates. A small smile, then he pursed thin lips and shook his head, as if such sweets were too decadent, not to be tasted. He pulled on a thick fur hat, tipped it at Claire and reached a frail hand for a cane.

In the window's reflection, Claire watched a party of German SS officers leave the Hôtel Emeraude. Their heavy jackboots cracked against the icy sidewalk as they marched toward the café. An officer, high ranking by the insignias on his jacket, paused behind her. His eyes flicked over her from muffled head to foot, dismissed her as nothing.

The café door opened, the Frenchman set the foot of his cane onto the sidewalk before him, as if testing his next stride. The officer didn't spare the man a glance and shouldered into him. The cane slid in between the Nazi's striding legs and tangled. He stumbled, windmilling his arms to catch his balance as he slid over the icy walkway and landed hard on his back.

Movement on the street froze. The soldiers guarding the hotel entrance, the men loitering in front of the restaurant, the people passing by. Even the chatter from inside the restaurant was silenced as if a switch was turned off. The old man's eyes widened in shock, his mouth dropped open. The Nazi lunged to his feet, brushing at the filthy slush soaking his uniform.

In one motion, the officer pulled a pistol from inside his jacket and fired a bullet into the old man's chest.

The frail body flew backward; the door shook against the hinges with the force of the blow. The fur hat skittered across the sidewalk as the man collapsed onto the cobbles. Blood turned the grey slush under him into a dirty copper brown. Kicking at the hat, the officer led the men into the café.

Claire released the handle of her cart and leaped forward. *Attendez*, wait, someone called behind her. She didn't. She couldn't. Dropping to her knees, Claire peeled off her scarf and pressed it against the wound.

He looked up to her, cloudy eyes gleamed over the pallor

of his face. "Ha." His voice was raspy. "I nearly brought that *batârd* down."

The old man was fighting back the best way he could. He may well have fought the Germans twenty years before in the Great War. Even here, bleeding in the frozen slush, he was a proud French soldier. Claire blinked back tears burning behind her eyes and smiled. "You fought a good battle today, Monsieur."

He choked on a reply, his breath a thin wheeze. Claire looked up for help.

Across the street, the soldiers guarding the hotel were staring, guns at attention. Everyone else had disappeared except for one of the men who warmed himself in the café's heat. Even he had retreated back into the building's shadows. He watched beneath a cap pulled low over his eyes.

"Help us. He needs to get to a doctor," she said.

His bearded face remained expressionless as he scrutinized her. He finally turned away, cigarette clenched in his mouth, gaze on the street. Biting back a curse, Claire turned to the old man. His grimace faded as he let out a long, hoarse sigh. His rigid body went slack. He was gone.

Claire sank back into the slush, feeling its bite as it soaked through to her legs. She heard panting, realized it was her breath. The cane rested half off the curb. The handle was ivory, gold-rimmed, an elaborate dog's head. Claire reached, felt the cold surface press into her skin.

Coarse laughter echoed from the café. A moment's amusement for them, she realized. The fear and anger she felt for the old man, the German soldiers, the constant struggle for life in this tortured city blazed together. She leaped to her feet, cane clenched in her fist, and strode for the door.

A strong hand grabbed her shoulder and yanked her back. The man in the shadows—the *connard* who hadn't lifted a finger to save the old man—was dragging her away from the café. Claire elbowed him hard in the ribs as he pulled her into an alley.

He cursed and let go. Under the sandy beard, his face was sculpted with sharp cheekbones and deep-set eyes. Those eyes. The English bastard that insisted Laurent send her away. Thomas Grey.

"You sorry—" Claire gripped the cane and swung it toward his head.

Grey caught the ivory handle. "Claire? What are you doing here?"

"You stood there and let—"

"There was no help for him." He tossed the cane across the alley.

She shoved hard on his chest. "You watched an old man die on the street."

"I watched an old man be murdered. We both did." He caught her hands and pulled her face close to his. "Tell me, Claire. Now. How were you in Hôtel Emeraude?"

"You don't get to ask me questions." She jerked herself free.

Harsh shouts rose from the direction of the restaurant. A truck engine rumbled. Grey motioned for her to stay put with a finger pointed at her face, then leaned his head out into the street. He grimaced then bit words off in his mouth. "Just go. Right now."

"I need to get my cart."

"No. Leave it. Go."

Claire brushed by him and peered into the street. A truck had brought more troops. They were filing into the restaurant. The sounds of breaking glass echoed off the stone buildings.

Grey tugged on her arm. "You—"

"Just shut up." Claire turned into the darkness of the alley and stalked away from the restaurant, away from everything.

The banks of the Seine forced her to turn. She walked mind-lessly along the brick quai toward the tall spire of Grand Palais. With every stride, the anger drained away, leaving her weak, her stomach churning. Marching into that restaurant would have been an idiotic thing to do. She would have been carted off, likely killed.

Brushing away frozen snow, Claire slumped onto an empty bench that overlooked the pont des Invalides spanning the Seine. How was she going to explain this to Madame? Now the money was going to have to buy a new cart. If one could even be found. The muddy water tossed and churned in its banks. Claire let out a long breath and closed her eyes.

Warm lips pressed against her cheek as the scent of Gauloises hit her nose. Her eyes jerked open and her hand flew up in a fist.

Laurent peered down at her, smiling. "Ah, *ma chérie*, you used to like that." He slid onto the bench next to her, parking the lost cart at her side.

Claire looked at the cart then back to him, trying to regain her poise. To see his smiling face so suddenly after the shooting, she couldn't think. His English sounded strange to her ears.

"Today must be the day for unexpected reunions," she man-aged to say.

"Yes. A surprise for everyone." He paused as two business-men walked past. "Where have you been, Claire? What have you been doing? We thought you left. Went back to New York." He shifted on the bench to rest one arm around her shoulder and the other on her leg.

Claire smiled grimly. Same old Laurent. But the touch felt good. And he still had those lips. "I've done a little of this, a little of that," she said, in her best French.

His forehead wrinkled, lips pursed. He was surprised. And, she realized, troubled.

Claire smoothed her dirty, soaked coat against her legs. She had planned on meeting him again in such different circumstances. A man on her arm, a fine dress. Jealousy was the intent. In truth, his expression read worry for her. She couldn't help that her cheeks were thin.

"Your French is very good," he said finally.

"*Merci.*" Claire extricated herself from his hands and stood. She gripped the cart, didn't meet his eyes. "I need to go, Laurent."

He plucked the handle from her hands. "By all means, *ma chérie*, lead the way."

The empty cart bounced along behind them as they walked in silence. Claire tried to strategize, but the image of the old man crowded out every thought. She rubbed her dirty glove over her nose to erase the memory of those damn chocolates.

Laurent watched her. "Grey told me he saw you. He couldn't believe it was you at first, but then when you glared at him as though you wished him dead, he was sure."

"A man died on the sidewalk. Grey could have helped."

"No. He couldn't. He was working."

"I've seen whores on street corners work harder."

He snorted, seeming impressed by the breadth of her language skills. "I'll tell him you said that."

Claire threw him a dark look. What the hell had Grey been doing hanging around next to a Nazi hotel? There were rumors of *Resistánts* banding together to make life harder for the Germans. But how could it matter how the Nazis slept or ate? She clamped her mouth shut. She didn't care what Grey heard.

"You didn't leave Paris. What did you do? Where did you go? The hotel today—" Laurent tugged at her arm. She slid out of his grasp without slowing, leaving him struggling with the cart and trotting to catch up.

It was another block to the flower shop. She toyed with the idea of continuing on to avenue des Champs-Elysées. Can't a girl do a bit of shopping, she would say. But then where would she go? Her shoulders sagged as she realized she didn't have the energy to lie. Not after this afternoon. She thought back to the moment on the street. The last wheezing breath. Grey's expressionless face. She turned and stared Laurent in the eye. "What was Grey doing?"

Laurent looked uneasy. He rooted in his coat pocket for a cigarette, a move Claire remembered. He lit a half-smoked Gauloises and took a long drag.

They stopped in front of the flower shop. He glanced up, expression puzzled, as though he had just noticed where they were. She waved toward the awning that read *La Vie en Fleurs*.

"This is where I've been." Claire straightened her shoulders, head up. She would not be ashamed. "I'm a florist."

Laurent's eyes widened. His mouth relaxed into a surprised grin. "Ah. You work with Madame Palain?" He shook his head and took a drag off his cigarette. As he chuckled, a trail of smoke escaped his lips. "You were making a delivery today?"

"Yes. It amazes you that much I can be useful?" Claire snagged the cart from his hand and rolled a tire over his foot as she opened the door.

His mouth crimped in pain and he shifted his weight on his heels, but he still struggled to answer her question. "No. It is Madame. She is very . . ."

"Proper, Monsieur Olivier." Madame stepped from the door and pulled her sweater tighter over her shoulders. "I imagine you were going to say proper."

Laurent blushed deep scarlet. "Yes, Madame. I was going to say that."

Claire looked back and forth between them.

Madame smiled at Laurent then at Claire. "I have offered suggestions to Monsieur Olivier in the past. I don't believe my opinion has always been welcomed."

Laurent chuckled, his head hanging like a guilty schoolboy.

Claire held back a snort. The florist was even more powerful than she knew.

Laurent looked up from his shoes. "Perhaps I can atone for some of my less refined days. I am having a small party. It would be my deepest pleasure to invite you both to dinner tonight."

A trace of excitement bubbled in Claire's chest. Another chance with Laurent? Then an equally fast quashing. A cavalier dinner invitation was hardly an offer, compared to the ones he'd whispered so long ago. "No. It would be impossible."

"*Oui*, Monsieur. It gives us great pleasure to accept your invitation," Madame said.

Claire glared at the florist, her lips biting back a protest. Madame didn't deign to notice. She extended her hand to Laurent, palm down, the way, Claire had learned, either an aristocrat or Madame Palain exited a conversation.

Laurent leaned down, a soft kiss with the propriety befitting a knight and his queen. "Perhaps you could find yourselves at my apartment at eight thirty this evening?"

"Of course. That will be perfect," the florist said.

Laurent looked back to Claire. "I can't believe you were here all along." He took one last drag from his cigarette and carefully snuffed it out with a finger and thumb, then replaced it into the tin in his coat's hip pocket. He stepped forward, lips pursed as though to offer Claire *la bise*, a kiss on each cheek.

She leaned away from him, her face nonplussed. "*Au revoir*, Laurent."

"Until tonight." He inclined his head to her then turned on his heel. "Here all along." He shook his head as he walked away down the street.

The florist hummed a tune as she maneuvered the cart against the wall in the back room. Claire marched straight to her.

"Madame, why did you say we would go?" Her voice was shrill to her own ears. "I can't eat his food. You don't know what went on between us. Before."

"If you knew Monsieur Olivier before, it is not hard to imagine what went on between you. He has spent a great deal of money here over the years. The address file of women he has sent flowers to is as thick as my palm." She grasped Claire's shoulder and tugged her over to the mirror lining the back room wall. "Look at yourself. What do you see?"

"I don't know. What do you mean?"

"You are a beautiful woman. You are in Paris and the only people you speak to on many days are Georges and I. And you are too thin. Don't be foolish. You will go to dinner, laugh, flirt and eat until you can't swallow another bite. There is a use, at times, for that kind of man."

"But, Madame, you're coming too, right?"

"Ah, Claire, I am not going. Monsieur invited you, not me."

"He invited us both. And you accepted. For. Us. Both."

Madame shook her head and sighed. Her hands dropped to her sides as if she didn't have the will to hold on anymore. "You must pay better attention, Claire. There was what was said and what was meant. You will never learn to be Parisian if you insist on conversing like an unschooled American. You are impossible." She left Claire alone in front of the mirror.

Soft yellow light glimmered from candles clustered in a silver tray in Claire's dim bedroom. Staring into the full-length mirror, she smoothed the grey wool dress over her hips and twisted her body to view her silhouette. The bulky fabric helped hide her thinness and almost gave Claire her figure back. She'd been so active trying to help Madame make ends meet in the flower shop, her skin, though pale, exhibited a healthy glow. A touch of crimson red lipstick was all it took. Not bad, but something was missing.

She laughed. Of course, how could she have forgotten? She tugged the top drawer forward until its face rested on her bent knee and groped around behind the drawer's backing until her fingers touched a hard bundle wedged against the wood. Her jewelry roll. Sitting on the bed, she untied the ribbon and unrolled the silk fabric.

In spite of herself, her pulse quickened. Diamonds. The necklace's weight pressed into her palm, stones sparkling in the faint light. She hadn't even thought of it since she put it away the day she arrived. She ran her hands over the sharp, cold edges. So ridiculously big! The pendant extended past the curves of her palm. Madame would pronounce it gauche. It was still ravishing. Claire slipped it on and let the pendant slip down toward the vee in her dress.

The touch of cold stones against her skin sent her mind back to the last evening she wore the jewels. Her final night at her brownstone in the city. Distance had faded the memory to a blur of men in tuxedos, women in diamonds and fur, and the orchestra playing Glenn Miller. Something out of a picture show, but the cold weight squeezing against her chest wouldn't let her forget how it ended.

Claire dropped the necklace back into the cloth, rolled it into a ball and tucked it back into its hiding place. She was smarter now. She'd learned. She wouldn't trade her life now, hungry and cold as she remained, to have that New York–socialite role back. Not for anything in the world. Including diamonds. Staring at the bare space the necklace left behind, she pulled a midnight blue scarf from the drawer and knotted it around her neck as Madame had taught her. Tonight she would be restrained. She would have impeccable poise. She would do and say as Madame would. She was Parisian now.

It was just a few blocks from the flower shop to Laurent's apartment on rue d'Artois, but the cold and memories of Claire's last trip down this street jarred her with each step. The blackout was in effect and the darkness of the city compounded her mood.

Claire arrived at Laurent's doorway at the moment she determined she would turn around and go home. Better to face Madame's chiding in the morning than walk in there again. Undoubtedly the sullen Englishman would be in attendance. It was clear in what regard he held Claire from their unfortunate meeting today. And she was confident she thought even less of him.

"*Excusez-moi.*"

Claire whipped around, bumping into the door. "Oh. It's you." She inspected Grey's dark bundled shape.

The muscles tightened in his freshly shaved jaw. His steel eyes narrowed. "I didn't expect you here."

"Really?" Claire pulled the flaps of the thick coat collar away from her face and fluffed her hair. "Perhaps you aren't in charge of the guest list." She rapped on the carved wood with gloved knuckles.

Grey slipped past her and opened the door.

She threw a smile back at him as she entered past him into light and music. "I'm sure your parties are a real scream though."

He slipped off his coat and held his hand out for hers. Claire shrugged her coat into his arms and inspected him as he turned away. His tailored suit revealed broad shoulders narrowing to a trim waist as he hung the coats in a concealed closet.

They walked side by side to the salon's doorway then paused and looked at each other. She wasn't about to enter the party with this bastard. He stood back from her, the hint of a smile on his lips. Apparently, neither was he.

"After you." Grey tilted his head toward the doorway.

Claire peeled back her lips into her coldest smile. *"Merci."* She entered.

The salon shimmered in candlelight. Men in tailored suits and women in soft dresses, the strains of forbidden jazz on the record player. A long marble-topped table reflected glints of flickering candles between the black-market bread, cheese and wine. Paintings in gold-leaf frames glowed like scattered embers in the light. Laurent's photos, framed in black, leaned discreetly against the wall.

It amazed Claire to think this place had almost been home. For a while anyway. She could almost imagine what it would have been like if she'd stayed. If she had helped throw tonight's fête. She felt a stab of sadness that she and Laurent weren't a beautiful couple, ensconced in a beautiful life.

No one seemed to notice her. Claire found an empty space next to the fireplace. She extended her cold hands toward the flames as Grey headed to a couple across the room. He kissed the woman on the cheek and greeted the man with the first smile Claire had seen on him. In spite of herself, she noticed how the grin sparked Grey's eyes and warmed his face in a way some might call handsome.

The man was short, stocky, with a burst of dark hair on the top of his head. He wore heavy trousers, faded tie, stiff collar and a sweater with the sleeves rolled up to reveal thick forearms. The woman was in her early forties, in a worn but impeccable brown tweed suit. After a moment of talk, the woman squeezed Grey's hand, left the men and approached Claire.

Claire's mouth dried up. What did Grey tell them about her? She took a deep breath and smoothed the wool over her hips. Poise, restraint, grace, she told herself. She pulled back her shoulders and arranged a smile as the woman faced her.

"Good evening, Madame Harris. I am Odette Berri. I am pleased to make your acquaintance." The woman extended a firm hand. Her pleasantries didn't extend to her face, kept politely neutral.

"Good evening, Madame Berri. Thank you."

"My husband, Jacques." She gestured toward the man speaking with Grey.

That was a surprise. Though Odette's suit was a bit worn, her manner appeared too refined to be married to the man next to Grey. He looked like a farmer fidgeting in his Sunday best.

Odette distractedly fingered a loose curl of wiry salt-and-pepper hair and glanced back toward the men as if thinking about rejoining them. "How are you finding Paris?"

Claire raised an eyebrow at the rather wishful attempt at benign conversation.

The woman glanced away and tried to suppress a grin. "Never mind." She met Claire's gaze. "You find Paris cold, hungry and beaten. Same as every other cold, hungry person in the city." Her eyes were an arresting green, with laugh wrinkles at the corners. "I hate inconsequential conversation." She nodded toward the table, still unvisited. Her eyes lingered on a platter laden with slices of cream-colored paste layered on toasted bread. "I wish Laurent would join us so we may begin. I haven't tasted foie gras or brioche in months."

A genuine smile found its way onto Claire's face. "I can't believe he has all this."

"It cost him." Madame Berri shook her head with a sideways look.

Claire shrugged, the *what can you do in these times?* expression the Parisians fell back on more and more. Still, her mouth watered looking at the table. "Thank you for asking, Madame Berri. About Paris. I do love it."

"Good." A grin tugged at her lips. "You may call me Odette."

"Thank you, Odette. Please call me Claire."

Laurent walked into the room with a woman on his arm. Unlike the other women in the room, she made no concessions for the cold weather. Early thirties, in a thin silk dress, deep green with fluttering cap sleeves. Dark hair cut short and fingered into place. Long emeralds dangled from her ears. Her thin silver heels cracked across the parquet floor.

Claire raised an eyebrow toward Odette.

"Couture. New, I'm sure." Odette's nose wrinkled, as if she'd eaten something bad.

Not Claire's style, but no denying the clothes were expensive. Nicer than could be found in stores these days. But the woman wasn't much to look at. Tiny eyes and a hard little mouth that seemed to search for reasons to turn down. It appeared Laurent had found himself a moneyed woman. Not what Claire expected to find this evening, but, she decided, good for him.

"Is that his latest?" Claire watched as they circled the room, welcoming guests, making their way toward the pair by the fire.

Odette's head swiveled toward Claire. "Oh . . . No. I wish. That—" Odette sighed. "That is his wife of many years."

A flash of heat tore through Claire's body. He had asked, almost pleaded, for her to leave her husband and move to Paris with him, and he was married? She willed her cheeks cool, her expression composed while thoughts screamed in her head.

Laurent smiled and said hello to Odette, then switched to English as he turned to Claire. "Claire. I am so glad you could make it. Was Madame Palain not able to join us?"

Claire smiled, anger adding warmth that wasn't there. Poise. Restraint. "Thank you, Laurent, for your kind invitation. Madame was indisposed tonight." And it's damn lucky for her she's not here. Claire offered her cheeks for Laurent's *la bise*, quick pecks, right and left, right and left.

He put an arm around the woman's shoulders and drew her forward. "I would like you to meet someone. This is my, eh, wife, Sylvie Olivier."

Sylvie's eyes flicked once down and up Claire's form. Her skin pinched around her lips as if she bit into a lemon.

Poise. Restraint. "Madame Olivier, I am pleased to—" Claire said.

Sylvie turned to Laurent. In a voice that cut across the room, she said in French, "From what I'd heard, I expected her to be more attractive, Laurent."

Claire felt Odette flinch next to her. An icy smile stretched across Claire's face. She's going to play it this way, eh? Claire responded in French, her tone loud and cheery. "That is so sweet of Laurent to speak of me. He never mentioned you at all."

Silence exploded across the room like a mortar. Claire arranged her most innocent expression. She knew how to win this game. Rising in position in New York society was a blood sport.

Grey coughed into his drink.

Claire kept her smile as Sylvie's eyes glittered and her pinched expression deepened. It was a standoff, and neither woman was going to back down.

Laurent retained his smile but his eyes twitched like a snared animal's. His discomfort was a small salve to Claire's pride. He will have to chew off more than his foot to escape this trap, she thought.

"This is a beautiful display you put together tonight," said Odette. "Laurent, would you like to open the champagne?"

"Oh, yes. Of course." He gestured welcome to the scattered guests in the room. "My good friends. Thank you all for joining us tonight. Please enjoy yourselves."

He steered Sylvie away. She took her seat at the end of the table without another glance back.

Odette hung back with Claire. Her tone was light. "You must try the foie gras. This is from ducks raised in Gers. It is worth it." A gentle squeeze on Claire's arm held more meaning. There is more here than you know, it implied.

As the guests gathered around the table, Claire found and slid into her chair. The seating arrangement had taken some thought, though it seemed to be explicitly to her disadvantage. To her left was Jacques, Odette sat to his left. Grey was across from Claire, between him and Laurent at the head of the table sat Monsieur and Madame Bruel.

Sylvie's cousin sat on Claire's right. He was introduced as Bertrand or perhaps Burcet. In Paris on business, he was middle management in Sylvie's family's textiles factory in Lyons. Sylvie sat at the end of the table to his right. The family resemblance was noticeable. They shared the little eyes and tight mouth, though on him it was muffled in the vacuum of his personality.

To Grey's left preened a young bird in burgundy organza. She was new to Laurent's group, a friend of Sylvie's. She leaned in to Sylvie's ear and whispered something that made her hard eyes glint.

Claire fortified herself with a glass a wine and watched the bird, also referred to as Babette, attempt to charm Grey. As the first plate was passed by, Babette rubbed Grey's shoulder with her bare arm. Puff pastries skittered dangerously toward the edge of the leaning plate. When he was forced to answer a question, Babette leaned into his face and cooed her agreement. With each attempt at seduction, Grey's posture became more erect, his expression more stern. Claire wondered how long until he climbed up on the table in self-defense. At least Claire wasn't the only one suffering.

Laurent presided at the head of the table. A side Claire had never seen, a stuffy aristocrat, too much self-conscious congratulation mixed with a host's graciousness. It almost bothered her more than the sudden appearance of a wife. But not quite.

They spoke of the weather, some inane story of a cousin's yacht in Nice running aground last summer while the captain charted a course across the cousin's wife. The couple, the story went, refused to be rescued from the listing boat for hours.

"Good. A captain must go down *in* his ship," Jacques pronounced, raising his glass.

Chatting wasn't easy. Every detail of life since last summer was imprisoned in the cold depths of the Occupation.

The mystery of how Laurent managed the feast was solved at the first pause in conversation. Business had doubled at Sylvie's family's factory, the cousin announced at Sylvie's nudging. The coldest winter in years, competition shut down. It was sad of course, but Grandpa's company must persevere through these difficult days. Nods of agreement and the conversation stalled. Grey's eyes darkened and he busied himself forming a forkful of puffed pastry and baked chicken.

After a moment of whispering between Babette and Sylvie, Babette turned to Claire. "You're an American. What is it you do that you haven't been shipped back to your own country?"

The attention of the table swiveled to Claire. She swallowed hard at the food lodged in her throat. Without the right papers, she wasn't legally able to work. Wasn't able to do anything, for that matter. Madame Palain turned a blind eye. *Vous travaillez au noir*, meaning she worked under the table. With a room full of strangers and Sylvie gunning for her across the baguettes, Claire couldn't risk answering and putting herself or Madame Palain in the German's sights.

Grey looked up from his plate for the first time seemingly in hours. "She is what they refer to as a socialite in the United

States. Apparently, Madame Harris is known to be particularly talented at important social activities."

Claire didn't know what to say. She wasn't sure where he was going with this. He very may well be insulting her.

"What does a socialite do, exactly?" Grey grinned now; he appeared to be enjoying needling her.

Claire rewarded him with an honest smile. "Oh, I usually throw extravagant parties, shop for diamonds and seduce"—Claire glanced at Laurent—"pitiful, dim-witted men. A bit tiresome, really."

A low laugh rolled over the table. Madame Bruel began a story about an American movie she had seen like that, *Hôtel Grand*. The cousin poured Claire more wine. Dessert was served, a runny cheese confection spooned onto crystal plates.

They laughed, drank and ate. Soon a feeling near warm camaraderie blanketed the table. The cousin—was it Burcet or Bertrand?—laid his hand on Claire's thigh when he yet again refilled her glass. Jacques and Odette excused themselves to get home to little Gerard.

"Grandma will have had her fill of him by now." Odette extended a warm smile to Claire as they left.

Monsieur and Madame Bruel also begged their leave; he was a lawyer and had an early case. The remaining group drifted from the table, the women to the chairs by the fire, the men near the window. The cousin eyed Claire before he took his place with Laurent and Grey, a thin pout on his face.

Claire turned to examine the painting over the fireplace. It had been brilliantly executed, tiny brushstrokes depicting two poor farm children gleaning the last stray bits of the harvested field. *"Très enchanteur,"* Claire murmured as she wondered why the hell Laurent hung such a depressing scene over his mantel.

Sylvie and Babette closed ranks around Claire. "Laurent said you didn't speak French," Babette started.

"I've learned."

"Strange you hadn't studied it in school," said Sylvie.

"Yes. Isn't it."

"I thought all American socialites went to finishing schools. Babette and I met in Switzerland at Château Mont-Choisi."

"How nice for you both." Claire took a drink and smiled, showing her teeth. "I was already finished." Claire was reminded of something her Mama said: *You gotta be careful, Claire, fighting with pigs. They like to roll around in the mud. You just get dirty.*

"*C'est vrai?* Well, in France it takes more than blue eyes and lipstick to interest a man of consequence," Sylvie said, eyes glittering.

Claire felt a pair of eyes on her back. She turned. The men were standing by the window drinking scotch. Laurent was pointing something out to the cousin on the street below. Grey was watching her.

She drank deep and emptied her glass. "I think I'm ready for something stronger."

Claire marched past Grey and placed a hand on the cousin's thick shoulder. Gazing deep into his eyes, she slid her fingers down his arm to tap the rim of his glass. She smiled, running a tongue over her lips. What the hell was his name? "Hello again, my personal bartender, how about some scotch?"

In short order, her glass was full, the scotch was building a warm fire in her stomach, and Sylvie and Babette, for the moment, stopped stalking her. They all retired to the stuffed chairs scattered around the window. Babette slid next to Grey. Claire leaned against the cousin, the most boring man she had ever met, and asked him about textiles. It was hard to feign interest and keep the conversation going. She still couldn't remember his name, and the drink had gone straight to her head.

She ran two fingers down his jelly-filled leg toward his knee. Sylvie and Babette were silent. Apparently, even in France it was in poor taste to insult the woman who was giving your cousin a small erection. Laurent lost the pretense of being interested in his wife, and his gaze kept falling on Claire. All that was ruining the pleasant fuzziness she felt were the burning cold glares from Grey.

"It's late. And time for me to go." Grey lurched from the seat, away from Babette's tangling arms.

The cousin's hand slid down her hip toward Claire's thigh. His pudding body pressed against her. A wave of nausea hit her. She swallowed. Cold air was needed. Fast.

Claire pulled herself free and stood. "I also must be leaving. I have a full day of shopping tomorrow." She looked over at Sylvie. "You know how tiring that is."

The cousin scrambled to his feet next to her. "I will take you home."

The scotch was burning its way up her throat. "Burcet—"

"Bertrand," he said, lips pushing forward in an angry pout.

"I'm sorry, I don't even know your name, but you are. So. Boring. And—" She shuddered and slipped away from his hands. "Don't." She waved him off. "Just don't."

"Claire." Laurent reached for her elbow.

She jerked her arm back, stepping away. "Laurent. Thanks for an . . . evening." Lurching from the salon into the hallway, thank God, the closet was open and her coat in sight. She skittered down the stairs as fast as she could go. A few wobbly strides across the hall and outside. Doubling over, she vomited into the cone-shaped topiary boxwoods.

"Let me take you home. You aren't well." Grey shrugged on his coat behind her.

"Damn." She hadn't wanted to lose dinner. Claire straightened up. It took a moment for her eyes to catch up to her head, but her stomach seemed to be staying put.

Grey handed her a kerchief. "It's past curfew. I'll take you."

Claire wiped her face with the cloth. She was relieved to find she hadn't thrown up on her dress or coat.

Laurent rushed onto the step, hugging his arms to his body against the chill. "Claire, you mustn't misunderstand this thing with Sylvie. We married when we were very young, in school. This is Paris. She doesn't even live—"

"Laurent," Grey said, a low warning tone.

Laurent frowned, then turned to Grey. "I deserve the chance to explain myself."

"Not now. You are needed inside."

Laurent sighed, facing Claire. "*Au revoir*, Claire. I was truly glad to see you again." He turned on his heel and hurried back in the door.

Grey watched him close the door and turned back to Claire. "I don't like anything that happened tonight. But"—he shook his head and tugged his coat collar up around his ears—"I'm getting you home."

"Really?" Claire said with as much venom as she could muster, pulling her coat tight around her. "I am not interested in your opinion of my actions. Nor do I need *or* desire an escort." She marched away, head high, saying a prayer she wouldn't stumble. She called over her shoulder. "Thanks for the kerchief. I will wash and return it."

She felt his eyes bore into her back. She glanced behind her. He hadn't moved from the sidewalk; his hands were stuffed in his pockets, his stare drilling through her. A warm shiver rose up her torso.

As she turned the corner, she heard him swear, *bloody Yankee princess*. A sharp ache dug into her chest. She was so damn tired of pretending to be someone she was not, of scratching her way up. It never worked. Not for long. The little barefooted farm girl was still there, inside her. *Bloody Yankee princess*. He had no idea. She breathed deep into the cold air, letting it burn away at the fuzz in her head and lungs.

# Chapter 4

## THE OFFER

52, rue du Colisée, Paris. November 28, 1940.

The click of a heavy bolt into the flower shop's ancient front door marked lunch break. Claire pressed away from the bench in the back room and stretched. She had hand-painted curved tree branches silver and gold all morning. They hung like long jeweled fingers from a wire stretched across the small room. Lunch wasn't in mind. Her stomach still churned from last night's scotch; she couldn't even look at the brined egg Georges had passed her.

It was easy to stay busy. The Paris Ritz called this morning. The hotel had lost their florist to the fighting, and their greenhouses had been requisitioned for growing food for the hotel. But apparently Marshal Goering, Field Marshal of the Luftwaffe and said to be running the Blitz against England from the hotel's Imperial Suite, demanded something lavish be done for the New Year. The staff at the Ritz turned in desperation to La Vie en

Fleurs. The contract was generous, much-needed money, and Claire's first opportunity to make masses of lavish arrangements. Overseen, of course, by Madame.

The florist left Claire mercifully alone this morning. She took one look at Claire's face and sent her to the back with gold leaf and paste. The branches were structural elements of the arrangement; small crystals would hang from them, like icicles in a golden forest. Tomorrow, Claire would be gold-leafing ceramic nuts.

Madame walked into the back room. She inspected each stem, her eyes inches away, her hands tucked behind her back. "Quite nice, Claire. I'm pleased. You show discipline."

Claire raised an eyebrow at the compliment. Discipline?

Madame smoothed a loose fleck of gold leaf with a fingernail as she spoke. "A party at the Ritz will be sophisticated, extravagant, no doubt. But La Vie en Fleurs brings a spirit of cultivated beauty—romance—to the night. That can't be bought. Only earned."

A loud rapping against the shop window made the florist pause.

"You seek artistry, Claire. But discipline must come first." Madame turned and left the back room.

The front door's bolt clicked. "*Bonjour*, is Madame Harris here?" asked a woman's warm voice.

Claire stepped around the corner, dusting bits of dried flecks of leaf from her dress. "Odette? What a surprise."

"*Bonjour*, Claire. I apologize for coming unannounced. Care to take a walk?"

Outside, trees shivered against a pewter sky. An icy wind gusted from the north in staccato coughs that pricked the skin. The women walked in silence. Claire inspected the passing buildings as they walked down rue Rembrandt toward parc Monceau.

Odette's mouth was pinched, her forehead creased. She spoke slowly. "I have known Laurent for seven years. Thomas introduced him to us."

It took Claire a moment to remember Grey's given name. She nodded.

"My husband works at *L'Express*. He is the foreman for the printing machines. We are simple, Jacques and I. Our social circles, we would never have crossed paths with Laurent, except for Thomas. Perhaps it is because he is English or because he is that kind of man."

Claire thought about the possibility of a man like Jacques at one of her Manhattan parties. He never would have been let in the door. "I see."

"I understand Laurent. He and I both had the same past. A few generations back, we were important. Some of us marry for love and accept who we are now. Others marry money, trying to get back to the place where we were raised to believe we belonged."

"I would say you made the better choice," Claire said, with a smile.

"*C'est vrai.*" Odette laughed. "Jacques can be a beast, and sometimes I think he would be better living in a barn. But he's good to me." She considered her words before continuing. "Sylvie is mean-spirited. It was bad enough Laurent was forced to bring her last night. He never should have invited you."

Claire shrugged. There were many things about that night she would prefer not to dwell on.

Ahead rue Rembrandt spilled into a small side entry of parc Monceau. Claire's eyes were drawn to the stately apartment buildings surrounding the park. In the dead of winter, the dark and shuttered windows looked down on the women through jagged branches of giant desolate oak trees. She shivered as much from unease as from cold.

Odette glanced back at Claire as she headed for the open gate of the iron-spired fence. "It will feel less exposed inside."

True enough. Once inside the park, Claire felt the calm dignity seep into her raw nerves. Hands bunched in pockets, they strolled along a side path tracing the park's perimeter. On their right, the buildings were a fanciful backdrop. Barren trees lined the paths they crisscrossed. Even dressed in a snowy winter grey, the park's architectural lines of trees and stone defined beauty. To Claire, parc Monceau was a stately woman, her well-bred bones showing through the ravages of the season.

Claire had come once before with Madame Palain, not long after the Occupation began. They walked beneath green spreading trees, past the grand rotunda, over a delicate bridge that arched over a finger of pond. Children chased each other along the water's edge, throwing bits of stale bread to the ducks. The mothers cajoled and ordered, *Martine, slow down; Jon Pierre, don't push your sister*, but the words rang hollow and half-hearted. Claire understood they were going through the motions. They were there because they were Parisians and, damn it, it was their park.

There was just one little boy at the bridge today. He skipped stones across the pond's half-iced surface. No bread, no matter how stale, could be wasted on birds. A nervous mother hovered behind them.

Odette turned onto a path beneath towering oaks. "Sylvie and Laurent separated years ago. Before we met them. Sylvie is a *connasse*, undoubtedly, but also useful, in a certain way."

"Really? For bringing your favorite foie gras to parties?"

Odette snickered. "Yes. But also for more."

They continued down a narrow curving lane that opened up onto a large oval pool and crumbling marble columns. Claire stepped up to the water's edge, breath suspended in her throat.

Odette smiled at Claire's reaction. "Good. I didn't think you'd been here yet."

Claire tore her eyes away from the view. "Thank you. It's beautiful."

Odette watched her a moment before continuing. "You haven't been able to leave the shop much, have you?"

Claire shook her head.

"These are dangerous days." Odette's eyes speared Claire. "Even more so if you don't have papers."

Claire started before she could cover her response. "What do you mean?"

Odette shrugged. "The way you arrived in Paris. At best your papers have expired, no? It wasn't hard to figure out."

Claire burrowed her hands deeper in her coat pockets.

"There is an option," Odette said. "We spoke of it this morning."

"We? Who is we?"

Odette pulled a half-smoked cigarette from her pocket and lit it, her hand cupped over the flame. She was either not at liberty or plain not willing to answer. "Sylvie is a collaborator. Her family's factory—wool, cloth. They are shipping it all to Germany. Not because they were taken over."

"For money," Claire said. That had been made clear last night.

The winter, she had been told, was the coldest anyone could remember. Coal prices had gone through the roof; most was hauled away for the German war effort. People froze in their beds nightly. The only way to get a coat was to take it off someone's back. Now it comes out the textile factories were shipping their cloth to Germany.

"What do you say to that, Claire?"

Sylvie left a horrible taste in Claire's mouth. It would be easy to say what Odette was fishing for. But, Odette deserved to know the truth.

"I knew industrialists back in New York. Successful, hard men; my husband was one of them. Sylvie's family is no mystery to me. My husband would let poor Americans die to make a buck."

Odette's eyes squinted as she tried to decipher Claire's answer.

"If you are seeking moral high ground, don't look to me. I have no high ground to climb onto, Odette. I gave that up years ago."

Odette nearly spit her reply. "You agree with what they do?"

"I'm wearing a coat that was probably made before I was born." Claire tugged on her lapel, shaking her head with a mirthless chuckle. "No. I don't. Her greed is despicable. It's just not surprising."

"So?"

"Sylvie and her family are puppets. The money? The Nazis are throwing them crumbs. It is easier to pay them, right now. What does that mean to the Nazis? They print their own money. If they wanted, they could seize the factory today."

Odette smiled grimly. "That is true."

Claire's voice softened; selling out was a topic she knew too well. "Sylvie has to spread 'em wide for her masters. She takes the reichsmarks left on the nightstand and pretends she is loved and respected. She's not."

"What Sylvie is doing, what you saw yesterday in front of the hotel—doesn't it make you want to act?"

Odette knew about the old man too? Claire took an unconscious step back. "I don't like any of it. But I won't get involved."

"You aren't curious about what I may offer you?"

"I don't think I'll like the price."

"Everything in life costs, Claire. You should know that."

Claire did know. And she was damn tired of paying with her soul.

Odette glanced about them. They were alone. "You cannot speak of this to anyone, you understand? You would be able to travel about Paris, about France, as safe as any other Parisian."

"How?"

"A false identification card. You would be American, of course, but married to a Frenchman. And gainfully employed. You could have a ration card."

The possibilities swam in Claire's mind. Bread. Meat. Potatoes. "How?"

Odette didn't answer. Eyes watchful, she motioned for Claire to walk with her. "You couldn't be Claire Harris anymore. You would have to become someone else. Could you do that?"

Odette didn't know how little she asked. Claire smothered a laugh. "The cost?"

"We wouldn't have offered if we didn't believe you would benefit. We ask little."

"Well?"

"The hotels. Crillon, Lutetia, George V, Emeraude, Meurice, the Ritz. The Germans hold them all, use them all. General von Schaumburg commands all of Paris from Hôtel Meurice. Goering directs the air bombing of England from the Ritz. Important things occur inside hotel walls. Things we need to know."

"I'm no spy."

"No. You're not. But you do get inside. That's not easy to do. All we ask is you note what and who you see."

"Dangerous."

"You'd give us a little report, anonymous, not traceable to you, dropped in a mailbox. What is more dangerous? The papers you have in your pocket right now would get you taken in, no?"

Claire took a deep breath. A bird chirped in the tree above them. They both watched as a man rode a bicycle down the path behind the ruin.

"I need to get back," Claire said.

Wordlessly, the women traced their way out of the park and down rue Rembrandt toward the flower shop.

Odette paused in front of the shop door. "Grey said you left your husband to be with Laurent. That is why you are in Paris."

Through the window's frost, Claire could make out the few tins of flowers, the plants, the soft grey walls. Above was *her* balcony, grey ice outlined the iron scrollwork. "No. Laurent wasn't the reason I came." She remembered their afternoons together in New York. "But he would have made a good way to pass the nights."

"*D'accord*. Women like him for that." A knowing grin lit Odette's face. She glanced at Madame through the glass and her smile faded. She slipped a piece of paper in Claire's hand. "A phone number. Think about it and let me know."

"I will." Claire stepped inside. She meant no.

Madame looked up from spritzing a potted ivy with an old perfume bottle filled with water. The air in the shop smelled faintly of roses.

Claire locked the door behind her. Hell, no.

## December 13, 1940.

A rare day of clear sky, the sun glared off shop windows. Up
to her elbows in dried hellebores, Claire watched through
the glass as a woman strolled by in a long fur coat, short blond
hair curled tight against her neck. Her hat was ruby red, a frothy
little thing perched on the front of her head, a silk ribbon tied
around the back to hold it on. She was on the arm of a German
soldier in the grey uniform of Wehrmacht. An officer on leave
from the real fighting or just lucky enough to be doing his bit for
the war while sampling the goods of Paris.

Behind them, a handsome man with coal black hair, a thick
blue scarf tossed around his neck. He walked with an arm slung
around the small waist of a woman wrapped in a tailored coat
to her knees, a small-brimmed hat pinned on her head. Behind
them, two older women in heavy-soled shoes and heavier furs.

Claire watched out her window all morning as the ice crystals melted from the glass panes and the icy street turned to grey
slush. At first a trickle, then a stream of shoppers on their way
to and from the shops on the les Champs, as they called the
avenue des Champs-Elysées. Reluctantly, perhaps, like a drunk-
ard pulled by his feet from the morning bed, Christmas season
had officially begun.

Madame had excused herself from the shop that morning.
To meet with the manager at the Ritz, she said, but Claire knew
a full afternoon away was more likely to escape Claire's mood.

A broken vase, crumpled gold leaf, a dropped potted ivy, and
cursing to go with each. Well, damn. She used to be one of those
women in Manhattan in a mink coat, an outrageous hat and an
obviously handsome, discreetly rich man on her arm. She had

paid dearly for the right, and now she was back on her knees in a shop?

This should have been the Christmas of dreams. Her first Christmas in Paris.

Her face ached from scowling. She glared at the cracks in her fingers, her calloused hands. They hadn't looked this worn since she was a girl. She smoothed the deep blue skirt against her legs. This was the best of two, and she just found a seam starting to fray. Laughter echoed off the window's thin glass. Claire didn't look up but felt shadows slide over her as more people passed.

The sharp pinch she felt in her chest reminded her it wasn't the flowers in front of her that shrank her world to the size of this shop. A gentleman died in her arms. Shot to death because of what? A cane?

Claire wasn't naive; she'd known desperate people in her life and more than her share of thugs. But the world was filling with an ugliness she had never seen before. She hadn't gone beyond the block in two weeks. And now she was stuck in a little flower shop staring at plants.

A knock on the window. Georges' smiling face peered in as he walked by, his arms full of bags. Even Georges was going to take in the Christmas sights of les Champs.

A flash of irritation, a broken stem, another curse and Claire threw down the half-full dried wreath. She had come too far to sit this one out, she told her conscience as she bounded up the stairs. Smoothing her hair, she painted her lips with a nub of lipstick and reached deep inside her closet.

Heavy softness enveloped her fingers. The sable. Claire had shoved it into the darkness the day she arrived. Too ostentatious for a flower shop girl, too close to her old life. As the winter progressed, she looked at it like money in the bank. A month ago, she'd even offered to sell it for food. Madame had gazed at Claire for a moment and patted the coat Claire held against her chest.

"Not yet," Madame had said. "We are not there yet."

Sinking her fingers into the fur, Claire stroked the collar against her cheek. Today, for a few hours, she could be the woman she came to Paris to be. She slipped on the fur and spun to face the mirror. Burying her rough hands in the deep pockets, she twisted from side to side. A hat would be preferred, better shoes, but at least the sable was damn decadent and completely covered her worn clothes. She smiled at the woman in the mirror. She'd missed being her.

Locking the shop door, Claire dropped the keys in her pocket and hurried down the narrow street. As she stepped into les Champs' wide-open avenue, she felt the first touch of the sun's warmth in months. She turned right, gazing down the wide, straight line to the Arc de Triomphe. On either side, rows of trees were slender bare fingers curled toward the sky. She moved into the meandering flow of people. The tightness evaporated out of her body as she strolled along.

A man in a dark suit waited in front of a luggage store. He watched her come and made a show of moving aside so she could pass. She swished her hips and glanced back at him from the corners of her eyes. Another block and the sight of a gown in a dress-shop window stopped her. Silver, shimmering silk, with thin straps. A jeweled orchid blossom in deep blue sapphires rested at the base of the low-cut décolleté.

Through the window, Claire could feel the touch of silk on her skin, the fabric warming against her breasts, the reassuring weight of the jewels. She sighed and smoothed her hair in the window's reflection.

Drifting strains of what sounded like "Oh Come, All Ye Faithful" pulled her away from the window. In front of a building on the pointed corner of les Champs and avenue George V, the red awning over the terrace door read *Fouquet's*. Where in the summer diners would have lingered in scattered tables, a five-piece orchestra played in white dinner jackets and black bow ties.

Claire pushed into the crowd gathered in front. A cello player, a violinist, and three guitarists. So Parisian, this could be any Christmas. A small smile formed at the edges of her mouth, shared by a tall, ageless woman to her right.

The song ended to applause and calls for more. The next song featured the violin and sounded a bit like "Silent Night." A pause and the next song started, a mournful tune, led by one of the guitarists. He was dark and thin, leaned over his guitar like a lover. His eyes closed, his face was a shadowed mask.

No one sang or spoke. The crowd was still as if a single movement would shatter the sound hanging in the air. Claire turned to the woman at her side, meaning to ask the name of the song. The woman stared at the guitarist, her perfectly painted lips mouthed words Claire couldn't hear, tears ran unheeded down her face. The tune was unmistakably French, like it should be coming from a dark corner of a smoky café. The guitar keened, echoed from the bricks. A chic couple silently passed an embroidered kerchief to the crying woman. Claire glanced to the left. The man next to her clamped his cigarette between tight lips, eyes misting.

Each note wove the crowd together into a living, feeling

fabric. Claire felt it too, a stirring in her heart, a warmth pierced with sadness. A certain Parisian melancholy. A weariness to be shared. To be carried together.

Claire glanced over her shoulders. The crowd had doubled. A car idled at the curb. A man craned his head out the window, his eyes vacant as he strained to hear.

"*Arrêtez*," a loud voice barked. Stop.

The crowd fell back on each side as a pair of French policemen pushed through. The two muscled men looked like prizefighters, holstered pistols belted over blue coats. The larger of the two turned to face the crowd. His nose had been busted against his face too many times; it was a divided lump plastered between his eyes.

"Enough," he said, his voice like grinding metal. "Christmas is for good Christians. Good Frenchmen. Who respect our father, Maréchal Pétain. Who fight the filth of Jews, Communists, immigrants." His mouth twisted as he looked over at the guitarist. "Gypsies." He glared out at the crowd, hooked his thumbs into his belt.

Claire recognized the type. He was a bruiser who had gotten his big break in the new world order and was going to rub these rich *bâtard* noses in it. These were the worst. They came from the gutters to carry out the work the police didn't have the stomach for.

"Play '*Maréchal, nous voilà!*'" he said.

Claire felt resentment ripple through the audience. *Marshal, here we are,* the song said. An anthem to Marshal Pétain, Chief of State of Vichy France. And whispered to be Hitler's puppet.

Claire's eyes were glued to the guitarist. His face still, he shifted his guitar, took a deep breath and strummed. After a few notes, his band joined him.

The policeman smacked his hands together and nodded at his partner. Around Claire, faces closed down, eyes became hooded.

The woman at her side turned and hurried away. In ones and twos, the crowd dissipated into nothing.

Claire drifted across the street, lingered at the corner, not ready to face the inside of the flower shop. There were bits of Paris still. Real Paris. Her throat tightened. In this villainy, in this worn skirt, these calloused hands—somehow this place was her soul's home. She hummed a bar of the melancholy song.

"*Madame, vos papiers,*" a gravely voice spit.

Claire turned. The officer who had stopped the song stood in front of her, his hand outstretched, palm up. Waiting for her papers. His partner waited, his thick lips turned down, thumbs stuck in his belt. "Now." The officer reached for her arm.

Claire's body went numb, her shaking fingers fumbled with the wallet in her pocket. She tried to smile at him but the grip on her arm disgusted her. Those hands had crushed or hauled off how many to their deaths? She couldn't meet his eyes.

"*Monsieur l'agent?*" a familiar voice spoke over her shoulder.

Monsieur Dupré, Georges father, stepped around Claire to face the officer. Georges trailed behind him, his face white. They both had arms full of bags, delivering an order to one of the apartments along the street.

Dupré's slender body and stiff posture looked fragile next to the bull of a man. He turned to Claire, shoving his bags into her arms. It was the first time she had seen him out of the shop. Precisely barbered dark hair, thin glasses hooked over his ears, and a mustache turned down at the ends lent him a slightly disapproving air. Claire clutched at the bags with numb hands, trying to keep the groceries from hitting the ground.

Dupré pulled from a bag a bottle of Château Mireille Bordeaux and a box of cigars. He faced Claire with a frown. "You stupid girl, take off Madame Austerlitz's coat before you ruin it. You were to get it mended, not wear it. She will have you blistered." He turned to the officer. "My neighbor's employee is not too hard to look at, but worthless. We have a delivery for Madame Austerlitz, wife of Kommandant Austerlitz, but I find I have brought more than was ordered. It would be inconvenient for me to go back to the shop. I am late because of this woman's laziness. Perhaps you could help?"

The policeman nodded to his partner, who grabbed the offering and pushed Dupré back with the other hand. He made a show of reading *Épicerie Dupré* printed on Georges' apron pocket, then glared at Claire. "I don't like you." He tapped a thick finger next to his eye. "I will be watching." He turned on his heel and the men walked away.

"Remove that stupid coat and carry something." Dupré took a bag from her hands and hurried down the sidewalk.

Georges paused as he passed Claire. "Come on!"

Claire tore the coat off, stuffed it in a bag and followed. Another block and they turned onto rue Balzac. Claire waited in front of a courtly four-story building while Georges and Dupré went inside. Shivering, she stared up at the white-shuttered windows and tried to calm her heartbeat. A moment later, the door opened and the men returned, empty-handed.

The jerk of Dupré's head brought Claire in line behind them. They walked single file down a narrow side street, until they spilled onto rue du Colisée. Dupré shook his head at Claire when she turned toward the flower shop and started to pull the keys from her pocket.

"Not yet. Come with us first." Dupré said.

She glanced longingly back at her balcony above the flower shop as she followed Dupré inside Épicerie Dupré. He told Georges to mind the register and led her to a small room in back.

His office was austere. A plank bench. A wooden chair with a worn cushion behind a small desk. A small framed photo of a smiling woman and dark-haired baby hung on the wall over his desk. Dupré motioned toward the bench. He stared at Claire over his glasses, his lips a compressed line.

"*Merci*, Monsieur, for your help." Claire perched on the bench and forced a smile on a face that was still numb.

"No!" His thin face twisted into a deep scowl. He turned to pace the small office. "No thanks for me. Madame Palain has said you show great promise. Thank her."

Claire wasn't sure how to respond. It was one of the nicest things she'd ever heard, but he delivered it like an accusation.

"She has put trust in you. If you were to betray that by bringing attention to her, that would be—" Dupré snapped his mouth shut.

Claire began to protest, but the argument died, unspoken. She fingered the coat on her lap.

"I know you have a problem," he said. "I would suggest you either fix it or be gone when that *flic* comes looking for you."

"Problem? I—" Claire jerked upright. How the hell did he know her papers were not good?

"I know Georges sneaks food to you. Food that you cannot buy without a ration card. I am not stupid. It is Madame's kindness to allow you to work." A woman's voice rose outside. The rumble of a man's voice joined her. Customers. Dupré sighed and stood. "Fix your problem. Or go."

Claire locked the shop door behind her and climbed the stairs on wooden legs. Her room, the tiny bed with iron railings, the dresser with chipped paint. The clouded mirror and the photo of her garden tucked in the corner. She had nearly lost it all. She still could.

Claire shoved the sable in her closet. Taking a deep breath, she faced the window. Across the street, the grocer considered her a worm. And, for the sake of Madame Palain, had saved her life. Over the rooftops, the Eiffel Tower stood in the distance, sunlight peeping through dark grey lattice. The beauty was astounding; it tugged at her heart.

Claire heard the shop door click open.

"Bonjour, Claire," Madame called up the stairs. "I have designs for the Ritz."

A slip of paper sat in Claire's trash, waiting to be burned. It wasn't about Laurent or Odette. It wasn't even about the cane. Claire was a part of La Vie en Fleurs now. Her new life was worth the risk. Wordlessly, she descended the stairs to the phone and dialed. "Yes," she said and hung up.

D ays passed. Claire heard nothing. Her nerves started to fray. Then one morning, a week later, she opened the doors at nine o'clock and found Odette waiting outside. Claire made an excuse to Madame, slipped on her coat and joined Odette.

The women walked for blocks before a word was spoken. Pleasantries seemed absurd and the truth, too dangerous to be said aloud. They took a left on boulevard Malesherbes.

"It is a good day to walk," Odette said.

Claire nodded. A chill in the air, but at least the sun was out. "We going far?"

"*Un peu,*" Odette said. A little. She flashed Claire a smile. "But perhaps we will take the Métro back, no?"

Claire grinned back at Odette. Freedom, at least a form of it, would be hers in the form of a little slip of paper.

"Have you been to the ninth arrondissement yet? Have you seen Cimetière de Montmartre?" Odette asked.

A cemetery? "Not at the top of my list, Odette."

"We will be near there. Not a place for us to see today, but you should visit."

"You French and your dead people."

Odette chuckled. "History surrounds us. You cannot open your eyes, not in Paris, and see something that wasn't touched by someone long gone." She took a sideways glance at Claire. "You, maybe, run from your ghosts. Here, they live among us."

Claire buried her gloved hands deep in her pockets. Odette had no idea how many ghosts trailed behind Claire.

Claire began to tire by the time they turned down rue Jean-Baptiste Pigalle. The buildings were old, sculpted grey stone, like any other neighborhood. But the flavor was dark and the neighborhood seemed to be sleeping off a long night. Unshaven men in tattered clothes leaned against doorways.

She peered into a darkened bar; the odor of stale cigarettes and sour wine wafted out. "Interesting place."

"Not much farther." Odette held her eyes firmly on the sidewalk in front of her.

Claire sighed. It reminded her of Fifty-Second Street in New York. A lifetime ago, before she was Claire Harris Stone, she'd spent many evenings at the Three Deuces, Kelly's Stable or the Spotlight. That was where she had first heard Billie Holliday. She could still feel the tug of the singer's forlorn voice in her chest.

This place, Le Renard Noir, might have been a jazz club once; she'd heard they had been big in Montmarte before the war. Not anymore. The Nazis had proclaimed jazz to be degenerate Negro-Jewish music and banned it.

They entered the faded lobby of an apartment building. Odette led her up one flight of stairs and down a narrow hallway to an odd-shaped door at the end. She knocked on the door hard once, paused, then rapped three more times.

"Yes?" a muffled voice asked.

"It's Danielle," Odette said, her voice low.

Claire looked over at her questioningly.

"Here, I'm Danielle," she said, under her breath.

The door creaked and opened. A teenage boy peeked out, bundled in heavy layers, the faintest line of fuzz across his upper lip. He peered up and down the empty hallway, opened the door wide and gestured them in.

The room was more of a janitor's supply closet than an apartment. Stacks of doorknobs, buckets and empty cans lined the walls. An unmade cot was tucked in one corner, a workbench piled with pipes and machinery in the other.

He glanced over at Claire. "This is her?" he asked Odette.

Odette nodded. "You have what you need?"

"*Oui.*" He grabbed a camera from the bench and snapped photos of Claire posing against a drab white wall. "Three hours."

Odette turned to Claire. "We'll come back." She poked her head out the door, then stepped out.

Claire followed; she glanced over her shoulder at the boy, now hunched over equipment at his workbench. He didn't look up.

"Danielle?" Claire asked as they stepped out onto the street.

Odette glanced at her watch. "There is a place we can wait." She read the frustration in Claire's face. "I will explain there."

They walked side by side back down the street. Claire peered into the windows of the shops and side passages while Odette kept her eyes ahead. Cabarets, bars, cafés. Cold-looking prostitutes loitered on side streets and followed them with their eyes.

"In here." Odette entered the church on the end of the block.

Claire stepped over an entryway into soft dimness. Burning candles and incense, wood, stone and age mixed together to form a musty smell Claire found oddly soothing. The ceiling rose in Gothic arches. A saint with sword brandished and monster wrapped around his legs adorned a high stained-glass window that radiated deep ocean blue, moss green and butter yellow. With her head bowed, Odette sat on a wooden chair.

Claire slid next to her, staring up at the ceiling. "Are we meeting someone here?"

"No. But it isn't wise to be the only women waiting on the street that aren't prostitutes."

"Oh. I see. Where are we?"

"L'Eglise Saint-Michel."

"Famous place?"

"Not really. Saint Michel was a dragon slayer. A popular man during times of war." Odette stared down at her hands folded in her lap. "I don't go to church, not anymore. But this place, I like, when I am here."

Claire nodded. The frayed fabric, the scuffed wood and the grooves worn in the floor from centuries of feet gave the place a melancholy dignity.

They watched a woman walk past them down the aisle holding a too-thin young boy. He clung to her arms, his dark eyes rimmed with sickness. The door closed behind them before Claire and Odette spoke again.

Odette looked up at the altar, her face thoughtful. "Gerard, my son, turned nine this summer. He is too much like his father to be a good boy. But he is right for the times. It is hard for the good boys to survive."

"I'd like to meet him."

"Perhaps." Odette heard the shortness in her own voice and shrugged lightly. "When I work, like today, I'm Danielle. It's too dangerous for me, with a family, not to hide my true name. As Danielle, if I were caught, the trail would end with me."

Claire thought of the old man in the street. If Odette were caught . . .

Odette turned to Claire, her face serious. "Normally, you wouldn't know who I really am. It is a risk. You're a risk, Claire."

Claire held Odette's gaze for as long as she could. "You came to me."

"Yes. We came to you because we need to know what you see. You're making a commitment to us. Perhaps to save your skin or your position. But you have a responsibility now, much greater than just to yourself." Her eyes squinted as she stared at Claire, as if she might be able to see inside. "And we seem to believe in you."

The door opened behind them. A man bundled in rags walked down the aisle toward the altar.

"Who's we? Laurent?" Claire remembered how he'd tried to speak with her as she left the party. She felt warmed by his concern, by his unexpected confidence.

"You have made an impression." Odette rose and walked toward the candles.

Claire watched Odette drop a coin into a wooden box. She lit a stubby white candle and set it in among many on the altar. Her expression was pinched, her head bowed. Odette had her own ghosts.

Claire looked away. Her gaze paused on the wall across from the stained-glass window. The light through the window painted soft swatches of blue, green and yellow onto the stone like an Impressionist painting. She marveled. So much beauty and evil stirred up in the same bucket.

As the afternoon shadows lengthened, they traced their way back to the apartment. After three knocks, the boy let them inside. He slipped the identification card in Claire's hands. As always, her eyes were drawn to the photo first. The shot was good, she had to admit. Not too good as to arouse suspicion, it wouldn't make the cover of *Harper's*, but she did look tempting as well as somewhat French. Her hair was nearly to her shoulders, a lock curled over her eye. Red lipstick kept her lips full. Her eyes skimmed over to the text.

**Nom: BADEAU. Prénom: CLAIRE.**
**Nationalité: AMÉRICAINE.**
**Adresse: 44, RUE DU MONTPARNASSE, PARIS.**

The card was stamped, dated May, signed at the bottom, and worn as if from months of wear.

"This is me? Claire Badeau?"

Odette nodded. "American, married to a Frenchman, Henri Badeau. This way, no one will question why you are in Paris."

"Is Henri a real person?"

"Yes. A writer. His family was from Toulouse."

"Handsome?"

"He was. He was called to the front last November. He died in June. You are a widow, Claire." Odette cleared her throat.

"You met in Paris, fell instantly in love, were married, and then he was gone." She looked to the boy. "The license?"

He riffled through papers on the desk and handed Claire a slip.

Odette spoke as Claire glanced over the paper. "Your marriage was recorded here, in your *livret de famille*, given to you by the official at city hall. Your name, your true name, is buried deep in the files there, impossible to find. Memorize the date, your home address. Make up the details." She looked over to the boy. "Well done. As always."

He hid a smile; his thin chest puffed out beneath layers of fabric.

"You'd better get back to school before they miss you." Odette pointed to a textbook half-buried under a jacket. "Don't forget your science book."

He lifted his chin; his eyes shot a squinty glare. Already a proud artist, Claire thought. What made the Nazis think they could control this world?

Odette turned to Claire. "Shall we take the Métro?"

The humid warmth inside the Métro station on boulevard de Clichy hit Claire like a hot bath. She trailed Odette beneath flickering lights through the crowded entry, down the stairs and through the dingy white-tiled tunnel. The train arrived as they reached the open platform. They pressed into the boarding crowd and sank into hard seats facing the door.

Cars had been prohibited for months. The Métro was bursting at the seams. It didn't run at all on the weekends. Protests over the loss of cars in the first months succumbed to grumbling as an early winter hit. Bitter cold overwhelmed a city reeling from fuel shortages. The only time many Parisians were warm was during their commute on the Métro. Young and old, rich and poor, they learned to put up with the ride.

Claire relaxed into the jostling as heat seeped into her core. She couldn't remember when some part of her hadn't been chilled. She breathed in deep. It smelled of cigarettes, oil, stale bodies and a faint whiff of perfume. It was about damn time.

They got off at Saint Lazare and walked down rue du Rocher. A couple of turns and they paused in front of a café. The faded sign read *Café Raphael*.

"A theater." Odette tilted her head toward the building across the street.

"I see it," Claire said.

"And next to the theater. A dentist."

Claire squinted. A sign embellished with the drawing of a tooth was propped in the street-side window of the building next to the theater.

"Dr. Rousseau. That's where you will drop your reports, in the mail slot to the left of the door. Always come a different way. Never at the same time. Write the name Danielle on the envelope. Sign it as Evelyn."

"Evelyn?"

"That will be the name you use. Can you find your way back to the shop now?"

Claire nodded. "What about the address listed as my home?"

"A decoy," Odette said. "Leave a note for Danielle here if you have news or need to see me. Otherwise, I will find you at the flower shop. You cannot tell Madame Palain about our arrangement."

"I have a dead husband and new name, Odette."

"I am confident you will think of something." Odette turned
to go, then looked back over her shoulder. A smile flitted over
her face. "I am pleased you have decided to contribute."

Claire sputtered. She argued with Odette's retreating back.
"I'm not. I am just noting a few things. That's all. Reporting a
party in the society pages."

Odette crossed the street and disappeared into a side alley.

Claire twisted Russell's wedding ring she wore on her right
hand. When she considered selling the fur coat early this winter,
Georges told her about a pawnshop not far from here. *Badeau.*
Claire tested the name in her mouth. Henri Badeau sacrificed his
life for France.

Madame Palain couldn't argue if Claire sold her ring to pay
for marriage papers. A soldier fallen in battle, his family needed
money. And she, Claire would say, needed to work over the
table. *Le system D.* A done deal. Claire pulled the ring from her
finger. A lie, not a life, but this would be her sacrifice for La Vie
en Fleurs.

Claire glanced up at the theater marquee and smiled. *Le
Voyageur sans bagage.* A traveler without luggage. Rather fit-
ting.

# Chapter 5

## THE NEW BADEAU

Paris Ritz, 15 Place Vendôme. December 31, 1940.

The truck's headlights reflected off billowing white flakes and illuminated the snowdrifts growing against the buildings. Worn tires spun and the heavy engine protested as the truck shifted down, crawling around the tight corner off rue Cambon into the guarded delivery entrance of the Hôtel Ritz. Claire watched from her perch in the passenger seat as the driver, Monsieur Bison, pulled the brake and reached for a wad of papers in his overcoat pocket, passing them to a waiting soldier in feldgrau.

The guard marked a list and waved them through a line of soldiers. Bison let out a shaky breath as he threw a tight grin to Claire. The truck crept into the hotel's snow-blanketed courtyard. Dark twin trails left by truck tires that had already come and gone that evening traced up to the loading dock.

Claire could only afford a glance at the graceful lines of the building, the stately high windows and the slivers of golden lit rooms visible through half-closed curtains, before the engine rumbled to silence in front of the dock. She slid out the passenger door. Bison met her at the back. With the flick of a lever, the door swung open with a clang.

A dim bulb lit the center of the truck, leaving the rest in shadows. Claire quickly scanned the interior, barely able to make out the wooden crates that butted against each other. Exploding out of each crate like firecrackers were pink hellebores, dried roses, burgundy lilies and winding branches gilded in silver and gold. The porcelain and silver vase rims that jutted from the crates reflected orange in the bulb's light. Nearly a month of preparation by Madame and Claire for tonight's fête.

She nodded at Bison. Everything looked to be the same as when they left the shop. He returned the gesture, apparently as nervous as she was about getting the flowers to Madame Palain in perfect condition. Craning her neck, Claire peered through the swirling snowflakes at the rows of windows that faced rue Cambon and what looked to be a garden. Feeling like a thief huddled in the darkness, she shivered down to her core in the bitter cold and slapped gloved hands against her body. The sound echoed off the walls and made her jump. Bison snickered around the cigarette in his mouth.

Double doors swung open and lights shone from a bright hallway. Attendants in white jackets pushed carts past the soldiers guarding the corridor and up to the truck. While the guards watched, Bison handed out boxes from the truck bed.

Madame waited inside the Ritz, preparing for the flowers' arrival. Claire's job tonight was getting the flowers, fresh, unbruised and unbroken, to Madame in the hotel's salon. A Herculean task that would have been impossible, except for the experience of Bison. With his stained overalls and cigarette dangling from the side of his mouth, he didn't seem like Madame's first choice. But he was good and steady, and he worked with a delicacy that belied his calloused, meaty hands.

He told Claire during the drive over this was the first job he'd had all winter. His other two trucks had been requisitioned long before; it was impossible to get permission to make deliveries at all. He hoped tonight was a sign things were going back to normal. *This cannot last,* he said, shaking his head as he ran his thick fingers over the steering wheel. He could not last, Claire knew he meant.

A boyish attendant pushed his cart against the truck bed and reached for a crate with one hand.

"You there, be careful, carry it like this." Claire handed him a vase brimming with ivy, placing his hands underneath the container. "Don't use the handles. Do you hold a woman by her wrists or her body?" She smiled as he blushed.

Claire supervised as Bison passed out more boxes. She tried to ignore the soldiers in the doorway, the way their eyes roamed over her like searchlights. A flash at the edge of her vision distracted her. She glanced up and noticed the pedestrians, bundled against the cold, hurrying along rue Cambon's sidewalk. She watched the broad back of a man in a long wool coat stride away. The gleam of a sculpted jaw reflected the streetlight as he turned the corner, a quick glance to the side. She squinted into the darkness, her mind on the pedestrian's angled face. It brought to mind the Englishman. Was he watching her?

"*Mon dieu!*" Bison cursed.

A vase of lilies laced with tiny faceted crystals tipped off the back of the truck. Claire leapt backward and caught it with one hand. She straightened and set the vase onto the waiting cart.

"*Faites attention,*" she scolded the attendant.

He put his cigarette back in his mouth and pushed the cart with both hands toward the hotel door.

"It will come out of your salary. Not mine," she said to his back.

Her gaze returned to the street. One of the German soldiers, a driver, loitered there now, hands in his pockets. He stared back at her. Claire hurried behind the truck.

A long hour passed. Hard gazes from the soldiers, countless more cart trips by the attendants, Claire nervously watching over each detail, and Bison finally reached the front of the empty truck bed.

He climbed down and swung the door shut. "Did you need a ride to the shop?"

Claire looked down at her grey wool coat, her mind on the dress beneath. Dark green, long tapered sleeves, buttoned up to her neck and ending in pleats well below the knee. Warm, pleasant and a kindness from Madame, but nothing compared to the cream-colored silk gown hanging in the back of the closet in her bedroom. Still, she felt the pull as if she were iron dust tugging toward a magnet. Surely she was dressed enough to take a peek inside. This was New Year's at the Paris Ritz. "No, thank you, Monsieur." Claire bit her lip to hold back the grin. "I will walk."

Bison lit a crumpled rolled cigarette. "You won't make it before curfew. I have authorization to be on the streets." His forehead wrinkled and he glanced toward the building as if he could see Madame Palain inside. Claire knew the florist expected him to take her home.

"You are so kind, Monsieur. I will be fine. We will be back to break down at six o'clock in the morning. You will be here, no?" She turned and went inside before he could think of another argument.

Passing the soldiers, Claire marched through the long hall toward the main lobby and the salon. Feeling a bit more like herself, she smoothed the curl over her brow, ran the stub of lipstick over her mouth and tucked a flower in her coat lapel. Her hands brushed the old wool of her coat and she thought wistfully of her sable hanging in her closet. This party could once have been hers.

The hall opened into an entryway. The opposite side was lined with open doors. An army of people in white jackets bustled inside. Perfect, she decided with a grin. No one would notice her just taking a look. Besides, she needed to have something to write Odette about tomorrow. What could be said about loading docks?

Claire peered inside the doorway and caught her breath at the sight. *Salon Louis XIV.* Madame had told her it was modeled after a château at Versailles. It truly was a testament to the Sun King. Pale butter walls, every surface embellished. Giant crystal chandeliers snowed light onto a long dining table set with silver and crystal.

Madame Palain held court in the army of bustling white jackets. She was the queen here, commanding with words and a wave. "These lilies, there, on this pedestal under the painting. Don't bruise the petals. Do you want them to turn brown?"

Carts heavy with stacked silver trays were wheeled past. The smell of the food inside made Claire's mouth water. An ice sculpture of two facing swans arched over a tower of champagne flutes. In the corner, an orchestra was setting up, all in tuxedos.

And the flowers. A smile crept to Claire's lips. They were magnificent. Two of her arrangements were paired on the mantel bordering an elaborate gilded mirror. Twisted gold branches looped out from the blossoming lilies like trails of golden fireworks, the dangling crystals their fire.

"Quite an operation, isn't it?" a low voice, smooth as bourbon, said behind her.

Claire started and turned at the sound.

He was slender, aristocratically so, in an expensive tailormade tuxedo. His thick black hair was parted with a knife and combed behind his ears. He smiled with his teeth, taking a drag from a cigar. "Beautiful, no?" he said, in the tone of a man who knew his worth.

This was the type Claire planned on finding in Paris. Rich, important, handsome, but judging from his eyes not so passionate or principled as to entangle. Times changed. She changed. But she couldn't help the anticipation that kindled in her stomach. She twisted toward him; her hand nonchalantly adjusted her coat to hint at what awaited inside. She nodded in approval. "Very beautiful."

He slowly took her in with his eyes. "Can I look forward to your presence tonight?"

In spite of herself, Claire was charmed. She let a slow smile grow on her lips.

"Perhaps I could offer you a drink? Or two?" He indicated the champagne table with the tilt of his head. "Madame . . . ?"

"Badeau, Claire Badeau," Claire extended a hand.

Madame Palain appeared at Claire's side. "*Pardon*, Monsieur. Madame Badeau is required in the salon."

"Of course." He bowed lightly.

She grabbed Claire's elbow and led her into the salon. Her touch was light but the grip was steel. "You didn't return with Bison."

"I wanted to see."

The florist looked at Claire's lipstick, the flower in the open collar of her coat. "Is restraint a word you are completely un-familiar with?" She bit each word as she said it.

"Madame Palain?" a man called from across the room, arms full with a large basket.

She composed herself, smoothing the irritation from her face. She pointed toward two large silver chalices brimming with lavender lilies. "Take these to the Place Vendôme lobby on your way out. Monsieur Brun will show you where to place them." She leaned in close. "Do not allow yourself to be alone with the Comte de Vogüé again. You could hardly have done worse."

Claire opened her mouth to argue, but the florist was already across the room. Another cart of champagne flutes wheeled past. Claire could almost taste the golden liquid, feel the bubbles play on her tongue. She sighed and hooked an arm around each chalice. With a final wistful glance around the room, she marched into the hallway.

It was easier to dawdle in the lobby. The flowers needed to be placed perfectly, one on the front desk, the other over the mantel in the seating area. Then there was flirting with the concierge, Brun. Shaped like a loaf of bread, thin hair parted on the side and swiped across a wide forehead. He wasn't so much to look at, but each man who passed called him by name.

Leaning over the desk, her face inches from his; she toyed with the chalice, rubbing a nonexistent smudge. "Who is Comte de Vogüé?"

A scowl flashed across Brun's face. "Important." He paused, staring down at the desk and squaring a stack of papers as if he stopped himself from saying more.

"What do you mean?" Claire said, covering the irritation with honey.

A long car rolled up to the Place Vendôme entrance. Bellmen on each side opened the lobby doors wide. Three couples strolled in, one after another.

"The guests. I must go." Brun scurried around the desk.

Claire swung to face them. She thought of her report. *Flirted with Comte de Vogüé, an important, perhaps dangerous and strangely charming man.* She pictured Odette bent over the note, a room of agents waiting with baited breath. She laughed to herself.

A Nazi officer came first, built like a Panzer tank with a wide neck bulging over the top of his uniform. A woman in a heavy mink was pinned to his side.

It was Sylvie. Claire froze. The officer's roving gaze flicked over Claire. She slid around the desk, bending down behind the flowers as his eyes followed her. He lit a cigarette as Sylvie spoke into his ear and adjusted her mink. They walked by; he glanced over at Claire. She turned her head, pretending to read the papers on the desk.

"Gerolf, I want to go in," Sylvie whined, her voice like a razor scraping over tender flesh.

The warmth Claire felt now coalesced into a cold lump in her stomach. *That* was who the party was for. Not for aristocrats and their stylish mistresses. Not self-made socialites on the run from the States. All this cultured beauty was for Nazi officers and collaborators. People like Sylvie.

It was past time to go. Claire ducked her head as she walked from the lobby. Running her hand down the molding of the long hallway as she walked, her eyes grazed the marble floor under her feet. You will see better days, she promised. She wasn't sure if she was talking to the Ritz or Paris or herself.

Claire stepped out the double doors onto rue Cambon and

welcomed the bite of the cold night air. Bison was long gone. Wrapping her coat tight around her, she scurried down the dark, empty sidewalk, plotting her course east then south, toward the shop.

The Ritz exuded the glamour Claire sought when she boarded the Yankee Clipper. Her timing was plain bad luck. But, damn, tonight she ached for this fallen city.

She shook her head to stop the thoughts. Her feet picked up speed as she cut onto the avenue that ran east, just out of sight of the Seine. Life was hard enough without worrying about the other guy. Without thinking about the big picture. She knew better.

She wrote and rewrote her report the next morning. In the end, the note was short and sweet. Sylvie and the officer, the Comte, the guards stationed by the door. Signed Evelyn. She addressed the envelope for Danielle and dropped it in the dentist's box on her way to the Ritz. After she helped Bison reload the truck, she celebrated a day of rare sunshine with a stroll along the river.

The Seine was unlike any other river Claire had ever seen. Like every bit of nature she'd seen in Paris, it had been so molded by human hands it became a civilized thing, more formal than any structure, a living monument to the elemental. With her coat bundled tight against the cold, Claire skirted patches of snow along the brick quai and gazed up at the Eiffel Tower, looming over the boats that chugged down the Seine.

Her day stretched before her like a promise. As long as she could keep warm, she would work upstream along the quai, passing the tower then the Grand and Petit Palais. At Place de la

Concorde, she would leave the river and cut through jardin des Tuileries. She was contemplating the splurge of a hot drink along the way when a man stepped out from the shadows of the pont d'léna and caught her stride.

"Grey." Claire said it like an unpleasant but unavoidable fact.

"Claire." His gaze rested on her a moment before he turned to scan the riverbank.

"Where's Laurent?" Claire said.

"I am your contact. Not him."

"That's a shame."

Grey closed his mouth on a reply.

They both were quiet as they looked up at the line of soldiers in front of the Eiffel Tower, their gazes on the banner draped across the tower's façade, *Deutschland Siegt an Allen Fronten*. Germany victorious on all fronts. They walked steadily until they passed the tower and the last guards.

Claire looked up to find Grey staring at her, forehead wrinkled in thought.

"What? Don't tell me a woman shouldn't be walking alone with all these soldiers about." She'd already heard that exact warning from Madame twice this morning.

A grin tugged at his lips. "I wouldn't dream of telling you not to do anything."

"Really?"

"You are too obstinate. You would do it just to be difficult." His slate eyes flashed.

Claire laughed outright, delighting in the smile that lit his rugged face. Surprisingly handsome, she decided, in a firm British way.

His smile faded. "I miss this." With the tilt of his head, he motioned to the city around him. "I miss walks through Paris."

Grey was a romantic? Impossible. Her face must have shown her wonder.

"Bloody hell. Why do you look so surprised? That is what Paris is for. *Flânerie.*"

"What does that mean?"

"*Flâner.* To amble. To enjoy. The pleasure in noticing all the details one wouldn't see scurrying about."

"My God, how French." Claire smiled like a child. "*Nous flânons.*" She rolled it around her tongue. His eyes met hers. Struck by the depth of his gaze before he looked away, she was glad for the air cooling the flush on her cheeks.

They lapsed into a comfortable silence, both taking pleasure in the rare sun, the river, the stonework, the quiet company. They strolled past the pont des Invalides and stared over the rows of treetops to the arching ironwork and glass of the Grand Palais.

Shrill whistles turned their attention to the pont Alexandre III, ahead. German soldiers had a man pinned against the bridge's railing over the center of the Seine. The man jerked free and flipped over the side, his arms flailing as he fell. A splash as he landed and thrashed feebly.

Soldiers charged off the bridge toward them as the man drifted past Claire's feet. Grey pulled her from the river's edge and pressed her backward against the far brick quai wall. He embraced her, his face tilted forward against hers in the appearance of a kiss, his back against the water. Her heart hammered, her hands gripped his broad shoulders.

"Don't watch them. Look at me now, Claire."

She fell into his fierce gaze. His dark eyes swallowed her, flecks of blue swam in the slate depths. Soldiers thundered by, jackboots ringing on the bricks. From the edge of her vision, she watched one man pause and finger his pistol as he examined

Grey's back. A shout near the river, and he turned and jogged away.

The soldiers gestured and cursed at the man struggling in the current's center. Shots rang out. Splashes erupted around him. He jerked and was still.

"He's dead," Claire breathed. The suddenness of it stunned her.

Grey slipped his arm around her waist. "Come on." He hurried them back the direction they had come.

She sank into his side, sick from what she'd seen, grateful for the strength that kept her upright. Out of sight of the bridge, he sat her on a bench facing the river.

He slid next to her and leaned close. "You alright?"

Claire glanced down and realized she was clenching his hand. She let go and gave him a small smile. "I'm fine."

He stared at the water. "Tell me about the Comte de Vogüé. Describe him."

"I don't know much. I honestly don't. Late thirties, dark hair, impeccably dressed." She paused. She wasn't going to say charming. Not now. "Who is he, Grey?"

"I don't know. Not yet. But he is important, you were right about that."

"And dangerous?"

"Likely."

"You didn't ask me about Sylvie. Or the Nazi she was with." Claire's mind was working, desperate to move past the shots, past Grey's eyes. "You are using her."

"She doesn't know what Laurent does, what we do, against the Occupation. Her Nazi Kapitän requisitions SS equipment and supplies. She boasts more than she should to Laurent."

"Pillow talk?" Claire said.

The barest of a grim smile. "She has no idea what a patriot she really is."

Claire shivered. There was no *flâner* in Paris, not these days. She looked back at the Seine. It churned slowly along as it had for centuries. "I need to get back to the shop."

Bison was wrong—nothing returned to normal. Although winter gave way to spring, which stretched into summer, there were no parties dripping with flowers, no large deliveries to be made. Just a little trip to Hôtel George V or Hôtel Emeraude or another nearby place to drop off a bouquet in the lobby, maybe flirt a bit. The goal was to keep going, to keep La Vie en Fleurs alive.

For Claire, even under the Occupation, Paris was like a university that summer. There were bouquets of zinnias, nasturtiums, marigolds, poppies, sweet peas and roses to create. Oh, the roses. Clusters of all colors, shapes and petals, but her favorite were the curvaceous shell-pink "Pierre de Ronsard" roses. She bundled them in a silver vase on her dresser, next to the photo of the garden.

From Odette, Claire learned the Nazis had one hell of a dress code. Each group had different caps. The collar patch signified rank and branch, whether Waffen-SS, Kriegsmarine or Luftwaffe. Shoulder straps showed rank, sometimes the unit and specialist. Then there were chevrons, badges, arm shields. The Waffen-SS, Luftwaffe, Heer and Kriegsmarine had different styles of eagles. Even the cuffs had to be examined; the smallest insignia could reveal the presence of an elite unit or special command.

Claire dutifully reported the uniforms she saw at each hotel in notes dropped at the dentist. More and more, her reports were interesting enough for Grey to meet her on her walks about the city. A few questions about her report, who she saw, if they were coming or going or staying put. How he knew where to find her, she never understood.

Still, as the days of summer stretched languidly, Claire found herself wearing her best dress, arranging her hat just so and listening for his footsteps behind her. A curt nod when he stepped in stride at her side, a short word about the day or the location, but his slate eyes glinted warmly.

They spoke of flowers and parks as they walked, shoulders touching, along the Champs-Elysées, traced their way through tombs at Cimetière de Montmartre, and meandered through the fountains and greenery of the jardin des Tuileries. They did their best to stay away from the roving patrols of feldgrau and the units of goose-stepping young fascists of the *Garde Français*. They did what the rest of the Parisians did: felt the sun's warmth on their skin, shared a lingering glance, savored another's soft touch through thin summer fabric. And tried to remember how it felt to be alive.

# Chapter 6

## THE WARNING

52, rue du Colisée, Paris. August 16, 1941.

Claire fell asleep with Madame's art book again. A painting of Venus, the goddess sat half-naked on a low seat in front of a temple, primped by the Graces for Adonis' seduction. Two Graces styled her hair; a third brought a net sewn with pearls. A cherub held her mirror while another fastened her sandal.

She dreamed the painting in flowers. The Fantin-Latour rose, with its soft blush pink petals, portrayed Venus herself. Trailing green Queue-de-Renard amaranthus were her robes. A gossamer web of pearls draped over the entire arrangement, displayed against a blue wall. The flowers replaced the Parisian artwork carted off to Berlin or hidden in dark corners. She woke smiling.

At Madame Palain's instruction, Claire pushed pails of asters and dahlias, all that remained, into one corner of the back room. On hands and knees, first a bucket of sudsy water and a brush, then rubbing with a soft cloth, Claire spent the morning polishing the stone floor. The floor shined. And Claire ached. Yesterday it was the walls. Tomorrow, she imagined Madame would want the countertops polished. By next week, if things didn't change, she would be out on the street cobbles with a toothbrush in hand.

Business had dried up. No celebrations for the parents, no little posies to lighten up a room. As the summer heat drained into fall, all the customers remaining were the occasional German soldier buying for his Parisian girl. Madame did not approve and charged them outrageously. What did they care? They printed up more Occupation money.

Claire was lining up the flower tins against the wall when the phone rang. She ran to the counter, Madame close behind. Claire forced herself to wait for the end of the second ring before she picked up.

"*Allô?*" Claire said. Not bored exactly, not rude. Just a touch inconvenienced by a call interrupting a very busy day. She examined her worn nails.

"Madame Badeau?"

Claire paused. "Yes."

"Of the flower shop?"

"Yes. You have an order?"

"I am calling for Comte Jean-Luc de Vogüé."

Claire swallowed. "The Comte?"

Madame frowned and reached for the phone.

"The Comte met you at the Ritz. It was on New Year's Eve. He found your flowers quite captivating that night."

With a stiff arm outstretched, Claire kept Madame away from the phone.

"Madame Badeau? Are you available to take an order? In person?"

Claire smiled at Madame. "Of course. Is the Comte planning a fête?" She nearly purred into the phone.

There was a pause. "Yes. For the winter. Are you available tonight?"

"I can reschedule my plans."

"Good. Eight o'clock, then. At the Ritz. Use the rue Cambon entrance."

Claire set the phone in the cradle and hugged Madame. "A party!" She smiled into the florist's disapproving frown. "It will be beautiful. I'll insist on roses, countless roses, all fresh flowers. We will hire Bison to deliver."

"I do not like you talking with the Comte."

Claire sighed. "How is he any worse than your hoteliers working for the Nazis?"

"The hoteliers have no choice. They only want to survive. The Comte chose his path for other reasons. One hears things. Why did he ask for you?"

Claire stretched her aching back. "He asked for me because I flirted with him. You hear *things*. I hear an orchestra and the pop of champagne bottles. I hear francs."

Madame folded her arms in front of her. "You are impossible." She gazed about the room, her forehead crumpled in thought. "Tell him no matter how small the event, he must show the French good taste and outshine the vulgar *Boche*. Also, tell him he must pay up front with francs, not those reichsmarks."

"Yes, Madame." Claire hurried into the back room. Inventory had dwindled and the room was nearly empty. Shears and pliers lined the wall, above rows of stacked vases and empty flower pails. Still they had options. She could see it now, the

theme would be Venus, and her flowers would take the place of
the unseen art. She had passed strings of glass pearls on display
at Le Bon Marché on the Left Bank.

Of course, the flowers would be *très cher*, very expensive, for
the Comte. The city was full of aristocrats like Laurent, pleased
that their ancestors managed to keep their heads through the
Revolution. The des Vogüés, however, also retained their money,
and the Comte appeared to be doing well through this reorder-
ing, cozied up to the Germans in the Ritz. He would be quite
able to make a significant contribution to La Vie en Fleurs.

Eight o'clock meant dinner and that meant dressing. Claire
bolted up the stairs. She pulled the blue dress she had bought
with her first paycheck out of the closet. It was a year old now
but still quite presentable. For the price of a posy, a cobbler
had reheeled her shoes with rubber from old bike tires. They
squeaked a bit when she walked but looked acceptable.

She examined her reflection in the mirror. All it would take
was a bath and a set. A small smile. Finally, a reason to dress.
The last had been Laurent's party so long ago. Warmth sparked
in her stomach as she felt again Grey's stare that night as she
walked away. She pulled her special notepad from behind the
dresser and jotted a note. She had time to deliver this to the dentist then get ready.


That evening, Claire threaded her way through fashionable
couples along rue de Rivoli. Sharp winds smelled of rain.
Black clouds waded through the darkening blue skies. A man
in a long raincoat sat on a park bench, newspaper tucked under
his arm. He appraised her as she walked toward him, adjusted

his silk tie, raised an eyebrow. A polite question, asked with his eyes. Perhaps?

Claire hid a smile. He was handsome, very French. Moneyed, by the shine of his shoes, the cut of his suit. She tilted her head to the side, the hint of a shrug, as she walked by. An equally polite refusal.

What would Grey make of that? Another Parisian experience to be savored on a walk? Or would his proper English jaw clench? She knew if he got the message, he would find her amidst the plants in the jardins des Champs-Elysées.

The garden unfolded on her right. She turned in and walked toward the large two-tiered fountain and pool where children used to float toy wooden sailboats. No children were there this evening, just a few scattered loners, taking the last few enjoyable minutes before curfew and their dreary nights. Not for her, not tonight.

She heard footsteps coming from the path through the trees. Claire slowed. The way Grey always found her on her walks, she'd turn and he would be there, hands in his pockets, coat collar turned up against the chill. He wouldn't even say hello, just start in conversation, something about the gardens or the day, his voice serious, dark eyes warm.

Claire turned, smiling.

It was Laurent. "You look breathtaking."

She frowned. "Hello."

He matched her stride, hands in his pockets, a cigarette in his mouth. "You are surprised to see me. You don't think I am a patriot like the others?

Claire shrugged, surprised at the depth her spirits had fallen. She hid her disappointment behind a doubtful expression.

"I do more than you know," Laurent said as if she had replied.

He caught her arm, pulled her to a stop. "Don't be mad with me, *ma chérie*. You must know by now why Sophie came that day. It isn't because I wanted her there. I wanted you there."

Claire looked over at him, wondering at his wounded tone.

His eyes were intent; he pulled the cigarette from his mouth so he could lean in close to her face. "Don't you remember New York? You are who I wanted."

She allowed him to pull her off the path onto a secluded bench overlooking the pool and the parterre gardens beyond. He sat facing her, one hand resting on her arm, almost protectively, almost possessively. She stared at his hand until he pulled it away. Even if he was the one who vouched for her with Odette, a long two years had passed since the New York he remembered. "Where is Grey . . . or Odette?"

"Odette is busy. There are important things happening, Claire. Grey is, what can I say—gone."

Claire sat up straight. "Gone?"

He shrugged, a small frown as though he were disappointed but what could he do? "He left."

"Where?"

"I cannot say."

"Tell me, Laurent."

He studied her, his eyes inscrutable, then looked away and sighed. Finally he spoke as if it pained him. "He went back to England."

"He what?"

"He had commitments. A woman and a child. A daughter. Grey is a steadfast sort of creature. A responsible man. They are getting hammered right now in London, the bombings." He shrugged then mimicked a lecturing Grey in his clipped French. " 'We all have duties, Laurent.' "

Claire looked away from Laurent toward the trees. She felt as though the wind had been knocked out of her. She kept her expression calm, chewed her lip. "I see."

Two policemen walked by. They eyed the pair on the bench but said nothing.

She stared at the pool, took a deep breath but didn't speak. Her insides ached. A mistress and child back in London.

"He's right. We all have our responsibilities. I have never forgotten you came to Paris for me." Laurent stroked her arm. "I know you, Claire. You're not made for work."

Claire's throat clamped down until it ached. She thought she'd seen something in Grey's eyes, the way he cocked his head and almost smiled when they walked together through the city. Like he wasn't just looking at her—he saw her. Had she only been lonely?

And now he was gone and Laurent was offering, what? Did the Comte's interest suddenly stir his competitive spirit? A surge of anger choked her. "Just advise me about the Comte."

Laurent scowled and started to say more. Finally, he nodded. "We investigated him after you first wrote. The Comte de Vogüé is a mystery. It seems as though he has always kept his dealings below the surface. The Ritz is the only occupied hotel the Nazis allow civilians to reside. They keep them on the rue Cambon side, but the Comte must be very important to the Nazis' military or business in order to stay at the Ritz. It could be very helpful for us if you made a good impression on him. I know you can do that. And then listen and look. Do as Odette taught you. We will await a report in the usual place."

Claire forced herself to listen. It felt as if her insides spilled out onto the stone below. She shivered, suddenly chilled. The bells from a cathedral chimed eight times. "I need to go." She began to walk toward the Ritz, toward dinner and whatever else she might find.

Laurent called after her. "Claire, not too good of an impression, eh?"

The soldiers on each side of the Ritz's back entrance off 38, rue Cambon said nothing as she passed beneath the small awning and through the double doors. She stood straight, head up, feeling strangely vulnerable without arms full of flowers. It was the back entrance, only Nazis rated the Ritz's front entrance on Place Vendôme, but still, it was the Ritz. Inside the long hallway, she passed a pair of doors on the left and right, and heard the murmur of voices, the smell of tobacco. Glancing inside the dimly lit bars, she saw a mix of men in uniforms and in fine suits, women in evening dresses. How hard would it be, she wondered, to get an invitation to the bar?

Moments after she introduced herself at the rue Cambon concierge desk, a suited man led her to the elevator. A hook nose on a thin face, he wore a lapel pin with the crest and crown logo of the Ritz. He introduced himself as Monsieur LeFevre with an expression that implied he'd seen better. He eyed her as the elevator ascended.

Claire kept her gaze on the gold elevator buttons, her posture straight. Apparently she wasn't the first woman the Comte had to dinner in his room. The doors opened on the fourth floor and, heart pounding, Claire walked through a group of Nazi officers dressed up for a night out. Claire ignored their stares and followed the man down a long corridor. He stopped in front of a room, perfunctorily knocked twice and pulled a key from his pocket.

"*Voilà.*" He opened the door with a flourish.

Claire followed him inside. The wood-paneled room was richly detailed, pale blue velvet upholstered sofa and matching armchairs. The walls and rugs were a tasteful grey blue. A small table and two chairs faced a tall window. Nothing personal, nothing of interest.

He pointed toward the sofa. "Comte de Vogüé has been detained on business. He will join you shortly." He nodded a curt good-bye and exited.

Claire walked over to the window. The sun was setting and the sky violet. Over shadowed rooftops, the gilded figures atop the Opéra glowed faint pink. Scattered pairs of headlights delineated rue Cambon, black outlines of thrashing tree limbs bent against the tugging winds.

Claire watched a couple cross the narrow street below. She frowned. So Grey had a family back home. Why the hell did she care? He never promised anything.

The couple on the street kissed beneath a blued-out lamppost and separated ways. Claire smoothed her dress over her curves and ran a hand through her hair. So Grey was gone. She was at the Ritz about to rendezvous with a handsome French aristocrat. This was why she'd come to Paris in the first place. It was hard enough to stay alive these days. How gauche to fall victim to a schoolgirl crush and risk getting shot over it.

Low voices sounded in the hall. The door clicked shut behind her. The Comte's figure reflected in the window pane.

"My apologies, Madame Badeau, for keeping you waiting."

Claire glanced over at the champagne chilling in a silver ice bucket beside the table. She arranged a devilish smile and twisted to face him, her hips cocked, chest out and one leg forward.

"I am sure, Comte"—she extended her hand—"you have many important things to attend to."

He cradled her fingers in his and brushed his lips over the back of her hand. He straightened, grip held, and admired her with a slight smile on his face.

She held his stare and examined him as he did her. He was dark. Lean, posture like a dancer, cigarette burning in his free hand. Polished hair, tanned skin and his eyes almost black in the shadows of his face. She saw lines around his eyes that weren't there at the party eight months ago.

"Please." He gestured toward the table, pulled out a chair for Claire to sit. He popped the champagne cork off the bottle and poured. "I hope you don't mind we are dining in tonight. With certain business, I prefer to have a bit of privacy."

Claire watched the bubbles rise in the golden liquid. The scent, like sunlight and berries, tickled her nose and made her mouth water. "We are honored you thought of La Vie en Fleurs for your business."

He sat across from her, his gaze on the window. He squinted through the smoke as he exhaled.

Claire studied him as she drank. He wore the trappings of money and power well, like a fine suit. But, there was something roguish there. As if underneath that polished surface, she would find an altogether different beast. It made her want to scratch.

A waiter knocked and pushed in a wheeled cart loaded with covered silver trays. Claire held her breath as the meal was unveiled. Thinly sliced roasted lamb, potatoes swimming in a caramel brown sauce and a steaming baguette.

He leaned back, lit another cigarette and watched her eat, his food untouched. "Have you been in Paris for the entire, eh, reorganization?"

Claire nodded. "Why?"

He shrugged. "You attacked the lamb as if you hadn't seen any lately. Forgive me. I am only making small talk."

"And you. Have you been in Paris?"

He snubbed out his cigarette and met her eyes. "Occasionally. I travel frequently, on business. I also have a family home near Saint-Malo. It is a good place to pass the time, with family. And you?"

"No family. Came to France for love, why else? But then there was war and, well, things changed. Paris is my home now." She glanced out the window as if the memory pained her.

The Comte examined her in the reflection. "There is always war, whether between countries or cities or men." He held his glass in front of him as a toast. "We're all soldiers in some manner. Only the foolish pretend otherwise." With a dark smile he drank.

The conversation dribbled on, about the weather and the tides of war. The meal ended and the Comte guided Claire to the sofa to talk business as a white-coated attendant cleared the table, leaving a fresh bottle of champagne chilling in a silver bucket. For later, Claire knew it implied. The Comte offered her a sifter of brandy and slid close.

The heat of the drink warmed her throat and stomach. She leaned back against the sofa, turning her body to display her curves. She smoothed the dress over her thighs, showing more skin than hiding. His gaze followed her movements. Smiling, she stared deep into his dark eyes. He reached out a hand and cradled her cheek.

He may well be dangerous, but he was a man. Her fingers caressed the pale blue silk upholstery. His sheets would also be silk, breakfast would be fruit and champagne. Maybe she saw nothing to report. So what?

One hand on her cheek, the other traced her shoulder, down her bare arm to rest on her leg. His palm was warm on her thigh; his smooth fingers softly caressed bare skin. His dark eyes glittered. For the first time tonight, he looked hungry.

Claire leaned back, gently removing his hand as she smoothed the fabric back down against her leg. She knew better than to lay all her cards on the table. Not this fast. "Ah, *mon Comte*." She ran her hand down his chest, firmly and slowly, pushing him back a few inches. "Please, tell me about this event."

He sat back and examined her quizzically, his mind calculating a shift in the game. "A celebration for a friend in November. Here, in the hotel."

"*Magnifique*. Is she a good friend?"

He raised an eyebrow, considered her real meaning. He nodded. "She is married now to the Minister of Finance. We have known each other for some time."

The wife of the Minister of Finance. That was going to be a very expensive party. Claire took a sip of brandy to hide her excitement. "Have you established the theme? Colors?"

He refilled her glass, the smallest smile on his lips. "I cannot answer these questions. Perhaps after some discussion . . ." He reached for her.

She stared into his eyes, letting him envelop her. Madame needed this deal. And Claire needed to make it happen for her.

She heard a light knock on the side door.

The Comte paused. "Yes?"

"I have news," a low voice said.

The Comte studied Claire for a moment. Finally he leaned back and stood. "Forgive me. Business." He walked to the adjoining door and disappeared inside.

As the door clicked shut behind him, Claire slumped back

into the couch. She stared up at the ceiling and tried to estimate the party costs over the fuzz of alcohol.

Low voices came through the door.

Claire walked to the mirror over the limestone fireplace mantel. She examined her reflection and frowned. She had looked better before leaving the house. Now, her eyes looked strained, her mouth tight.

Laurent's words drifted up in her mind, riding on the smoke of the fire building in her stomach. Sure, the Resistance gave her papers, but they risked her life in return. Madame Palain gave her a new life. A place in the world where she could create a beauty that didn't offer up regrets.

Claire glared at her reflection. Tonight was important. She owed it to La Vie en Fleurs. She smoothed the lock of hair over her brow. Like it or not, this was what she brought to the table.

In the mirror, she noticed the door into the next room swing open a crack. A corner of the bed, a dark wood desk against a damask fabric wall. She watched as the Comte picked up a phone from his desk, his back to her. He asked to be connected to Room 527.

I owe Madame, not them, Claire told the voice in her head that urged her to listen. She looked back at her reflection and pinched her cheeks to force color into her face.

The Comte dropped the phone into the cradle with a curse. A low voice—the visitor was still there, out of Claire's sight. The Comte jabbed at the air with a slip of paper held in his hand. "We must report this tonight. It cannot wait."

Claire glanced back at the couch, willed herself there, a drink in her hand. Instead, her gaze was locked into the mirror's reflection. In the next room, the Comte impatiently crumpled the paper in his fist and dropped it into the trash can. Claire pulled her eyes away from him and turned toward the brandy on a silver tray near the sofa. She was refilling her glass when the Comte came through the door, pulling it firmly shut behind him. She caught his eyes and smiled.

His lips returned the smile, but his eyes were hard. He walked over to her, rested his palms lightly on her shoulders and brushed his lips against the curve of her neck. "I regret to say I must attend to—"

"Business?"

"*Oui.*" He glanced around the room. His gaze paused on the champagne in the bucket, then her. "Pressing business. It will take an hour, no more than two."

It was an offer, Claire knew. Discreetly French. Would she like to be here when he returned?

She leaned in and kissed the Comte lightly, slowly on both cheeks. "I hope we can continue our discussion in the future."

He studied her. "Next week?"

Claire smiled. "Next week, then."

"You will want to freshen up," he said, tilting his head toward the bottle. "I will send LeFevre up to procure a ride for you."

He strode out into the hallway. She heard the visitor's voice in the hallway, the Comte's reply, then the voices faded away.

Claire drained her glass and slowly exhaled the warmth. The brandy was good, no doubt, but champagne was what she missed most of all. She glanced over at the bottle chilling in ice. It would fit in her coat pocket.

Her gaze was pulled toward the closed side door. Just beyond it, a crumpled piece of paper nestled in a trash can. Damn the Resistance, she thought through a flash of anger. She owed Madame. She wanted to owe them nothing.

But.

She had to know.

In three strides, she was at the door bent over the lock. It was old, the handle worn and the mechanism bent over the decades. Claire put her shoulder against the door and pushed hard. A grinding click and she was in the office, the crumpled note clenched in her hand. She smoothed it open on the desk with her palm.

In rough French script, hastily written and ink-smeared, *Resistance groups converge for meeting in Paris 17-08. Leader coming from south. Carries names and plans.*

Claire sucked in a breath and sank into the seat. Laurent said Odette was busy. A leader who knew all. And along the line a traitor who betrayed everything.

The door in the next room opened with a snap. Claire straightened, grabbing the phone in one motion. She faced the door as LeFevre entered. She eyed him with irritation. "So, you finally made it." She flipped the handle back onto the receiver.

He cleared his throat, the same smirk. "So things did not work out?"

She rose from the seat, curving her body around the chair like a dancer. One hand slid across her bare skin in the vee of her dress, her fingers tugging gently at the fabric as though she might shrug the dress off.

The smirk disappeared as LeFevre stared at her fingers hooked on the dress's neckline. Behind her body, the other hand crumpled the paper into a ball. She released the note from her hand over the trash as she walked toward LeFevre.

"Things worked out just fine. My car, please." Claire retrieved her coat and the bottle of champagne. She smiled at him as she slid the bottle into a coat pocket.

He didn't say another word as he led her downstairs. The

waiting car was a plain sedan; the driver French, his pink Nazi-stamped permit displayed on the dash. Claire slid into the backseat. The interior was dark and smelled of burned oil and Gitanes.

*17-08.*

This leader was coming tomorrow. The scene played in her mind like a gangster movie. Odette stood in a deserted square. A car full of Resistance fighters bristling with guns turned onto the street. The leader in the backseat, swarthy, grim, chewed on a cigarette while he mulled over plans of attack. In the shadows, line after line of German soldiers, rifles ready. Odette would be lucky to die in the square. They all would be.

The brakes ground as the car pulled up to La Vie en Fleurs. Claire opened the door before the tires stopped, composing the report in her head. The driver called out *Bonsoir, madame*, but Claire didn't look back as she slipped inside.

After this, she would damn well be even. She would have paid off her new life. Claire Badeau would be a free woman.

Claire's hand trembled as she stuffed the scribbled note into the dentist's mail slot. Addressed to Danielle, the script imprinted into the paper with the force of her pen, *I have important news. We must speak. Evelyn.*

It took too long to get here, slipping through the shadows after curfew, her pulse hammering, heels echoing like hammers on the bricks as she ran. The office was long closed. She only hoped Odette would get her letter in time.

The sky opened up and heavy drops of cold rain spattered the avenue. Claire looked up and down the street before she skittered across, choosing her steps over the puddles. Staying under the dark eaves, she hurried back to the shop.

* * *

Within an hour after the shop opened the next morning, a man called in an order. *A large posy of white flowers. Delivered immediately to an address in Saint-Germain, the sixth arrondissement. An extra twenty francs if it is there in an hour. For Danielle.*

Claire practically dashed from the shop, flowers in hand. She took the Métro to Vavin. The address, she discovered, was a café. Café des Trois Spiritueux. Odette sat at a table near the door, playing with a cup of coffee and an unlit Gitane. Claire took the empty chair across the table and dropped the posy on her folded napkin.

Odette stared down at the flowers. With a crooked smiled she held them up to her face and inhaled deeply. "It amazes me."

"What does?"

"It is impossible to get a cup of real coffee, much less a fresh vegetable, in all of Paris, and yet you do this." Odette cupped a snow-white blossom in her hand.

Claire shrugged and smoothed her skirt over her legs. "Madame orders from growers from the south, near Grasse. Besides—I took these from a bouquet going to a Kommandant Daecher's mistress. Feel better?"

A smile played at the corner of Odette's mouth. She signaled the waiter. "Something warm?"

Claire shook her head. She wanted to get this said and get out.

"You'll sit and stir it around the same as I am. We need something to do." Odette smiled her thanks as the waiter set a cup in front of Claire. "Now. Speak."

"This is safe, here?" Claire looked around at the scattered tables; the diners leaned over their lunches.

Odette smiled grimly, her eyes flicked over the café. "You would be surprised at this place. Talk."

Claire quickly ran through what she heard. *The meeting in Paris. The leader from the south.*

Odette's face faded to a chalky grey. She reached for a cigarette. It took three tries to light it with trembling fingers. "It is true."

"Now that you know, you can make adjustments, can't you?"

Odette didn't reply. Her face was composed but her eyes blinked fast as she thought. She focused on Claire, her lips pulled back to the slightest toothy smile. "Yes. We can." Odette gathered the posy and stood. A nod to the waiter. "Come."

Claire rose and followed her outside.

Odette pressed the flowers into Claire's hands as they walked. She spoke under her breath. "You must take these flowers and meet someone, warn him."

Claire stopped abruptly. She heard what the Nazis did to *Resistánts*. The torture, cutting, drowning, praying for death. "No."

Odette flipped around to face her. "No?"

"I already risked too much. I'm not like you. I won't go further."

"Claire, you don't understand. There is a traitor. They may know me. They see me and it's over. There is no time to find someone else. You must."

"*You* don't understand, Odette. I heard something important. I told you. I kept my part of the bargain. No—you find another little soldier." She shoved the flowers into Odette's midsection.

Odette glared. Claire opened her fingers. The posy hit and bounced off the uneven bricks of the sidewalk. Flowers and petals burst from their ties and rolled into the street.

"You could have written everything down in your report last night, risking the traitor would see it. You didn't. You came here today. You care, *mon ami*. You may not want to, but you do."

Claire leaned in, her voice a harsh whisper. "Caring for something and dying for something are two completely different things. Don't get them confused."

"It would be a mistake to walk away from us." Odette picked up the flowers. Her face was blank, eyes fixed on a single white ranunculus blossom she threaded back into the bouquet.

Claire's anger snuffed out like a cigarette butt tossed in the snow. Would they kill her? Damn. They just might. But she wasn't about to start following orders. "I could walk away, all right. Straight to the Ritz. The Comte would be pleased to see me. He enjoys a good chat. That would be a hell of a mistake too, wouldn't it?"

Fear flickered in Odette's eyes. "Yes. That would be." She held the crumpled flowers out to Claire, a note of pleading crept into her voice. "Claire. This is more important than I can say. For *all* of us."

"Oh? Grey too?" Claire said flatly.

Odette scowled.

Must have hit a nerve, Claire thought grimly. "Is it true? Did Grey go back to England, like Laurent said?"

Odette sighed. Her lips pressed into a thin line. "He did."

A cold sliver jabbed Claire in the chest. He was the same as all the other bastards she'd run across. And now Odette. Kind, genuine Odette demanded she risk her life for them, or what? Death?

Taking a deep breath, she plucked the posy from Odette's hand and hooked it in the crook of her elbow. She was through with every last one them. After she saved this *connard*, she'd tell them all to go straight to hell. She might not wait until next week to see the Comte. She was getting so tired of wool scratching her raw she dreamed of silk in her sleep. "Tell me what I need to do."

Less than an hour later, she climbed the stairs to the upper level of Gare Montparnasse to await the inbound train from Lyon. The concourse was huge; high ceilings beyond view, lines of tracks butted up against platforms accepting trains from all parts south.

She re-read her instructions from Odette, which were mercifully short. At 11:45 the train from Lyon would arrive. Among the passengers would be an older gentlemen wearing a red-striped scarf. He was called Christophe. She must get him safely to an address she memorized and tell him what she heard.

The hall was surprisingly crowded with families dressed to travel south. They could not be mistaken for summer holiday travelers, their clothes too worn, faces were too still, eyes averted from soldiers, from each other. They were the desperate Parisians with the right papers to join their families in the unoccupied zone, where the fascism was cloaked in the trappings of "Father Pétain" and people managed to keep a bit of the harvest away from the German army.

Claire pushed through the crowd toward the row of platforms. Nearly tripping over a stack of luggage, she bumped into the side of a soldier in feldgrau. He spun to face her, his arm poised to strike. He saw her, paused, then *saw* her. His arm dropped.

Claire watched his eyes run from her face to her feet and back up again. Wehrmacht Heer, regular German army. Not to say they wouldn't kill you, but they didn't seem to enjoy it quite as much as most of the SS. And for the Wehrmacht stationed in Paris, their most passionate conquests were usually more directed toward bedding French women than wiping out the existing world order.

Claire smiled at him, tilted her head to the side and let her hair fall back from her face. *"Pardon."*

His eyes flickered in surprise and he smiled back, the face of a man too young to expect attention and too inexperienced to doubt it.

She glanced at the table next to him. Two bored soldiers sat in metal chairs; they rummaged through a suitcase open between them. One held a shirt crumpled in his fist, his other hand deep in the suitcase. His partner smoked a cigarette, only half watching the contents get tumbled about. A tired traveler in a rumpled suit stood in front of them. His face was red and lips puffed out indignantly, but his rigid posture exposed his fear.

The soldier at her side spoke to the seated men. Both looked back to her, a smile hidden behind their lips. Claire turned and walked slowly toward the tracks, swinging her hips as she unbuttoned her coat. She paused on the platform marked *Lyon*, next to the empty tracks. She shrugged the coat off her shoulders and glanced back. All three soldiers stared at her. Well, if she had to be noticed, at least they liked what they saw. All she had to do was drop the flowers in front of the soldiers on her way out and show them some skin, and this Christophe had a free ride. She smiled. Odette had picked the perfect woman for the job.

She looked down at the bouquet cupped in her hands. Ranunculus. She knew it as a buttercup, when she was young. Given to another, it meant *I am dazzled by your charms*. Come to find out, a perfect choice for the day.

As she leaned back against a bench and applied her lipstick, a train pulled into the station one platform down. *Montpellier* snapped up on the board. SS soldiers strode out from an invisible doorway behind her. A dozen or more spread out into the crowd. They surrounded the platform, their faces masks, bodies poised like blades. Silently, they watched each person disembark and thread past them. Claire glanced back to the Wehrmacht soldiers who gripped their guns and stood. They weren't expecting this visit.

Claire adjusted the bouquet in her hands. She glanced back down the stairwell. The exit was clear. She could walk away.

But she didn't.

She knew how much the SS had been told. They were in the station because they expected a threat from the south. The fact that they are standing at the other platform proved they still don't know which train and they didn't know who.

Claire watched the SS scrutinize each passenger. A captain stood back a few steps, his eyes darted from person to person, face expressionless. He watched a businessman in a faded blue suit carrying a briefcase, his head down, walking too fast. The captain nodded his head. With military precision, two soldiers closed the gap between them, leaving the man pinched in the middle. Each grabbed an arm and marched, half dragging him between them, toward the door. A third soldier grabbed the abandoned luggage and strode along behind the others, stepping over a lone black shoe.

Claire turned her head away, her stomach queasy. He probably wasn't going to get a chance to miss that loafer. Remaining passengers hurried by, avoiding the eyes of the SS. A small girl stopped to pick up the lost shoe. Her mother jerked her arm and scurried away.

With the tilt of his head, the captain indicated another man.

Two more soldiers moved. She heard the man pleading as he was hauled away. *I have Ausweis. I have papers.*

Claire looked down at the flowers in her lap. The petals trembled. Why the hell was she in the middle of a SS raid? She forced her eyes back to the captain. What was he looking for? Men traveling alone? People without obvious reasons for arriving in Paris?

The train from Lyon rumbled in the station. The remaining soldiers regrouped on her platform, spread out in a semicircle facing the train. They were a step in front of her; she smelled the sharp smoke of German Roth-Händle cigarettes on their uniforms.

The time to get out was now. Claire stood, tugged at her dress and smoothed her hair, stared hard at the exit, but her feet wouldn't take her there. She planted a smile on her face and slipped in between two soldiers.

The doors opened and travelers streamed off the train. All blanched when they saw the uniforms; their strides faltered then picked up again as they hurried by. Claire watched the officer. His eyes zeroed in on a man, plump with a receding hairline. He looked offended when they pulled him aside. A loyal Vichy man, no doubt. He was hauled away, struggling. Not so loyal for long.

The skirmish was forgotten as her target exited the train. He was wiry, shorter than she'd expected. Thin glasses rode on a hawk nose. His thick head of white hair was carefully combed. A trimmed mustache lined a serious mouth. He carried a valise; a coat was slung over an arm. A red and white striped scarf was tied around his neck.

Claire saw the officers eyes flick over toward him.

"*Mon cheri!*" Claire threw herself in his arms. "Kiss me," she whispered, her mouth on his cheek.

Surprise flickered in his eyes but he recovered, gamely pulling her into his arms and planting a dry kiss on her lips. He tasted of tobacco and coffee.

Her arm anchored in his, she pulled him toward the soldiers. "*Excusez-moi*," Claire said, her tone light, and led with the flowers held out in front of her chest.

The SS in front of her didn't give way. With her momentum, she pressed up against him, felt his gun against her thigh, the patch on his uniform pocket scratched her collarbone. She swallowed the bile that surged in her throat, looked up and smiled through the burning that threatened to choke her.

His hard stare flicked down on her, a tongue slid through thin lips like a snake tasting for fear. Her smile was pinned on; the blood pounded in her ears as she held his gaze. He stared for another moment then shoved her away with a stiff arm.

She pushed Christophe through the gap created in front of her. Out of the corner of her eye, she saw the officer turn his head toward them. One nod and they were dead. The young Wehrmacht soldier from the table of feldgrau moved to block their path, his eyes on Christophe's case.

"What about a search for me, soldier?" She turned her head; the officer was watching. She had to make a friend and fast. She leaned in to the soldier, licking her lips. "A girl needs to make a living. But—" She slid out a blossom and set it on the table in front of him. "You look so strong. I haven't had a good search in ages."

His eyes widened. He said nothing, but nodded his head sharply.

She glanced back at the captain. Another poor soul was getting dragged away. She faced the soldier. "You'll be here later? After they leave? What's your name?"

"Günter. Leave your grandfather at home."

Claire turned to walk away.

He grabbed her arm. "And you, your name?"

"Evelyn. Don't forget me." One last smile and Claire reached for Christophe. She looked back as they reached the stairs.

The captain was watching. He nodded. The SS soldiers moved.

Christophe spoke for the first time, the immaculately smooth voice of a learned man. "I suggest we run."

They charged down the stairs, pressing through the crowd. Claire jerked Christophe into a tiled hallway off the main passage.

"Where are we going?" he gasped. He wasn't up for a sprint.

"I don't know." Claire pulled him around a sharp corner. The hallway ended past them at a closed door. They pressed themselves against a wall. Christophe reached out and rattled the knob. The door was locked.

Across the hall, a thick, wirehaired woman hunched over a mop in a dirty puddle flecked with suds. She paused mopping and looked up, her eyes dull. A low shout echoed from the main corridor. The woman stared.

Claire peered around the corner. A group of soldiers ran past. The captain walked by, paused in the hallway and looked down toward them. Claire jerked her head back and faced the woman, pleading for silence with her eyes. One word, one look. She was with a known *Resistánt*. They would both be dead.

Christophe struggled to catch his breath. He spoke softly to the woman, as if to a child. "Madame."

A shout echoed down the hall. Heavy footsteps pounded closer. The woman reached a gnarled finger toward them.

"Madame," Christophe said, his voice cracking.

She lurched past them to a second locked door nearly invisible against the white tile wall. With the flick of a key, the door opened.

Claire and Christophe charged into the darkness. The door clicked shut behind them. They held their breath, heard the footsteps pass. The other door rattled as the soldiers tried the lock.

Claire held one hand in front of her; the other clutched Christophe's arm.

"Are you alright?" Christophe said.

"Better now. Do you have a light?"

"Yes. Hold on."

A match flared. The flickering flame lit their faces. The tunnel was dark and wet. Moss-covered concrete walls led away into the distance. The air smelled old and sour.

"Where the hell are we?" Claire tightened her grip on his arm.

"Think of it as a wine cellar, my dear, and we are on our way to an exceptional Bordeaux. Say a Latour '29?" Christophe's teeth glinted.

Claire grinned weakly. "How about champagne? Bollinger, Grande Année?"

"I think a bottle of each would do nicely." He took a step forward. "Did you say your name was Evelyn?"

"Yes."

He nodded, as if she answered an important question. "Well, Evelyn, we better get moving. I don't know how far back the vintner keeps the good bottles."

Light was fading as they crawled out of a vent hole near the Métro's rue d'Odessa exit. They had walked underground for hours, arm in arm, each foot testing the next step, the only sounds their footfalls and the relentless drip of water down the carved rock walls around them.

Once outside, Claire and Christophe slipped into the rush of people trying to make it home before curfew. It was pitch dark when they entered the apartment building on rue Férou. As Odette directed, Claire led Christophe up three flights of stairs, then knocked softly on the door marked 33. "It is Evelyn."

The door opened an inch. "*Entrez,*" a low voice commanded.

They slipped through the entry into a dark room. The lights flicked on and they stared into a ring of pointed gun barrels. A tense breath then a thick man, one cheek puckered with a curved scar, pushed through and hugged Christophe. At that, the men lowered their guns and joined in greeting Christophe or as they called him now, Monsieur Kinsel.

Claire allowed herself to be pushed aside in the rush. Even she knew Kinsel was famous. She had read articles in *Le Temps* about this mysterious criminal who set up a network of alliances throughout southern France. What the Nazis would have done to her if she had been caught with Kinsel . . . Her knees wobbled and she sagged against the door, seemingly forgotten. And, for once, grateful for the lack of attention.

The men took turns shaking Kinsel's hand. In crumpled overalls and pressed suits, they all shared a hard-eyed look. A familiar face pushed through to Claire.

Jacques squeezed her shoulder, his normally sardonic face subdued for the occasion. "Evelyn, I will see you home."

Claire glanced back as he opened the door. Kinsel was at the table, a glass of wine in his hand. He raised it to her in a toast. She blew him a kiss as she stepped out.

It was after midnight when they reached the flower shop. Jacques waited in the shadows, his eyes on the street as Claire fumbled with the lock. In the darkness and her exhaustion, it took two tries to get the damn key in place and the mechanism to click. She turned back to him as the door swung open. "Thank you, Jacques."

He shrugged. "For *une femme américaine*, you have *des couilles*." He slipped into the darkness and was gone.

Claire crept up the stairs to her room, her feet aching, body heavy. She couldn't help but smile in the darkness. She had paid her debts. They damn well knew she was more than a Yankee princess. As Jacques said, she had balls.

# *Chapter 7*

## THE PRICE OF ELEGANCE

52, rue du Colisée, Paris. September 1, 1941.

A sweltering late summer day. The air trapped in the alley behind the shop cooked between the buildings. Bricks baked underfoot in the late afternoon sun. The sour scent of rotting vegetation and steaming trash settled on hair and skin. Claire wiped the sweat from her neck with a grubby hand. With a heave, she slung decaying flowers into the rubbage bin. Dropping the empty bucket at her feet, she picked up the next.

Eleven days ago, a *Resistánt* shot and killed a German officer at the Barbès-Rochechouart station of the Métro. Then the reprisals started. Nazi sweeps pulled people off the street. There were rumors of a planned public execution. Ten people, fifty people, a hundred, lined up and shot. No one knew. They held their breath and stayed inside. German soldiers weren't walking alone anymore, not pursuing lonely girls with dinner and flowers.

Even the Comte disappeared. The promised second meeting

should have been nights ago. Instead of a car to pick her up, his assistant called. Apologetic but brusque. Apparently used to finishing what the Comte started. *Thank you, Madame, for your interest, but regrettably the situation is somewhat changed. The Comte will keep your services in mind.*

Madame Palain was relieved. "We will do without his money."

But Claire knew what the loss meant. She said nothing when Madame pursed her lips and frowned, smoothing her hair in the tight bun she wore low on her nape.

They did need his money.

In the heat, what flowers Madame managed to buy slumped, unpurchased, in tin buckets. Claire tossed those that started to rot into the garbage. Claire cursed at the slimy daylily stems that slid from the bucket and splattered green sludge on her dress. With the Comte's party, the shop would have been set at least until Christmas. Was this the big Resistance Christophe came to Paris to lead? A single German midshipman dead, what good did it do? The entire city suffered for it.

Several turns of the decrepit water faucet handle in the alley and warm water splattered onto the bricks. Claire rinsed the worst from the buckets and carried them rattling against her legs back inside the shop. She paused as she saw Madame locking the front door. Another day without a customer. With the money from the pawned wedding ring long gone, they wouldn't survive many more.

Claire wiped her neck and arms as she leaned against the cool stone wall in the back of the shop. Madame started her closing routine. Claire watched her go through every bucket, every plant, a slight nudge here or there, inspecting the counters, the floors. Without looking at Claire, the florist gestured to the floor under the shelves. "The stones have sweat in the heat and collected dirt. It will need to be mopped in the morning."

Claire usually found the routine endearing. A daily lesson in observation and discipline. Tonight it was grating. "You think someone is going to notice?"

The florist straightened, her shoulders pulled back. Claire waited for her to respond in her modulated voice, offer some quaint lesson in living that would, tonight, make Claire sneer.

Madame ran her hand over the wall as she walked to the front and paused in front of the window. When she finally spoke, it was in a quiet, dreamy tone that forced Claire forward to hear.

"My mother was a baroness. The Baroness du Vinen. A title, but not the means. Still, I was given the best education at Sorbonne. Art, literature, culture. For the purpose of charming and marrying an important and wealthy man. I admit I was a disappointment to my mother. I married a professor of engineering. An educated man. A gentle man. But a man of simple tastes."

Madame never spoke about herself. Claire stepped forward, enthralled.

"We lived in Paris, a small apartment across from jardin du Luxembourg, near the university, his work. After only nine months at the university, my gentle engineer was called to fight the Germans. Another soldier fighting the Great War. Months passed. I cherished his letters. But without his salary, without the university, I had nothing. And one day, I passed by this place. The suitcase in my hand was all I had left." She stroked the petals of a peach-colored rose. "I had no experience, no references. Monsieur Russo saw something in me, I think. I became his assistant."

"He was the owner?" Claire said.

"Yes. The preeminent florist in the arrondissement. A celebrated artist, like Renoir or Seurat. But that was the Great War. Times were not easy. Still, he believed in this place." Madame smiled gently, her eyes gazing through the years. She tucked a slender green cherry branch behind three ruffled rose blossoms.

"My husband did not survive the war. I was devastated, of course, but no more so than many others. I gave my heart and soul to this place. When my mother died, I inherited a bit of money. Monsieur Russo was tired, his hands stiff. He sold me the shop on very lenient terms. He knew no one would care for it like I would." Madame turned to Claire, enunciating each word. "He knew I would never let it fail. Elegance endures. It must."

Claire gulped, wrestling with the knot in her throat. She scuffed a toe at the grit beneath the shelves—it *was* there—and bit her lower lip. She concentrated on the pain until the tightness in her throat relaxed.

Madame pulled her bag from under the counter. *"Au revoir, mon ami."* She kissed Claire good night and glided into the evening shadows.

Claire climbed the stairs and threw open the windows to her room. She pulled the garden photo from the mirror's edge and sat on the open windowsill, her feet resting on the balcony. She squinted at the picture in the dimness.

The dark violet sky lent the image a mystical air. The verdant beauty of the garden, the wise serenity carved on the statue's face was like cool water on Claire's overheated emotions. Her marriage and high society life was dead, her affair with Laurent a memory. Yet this little photo not only survived but had grown more real. A place, if only in her mind, that welcomed her like the first sun of spring.

Claire peered down at the deep blue awning below the balcony at her feet. The faded lettering of *La Vie en Fleurs* looked murky grey against the dying light.

Everyone saw her beauty, Claire knew. They always had. But Madame saw something more. Something worth saving. Claire felt a surge of heat in her chest. She straightened her shoulders, felt a warmth spread throughout her body.

Beauty might be a gift to our souls from the heavens. Luxury, purchased. But suddenly she understood. There was strength in elegance. Claire wouldn't let the shop fail. And she knew, first thing in the morning, before Madame arrived, she would mop the damn floor.


Avenue Montaigne. September 26, 1941.

The midday sun felt thin, hinting at fall's chill. The pressing heat of summer was a memory. Broken clouds stirred over the city. It would pour by nightfall.

Claire breathed deep at the scent of rain in the air as she walked slowly by the Théâtre des Champs-Elysées. The façade of the theater was beautiful, pale white carved limestone. A mix of Art Deco and classical styles, a good five stories tall, judging by the windows of buildings on each side. The gold-framed windows were oversized. At the end of avenue Montaigne, Claire crossed Place de l'Alma and meandered along the Seine toward the Eiffel Tower.

Madame Palain was out today. Another day spent in line to get her *Ausweis*, her permit to travel south to Nice in the unoccupied zone. They had no business to speak of, but the florist wanted to ensure they could procure stock for the long winter ahead.

Claire went to the Hôtel Emeraude to see Leluc. She wore the thin pale blue dress she knew he liked, forced a gay tone. Surely such a distinguished hotel would need increased orders for the holidays. A deposit would be available now, perhaps?

"I will need to check." Leluc hedged, his expression pinched, as he sat back in the chair behind his desk. He meant no.

Claire had learned there were many degrees of *No* in France. She played with the curl over her brow, settled a hip on his desk and twisted her body about to face him. "Ah, Monsieur, in times like these, a gift of beauty would mean so much."

A sigh rose from his feet, then Leluc relented they might need something soon. He pulled a small pile of francs from his desk. "The gift of beauty."

Claire judged the thickness as she slipped the money in her pocket, offering Leluc *la bise* good-bye. Enough to keep the shop going for a few more days but nothing more.

She squeezed the bills as she turned into the park at Trocadero, in the shadow of the Eiffel Tower across the Seine. She traced her way along the looping paths through the broad leafy trees. A beautiful fall day, she was in no hurry to face the empty shop.

She heard footsteps approach. She turned, hoping to be met by Grey's steel-colored eyes and a bemused smile. An older man hurried by her. Thin white hair, hunched shoulders.

Claire sighed. She wasn't angry at Grey. Not anymore. She thought back to the day they walked nearby and remembered the force of his gaze, the steadiness of his arm around her waist.

She wished for his company. He would let her be. What? Herself? Perhaps. Or someone close to it.

The papers said half of London was destroyed in the Luftwaffe bombing. She hoped it was propaganda. Then she dug out

Madame's hidden radio and listened to the BBC one night in bed. Thousands *had* died. But London stood strong.

For the moment, the Nazis had turned their attention away from air raids over England. Still, she didn't doubt Grey had gone where his strength was needed most. No. She wasn't angry.

An hour lost in mindless reverie, only her feet noticed the distance she traveled back to rue du Colisée. As Claire unlocked the shop door, she heard the phone ringing. She lunged for the phone.

"*Allô?*" Claire gasped.

"La Vie en Fleurs?" a low voice said.

"Yes." Claire grabbed the notebook and pen under the register, tried to calm her breath.

"I would like to place an order for Christophe."

A message then, not a paying order. Claire crumpled the paper in her hand.

"A white posy. Delivered to 17, rue Perrault. Take the Métro to the Louvre station." The line went dead.

Claire dropped the phone in the cradle and examined the shop. The long, barren shelves, the stack of empty tin buckets. The few flowers they had were artfully arranged on a center table, but they might well die there and join their brothers in the rubbish. La Vie en Fleurs couldn't go on this way.

She hadn't been able to swing a deal with the Comte. She would just have to try a different route. Resolution squared Claire's jaw. This dirt farmer's daughter had survived worse times. And she'd learned a thing or two since then.

A vase of white sweet peas intertwined with a single shell-pink rose caught her eye. Not exactly a white posy, but . . .

\* \* \*

Claire climbed aboard the Métro at the Saint-Philippe-du-Roule station. She settled back in the seat, resting the paper-wrapped bouquet on her lap. A young woman in dirty brown trousers sat across the aisle. She looked about fifteen; her face still held the roundness of a child. Only unmarried women were allowed to work. Or widows. With so many men gone, Claire imagined the girl on her way home from a factory.

The girl stared at the flowers the hungry way Claire used to stare at jewels, but she wouldn't meet Claire's eyes. These days no one met one another's eyes. They still waited for the retribution to end. For the guillotine to drop.

At the Tuileries stop, two police officers came aboard the car. They walked down the aisle asking for identification. Claire slipped hers out and held it in front of her without looking up. After a moment, they passed on.

The air smelled of rain when she exited the subway at the Louvre station. Odette waited out front.

"Where's Christophe?" Claire asked, not bothering to appear to be pleased.

"Nearby."

"What? Worried I wouldn't come if you used your own nom de plume?"

Odette shrugged, her lips pinched like her face ached. "You must understand why I pressed you to act." She looked around. "Let's walk."

They strode side by side along rue de Rivoli, turned onto rue Perrault.

"We are in a war, Claire. I must sometimes act as a soldier, not as a friend."

Claire nearly stopped at this. After Odette threatened her? "A friend?"

"Yes."

Well, at least Odette sounded ashamed. The way Claire had saved their skins, she should be. "A friend who doesn't act like one," Claire said. "What would you call that?"

"Pained," Odette said.

They turned to face a large church. An imposing bell tower, ornately carved stone colored soft pink against the cloudy sky. Gothic spires pointed out from the corners. An enormous stained-glass window overlooked the oversized wooden doors.

"Saint-Germain l'Auxerrois." Odette motioned for Claire to step inside.

Claire led the way down the center aisle of small wooden chairs. Odette touched Claire's arm and pointed toward a man sitting near the front, next to a thick stone column at the end of a row. It was Christophe. Kinsel. His head was bowed. Claire sat in the chair next to him, arranged herself on the braided fiber seat and held the flowers in front of her. Odette crossed herself and walked away.

Christophe opened his eyes and faced Claire. "*Bonjour*, Evelyn. I hope you are well?" He took the flowers and set them carefully on the seat next to him.

Claire held his gaze, kept a faint smile on her face. Pleasant, was what she called the expression, perfected by Madame. As if daring the recipient to offer something wonderful, with a warning not to disappoint.

"I am well, *merci*." Then added as if an afterthought, "Of course we have lost a great deal of business, due to the latest unpleasantness."

"Things will only get worse." He stared at the golden cross in the nave below the windows. "There will be more attacks. More reprisals. Many innocent people will die. Nazi evil sets no boundaries." He turned to face her, head on. "Do you know what is happening on the streets as we speak? A mass arrest of Jews. Why? In retaliation for acts against the occupying power. Thousands of people—thousands—are being pulled out of their homes. Taken away to Drancy. Nazis call the Jews vermin. What do you think will happen to them next?"

Claire shrugged, her chest heavy. When she was a child, her father drowned what he called vermin inside an old burlap bag in the cow pond. *You don't waste bullets on vermin,* he'd said.

"Who is implementing this Nazi order? The Parisian *flics,*" Christophe said. Our police. "There was a time when we could believe this would pass. A few months perhaps, then our life as the French would return to normal. But the Nazis want to remake the world. There will be nothing left of our life. Join us."

Claire ignored the ache in her throat. Christophe wasn't wrong. But this life she had, like a spring bud, was so young, so fragile. "The risk—"

"Yes. Always. But we do what we can."

"You are asking me to endanger the shop."

"Your position there gives you access to what we need. It is necessary."

Necessary. A good word. But then, Claire knew what was necessary. He was trying to get her riled up, as if she were a soldier before battle. But she knew what she fought for today. She made as if to rise from the chair.

"What do we fight for, Claire?"

"*Liberté, égalité, fraternité,*" she said. Liberty, equality, fraternity. The motto of France. At least before Pétain. She met his eyes, her voice sweet. "Expensive, these things."

He closed his mouth on his reply and appraised her. His eyes cold, like steel bearings. "The price is high. In lives or in treasure. You were offered one. Not both."

Claire fought the urge to backpedal. A dark hardness stirred in his eyes. She knew what happened to people who turned against the Resistance. No torture, but death just the same. But she also knew what this money could buy. Desperately needed food for Madame, perhaps even replace the pair of shoes that Georges outgrew. She ransacked her mind for a weapon. Real or not. She smiled, her mouth sweet, eyes cold. "Yes. But that is the manner I work, Monsieur Kinsel." His real name bled out between her teeth. "The circles I move in. I meet interesting people. Like Comte Jean-Luc de Vogüé."

"I am familiar," Christophe said.

"He too appreciates my particular abilities. And has made a proposal of a certain nature. I am a businesswoman. I must weigh all offers on the table."

Claire held her breath as Christophe leaned back, crossed his legs and adjusted a pant leg. Either she had him where she wanted him, she thought, or he was about to kill her.

"And?" Christophe examined her face. "What is your price?"

This was for Madame. She smiled at him, fingered a button on her coat. "Six thousand francs."

A small smile, too tight. "You are quite confident in the importance of your *particular abilities*. Perhaps you haven't yet been introduced to your own limits."

"You, Monsieur, have personally benefited."

He shrugged, the slightest nod. "Perhaps. Two thousand, then."

"*Tellement petit!*" So little. A dramatic sigh. The smallest shake of her head.

"A generous offer. And only because of the courage you displayed at the train station," Christophe said, his quiet voice strained.

Claire smoothed the skirt against her legs and stuffed back the doubt that snaked into the edges of her mind. There was no room for doubt or conscience. Not now. "Four thousand francs. On the first week of every month. I will let you choose the manner of delivery. That is your area of expertise."

He stared at her a moment longer, the skin around his eyes tight. "Very well. One day, Claire, you will understand. And then you will sacrifice everything for something greater than the indulgence of a few sparkling diversions."

Claire exhaled slowly, kept the smile. One day inferred she would see tomorrow. And Madame and the shop would survive.

"In addition to your reports, you will get phone orders, like you did today, for certain locations. On the route, you will be handed a message to slip inside the flowers. You won't see me again."

"*Vive la France,*" Claire said, her mouth dry.

He reached down for the flowers and turned them over in his hand. "Very beautiful. You are a talented woman. For the price, you'd better continue to impress." He walked out.

Claire sat back in the chair and took a deep breath. The church smelled of incense, wax and the wear of hundreds of years. She would have prayed, if she were the type. Instead she pulled out a pocket mirror, smoothed her hair and applied her lipstick. She puckered her lips at the serious face staring out at her.

She would have been happy with three thousand.

Still, she did the right thing. She knew it by the warm fire she felt deep in her chest. Madame had given her a new life, and she, in return, would do everything in her power to save her friend. But Claire Badeau better be damn careful.

Two weeks later, Claire swept the sidewalk in front of the shop as the sun dipped into the horizon. A stiff breeze whipped hair into her eyes and tossed fallen leaves faster than she piled them. Still, she hummed as she worked.

That morning, a small boy selling newspapers approached Claire as she opened the shop for business. Inside the day's edition of *Le Temps*, a small bundle. Her heart in her throat, she finished sweeping, then went inside and up to her room. The size of a cigarette case, wrapped in tattered paper. Too small to be a bomb. She ripped into it.

Four thousand francs, in one-hundred notes. Half she tucked behind the dresser, the other went into the till. *An order from the Comte,* she told Madame, *a regular payment.* They were to give flowers for the War Relief Committee. A Frenchman underneath it all, he must feel sympathy for the wounded French soldiers. *At this price,* Madame asked, amazed. *Madame, he is not that good of a Frenchman,* Claire told her. *For him, the price was doubled. His money is better with us than with the Germans.*

Gripping the broom, Claire smiled again at the memory. Tonight she planned a special surprise for Madame. Georges had just dropped off a box by the door. Nearly like the old days, a bottle of wine, a loaf of real bread, a square of cheese.

A man passed by, head down, hands in pockets. Thinning grey hair, sharply drawn mustache. A polite *bonjour* as he stepped around her broom.

A flash of warm recognition and Claire grinned. "Monsieur Oberon?"

He looked puzzled. "Madame?"

"I am the woman you picked up on the road and brought to Paris almost a year and a half ago. Claire, Claire Badeau."

A wan smile crinkled the corners of his eyes. "Ah, Madame Badeau." A nod at the name change. "Of course."

"I am so pleased to see you again. I've thought of you and your wife often." He looked thinner, she thought. Worn around the eyes but well enough.

"Oh? How kind. Your speaking has greatly improved."

"It is a constant effort. How is Madame Oberon?"

"She is well," he said, though Claire wondered at the tone.

"And your son? Michele?"

A muscle in his jaw ticked. Claire knew the answer before he formed the words.

"He was killed in the fighting. We heard last summer."

"I am so sorry," Claire said. Knowing words weren't enough. She remembered the grainy photo Adele had shown her, tattered from the years. The family kneeling in the sand on the beach, a grin took up the boy Michele's entire face. His smiling parents were draped around either shoulder like a loving blanket.

"Please, wait one moment." She dropped the broom against the doorway and bolted inside. She pulled out a dozen roses, white for honor, light pink for sympathy, wrapped them in silver and white paper. On the way out the door, Claire passed Georges' box.

The Oberons might have saved her life by giving her a ride to Paris. But more than that, they offered her compassion in the form of shared sandwiches, friendly though stilted conversation, a warm embrace. She tucked the roses inside the box and walked out the door out with it in her hands. "For you," she said.

His gaze flicked over the bread loaf, the wine bottle, the flowers. "That is too much. I could not take it."

"Monsieur, I have not forgotten your generosity that day. Please allow me to repay you and your wife. Please." She held the box in front of her.

He reached out tentatively, his face slack, eyes moist. "*Merci. Merci beaucoup.* Adele will be so pleased. It has been a difficult time. Things—" He cleared his throat, forced a smile, met her eyes. "Adele would welcome your company. The house feels so empty now."

Claire swallowed the knot in her throat. What could she offer Adele besides flowers? A smile and a kiss on his cheek, her regards to his wife, and she watched him walk away.

Across the street, the policeman who stopped Claire last December stepped from Epicerie Dupré. He caught her gaze and pointed a thick finger to his eye. Claire grabbed the broom and walked inside.

Madame Palain examined her. "Who was that gentleman, Claire?"

"An old friend."


Jardin des Tuileries. May 16, 1943.

The sky was deep blue and the air filled with the fragrance of blooming flowers. Gnarled chestnut trees, their heavy limbs weighted with vibrant green leaves and waving wands of white flowers. Claire could feel spring down into her bones as she entered jardin des Tuileries off rue de Rivoli.

It was a season she thought would never come. It didn't seem

possible Paris had another spring in her, given the death and war
boiling over the whole world.

Children kneeled on the edge of a large octagonal pool. With
*Maman* keeping a watchful eye, they dangled over the water
directing small wooden sailboats with prods from worn sticks.
Claire wondered how many of their papas had been killed or
were prisoners in Germany.

She ducked into an *allée*, a perfect green lane of trees and
shrubs. Birds chirped over her head in the manicured planar
trees. With the bouquet of white roses in her arms, she could
almost imagine this as a perfect spring day in Paris. Glinting
through the branches, the sun traced a lace of light and shadow
on the grass beneath her feet. The air smelled sweet, of fresh
growth, roses and jasmine, and moist earth. She headed toward
the carousel midway through the park.

Of course, if this were that sort of Parisian spring day, she'd
be meeting a lover.

She glanced down at the roses in her arms. The worn envelope that was slipped inside at the Métro station was hidden and
secure. But even after a year of passing messages, Claire couldn't
help but feel a wave of irritation. She had worked hard on this
bouquet. It came out particularly well. Roses with peonies, white
on white, with a bit of green ivy wound around and peeking out.
It would look so elegant in a silver vase. She hoped whoever
dug the package out would at least take a moment to enjoy the
beauty before they tossed it aside to carry out whatever orders
the flowers hid.

The light gravel crunched softly under her feet. At the end of
the *allée*, the golden dome of Les Invalides posed against the blue
sky in the distance. Finches flitted between branches overhead.
Her face relaxed into a soft smile, her pace slowed.

"Charming place, isn't it?"

Claire started, felt her heart leap in her chest. Another stride and she managed to hide a smile. She turned to Grey, her face blank. "This is a surprise."

He wore a thick grey wool trench coat over an unraveling black sweater and worn grey pants. His boots were scuffed and looked as though he had walked through a pond to get here. A beard masked his sharp cheekbones and strong jaw. A dark cap was pulled low on his head. Harsh lines radiated from the shadowed edges of his eyes. He may have basked in his lover's arms these last few months, but it didn't look like it suited him well. His dark eyes stared so intently at her face, a warmth crept up her neck. She turned away from him and continued her stroll.

Grey took two long strides, fell in beside her. He started to say something then strangled the words before they escaped. After a few moments, he spoke. "Things have changed since we last met."

Claire turned to look at him, searched his face. She was prepared to handle a dangerous delivery with grace. The codes for each situation, all memorized, were on her lips. But, Grey. Feelings she'd muzzled came surging up inside her like hungry dogs. She couldn't decide what to say; she said nothing.

"The war, I mean. The Americans," he said.

Business, of course. She had heard about Pearl Harbor the day after it happened from a Nazi soldier. A grinning Wehrmacht, who checked her papers at Hôtel Emeraude. *Ah, Américaine, eh? Your navy sank yesterday.* She shrugged at Grey. "It was inevitable, I suppose." She had made her own peace over the months. Her war was here.

"Perhaps. But I am glad the Americans have joined the battle." He rested his hand on her arm, for just a breath.

The heat from his hand warmed her skin even after he moved away. Her whole body was sensitized; she felt the breeze on her legs, the sun on her face. They turned left where two *allée* crossed, and headed toward a tall statue at the far end. Just another Parisian couple finding peace where they could. Claire stole a look at him out of the corner of her eye and caught him doing the same.

A smile at the edge of his mouth then. "This is one of my favorite places."

Claire felt something unclench inside her. "Tell me, Grey, what is it about this place you like?"

"Louis XIV resided at the Tuileries Palace while Versailles was under construction. His garden designer, the great André Le Nôtre, laid out parterres for the Tuileries in 1664. But when Louis left, the palace was virtually abandoned. Its gardens became a fashionable playground. During the Revolution, Louis XVI and his family were forced to return from Versailles to the Tuileries under house arrest. They fled through these gardens in an attempt at escape. In front of an angry mob."

"That didn't work out so well for them." Claire smiled. Even she knew they ended up on the guillotine, their reward for the same beauty she enjoyed today.

"But the gardens remain for all. And children play." He gestured with his head at an elderly couple on a bench. The man had his arm around the woman's rounded shoulders; their heads leaned toward each other as if they were sharing a secret. "And lovers . . ." He glanced at Claire then and looked away.

"What happened, Grey? Why did you leave?" Claire surprised herself with the question.

"The less one knows, the better."

"Not always."

He looked at her as if judging the weight of her words. "I heard about what you've been doing. What you did."

"And?" Claire scanned his face. She couldn't tell from his expression how he felt about her arrangement with Kinsel. About her. She was surprised to find she cared. Still. Damn.

A few more steps before he spoke. "The British government made a very tentative but very intriguing offer last fall."

"To you?"

He smiled. "Not me specifically. A voice whispered in the wind, so to speak. But several of us were convinced they had some things that would be very useful."

"Like?"

"Money. Guns. Radios. Information."

"All the essentials," Claire said.

"No. Not even close. But worth a trip."

Claire hid a smile as she toyed with the bouquet in her arms. "So, all you were doing was running guns and trying to topple the Nazis? I heard much worse about you."

He looked away.

She nearly chuckled. "A woman and illegitimate child in London. That was your official story, you know."

He jerked his head back, as if stung. Claire felt as though the air was sucked from the sky around them. He didn't even try to deny it.

She breathed past the sharp ache in her chest and mustered a smile. "Well, then. This is for you."

He took it, his eyes on her face. "It is beautiful."

"*Merci,*" she said, her mind on the envelope inside. It was like a loaded gun. Whose death it may cause, she didn't know. Hopefully not his.

He stopped under a tree, turned to face her. With the tilt of his head, Grey indicated the few people that lingered in the park. He glanced at his feet before meeting Claire's eyes. "You know we are supposed to be lovers, walking together. For show. Before I go, perhaps?" He leaned down toward her, tilted his head.

Claire leaned up to him. His eyes were open, searching hers until their lips connected. She concentrated on his mouth, soft but probing. This was what you cannot have, she thought, her mouth drifting open.

He pulled her into him, crushed his mouth into hers, tasting her. Hungry lips, one hard arm around her shoulders, the other tight around her waist. The warmth of his body radiated through her dress. A slow vibration started in her toes, rose up through her body. She felt lightheaded; her body responded as her mind tried to piece together who he was, what he was to her. Yes, she thought. Then, a chill cut through her. A woman and child.

Claire jerked backward, pulling free from his grip. He dropped his arms and straightened. The line of his mouth thinned, his jaw clenched. She couldn't read his expression. Angry at himself or at her refusal?

"You take your role too seriously, Monsieur." Claire smoothed her dress against her hips. Embarrassment turned to anger. Because she left her husband to come here, because of Laurent, he expected her to line up behind whatever woman he had set aside?

She knew better than to let herself feel this way. She swallowed the hurt, the embarrassment. She would face that later. Alone. She pointed at the bouquet. "Take care with that, Grey. And put those flowers in some water, would you?" She walked away without waiting for his reply.

51, rue des Ecoles, Paris. August 11, 1943.

The flickering light of the movie projector illuminated the scattered audience in the Le Champo cinema. As far as Claire could tell, they were mostly students from the nearby university, amorous couples taking advantage of an hour of darkness in front of a movie screen. She doubted most in the room even knew what film they were watching. A matinee showing on a Tuesday afternoon was not a bad place for a meeting, she decided.

She slipped down the center aisle, crouching below the shimmering image projected on the screen. *La Nuit fantastique* had already started, but she didn't mind being late. At least she had missed the Nazi newsreels. She read the papers and couldn't stand to see a live-action shot of goose-stepping soldiers, the announcer proclaiming another city in Eastern Europe defeated by the Nazi war machine, victorious on all fronts.

Claire slid into an empty row halfway to the front and settled back in the stiff wooden seat. She took a moment to arrange her coat, scanning the audience around her. It had been a phone call today during lunch. The voice crisp, *Are the ranunculus in season? I want two dozen red, please, next Monday, at this address.*

Ranunculus was her latest code for meeting, no actual flowers needed. Red meant immediately, so Claire made an excuse to Madame Palain and hurried out the door. The address was in the Latin Quarter; Claire was careful and changed trains at Châtelet and again at Saint-Michel. Exiting the station at Cluny–La Sorbonne she stepped into a pooling crowd.

A large truck was parked at an angle across boulevard Saint-Germain, the canopied bed butted up to a restaurant. Two policemen charged out, a bloodied man in an apron suspended from their arms. Behind them, two German soldiers herded out a string of patrons, some with napkins still clutched in their hands or trailing from their chins. All were loaded quietly in the truck.

As the truck engine rumbled to life, the police turned to look over the crowd watching from the sidewalk. Claire slipped backward between two heavyset women deep in a whispered debate over the raid: *He must have been doing something wrong. No, he merely fed the wrong stomach.* She circled the block, head down, before she was able to turn onto rue de Ecoles and find the theater.

It didn't look like she'd missed anything. Two rows in front, a couple were getting to know each other from the inside out. Several chairs down and one row behind her an older man, shaped like a dinner roll, was wedged in the seat. He wheezed loudly and shifted from side to side. She couldn't tell if it was nerves or if he was trapped between the armrests. Claire said a prayer he wasn't her contact and turned back to watch the movie.

On-screen, as the main character slept during his night shift at the flower market, a mysterious woman floated through the scene in a diaphanous white gown. Claire liked the dress, it would make a hell of a nightgown, but the story made no damn sense.

Claire scanned the audience again. She missed those fast-talking screwball comedies she used to sneak away to on Sunday afternoons. She smiled, imagined Cary Grant in that role, *Excuse me, Madame, but your frills are caught on my cuff link.* Or Irene Dunn as the mysterious woman in white. Kicking him with a toe, *Sell many flowers down there, Van Winkle?*

Odette slid in next to her, lit a half-smoked Gitane and settled back in her seat. They watched the movie together for a few scenes.

"You are well, I hope?" Odette breathed out with a trail of smoke, her face toward the screen.

Claire shrugged. "*Pas mal.* And you, Danielle?"

"*Pas mal.*" Not bad, she said.

A heavy wheeze from the man behind them.

Claire tilted her head to Odette, who nodded. They moved to the end of the row.

"Interesting place to meet." Claire sank into her new seat next to Odette. "I hope you didn't choose this because of the movie."

"No. Not the movie. But this is most secure. Most circumspect." She studied Claire's face. "You must earn your pay."

Claire's heart thudded heavy in her chest. She kept her gaze on the screen and her tone even. It wasn't unexpected. "Of course."

"Have you heard of *Foyer du Soldat*?"

Soldier's Hearth? Claire shook her head.

"They are an American organization from the Great War. In Paris, they currently collect food and toiletries to provide to captured Americans and Allies. With their Red Cross armbands, they go to hospitals and prisons. Tomorrow morning, at nine o'clock, you will wear an armband and take a package to an American man held in custody." Orchestra music welled from scratchy speakers. Odette paused, frowning until it died away. "He is on your donation list, nothing more. His name is Mathew Nash. A rich playboy."

"What's in the package?"

"As you tell them. A couple of shirts, bread, tobacco." Odette reached into her coat, pulling out an envelope she slipped onto Claire's lap.

Claire ran her fingers over the envelope, traced the outline of a heavy fabric, felt a cold slender tube. The armband, she guessed. The other?

"Of course, they won't let you see him. They will take the package and tell you to go. But on your way out of the lobby, you will see a large bas-relief carving, on the wall to the left of a corridor. The hall is guarded. The lobby is not." Odette glanced toward the package in Claire's lap. "You will slip the small glass vial into a crevice in the lower left corner of the carving."

"Then what?"

"Give them that special smile and walk out the door."

"What is inside the vial?"

"Pills."

It took a moment for Claire to process this. Not medicine. Cyanide. Someone had been captured. Someone important. Someone who couldn't afford to tell secrets. Claire was their angel of death. A flash of anger, she welcomed the heat, banked it against her fear. "Who? The American?"

Odette shook her head. "He is an innocent, mostly. This is for a patriot."

"You give up so easily on a *patriot*?" Claire twisted the last word in like a knife.

Odette faced Claire. Her eyes were dark and sunken; they shined glassy in the flickering light. "He will never see the sky again. There is nothing we can do to change that. All we can do is stop his suffering."

"And keep him from talking." Unease crawled up Claire's skin. "Where is he?"

"Rue de Saussaies."

She felt a cold sweat damp on her neck. "You don't expect me to go into Gestapo headquarters as Claire Badeau?"

"That is exactly what we expect."

"They'll check my papers," Claire hissed. "What if there is a problem? It will destroy my identity."

"It is our identity. We paid for it." Odette sighed and looked away to the movie screen for a moment. "You will be given the American's package on your walk there in the morning. You will arrive just after they open. Your armband and your list of prisoners are in the envelope in your hands. Look official. Look American."

"What happens to Mathew?"

"He is privileged. And well connected. He will be free in a few days. An older and wiser man."

Claire's instincts were screaming. Stand up, walk away, a voice shouted in her head. She opened her mouth to argue, to question, to put an end to this grievous mistake.

"May God be with you, *mon ami*." Odette rose and walked out without a glance.

Claire clamped her mouth shut and ground the corner of the envelope between her fingers, slid a finger into the crease. A gentle shake and the vial slid into her hand. She held it up as high as she dared into the light. A quarter of the size of a tube of lipstick, the pills were two dark gems, their glass coating shining black against the white tissue paper that held them in place. They gave her two pills, she thought, not one. She slid the vial back into the envelope. Her head sank back against the seat. She knew what it meant. One for the patriot, another, if necessary, then, for her.

*You can be brave when you know you are dreaming,* the man said on-screen.

That night, Claire curled up inside the open windowsill of her balcony, her forgotten blanket puddled around her legs on the wood floor. A siren shrilled in the distance. She shivered as a dark chill ran through her. Rue du Saussaies was where life ended. Where one prayed for it to end. She was no *Resistánt*. Her life wasn't to be thrown away.

Her gaze turned toward her dresser, hidden in the darkness, and the bundle strapped behind it. She imagined the cold weight of the diamonds in her hand. Her nest egg, the Cartier. She could take it and run, pay her way to be smuggled over the Pyrenees to Spain then God knew where.

A soft breeze against her cheek called her attention back to the brightening city. Her body softened as her eyes feasted on the dark lace of the Eiffel Tower against a violet sky that shifted to cobalt, then intensified to a luminous powder blue. Her heart ached in her chest. The beauty here had entered her soul. Running would feel like death. She couldn't abandon Paris. Not today.

Claire rose early and readied the store, changing water in the buckets, tidying the back counters and shelves, trimming back weakened stems and curling leaves, polishing the counter and dusting the register. On a fresh pad of paper by the phone, Claire left Madame Palain a note, *A friend needs assistance, not sure how long it will take*, and locked the door behind her.

The woman Claire saw in the shop window's reflection was so very foreign in the red suit she left New York in more than three years ago. She fingered the vial she had tacked with thread into the fold of her jacket cuff.

She chose to walk along les Champs to gain distance from the shop and to pass the Palais de l'Elysée and gardens along the way. A hot August morning already, the sun was heavy in the sky and the air was liquid gold. The brick wall guarding the empty palace and garden loomed well over her head, but she could smell through the hedge the sweet blossoms on the chestnut trees and the flowers blooming unattended inside.

Claire was handed the package on avenue de Marigny by a slender man in a suit striding in the opposite direction. She tried to see his face, but only noted a thick mustache and faded blue tie before he was gone.

Held tight under her arm, the package compressed against her ribs. It was soft, with the faint smell of tobacco and fresh bread, wrapped expertly in brown paper and tied with twine as if directly from Le Bon Marché. She imagined the shirts were silk, exactly the luxuries an American might require for an extended, unexpected stay.

Claire tried to swallow but her mouth was too dry. She'd hoped Grey would bring the package. His eyes would be serious today, the color of stormy skies. Walking close but not touching, his voice low, words precise, he would have described the gardens, naming each plant, dating each structure. How he knew these things, she didn't understand, but she would have loved to be unafraid, if just for a moment.

Claire slipped on the armband. Within a hundred feet of turning off rue du Faubourg Saint-Honoré onto rue de Saussaies, she passed three restaurants, a bar, a jewelry store and two fine hotels. A much smaller street than Champs-Elysées, she decided, but an expensive neighborhood, nonetheless.

The building at 11, rue de Saussaies was as beautiful as any other around it. Six stories, grey stone-carved balustrades on wrought-iron balconies. But thick iron bars covered street-level windows and heavy metal doors towered over the SS guards standing at attention.

The man in front of her was searched before he entered. Claire produced her papers for the soldiers, was scrutinized thoroughly and waved inside. As the doors banged shut behind her, the emotion drained from her body.

The lobby was large, with raised ceilings and long stone walls. In the far corner, three Nazi officers worked behind a broad wooden desk. A short line had already started to form in front. Details clicked through her mind like photographs as she walked over to join the end of the line. The floors were white marble. Marks on the bare walls showed where art had once been.

The man in line in front of her wrung his hat in his hands, shuffling his weight from one foot to the other. His blue worker's uniform reeked of an acrid oily smoke that made her eyes water. A factory worker, then. An informant, perhaps: *Francois is the one who pissed on your wires and shorted them*. He wouldn't be the first to turn another in for a crumb. Nor the last. You will find the Nazis very ungrateful, she silently told him, and hoped he would get a taste of a dark cell in back.

The soldiers behind the desk snapped to attention when an officer entered the lobby behind her. Tall and slim, his lapel and shoulder patches marked him as the equivalent of a major. The red swastika armband was a splash of blood against his feldgrau jacket. A patch low on his sleeve read SD. His peaked hat was pulled low over his face, but there was something familiar in the set of his mouth.

She turned her head away from him and kept her eyes on the floor as he strode past and disappeared behind a column. After counting to ten, Claire risked a glance behind her.

There it was at the far end of the lobby. As Odette had said, a stone carving covered a wall to the left of a long corridor. The sculpture was nearly covered by a large swastika flag suspended between columns on each side. Less than five feet from the carving, the hallway was guarded by four soldiers, hands on holstered pistols.

"Madame." The voice was sharp, irritated.

Claire stepped up to the counter, a deferential nod to the man waiting behind. She got a good look at him and suppressed a wince. His head came out of his stiff uniform collar like a mushroom. His heavy lips were pinched and his glasses magnified mean little eyes. He radiated hatred.

She formed a smile and slid the package onto the desk. "Claire Badeau. I have a package for one of your, eh, guests, Mathew Nash," she said slowly, in bad French with an American accent that would make Madame Palain shudder.

"What is it?"

"Bread, tobacco, a couple of shirts." She leaned forward, a certain amount of concern for the innocent American showing in her tone, the tremble of her lip. "I would hope Monsieur Nash could remain comfortable until this can be worked out."

An open sneer. "Your identification."

Claire slid her papers across the counter and said a silent apology to *Foyer du Soldat*.

With two fingers he flicked her identification from her hands. "Address?"

Claire recited the address listed on her identification card. He wrote on a form and barked something in German. The soldier next to him took the package and her papers, disappearing between the guards down the hall.

"Sit until you are called." The angry mushroom motioned the next person forward.

"Wait." Claire leaned over the counter, fear made her speak. "Can't I just leave the package and go?"

He silently pointed to the chairs lined up against the far wall. Her legs wobbly, Claire found a seat.

An anxious hour passed as she waited. Two guards were replaced by two more. The line in the lobby grew. It looked so civilized, she marveled. So bureaucratic. A slow-moving government line seen in any city. But on the other side of these walls were room after room of Gestapo torture chambers. She imagined the darkness, the pain. Her concentration wavered; she felt the fingers of fear hook into her stomach. She glanced toward the door facing the street. Her body itched to walk out. But if she made it, what about Claire Badeau?

A grip on her elbow startled her. A crisp voice, textbook English. "Mrs. Badeau, come with me."

Claire looked into the face of a German officer. His dark hair slicked back, thin face overwhelmed by a scar that traced down his cheek. She reached for her purse and straightened her skirt as she stood, taking an extra moment to think. This wasn't supposed to happen, she was sure of it.

Her heart raced as she was guided toward the guards and the hallway. She estimated the distance as she neared the banner, prepared to jerk free. Her hand brushed against the vial in her cuff. A sharp wrench on her arm threw her off balance, she stumbled into the officer.

He guided her into the corridor, then turned into an office, an unknown insignia over the doorway. He locked the door behind them. Motioning for Claire to sit in a wooden chair, he moved to the chair behind a heavy oak desk.

His stare tracked over her as she perched on the chair. She slid her shaking hands out of sight beneath her legs. Her identification and the package were piled neatly in front on him.

"Mrs. Badeau," he said.

She held her breath and waited.

He watched her, unbuttoned the top button of his jacket, his lips formed the slightest smile. "I am Kapitän Heydrich."

He meant to calm her, she realized, to show her he meant her no harm. She bit off a hysterical laugh in the back of her mouth. He might actually believe she was Claire Badeau. A meddling American on a mission of mercy.

"Mrs. Badeau, why have you come here?"

"Kapitän Heydrich," she said with a smile, "do you mean Paris or this building?"

"Both."

Claire leaned forward in her chair. "I married a Frenchman. He died. I stayed in Paris because, well, I don't like being lonely."

His eyebrows raised a fraction as he realized what she meant. "Does Paris meet your needs?"

She let a flush roll up her cheeks, an embarrassed grin. "It is improving."

His lips twitched toward a smile as he lit a cigarette, accepted the compliment for the entire German army. "And why are you here today?"

Claire shrugged. Not too interested, Odette had warned. "I am a member of *Foyer du Soldat*. I have a list of prisoners to deliver packages to. Food, necessities." Claire pulled the slip from her purse and dropped it on top of the papers on his desk. "Mr. Nash is on my list."

"Do you know Mathew Nash?"

Claire shook her head and pointed toward the list.

With the cigarette, he gestured at her identification card in front of him. "How long have you stayed at this address?"

"Since May 1940."

"Your neighbors?" he said.

"What about them?" Claire fought to keep her voice smooth. These questions weren't part of the note and not part of the plan. This had to be wrong.

"They know you?"

Claire smiled at Heydrich, glanced at her watch. "Kapitän, I understand you have an important job to do, but I do have a lunch date. Perhaps you could see that this package gets to Nash for me, and I could be on my way?"

He stared at her, his expression didn't change. She saw suspicion in his eyes.

She smiled at him then, lowered her tone. "You do have my address. You could always come by some evening if you had any other questions."

He leaned back in his chair, took a deep drag of his cigarette. "Perhaps." He grabbed her papers and the package, and walked to the door. He turned and looked back at her, buttoning his top button. "Wait." He left and locked the door behind him.

Claire released the breath she'd been holding. Muffled voices grew and then receded down the hall. Claire shot off the chair, across the room, and pressed her ear against the door. Silence. She rattled the handle. It didn't budge.

She'd roomed with a girl once who could pick locks with a hairpin. A useful talent when they were kicked out of their apartment. But Claire didn't have a hairpin. She turned to the desk.

The first three drawers were locked. The fourth slid open with a bang. Once her heart started beating again, she found an expensive fountain pen, a pack of cigarettes and one paperclip.

Claire bent it and stuck the pointed end into the lock. She pressed her ear against the door and shut her eyes, relying on her fingers to tell her when something gave. A loud snap startled her.

She dropped the paperclip, fell backward and smacked the chair with her hip.

The doorknob rattled, then turned. Claire shoved herself onto her chair. She landed in the seat as the door opened.

"The package was delivered. Mr. Nash sends his warmest regards." Heydrich closed the door behind him.

It took everything she had to smile, nod her thanks.

He locked the door and leaned back against it, her passport and identification card held up in front of him like a game of keep-away. "Your lunch appointment?"

"Of course." Claire stood, smoothing her skirt. She reached for the card.

He grabbed her hand and jerked her toward the wall. The door rattled on its hinges as she hit, the wind knocked out of her. He pressed her, his free hand reached under her skirt. His seeking fingers slid beneath her underwear and hooked upward between her legs. A sharp pain burst inside her as he jerked up hard with his hand.

"I have questions." He smiled at her as she squirmed. His fingers rigid, his hand thrust up again. Claire bit down on her bottom lip.

"You like that, lonely Fräulein?" He shoved, nearly lifting her from the floor.

Claire stiffened; her body lead, all her awareness concentrated on the pain in her mouth. His face inches from hers; she watched beads of sweat break out on his upper lip.

His mouth twisted, his eyes closed. Another jerk, and he let out a satisfied breath and pulled his hand away. With a decorated sleeve, he wiped the sweat from his face. "I have many questions." His mouth drew close, as if to kiss her.

Yanking away, Claire slammed her head into the wall behind her.

A small smile, the slightest regretful shake of his head, and he tucked her papers inside her shirt. "Later." He promised, reaching for the door.

Loud voices, one hoarse, rose outside the door. Heydrich sighed and gripped her left arm. They heard a scuffle, the crack of bone on bone, and the voices faded. He pulled a key from his pocket and opened the door, pushed her ahead of him into the hall.

Claire stared at the banner as he locked the door behind them. About fifteen feet, she guessed, to the lower left corner of the banner and behind it a certain crevice. The four soldiers guarding the hallway faced the other direction.

The blood pounding in her ears, in one motion Claire swept her free hand past her captured elbow and jacket cuff, hooking the vial with her finger. She palmed the vial in her free hand. Heydrich dropped the keys in his pocket, pleasant smile returned to his face, and started toward the lobby with Claire at his side. Two steps before the banner ended, Claire tripped and fell hard against the wall, tangling Heydrich with her legs. He stumbled to the floor next to her.

She kept her palm closed on the vial to take the impact. Don't break the glass in your hand, she ordered herself as the pain shot up through her knuckles. Blinking the tears out of her eyes, she stretched to the banner, slipped her hand underneath, felt a smooth crevice under her fingers and released the vial.

"*Was zur Hölle!*" Heydrich lurched upright.

He slapped her with the back of his hand and shoved her past the soldiers into the lobby. Her legs wobbled as she stepped, free, out onto the sidewalk.

"Claire!" a voice called out from behind her. "Claire Harris Stone!"

The guards' gazes flicked toward her. She forced her feet to move. One shaky step after another, she turned left from the doors and hurried down the sidewalk, darting inside a restaurant's shadowed entry.

A man burst out of the Gestapo doorway. Feldgrau uniform, red swastika armband glinting in the sun. The officer that had passed her as she waited in line. Her body went cold. She knew who it was. The German she'd met in New York. The businessman. Alby. Albrecht von Richter.

"Claire," he shouted again and started her direction. Two soldiers followed.

She hurried out of the restaurant doorway, head down staring at her watch, then scurried into the street. Behind her, she heard the squealing of tires, a crash and shouting. She glanced back as she slipped into an alley.

A delivery truck had swerved around von Richter and hit a streetlight. The driver held his cheek with one hand. Von Richter was pounding on the crumpled hood of his truck, the guards had their guns pulled.

Claire turned and ran. At the alley's end, she nearly gagged from the smell of a pile of rotting trash in a boarded-up doorway. A quick glance behind her, and Claire slipped off her armband and red jacket. Holding her breath, she dug down into soggy, dirty papers, rotting food, a dead rat. She shoved the armband inside, then the jacket.

Claire joined the flow of pedestrians onto rue d'Anjou and clamped down on thoughts that threatened to spin into darkness. Von Richter was here and he'd recognized her.

Only one thing she knew for sure. Grey was the truck driver.

* * *

An elderly man with silver hair scrutinized roses at Madame Palain's side as Claire entered the shop. "They are a young couple, a small ceremony. This small thing I can give," he said.

"Of course, Monsieur, I understand." Madame's eyes washed over Claire as Claire passed them without a word and hurried up the stairs to her room.

Shutting the door firmly behind her, Claire turned on the faucet over the washbasin and stripped down as it filled. Don't think, she commanded herself. Her mind fastened on the cotton rag she dipped in the cool water, working a thin sliver of soap into a lather and methodically scrubbing her skin until it glowed red.

"Claire," Madame said from the bottom of the stairs.

"*Une minute.*" Claire grabbed her towel, dried herself and slipped on a clean dress. She leaned out the doorway, found Madame waiting on the foot of the stairs. "Yes, Madame?"

The florist scanned Claire's face, her expression worried. Her mouth opened to speak, clamped shut. A determined frown and she tried again. "Your friend?"

"It seems as though my friend is going to be better. Thank you, Madame."

Madame nodded as if relieved, but kept her eyes on Claire. "I am going to close up early this afternoon. We have been paid with a chicken. I will make *coq au vin*. Would you care to join me?"

Claire clenched the doorjamb, felt tears form in the corners of her eyes. Madame worried for her. It was a grand offer of discreet compassion, of conversation with nothing said but much heard. Claire had to clear her throat before she spoke. "Thank you, Madame, but no. I have some reading to do."

Madame watched her, nodded deliberately, as if that were a reasonable excuse. "Of course." She disappeared from view.

Claire leaned back against the door and sucked in a ragged breath. The sun glinted in the window, illuminating dust motes. The oak parquet floor was golden in the light. Safe.

Steps creaked on the stairs. Claire straightened, the forced smile returned. Madame stopped in the doorway; she held a delicate crystal bud vase. In it, one exquisite pale blush rose. "For your reading, then," she said, handing Claire the vase, a quick kiss on each cheek, before descending the stairs.

Claire centered the vase on a silver tray atop the dresser. This was the grace that Madame practiced. Claire still gazed at it when the front door thudded shut and the lock clicked into place.

A heavy silence filled the empty shop. The weight of it pressed the air from her lungs; her pulse began to race. Avoiding her reflection, she plucked the garden photo from the mirror's edge and drifted toward the bed. The mattress creaked as she curled up into a ball on top of the covers, the way she slept as a child. Head resting on a pillow, she held the photo in front of her face.

She could smell the sweet fragrance of apple blossoms and lush grass. She could feel the tree's rough bark under her fingers, the smooth cold marble of the statue, the goddess' knowing stone eyes looking down at her. Time slowed then stopped.

Claire slept.

She awoke in darkness, heart thumping. She sat up, unsure of what woke her. A sharp tap on her half-open window and a small pebble rolled across the floor. Claire tiptoed to the window.

The stars were out, a sliver of a moon. A dark form looked up from the shadows in the doorway of Dupré's store. Claire leaned back against the wall in the darkness. The Nazis would have busted in the door and pulled her out by her hair, she told herself. She peered out again. There was something familiar.

Claire hurried down the stairs. She felt her way across the dark shop and unlocked the front door. A moment later Grey slipped inside and clicked the door shut behind him.

"Away from the windows," he said, motioning with his head.

Claire led him to the back of the shop, up the stairs to her room.

As he stepped in behind her, she became intimately aware of his body next to hers, so near her still-warm bed. She slid away from him, closing the shutters. The room fell into darkness. Fumbling with a match, she lit a candle.

"A Sturmbannführer recognized you," Grey said, his voice hard.

Heat churned up inside her. After all she had faced, she was to be examined by Grey?

"Claire," he said, as if commanding a stubborn child and moved close.

Her calves smacked into the bed as she jerked away. "Go to hell," she said, her voice shaking.

"How did he know you?"

Up close, Claire saw his cheek was swollen and red. A memento from the streetlight or the Nazis. A stab of guilt she brushed aside.

"He is a Sturmbannführer, for god's sake. The SD on his armband is Sicherheitsdienst. Nazi intelligence. Who is he to you?"

"Your concern for my welfare is overwhelming," Claire said, in spite of herself, her voice cracking.

Grey stopped and stared at her. His frown gave way to concern. His eyes scanned her face. "What happened in there?"

Claire felt the start of a sob, covered it with a laugh that came out too loud. What could be said? His bruised cheek was so close. What happened after she ran? She shook her head as if shaking off the question. "I completed my mission. What does it matter?"

He stared at her like he didn't believe her. A breeze rattled the shutters against the window frame.

"His name is Albrecht von Richter," Claire said.

"And he knows you?"

"From New York. From before. I hadn't seen him since I left."

"How well does he know you?"

Claire shrugged.

"He was very intent on finding you."

"He was in a business deal with my husband."

Grey stared, his eyes were nearly black, mouth set. He didn't believe her, she could tell.

"Well. It's true. And he couldn't have been positive that it was me."

"He was sure, Claire."

"But my identification said Claire Badeau. I gave them an address in Montparnasse. Nothing tied me here." She hated the note of pleading in her voice.

"He knew you. Personally. You weren't just some grainy photo on an identification card. An SD Sturmbannführer can tear the city apart brick by brick to find you. Everything we've built could be destroyed."

"I didn't ask to go to goddamn Gestapo Grand Central."

He sighed, shook his head. "You have to leave here, tonight."

"No."

He reached for her, then stopped. He pointed toward the window. "We are hiding people who will die unless they get out of France. Their escape line has been compromised. We are their only hope."

Claire stared at her hands.

"Tomorrow morning, before daylight, I will drive a truck into the countryside. A simple farmer on his way home. But with a wounded American pilot and two civilians hidden inside the truck. In a few days, they will be transported out to freedom."

"So?"

"A farmer needs a wife. And the civilians, well, they need a woman."

"Need me for what, exactly?" She didn't try to hide the frustration in her tone.

"They are girls, Claire. Young, too young. At the farm, I can't—"

"I am needed here."

"We need time to try to get a handle on von Richter to try to contain the damage. It doesn't have to be forever if you leave tonight."

She didn't believe him. Sneaking away in the darkness always meant forever.

He looked around. "You may bring a small bag."

"What about Madame Palain? I need to tell her good-bye."

A quick headshake, no.

"A note, then," Claire said.

His jaw twitched. "Nothing. In this, that is the kindest farewell that can be offered. I'll be below, when you're ready."

She stared at the room through the flickering candle. Her window and Paris outside. The dresser Georges had found and carried up the stairs on his shoulders. The mirror Madame brought Claire from her own bedroom. The single rose posed on the silver tray, *un petit monument* to La Vie en Fleurs.

Claire packed three dresses, a thin slip, a toothbrush and panties. Flipping a drawer upside-down, she retrieved the jewelry roll and a wad of francs. The Cartier's sharp edges pressed through the fabric into her skin as she gripped the silk roll.

If she took the necklace, it meant she wasn't coming back. She strode to the window, swung open the shutters. A quick scan of the street to make sure it was clear and she leaned out over the ledge and jiggled free a loose stone cornice. She pushed the necklace then the money in the opening as far as her fingers could reach then slid the stone back into place.

In this shop she'd discovered a family in Madame's gentle guidance, in Georges' sweet friendship. She'd found her own worth, a gift with flowers more lasting than a pretty face and supple body. What she had created here mattered. More than her Oklahoma farmhouse or Manhattan brownstone, the shop was her home. She was damn well coming back.

Claire slipped the photo into her jacket pocket and plucked the rose from the vase. She met Grey at the bottom of the stairs and took one last look around. Flowers in tin buckets posed against the walls like vain ballerinas. Her eyes were hot, her chest hurt.

Grey took the case from her hand. "Claire," he said, his voice gentle.

She looked up at his face. "Did it work? What I delivered at rue de Saussaies?"

"It did. Our man inside was able to pass it to the person in need."

"Who was it?"

He shifted the bag in his hand and cleared his throat. "His name was André Paldiel. Our forger. He made identification cards."

Claire's breath caught in her throat. "The boy? The teenager?"

"Yes." His gaze held hers, his eyes dark with pain.

The constriction in the bottom of her throat choked her. She fought the urge to reach for his bruised cheek and instead stroked the rose's soft petals with the tips of her fingers.

"Alright, then." Claire tucked the blossom in her lapel and led Grey out. Locking the door behind them, she shoved the shop keys through the mail slot.

They clattered as they hit the stone floor.

"This way." Grey slipped into the darkness against the building.

They kept to the shadows for several blocks and found a car idling in an alley. Grey opened the door and they got in the back. The car was old, torn seats scratched the back of Claire's legs. It smelled of stale sweat and cigarette smoke.

The driver glanced back at them in the mirror. He pulled the car into the street and turned into another alley. Claire studied him in the rearview mirror as he drove. He was short and stocky, his face set in a resigned frown. His beret was pulled down low; a handmade cigarette smoldered between creased lips.

Claire held her bag on her lap, her gaze outside. In the narrow alleys, it was as if they were gliding down dark, sinister canyons, neither the Arc de Triomphe nor the tower was visible. She brushed her hair from her face. Her fingers smelled of roses. She closed her eyes and let the empty darkness swallow her.

# Chapter 8

## THE ESCAPE FROM PARIS

18th Arrondissement. August 13, 1943.

Claire awoke to tapping on glass. The car was parked, engine silent. Grey was gone and the driver was peering in at her through the passenger window. He jerked his thumb toward the building next to them.

Body stiff and eyes gritty, Claire climbed out of the car. The brightening sky revealed a row of warehouses. She picked up her bag and walked through an open door. The dusty building was empty but for one beaten-up old farm truck. Smoke-green, a bent radiator grill, and wooden slats over the truck bed.

Grey slammed the truck's back gate closed and walked around. "Your case," he said, reaching for her bag then dropping it in the cab behind the seat. He held the door for her and offered a hand. "Ready?"

Claire hitched her dress up above her knees and scrambled up into the cab. She slid back into the seat and stared down at Grey, one eyebrow raised.

The edges of his lips turned up as he swung into the cab and turned on the ignition. With a coughing rumble and a black cloud of smoke, the truck came to life. Grey needed both hands to shove the shift lever into first.

"Where are they?" Claire turned to look behind the seat for the escapees.

Grey let out the clutch to the sound of grinding metal. They rolled through the doors. "Safe."

Fifteen minutes of steady driving took them to the northern edge of town. It was the industrial side of Paris Claire had never seen. Smokestacks, factories and cavernous warehouses. Claire rolled down the window to weaken the smell of burning oil inside the cab, but here the air was a mix of smoke, oil and acrid chemicals. Hunched men and women hurried like ants to join the morning shift.

The air tasted metallic on her tongue. "What is this place?"

"Paris' war effort for the *Vaterland*," Grey said, his mouth twisted. "Ironworks, steel, pharmaceuticals."

They pulled over at a checkpoint, north of Saint-Denis, where a few cars and trucks waited off the road's edge. A gendarme stepped up to the window, scrutinized their permit and listened to Grey's story. *Sold all the season's beets, going home to the farm north of Beauvais.* Claire was amazed by Grey's perfect farmer's French. He was as English to her as Prince Edward. Hell, even more so. But today, just a simple French beet farmer.

A second gendarme opened the back of the truck. His heavy boots thumped around the empty truck bed. After a moment, the truck shook as he jumped to the ground. The gendarme at the window motioned them forward. Claire sat back and exhaled as Grey accelerated back onto the road.

The sun broke free from the horizon as they pulled onto a smaller road and headed northwest. She kept her gaze out the window. Open farmland, giant strands of heavy trees, a small village in the distance, church spire puncturing the sky. Madame Palain would have arrived at the shop by now. Claire rubbed her burning eyes.

The engine growled as they lumbered over hills. They turned onto a hard-packed dirt road. The truck jumped and swayed as they bottomed out over a deep hole. Grey flinched and cursed. After the truck righted itself, he stretched an arm behind to the back wall of the cab and rapped hard twice.

A moment and two raps back.

"You still don't trust me?" Claire said.

Grey could only spare her a glance; he struggled to keep the truck on the road. "If we were searched, it would be better for you not to know."

Claire tightened her lips; she stared back out the window. They'd squandered her life, and still, she wasn't trusted.

"Claire—" Grey cleared his throat, let the truck coast to a stop. "I, we, didn't expect you would be questioned. There was no reason for them to suspect you."

"So what happened, then?"

"You caught somebody's eye. It wasn't your fault." He shoved the shift stick forward, the gears ground. "I'm sorry I ever got you involved in this."

"In rue Saussaies?"

"In everything."

Claire leaned back in her seat, settled her chin in her palm,

her elbow wedged against the door. "Thank you." She stole a
glance at him out of the corner of her eye when she realized what
he meant. Grey was the *who* Odette referred to that believed in
Claire, but never named. Not Laurent. Well, damn.

The truck bucked over a road that grew more narrow and rutted. They entered a dense forest, towering trees cut out the
sky. A steep climb, the engine protested and they crested the top
of a hill. For a moment they were above the trees in the bright
summer sun. Before them lay more woodland, then open farmland and orchards. In the distance a small village was tucked
inside a thick forest.

"Lyons-la-forêt. But we are going there." Grey pointed toward a dense grove to the north.

"Secluded," Claire said.

Grey grinned. "No formal balls for you."

Claire threw him a dark glance. She had the awful feeling
she was being hauled back to the French version of the farm she
had escaped from long ago, the rebellious pig being dragged to
slaughter.

They descended back into the forest and its shade, crossed
over a heavy wooden bridge, then turned onto rutted tire tracks.
Another half hour of bucking, and they pulled into a dirt farmyard. The house was a ramshackle thing backed up to the trees,
constructed from bricks and heavy timbers in the Normandy
tradition. Heavy dark beams crossed the walls; too many hard
seasons had made the high-peaked wooden roof cant at an awk-
ward angle.

A tilting barn of the same construction sat across the yard.
A small orchard on one side, surrounded by a half-fallen fence.

Many of the trees had broken branches or leaned wildly. It must have been years since this place was guided by a human hand.

They parked next to a rusted wooden wagon, listing wheels half-buried in farmyard muck. Claire slid out of the truck, dropped to the ground and glared at the dust that swirled over her legs. She struggled to swallow, her mouth suddenly dry. She could taste the weariness and despair in the dirt.

"Never been off the pavement before, princess?" Grey said.

Her ears buzzed and eyes ached. "Never," she said, venom lacing her tone. She slammed the passenger door closed.

Grey grabbed a crowbar from behind the seat and clattered into the back of the truck. Claire watched him pry at a thin board on the floor against the cab. A snap and an entire section of floor gave way, leaving an opening just large enough for a body to wriggle through.

Out of the darkness slid a slender teenaged girl, dark haired, a prim grey dress, ruffled at the neck. She held a leather mono-grammed duffel and a wide briefcase. She turned around and reached in behind her. A small girl, maybe four, scrambled out. Her hair was the color of wheat, her face tear-streaked and her blue eyes red. A hand was shoved against her mouth, small snif-fles escaped. She wore a blue dress that ended in ruffles above her knees; the fabric was wet below her waist.

The dark-haired girl scooped the young one up and strode across the truck bed. She ignored Claire's outstretched arms as she clambered down and hefted her bags.

Grey reached deeper into the opening, turned back to Claire. "A bit of a hand here?"

Claire scrambled to his side. When her eyes adjusted to the darkness, she could see the compartment was just bigger than a bathtub. It smelled of sweat, urine and blood. Blankets had been tacked up along every surface. A man lay stretched on his back, his arm and shoulder swathed in bandages. His eyes were closed.

"He's passed out. We need to get him inside."

Claire shimmied inside the opening and reached for the man's shoulders. With Grey half in, tugging on the man's legs, and Claire at his head, they slid him out feetfirst.

Grey handed her a key and motioned toward the house. A medieval looking thing, but the heavy front door screeched open. The small windows next to the door didn't offer much light. Claire lit the nub of a candle that sat on a table near the door.

The inside wasn't nearly as decrepit as the outside. Not too long ago, someone had taken a stab at making it livable. A small front room, chairs along the wall. One doorway opened up to a kitchen with a wood-burning stove and a cupboard, the other to a small bedroom, empty but for a low cot along the wall.

Claire turned back to the girls, created her most reassuring smile and waved them in, the little one still sniffling. She handed the candle to the oldest and hurried back outside to Grey. Between them, they hauled the man inside, depositing him on the cot.

He was surprisingly heavy. Stocky but not fat. His cheeks were drawn, but his face was young and strong and reminded her of her brother, Willy.

"I'll try to help him if you'll bring in the box of supplies and settle the girls in." Grey started to peel away the bloodied bandages. He was unbuttoning the man's shirt as she left him.

Claire pulled closed a tattered curtain across the doorway. The two girls faced her, hands gripping each other. A united front against, it must seem, most of the world.

"Hello, I am Evelyn," Claire said with her warmest smile.

The older girl scrutinized Claire before she spoke. "I am Marta Decler. This is my sister, Anna."

Marta was slender, almost fragile. Her lips were the only part of her that looked soft. They turned down into a pout. Her eyes were guarded and dark. She stared up at Claire through thick coal black eyelashes.

Anna was soft where Marta was thin. Plump pink cheeks, round dimpled knees, her big blue eyes dripped tears. She sniffled again. "I'm hungry."

Claire shut her eyes, steeling her nerve. Pa must be snickering in his grave, she thought. "Well, then. Let's see what we can find."

Marta changed Anna's dress while Claire brought in a wooden crate from the truck. It held small tins of chicory, flour, sugar and salt, a bag of potatoes and a jar of brined eggs. Claire gave each girl an egg then went outside to the orchard, filling the front of her dress with apples. She found a knife and arranged slices on a chipped plate for dessert.

Grey shook his head when she offered him food. He lit a cigarette and smoked it on the doorstep as the sky darkened, then returned to the bedroom. Exhausted from the drive, they all sought sleep. The men got the bedroom, the girls the living room and Claire the kitchen.

She rolled up in a blanket on the kitchen floor, her back to the stove, an arm folded under her head. It was musty inside; the air had been cooped up too long. Claire felt the weight of it, like history, bearing down on her, pressing her into the floor. When she closed her eyes, she could smell the Oklahoma dirt and feel the weight of her mother's wasted body in her arms.

Anna cried out in her sleep like a wounded animal. Marta soothed her in a low voice that sounded like a song. Claire rubbed her eyes, pulled back to the present. She fingered the rose she'd taken from the shop, the dying petals limp against her skin.

She swore long ago she damn well wasn't going to end up faded and broken, surrounded by dirt. Paris was her life, never a place like this.

The next morning Claire woke to the golden red light of a promised sunrise tracing patterns in the window's wavy glass. She passed the girls wrapped in a blanket on the floor. Anna was curled against her big sister's stomach. Her baby face innocent, a thumb inches from her mouth, poised to be sucked. Marta's arm was wrapped protectively around her. Even in slumber, Marta's face was serious.

Tired hinges creaked as Claire stepped through the door. She sat on the worn boards of the bottom stoop and watched the sky shift from indigo to pale blue. The farm was bordered on the north and west by dense forest. To the east and south, open farmland rose into rolling hills. The morning air was fresh and smelled of damp earth. A flock, a murder, of crows flew overhead. A breeze cooled her and nuzzled the trees, leaves whispering softly.

She knew this time of day, how it felt. It had been her chore to haul in water from the well, to milk the cows and let the chickens from the coop before she sat down for breakfast with Mama. By then Pa, Willy and Hank would be in the pastures or fields, and she wouldn't see them until nightfall. *Stop dawdling, you worthless thing*, she heard Pa say. *Get something done*. She was glad the bastard was dead. Her seeking eyes found the well, tucked up around the corner from the house, and her feet began moving toward it, stirring up little puffs of dirt with each step. You think you've won, she whispered to him. You haven't.

Two buckets hung over the side of the well next to a coiled

length of heavy rope. Hooking the first onto a rusted metal hook and gripping the line, Claire lowered the bucket until she heard a splash, felt the rope go limp and then heavy. She spit into her palms, gritted her teeth and pulled, hand over fist. Her arms were burning before the bucket was level with the well's wall. Bracing the rope around a shoulder, Claire reached out and pulled the bucket toward her to rest on the wall. Tugging the handle free, she wrestled it to the ground.

Dipping her burning palms into the water, she flinched at the bite on open blisters. It was shockingly cold on her skin, smelled earthy and sweet. She splashed water on her face, rinsed out her mouth, then took a long drink and felt the chill roll down to her empty stomach. It was good, clean of taint and grit.

She filled the second bucket and was working her way toward the house, one in each hand, when the door opened. Grey scanned the farmyard before his eyes lit on Claire. He couldn't quite conceal his surprise before he hurried to her side. Claire was gratified when he hefted the buckets and exhaled under his breath.

"I didn't see you inside when I awoke," he said.

"Thought I made a run back to Paris?"

His brows knitted as he tried to read her expression. "You just might."

Claire held the door open for him. "Don't slop when you go inside."

They walked silently by the sleeping girls. Claire motioned for Grey to set down the pails next to the stove. She found the chicory and got a pot brewing.

He watched her, his lips curled into the faintest smile.

Claire found the cups in the cupboard. Old patterned china, each cup a different color and shape. She filled three, didn't spare him a glance.

"How—"

Claire handed him a cup.

They heard a low groan from the bedroom. Grey stared at her a moment before he turned and disappeared behind the curtain.

She took a sip of the coffee, not bad, and carried the third cup into the bedroom. The American was sitting upright. His face was pale, but his green eyes were bright. He took the cup from Claire with both hands, drank, then smacked his lips and blinked as though he couldn't believe his eyes. He broke into a grin and spoke, the drawl of a southern boy. "Thank you, ma'am. This is the prettiest coffee I've ever tasted."

Claire smiled, blushing in spite of herself. "Well, hello, fly-boy."

He seemed surprised she was American, though he tried not to show it. He leaned back against the wall, took another sip, a deep sigh, then drank her in with his eyes.

Grey frowned at the soldier's unabashed gaze. "Captain Walker, this is Evelyn."

"I am very pleased to meet you, Evelyn," he said.

She turned to Grey. "You didn't tell me this flyboy was such a charmer."

Walker gritted his teeth but managed a smile; exhaustion showed on his face. His shoulder slipped down the wall toward the cot.

"Take a rest, Captain." Grey grabbed the cup before it tipped.

They watched Walker settle into the cot; his eyelids drooped, then closed, his breathing slow and regular.

Grey motioned toward the curtain. Claire walked out ahead of him; they passed the girls, now sitting quietly on the wooden floor. Marta sat legs crossed, Anna in her lap. Neither girl looked up as Marta drew a silver-plated brush through Anna's pale hair.

In the kitchen, Claire rummaged through the tins. "So, who is he?"

"Captain Walker is a transporter. He pilots a bomber and drops people and supplies at night. He was shot down two weeks ago in Belgium and somehow managed to survive. The Americans need him back."

"Makes sense," Claire said. "What about the girls?"

"Someone important made arrangements for them to get out, though no contact has been made since. In the next few days, a messenger will notify us as to what we need to do. The twenty-third is a new moon, perfect for transport."

"Escape," Claire said. America for them and Paris for her.

Golden summer days passed into sultry nights where the moon waned to a crescent. Life fell into a quiet ritual marked by the rising and setting of the sun. The sky was golden, sun sinking behind the dilapidated farmhouse, as Claire shaded her eyes and stepped from the shadowed forest into the farmyard.

Anna tugged on Claire's fingers as she skipped next to her, her small face rosy and free hand clenching wildflowers. The radio crackled from the house as Captain Walker entertained Marta with a story full of curses and *slang américain* from his self-appointed station propped up on the doorstep in the shade.

Claire felt a gaze on her. She looked up to see Grey leaning against the open doorway of the barn, his shirt untucked and half-unbuttoned in the late afternoon heat. He'd left before sunup, his day spent scouting the roads for any sign of soldiers or the expected messenger. He watched her, a cigarette in his mouth. His slate eyes were a palpable force on her skin. A warm shiver ran down her spine.

"Look at what I have," Anna shouted, waving her chaotic bouquet toward Grey.

He smiled at Anna. "Well done."

"Ask Grey for water for your flowers. I'm going see how our stew is coming." Claire flushed as she turned toward the house, relieved at the break from his gaze.

She slipped past Marta sitting on the stair next to Walker. The girl hung on the pilot's words, chin resting in her palms, black lash-rimmed eyes open wide, offering the rarest smile.

Claire passed the china cups and empty food tins bursting with riotous purple, white and yellow blooms decorating every surface on her way to the kitchen. A rabbit simmered in a pot with potatoes and flour on the stove. Claire reached for a scarred metal spoon and leaned in for a taste. Not dinner at the Ritz but not bad either. A recipe she'd learned from Mama back when she had to stand on her tiptoes to see inside the pot.

"Smells delicious in here." Grey stepped up behind her; his muscled chest brushed against her back as he peered over her shoulder at the stove.

Claire felt the warmth from his body, smelled the mix of tobacco and sun. The blood rushed from her head. She gripped the spoon and concentrated on stirring. "Thanks to you."

He grinned, head tilted forward to examine her face. "I didn't think Yankee princesses knew how to cook rabbit."

Claire flushed at his stare and kept her eyes on the stew.

He gripped her hand, stilling the spoon. "Really, Claire, tell me, how—"

"Evelyn," Anna cried from the doorway. "May I fold the napkins tonight?"

Claire stepped away from Grey, grateful for the reprieve. She handed Anna the squares she'd sewn from an old grain sack. "You remember how I showed you?"

The little girl nodded, her face serious.

Claire turned to Grey and handed him chipped china bowls from the cupboard. "I assume a proper British gentleman knows how to set the table?"

He raised an eyebrow, but his expression was admiring. "I'll manage."

A week passed, the new moon rose, a shadowed presence in the dark night. After dinner they sat in the living room gathered around the radio's crackling tunes. At 9:15 they tuned the radio to the BBC and fell into silence. The opening measure of Beethoven's Fifth Symphony sounded the rhythm of Morse code signal for *V*, as in victory. Then the *messages personnels*, read in perfect French. Simple sentences about Jacques's vacation in Lyon, Murielle's new baby, a few lines of poetry. In truth, they were prearranged messages designed for certain ears, alerting agents of missions starting or aborting. Grey listened with eyes closed.

"Anything?" Walker asked as the broadcast ended.

Grey shook his head. At the anxious look on Marta's face, he tried a smile. "It hasn't been too long. They'll have more chances."

As Marta returned to brushing Anna's hair, Claire offered Grey an appreciative smile. *Thank you,* she mouthed. He nodded, but his grin faded as he looked out the window into the darkness.

After settling the girls on top of their blanket-bed, Claire joined Grey on the crest of a rolling hill above the farm. A lone oak tree stretched its branches above them. The night was balmy. Tall grass swayed, whispering in a warm breeze that didn't cool.

Faint lights from Lyons-la-forêt glimmered in the distance, but his eyes searched the black sky. "The plane should've landed tonight. Our messenger should have been here by now."

"What happened?"

Grey scowled. "I don't know. Our messenger is local. He's supposed to lead us to the drop point in an open field somewhere out there. We light signal fires. The plane lands; we pull off our supplies and equipment, and load it inside the compartment in the truck. Walker, Marta and Anna take their place on the plane."

"Could it still come?"

"It might. But these things are bloody difficult to plan, and after tonight they'll have a moon to deal with. They'll either have to wait for cloudy night skies for cover or"—he looked at Claire—"the next new moon."

Claire ran her fingers over her calluses. She waited for the old surge of trapped despair, but found, to her surprise, her thoughts were on Marta and Anna. A sigh of disappointment for them. "But they will come, won't they?"

She felt more than saw Grey's shrug in the darkness.

"I know Walker is important to them," he said.

"And the girls?"

"Well, they don't weigh much, do they?"

She saw his teeth flash white, heard a low chuckle. In her mind, she inventoried their supplies. The food wouldn't last. "They will weigh a lot less in a month. What other options are there?"

"If the girls or Walker had the right papers, special *Ausweis*, they could take the train south, pass the soldiers at the demarcation line, then cross the border into Spain in the comfort of a car. But those papers are impossible to get, and the bribes would be enormous. More likely, more common, they could be smuggled past the demarcation line in hidden compartments, under loads of rotting vegetables or rancid meat. Then, they would make their way south, sleep in barns, ride in wagons or walk, until finally they bribed a farmer to cross his land to bypass the French border guards. Then they must hike over the Pyrenees into Spain." He shook his head, his mouth tight. "Not an easy journey for girls or the wounded. And even then, if the border guards in Spain catch them without the correct papers, they will arrest them and notify the Gestapo."

Claire examined the edges of Grey's face, dimly visible under the stars. From his tone, what was unsaid, Claire knew he'd suffered much of that to reach London. Something she named admiration stirred in her stomach, doused with a single thought. "You must love her very much." She choked on the word, *mistress*, and said instead, "Your child."

His eyes were black and probing in the darkness. "Abigail isn't mine."

"What do you mean?"

"It's war, dammit. Things happen and we can't control the outcome. We can't control people, even when we know what they are doing is wrong. Hell, we can't even control ourselves. She lacks a father. But it's not Abigail's fault," Grey said, as if it were an argument he'd had too often before.

Laurent's words echoed in Claire's mind, *A woman and a child. Grey is a steadfast sort of creature. A responsible man.* "And so you're responsible for her, aren't you?"

"Always," Grey said.

A wave of sadness, like the tide, rose up and submerged her.

"I don't think anyone is getting rescued tonight." She turned and walked to the house alone.

She rolled up in a blanket on the kitchen floor, her gaze on the window. The stars were streaks of light in the wavy glass. She heard the door creak open and the curtain rustle as Grey came inside. Always, she thought. How would it feel to be promised *always* by a man like that?

The next morning, Grey disappeared into the forest to gather bird eggs with Anna riding on his shoulders. Walker made slow circles in the farmyard, gaining strength through willpower and sunlight. Marta watched from the step, her face shadowed.

Marta's face mirrored old feelings Claire knew, a caustic mix of longing and despair. For Claire, childhood had been a longing for a better life, of seeing the world, despair at never getting off the farm. Marta had seen the world, too much of it, perhaps. Claire wondered if the young American soldier was the target of Marta's longing for the strength he offered, or for the promise of a new life in a free country. Misery etched her young face.

"Marta, come pick flowers with me," Claire said.

They walked side by side along a path that edged the forest, at the base of the rolling hills.

"I miss Paris," Claire said, a way to begin. "Did you live there?"

Marta leaned over a grouping of primrose. "We left Poland when I was nine, so six years in Paris."

"A long time. You could be called a real Parisian, then."

"I suppose. I am Polish too. I remember it before things got bad. We were very happy there."

Claire nodded. She knew Paris was full of refugees that fled countries suckling fascism for years before Hitler's armies marched. Jews had taken the brunt of it, many landed in Paris.

Marta tugged at a few of the blooms, just opening, and handed them to Claire.

Claire slid the ends into the thin layer of water at the base of her bucket. "Were you happy in Paris?"

"My mother was. Very happy. My father was not." Her cheeks colored. A delicate subject. They walked for a while in silence before Marta continued. "My mother is an important modernist artist. She paints, *painted*, portraits of the wealthy in Paris. She loved it. The parties, salons. It was very glamorous, you see, and my mother is very talented, very beautiful. But my father is different. He's like me."

"Thoughtful," Claire said.

"Provincial and prudish were her words," Marta said, with a touch of humor. Her face darkened. "After the Nazis came to Paris, my father fled to Marseilles. This spring, he wrote Mother a letter. He arranged for Anna and me to go south to a country house with mother's paintings. To be safe. But mother thought it was silly. She said she wouldn't let her paintings be snuck out of the city like gypsies. We were Parisians now."

Over the crest of a hill, a thick growth of delicate purple hyacinths blanketed a slope beneath a green canopy of beech trees. Claire chose a grassy spot beneath the branches, setting the basket at her feet. She leaned back against a thick trunk and patted the ground next to her.

Marta sat, her face scrunched up into a scowl. She plucked a flower and crushed the petals, one by one. "But I couldn't go to school anymore. Anna and I stayed inside with Madame Russo, our servant. Mother said the Nazis wouldn't dare bother her. She still painted for those who could pay, and many nights went out."

The muscles in Claire's back relaxed against the trunk,

warmed from the walk in the sun. The soft breeze and touch of shade was pleasant on her skin, but she felt a chill with Marta's listless tone. "What happened?"

"One morning, it wasn't quite light yet, I was watching out the window, waiting, like I always did, for Mother to come home from a party. Police stopped her on the street in front of our house. I recognized one of them, his father was our *boulanger.* They made her open the door. I heard them downstairs. *Where are your children? Where is your husband, Jewess?* Madame Russo rushed in our room—her face was so pale. She grabbed Anna from her bed. We ran to the side door. There were two cases there, waiting. We snuck out into the courtyard. Mother screamed so loud at the men. So loud. Madame Russo made us climb over a fence into the alley and run." Marta's face was still, but large tears rolled down her face unheeded as she stared at passing clouds. "Father knew they would come. He had ordered Madame Russo to pack our bags and be ready. She hid us in a neighbor's cellar. But father never came for us."

"Your mother?" Claire asked.

"Madame Russo told me the police took all the Jews they could find in all of Paris. They hauled them away in our school buses. They were shipped away to Germany on a train." Marta wadded the flower stem in her fist then dropped it into the grass. "I know my mother isn't coming back."

Claire rested her hand on Marta's arm.

"No. I don't miss Paris," Marta said.

Marta sank silently into her arms. Claire's heart ached. Months ago, Christophe had told her about the roundups. Perhaps she'd wanted to believe that he was just trying to draw her into his fight. Madame Palain and the shop had to come first. But thousands of people? Her fists clenched as she absorbed the girl's agony, her betrayal by the world and her own anger at herself.

A breeze blew a lock of hair in Marta's face. Claire brushed it from her eyes. At that simple kindness, the girl shuddered and released deep, wracking sobs. Legions of puffy clouds marched overhead as Claire rocked her in her arms.

Marta grew soft against her, sobs fading to breaths. She pulled her head away, swiping futilely at her eyes. "I'm sorry," she said, her cheeks red from tears and embarrassment.

Claire wiped the girl's face with the hem of her dress and looked deep into her eyes. "I am your friend, Marta. Truth, no matter how sad, is meant to be shared among friends. I am grateful you chose to tell me. And please, call me Claire."

Marta nodded, her eyes taking in Claire as if for the first time. Hand-in-hand, they meandered back toward the farm, picking hyacinths and white anemones until the bucket was full. Marta wore a crown of braided flowers in her hair and a fragile smile when they got back to the house.

Anna's laughter sounded like a bird's trill as she and Grey returned from the forest. Grey cradled a bag bulging with eggs. Anna's hands and pockets were stuffed full of rocks and leaves. She held a leaf up before her. "*Fagus sylvatica,*" she pronounced.

Claire turned to Marta. "How would you like to help me cook an omelet?"

Another week passed, supplies dwindled to crumbs. Claire woke hungry, an old memory in her mouth of the taste of fresh tomatoes still warm from the sun, the deep ache in her shoulders from picking vegetables all day in the blazing August heat. Her eyes flew open and she jerked upright. "A kitchen garden," she whispered.

They were on a small farm, too far from town and too poor to shop for more than the essentials. A kitchen garden would have been a necessity. Her body felt what this time of year was on a farm. Harvest. That morning, Claire instigated the hunt.

A game for flagging spirits, the prize for finding the garden was a kiss or a spoon of sugar, the victor's choice. Anna giggled and slid her fingers into Grey's hand. A smile and he led her outside. Walker teamed up with Marta, leaned on her shoulder and hobbled out the door.

Claire scoured the barn for a shovel or trowel while the search continued outside. Climbing the ladder to the darkened hayloft, she felt her way across the room and swung open the heavy door overlooking the yard. Sunlight revealed the room empty except for a bundle of rusting tools and bits of straw pushed into the corners. Claire gathered a bent rake, two chipped shovels and a pick, then watched, from the doorway, the scene below.

Grey stood nearly motionless, his eyes studying the sky then the ground, while Anna kicked up dust next to him. Finally, they set off hand in hand, working their way through clumps of low brush alongside the road. Walker leaned on a fence post next to the orchard, wiping sweat from his eyes as Marta thrashed through the grass behind him.

"Here, here," Anna cried.

Marta burst into a run and Walker stumbled along behind. Claire slid down the ladder and caught up with Walker. They found Grey on his knees between low brambles. His shirt clung to him in the heat as he dug into a tangle of vines and grass with his hands. An exhale and he leaned back. "Look, Anna, what is this?"

The little girl jumped to her feet, holding it aloft like a trophy, dancing from one foot to the other.

"A dried-up squash?" Marta couldn't hide her disappointment.

"No, better. A marker," Claire said. "Like a treasure map. Take a rake and poke through these bushes. There may be tomatoes, green beans, onions, garlic, or other vegetables hidden there."

Grey nodded; he understood. "Plants that reseed themselves year after year. Smart. How did you know?"

"Lucky guess. Your prize?" Claire said.

"Sugar, sugar," Anna yelled, jumping up and down.

"The lady chooses." Grey bowed toward Anna with a benevolent smile.

Claire pointed them toward the tools in the barn and led Anna into the house. As they stepped inside she heard Walker say, "Sugar is sweet for Anna, Grey, but you are a goddamn fool. The sweets you want come with a kiss."


That afternoon, a meal of fried squash and apples, and the garden still held much more. Marta and Anna sat at Walker's feet, learning words for their journey: soda pop, square and jitterbug.

Claire made a plate for Grey, found him inside the barn, the upper half of his torso hidden inside the open hood of the truck.

"Food." Claire laid a towel over a board, setting the plate on top.

A curse from deep inside the engine, and Grey reappeared, arms black up to his elbows. He jumped to the ground, wiped his hands on a rag, sniffed the air and grinned.

"A problem with the truck?"

"Not really. An oil leak, I think, but we must have reliable transport out of here, whether we make the drop or not." He took a bite of squash, savored it and smiled. "Thank you. Are you a secret mechanic, as well?"

Claire shook her head.

"Neither am I. I admit to using a driver, before."

"So did I. Well, my husband's." Claire circled the barn, peered into the dusty stalls that lined one wall and examined a tangle of dried leather and iron hanging from a rusted hook on the empty tack room door.

"Do you miss him?"

Claire laughed. "My driver, terribly. My husband, hell no." She pulled the tangle off the wall. A plow harness, the leather cracked from age. She examined it. The thread had rotted and once-tight seams split open in her hands. "I don't understand this place. This was good leather and well made. It would have been too valuable to leave behind, if they'd had a choice."

Grey walked over next to Claire. "Who are you? Who are you really?"

She stared, swallowed by his gaze. "A bloody Yankee princess."

"No. That is what you show, but underneath." He shook his head, forehead wrinkled as if he didn't understand. "I'd heard of the courage you showed in Paris. I saw it. But here, you've shown heart, grace." He reached out and stroked the back of her hand. "Who are you?"

Claire felt herself falling into his eyes; she stepped back from the precipice. A deep breath, something ripped free inside her chest. "A plow horse, then, who dreamt of champagne and diamonds. And did what it took to have it."

Grey tugged the harness from her hands, dropped it onto the packed dirt floor and reached for her. Claire met his hands with hers, softly pushed them away.

"I was born Clara May Wagner on a dried-up farm in Greenville, Oklahoma, population 317. My family were sharecroppers, worth less than our plow horse. Dirt poor. After my mama died, I got a chance to leave and I took it."

"To New York?"

She nodded. "I taught myself how to dress and how to talk. To drink and lie, to make a man feel important. I became Claire Harris, with a pedigree I'd stolen from a dead woman in an obituary."

"Your husband?"

"He didn't know. We had an arrangement. He needed a blue-blooded wife to become respectable. I needed money. I had certain abilities he put to use."

"Albrecht von Richter?" The anger was clear in Grey's voice.

Claire shrugged. "Among others. The drinks flowed and I made certain businessmen feel very important."

"He made you—"

"Not that. Hinted, but no, sex wasn't part of the deal." The thing inside burst free, left her throat aching but her mind crystal clear. No matter the cost, she needed Grey to see her as she really was. "I'm Clara May Wagner, runaway daughter of a dirt farmer."

He caught one hand. With a callused thumb, he wiped at a smudge of dirt on her knuckles. His warmth sparked her skin. "You are so much more, you have no idea. There is a fire banked deep inside you. I'm sorry I was so wrong about you."

His eyes were the color of slate and drilled deep inside her. Heat flooded her core; her lips sought his; her free hand slid behind his neck. He pressed her backward against the wall, cupping the back of her neck with one hand, his mouth tasting hers. He smelled of sun, oil and tobacco. She melted into the hardness of his body. The heat from his breath woke the skin on her face, then her neck as his lips tasted lower. His hand slid to her hip, then under the hem of her dress.

Anna's laughter drifted from the house.

"Not here," Claire said, her voice breathy.

"The hayloft." Grey held out his hand, palm up, his expression serious. "Join me?"

A hundred responses flashed and died on her lips. The truth was this life was uncertain, darkness was always too close, and she could be sure of nothing.

Except for this.

She took his hand. His grip was tight. He followed her up the ladder.

Lines of sunlight illuminated the loft floor through warped boards overhead. They faced each other. He watched her pull her dress over her head and slither out of her panties. She slid her fingers over the muscles in his stomach and up to his chest then slowly freed each button until his shirt fell open. She peeled it from his shoulders.

Their breath was loud in the hot liquid air. He ran his fingers over her lips, over the curves of her breasts, his palms flat against her waist, her hips. He pressed her backward against the wall. She gripped his belt buckle and pulled, fumbled with his zipper, then was rewarded with a low moan.

Her hands rested on his shoulders. With the wall at her back, his hands lifting and guiding her hips, her legs opened.

His lips and tongue found the soft skin of her thighs. She shivered at the sensation and pulled him up to face her. His gaze was consuming as he traced her lips with a finger. With a glint of a smile, he pressed her against the wall. She shut her eyes, held him close, felt his breath on her neck, their sweat mingling, her fingers in his hair as she accepted him inside her. Their breath combined in a rhythm that took over all thought. An exquisite pressure mounted until she cried out. He responded, gripping her tighter, driving her against the slats. Pleasure exploded in waves that rippled through her body then his.

Afterward, they lay on the floor, his shirt, her dress stretched flat beneath them. More gentle now, he explored every inch of her with the tips of his fingers, then his lips. The cadence of their breath and their bodies became music, a world for them alone. They were drowsing, limbs intertwined, when they heard a burst of static from the radio inside the house, then strains of a song too faint to make out.

"I miss music," Claire said drowsily to Grey's neck.

He rolled over to face her, head propped up on an elbow. "Let me guess. Jazz?"

Claire smiled. "Billie, Ella, Louis."

His eyes closed, with a finger he traced a line on her stomach, his voice a low whisper. "Just when you are near, when I hold you fast, then my dreams will whisper—"

Walker whooped inside the house. They both jumped, sat up, stared at each other a moment then leaped up to slip into their clothes and stumble down the ladder. They didn't look at each other as they raced across the yard.

"Our boys have landed in Sicily," Walker yelled, his face beaming, as they stepped inside the door.

Anna bounded over to Grey. "Bombardier to pilot," she said triumphantly in English.

"It won't be long now. You'll see." Walker looked at Grey a moment then at Claire. "Shucks," he added under his breath.

Claire ran a hand through her hair, found bits of straw. She caught Grey's eyes and noticed his shirt was misbuttoned. To cover the flush on her cheeks, she went to the kitchen to start dinner. She felt his stare as she walked away.

As she stirred tomatoes into a stew on the stove, she hummed the Billie Holiday song that Grey whispered in the barn. The spoon froze, midair, when she remembered the next line. *You're too lovely to last.*

The full moon lit the sky and still no messenger. They gathered around the radio during the nightly broadcast on the BBC for a coded message, for any news at all. But there was nothing. Grey, Walker and Claire debated the next step. They couldn't take the truck back into Paris empty, Grey would need to buy a load of something and bury them inside. But where would that leave the girls? Claire couldn't imagine sticking Anna back into that hole in the truck, the girls ending up trapped in Paris. *I can't stay here forever,* Walker told them, glaring back and forth. Claire knew what he meant: *You know you can't either.*

And they did know.

The next morning in the still shade of the forest, Claire found Grey. Or he found her. It didn't matter. On a blanket laid over a bed of leaves, she slipped her hands beneath his unbuttoned shirt and traced the lines of his chest beneath her fingertips. Let the beating of his heart warm her palms.

He slipped the dress over her head, pressing fully against her as though he needed to feel all of her to know the moment was real. He cupped the back of her head and covered her face and stomach in tender kisses. She guided his other hand between her thighs then reached for his loosened waistband. His breath was hot on her neck as he slid between her legs. She smiled and bit her lip against the moan. A day had been far too long. Their moments together so short.

Afterward he cradled her, his body warm and solid against her. His soft words died away at the drone of bombers flying overhead. Claire reached for him to drown out the sound with their bodies. But her heart ached as she stared into his eyes. He might belong to her now, but for how long? And damn it, but it was hard not to care what would come next.

That night after dinner they tuned the radio to the BBC. Grey jotted intently on a small pad of paper. His frown deepened as the broadcast faded to static. Walker turned the radio off. The click echoed in the silence.

"What did you hear?" Marta asked.

"I don't know," Grey said finally. "And I damn well should," he added under his breath. He stalked out into the darkness.

Claire helped the girls get ready for bed then slipped out after Grey. The heavy summer air was still. She found him on the hilltop above the farm, leaning against the lone oak tree, his eyes on the night sky. She rested a hand on his arm. His muscles were taut beneath her grip, his jaw clenched.

"They should have told us something by now," Grey said without looking at her. "A messenger. A broadcast. But bloody nothing."

Claire felt the frustration, the anger in his body. She faced him, sliding her arms around his waist and pulling herself close. His heart pounded against her. Steadfast Grey was desperate. She felt a surge of dread rising in her core.

Grey looked into her eyes. "How many days can we stay here, Claire? How many more?"

She pressed herself against him and stared up into his shadowed eyes. She had to respect his need to get Walker and the girls safe, to get his job done. Her own worry for the girls grew daily. But leaving meant losing these moments, losing Grey. Was he so desperate to escape her, to return to his lover in London? She tamped down the fear that bubbled in her now. She knew better than to think of a future with Grey. She *damn well* knew better. She pressed her lips hard against his.

Grey responded by devouring her with hungry kisses. He pushed her against the tree. The bark bit into her back. Her skin was on fire, heat building inside her. He stared into her eyes as he entered her. She gripped his shoulders, pulling him close, letting his strength fuel her. His rhythm was the ticking of a clock against them. She concentrated on their heartbeats, their breath. It was this moment that mattered. That made her feel whole. Safe. Only this moment. Time slowed and gave way to ripples of pleasure.

A warm breeze dried the sweat on their skin as they lay cupped together in the grass, their gazes toward the faint lights from Lyons-la-forêt in the distance.

Grey brushed the hair from her face. "Claire, I . . ." His words trailed to silence. "Thank you," he said finally. He wore the ghost of a faint smile as he covered her with his discarded shirt.

In the depths of his slate eyes she saw tenderness, gratitude and, yes, something more. A warmth spread through her chest. She felt such simple joy; she had never been so alive.

*In love,* a soft voice whispered in her head.

No, never that. She shoved away the thought. She was too damn smart to let a few fleeting weeks, a *liaison de la guerre*, make a fool of her. In truth, it would be good for all of them to escape this place, this deception. But not yet. Not tonight. She slipped the shirt from her body as she reached for Grey and let the cadence of their breath smother her worries.

They lay intertwined until the sky began to lighten around them. An intimate form of *flânerie*, of the body and the heart.

The moon waned to a crescent. Weeks passed, the summer heat descended and broke. The sun was bright, the sky a translucent blue. Claire and the girls spent the morning in the forest among birdsong and whispered laughter. Claire and Marta each carried a sack of berries. Anna trotted between them, her mouth stained deep purple.

Claire paused at the edge of trees behind the farmyard and motioned for silence.

"They've found us?" Marta whispered, reaching for Anna's sticky hand.

The farm looked as it always did. Building listing to the side, brush overgrown. But there was a stillness in the trees. The yard was too quiet. The skin pricked on the back of Claire's neck.

"Wait here." Claire set down the bucket and snuck forward.

The door was closed; Claire crept around under the window, past a dented bicycle with the spokes covered in mud. She held her breath and listened.

"This is not the plan," Grey said, anger radiating in his voice.

A new voice, a mix of bluster and fear, spoke in a provincial dialect. "My job is to take you to the drop at the appointed time. I do not make the decisions, Monsieur. I cannot control the *pilotes anglais*."

"Tell him, Grey. No deal." Walker interrupted in English.

Grey answered Walker. "I can't do that, Captain. We must do what we can."

Claire slid back from the windows, let her voice rise. "I'm back."

Chairs scraped across the wood floor, the door opened. Grey leaned out, the lines around his eyes tight, jaw tense. "Come inside, Evelyn, and meet Monsieur Citron."

A farmer with hair like a ragged bush stared at Claire as she entered. His hands stuffed in his pockets, he smiled, the smallest bow, but his stare appraised her like livestock. "I see," he said to Grey.

Walker leaned against the wall, glaring. Grey led her outside. Claire motioned to Marta to stay in the trees as she crossed the yard and followed Grey inside the barn.

"The plane is coming. But they won't offload any cargo. They'll take Walker. Not Marta or Anna." Grey's face was hard.

"What do you mean? They can't do that."

"They can. Only the pilot."

"No. You can't accept this."

"I have to. I'll drive Citron and Walker to the point, as directed. When I get back, we'll figure out a way to get everyone out."

Claire paused, replayed the conversation in her head. There had to be a way to change this. But something didn't fit. "Citron said *I see*. What did he mean?"

"It doesn't matter now."

The way Citron looked at her. It was as if he was judging her worth. What had he expected? Suddenly it made sense. Grey had made another arrangement. For Claire. A deeper wave of anger shook her. "You were going to send me away too."

"It's not safe for you in Paris anymore." His eyes met hers. "I want you all safe, cared for, away from here."

"You lied to me. I have a life in Paris."

"Von Richter wanted you, Claire. In Paris, he would eventually find you. If he learned you were a *Resistánt*, he would take you deep into rue des Saussaies, and you would pray, you would beg, for someone to make the pain stop."

"Marta and Anna are alone today because they weren't helped. In Paris. I helped save Christophe. I helped you. I'm not leaving."

"You've done enough." He gestured toward the house with the tilt of his head. "Think of the girls. They need you."

"When do you leave?"

"Tonight."

Claire stalked away.


While the men plotted in the barn, Claire settled the girls in the kitchen, buckets of water at their feet to wash the berries. The girls were quiet.

Claire prayed for Madame Palain's graceful words, but nothing came. "Walker is leaving tonight. Only Walker."

Marta's body went still, dripping berries cupped in her hand. Her eyes turned toward the floor, she reached for Anna. Claire read the tenseness of Marta's shoulders, her knuckles white where she gripped Anna.

The sight pierced Claire. "I promise you're going to get out of France. I promise you will be safe."

Marta nodded, but her expression didn't change.

*　*　*

That evening, Claire and the girls watched Citron and Grey prepare the truck. As the sun set, Walker hugged Marta and Anna good-bye, a kiss for Claire, then climbed into the truck.

Claire turned to go inside. Grey caught her arm in the doorway. "I don't have a choice."

Her eyes caught the glint of a pistol tucked inside his belt, covered by the hem of his jacket. She swallowed the fear surging in her stomach. "I do."

"It'll take one day, two at the most. Then I'll be back for you and the girls." He bent toward her, his lips brushed her cheek.

When she didn't respond, he released her and walked toward the truck.

Claire's heart splintered inside her. She ran, catching Grey as he moved to climb in the driver's seat. She pulled him close and her lips found his in a deep, ravenous kiss. "Promise me, Thomas Grey."

"I promise."

# Chapter 9

## THE BETRAYAL

Lyons-la-forêt, Normandy. October 26, 1943.

Three days had passed since Grey left them. The autumn grass blazed golden in the morning sun. Claire stood with her back pressed against the twisted oak, surveying the rolling hills and shaded forests for any sign of human movement. Any sign of Grey.

She closed her eyes and heard only the cawing and fighting of crows in the field. She slid down the gnarled trunk to a seat in the grass, felt the cool strength of the tree support her. The sun's rays soaked into her skin as her mind wandered, lighting here and there on single moments or sensations: the feel of Grey's arms enveloping her, translucent flower petals against the light streaming in the flower shop windows.

The farm behind her was deserted. The girls asked to "wash clothes" this morning. Claire knew they were wading and throwing rocks into the deep pools of the stream, but she let them go. She needed to be alone.

She'd waited for Grey's return all yesterday, trying to work, trying not to snap at the girls. By this morning, she gave up on appearing unconcerned and came to watch for Grey as soon as the girls were out of sight.

What then?

The way Grey looked at Claire with his slate eyes burning, his smile as he watched Anna play. There was a warmth there. A depth. God, but she wanted to believe he was coming back.

The rumble of a heavy diesel engine startled Claire. Her eyes jerked open and she stumbled to her feet.

An army truck slid to a stop in the farmyard. The doors opened and three soldiers piled out. They wore feldgrau but the twin lightning bolts on their helmets and collars caught the sunlight and revealed them as Waffen-SS. An officer, in SS collar patches and shoulder stripes, stepped on the running board and hopped onto the ground.

Two soldiers rushed toward the house, rifles at the ready. The officer stood by the truck. He lit a cigarette while the soldier at his side fiddled with his gun and peered into the dark doorway of the barn.

Claire slid behind the tree, her heart thudding in her chest. The girls were noisy, splashing in the river. You could almost hear them from the house. Crouching low, she slipped backward off the crest of the hill, then threaded along the base, submerged in the grass. Scrambling over roots and rocks, she circled the yard toward the tree line.

A shout echoed and Claire dropped to her stomach, her breath held. After a long moment she peered through the grass. The soldiers came out of the house. They conferred with the officer and turned toward the barn.

She scurried on hands and knees toward a fallen tree near the edge of the forest, cursing as her shins scraped against a splintered branch. Breathing fast, she scanned the clearing. Two soldiers disappeared into the barn. The officer faced the house. The remaining soldier was gone. Claire measured the distance with her eyes.

A shrill cry behind the house and her body froze. The girls. They'd come back. A burst of sobs, frightened and thin. A smothered crying in the yard, then a scuffle. Claire recognized the high-pitched sobbing. Anna needed help. Anna needed her.

A current of heat ran through her, a sensation so fierce Claire wondered at it. Rage pulsed inside like her body would explode. She stood, pulled back her shoulders and strode toward the soldiers.

They turned to her, fingers pressed against triggers. Anna was a sobbing pile in the middle of the yard. A soldier towered over the girl, his hobnailed boot raised to stomp. The officer leaned against the truck; the two remaining soldiers stood at the edge of the clearing, facing the river.

"*Bonjour.*" Claire hurried into the clearing, hips swinging. Her voice was low and welcoming as if a handsome neighbor had come to visit.

The officer spoke a command. Except for the soldier standing over Anna, they converged around Claire. She stopped and arranged a pose. One foot forward, hands on cocked hips, a half smile pulling at her lips.

The officer was trim, in fighting shape, dark hair combed back in a perfect wave. Bored eyes and thin lips turned down in a displeased sneer. He barked a command in German. Claire didn't respond. He backhanded her across the face. She spun backward, slamming face-first into the hard ground.

Darkness crept around the edges of her mind but she fought

for consciousness. She looked up at the officer through the hair that had fallen over her eyes, forcing down her anger. He spoke to his men, his tone disinterested. The solider guarding Anna laughed and leaned back against the truck's grill. His gun was pointed at the little girl, his gaze on the show.

Claire pulled herself to her feet and straightened her rumpled dress, frowning at the marks on her dress and knees. She rubbed the back of her hand across her aching mouth and tasted blood and soil on her tongue. With as much poise as possible, she spit out a wad of dirt. Her eyes flicked over the edges of the yard. Where was Marta?

The officer spoke again, his voice commanding.

Claire smiled at him through the pain. She knew only one phrase in German. From Albrecht von Richter. Perhaps useful. She licked the blood from her lips and took a step forward. *"Ich will dich."* I want you.

The officer studied her with cold eyes. The soldiers at his side smiled, nodded. The soldier to her left reached for her. He spoke over his shoulder at the others, pulling her toward the barn.

*"Nein."* The officer glared.

The soldier frowned but released her.

Claire smiled at the officer, lifted the hem of her dress up to her thighs. She took a step back toward the barn. *"Ich will dich."*

A quick command and the officer sent a soldier into the barn. After a moment of searching, he reappeared, a shrug. The officer sheathed his Luger in the holster at his hip. With the flick of his head, he and the other two soldiers shoved Claire inside. The man watching Anna shouted, the complaint clear in his tone. The soldiers walking into the barn laughed back over their shoulders.

Claire walked over to the hay piled loosely next to the empty stalls and patted the surface with a hand. The officer took a step closer, still not committed, hand firm on his holstered gun. As the other two soldiers watched, Claire pulled off her dress over her head and let it drop onto the ground. In one movement she kicked off her underpants.

He examined her, his lip curving back like a cat eyeing a trapped mouse. It was plain how much it pleased him, the white skin, the taut body, the curve of her hips, the tawny swirl between her legs.

She ran her hands through her hair, let her fingers slide down her cheeks, over her breast, down past her stomach. "I remember the taste of dirt," she said, her voice low like a promise.

His forehead wrinkled as he tried to understand. He moved closer.

"Of all the things I've tried to forget, I still remember that specific taste." Slowly, Claire reached out, resting her fingers on his chest until she felt the heat from his body through the fabric of his uniform. Her fingers trailed down his torso.

He struggled to keep his breath calm. His fingers clenched the gun handle.

"When I was real little, I remember Pa's big hand picking up a fistful. He'd let it slide out between his fingers, like he could feel what would grow from it."

He looked at her questioningly. Claire smiled. She moved her hands toward his belt and began to unbuckle it. He held completely still, watching her hands.

"Like he was caressing it." Claire slid her fingers between his legs and rubbed the tightening fabric.

A muffled grunt escaped his closed mouth.

She leaned in, murmured into his ear. "Then the drought came and the winds started. The dirt came alive. It didn't lay there nestled with growing things. It howled and wailed. It flung itself at the world." Claire looked into his eyes as she took a firm grip on him, cupping him in her palm.

He watched her, enthralled, his eyes half-closed. His tongue flicked over his lips.

"It baked in the sun, then peppered us until the livestock went mad. It burned and stung our eyes, tore at our skin, and filled our ears and noses with grit." Claire gripped him harder with her right hand then unbuttoned his trousers with the other. "And even inside at night when the dirt settled into the parched ground to rest, we could never forget its presence. Because everything tasted like dirt."

His breath whistled from his mouth. Grunting, he dropped his pants and grabbed her with both hands, shoving her back into the hay.

Claire looked into his eyes and pulled his hips toward her open legs. "You could say all the things I've done in my life were so I'd never have to taste dirt again." Her left hand slipped down his side. Her fingers reached for the cold touch of steel.

The Luger roared. His heart exploded as a bullet tore through his chest. He collapsed on top of her. Claire jerked the pistol free, pointed at the soldier next to her and fired. He grabbed at his chest and fell backward. She pointed at the soldier ducking inside the doorway and fired again.

A flash from the doorway and the officer on top of her spasmed; the impact of a bullet knocked the wind from her chest. Gasping, she pushed him off and rolled beneath the raised wall between the stalls. She peered back at the officer. He stared at her, blinked once. His mouth hung open, sneer gone. Then his bored eyes stared at nothing.

She crawled across the stall, Luger clenched in her hand. She held her breath and listened. A soft groan from the soldier by the wall. A gurgle faded to silence.

Willy used to take her hunting on Sundays when their parents went to church. He was the cowboy and Claire always the Indian. She had better aim.

Claire heard the faint squeak of a rusted hinge. The soldier was in the empty tack room, looking for another way out. There wasn't one. Gritting her teeth, she slid under the partition into the next stall. She inched forward on her knees to the doorframe and gripped the Luger with both hands. The barrel, motionless, was pointed at the tack room doorway. A slow breath in. Breath out. The air hissed over her tongue as she tightened her finger on the trigger slowly, deliberately.

A torso came into view. Feldgrau. A wide, black leather *koppel* belted around a thick waist. She aimed at the eagle on the metal buckle, swastika clenched in its talons. The gun barked in her hands and the uniform burst open in grey and then red.

The soldier outside shouted. Anna screamed. Claire raced to the door and peered out, her form hidden in the shadows.

He faced the barn, his rifle pointed at the wide doors, half his body shielded by the cab of the truck. The little girl was prone on the ground beneath his boot, her cries muffled into the dirt.

Claire rushed to the dead officer; his white buttocks peeked out between his long shirt and lowered trousers. She wrenched the shirt from his body. Blood ran down her arms as she wadded the shirt into a ball around the pistol gripped in her hand. She pressed the shirt against her stomach, felt the blood drip down her legs.

The soldier cursed. Anna wailed.

Claire sucked in a deep breath and dropped to her knees. She crawled into the farmyard, moaning, her hand clenched to her stomach, dragging her legs behind her. She kept her gaze on the dirt in front of her, body clenched as she waited for a bullet that didn't come. Just outside the doorway, she collapsed, body limp, her eyes open to slits.

The soldier pointed the rifle at Claire. His face was twisted in hate, his boot poised over Anna's head to stomp. Inside the bundle of bloody fabric, Claire pulled the trigger. The pistol jerked in her hand; he fell behind the truck. Dirt and rock chips exploded from the ground in front of her face from the impact of a rifle bullet.

"Hide, Anna, behind the wagon!" Claire rolled to her knees, aimed at the dodging boots she saw under the floorboards and pulled the trigger once, then twice. The third time and the chamber clicked. Empty. She fell back inside the door listening for his shots.

The dead soldier inside the barn door was slumped on top of a gun strapped to his back. Claire kicked him over and wrestled it free. Longer than a rifle, the wide barrel was slitted along the side, a line of bullets in the assembly over the handle and trigger.

Claire pressed the butt against her shoulder and cocked the trigger. Leaning out the doorway, she squeezed the trigger. Bullets spewed in a roar that sounded like tearing canvas. The recoil knocked the air from her lungs; she fell backward to her knees.

The truck engine churned to life. Claire charged into the yard and pointed the machine gun at the soldier through the windshield. He jerked the wheel as the truck lurched forward, accelerating toward Anna.

Marta broke from the trees, screaming. Anna looked up at her sister then stumbled under the rusted iron toe of the wagon. The truck hit, then skidded down the side of the wagon bed. The heavy boards groaned as they were splintered by the force of the metal fender. The truck broke loose and tore out of the yard.

Claire dropped the gun, running. Anna was crumpled in a pile under the shattered but still standing wagon; shaking and crying; her little fist balled and stuffed in her mouth. Marta crawled under the wagon and pulled the girl to her. Claire dropped to her knees and hugged them both.

"Are you hurt? Are you hurt?" Marta said, holding Anna too tight for her to reply.

Anna looked up at Claire, her cheek was bruised, and tiny teeth marks dented her pudgy fingers. "You're not wearing any clothes."

Claire's legs gave way and she crumpled into Marta. They both slid to the ground, Anna tucked between them. She felt their bodies against her skin, inhaled the smell of dirt and blood and tears. She gave herself a couple of breaths to stop shaking, then stood, pulling them to their feet.

Claire stared down the road. "Marta, go pack your bags. Quickly. They'll be back."

Claire pushed the girls inside the house then turned back toward the barn. She retrieved the empty Luger and wrapped her discarded dress around her. Gritting her teeth, she kneeled next to the officer and rummaged through his pockets. There was a tin of bullets and a wallet. She flipped open the wallet and found his identification, the unsmiling photo of a woman and a thick wad of Occupation reichsmarks.

His skin was chalky, his eyes blank. Blood was everywhere. She started to shake, then doubled over and vomited. After a breath, she reached for the bullets and the money, covered her face against the smell of blood and gunpowder, and ran.

In the kitchen, she dunked a cloth into a full bucket and scrubbed at the dirt and sticky blood that was starting to dry on her skin. She could hear Marta talking to Anna, shoving things around in the other room.

"Claire?" Marta waited in the doorway, cases in one arm, Anna in the other.

Claire pulled a dress over her head, slipped on shoes. Wrapping up the rest of the food in a cloth, she reached for her bag.

With the girls waiting by the door, Marta's eyes on the road, Claire glanced around the house. Nothing could be left behind to reveal identities. No signs of Grey. No signs of the moments they shared. Not a word of the stories that Captain Walker told. Just dead Nazis in the barn.

She led the girls out of the clearing, toward the forest.

"Where are we going, Claire?" Marta said.

"There is only one place where I know people who can help us. Help you."

"Paris," Marta said, her voice soft and grim.

"Paris." The city Claire loved, where she found beauty and self-worth. The city where Marta's life was destroyed. The world had gone mad.

Claire reached down to the dirt, squeezing a handful in her fist. The faint smell of rich, peaty earth, it crumbled through her fingers onto the ground. Another glance at the farm, and she led the girls into the trees.

The forest was shadowed, the sun slipping below the treetops when they heard the whine of an engine. Claire's shoulder throbbed. Without looking she knew it was bruised. The price of firing a machine gun. Her other arm ached from carrying Anna for the last few hours, but the girl finally slept, her cheek red and swollen. Claire winced as she set Anna onto the ground next to Marta, motioned for them to remain still and crept to the edge of the trees overlooking the road.

The asphalt turned in a serpentine bend below. A motorcycle sped by, the soldier crouched low over the handlebars. Claire watched him go then slid down the slope to the brush next to the road. A Nazi messenger. Was he reporting what happened at the farm, starting a hunt? She couldn't believe it was a random search. They were betrayed.

In spite of herself, her thoughts flashed to the gun hidden in Grey's waistband. A darkness rose up inside her like a tide. He wasn't coming back.

A low purr snapped her to attention. The sound grew as a car drove into view in the distance. The little green Fiat slowed as it approached the bend. Squinting, Claire made out a lone man inside. She crawled closer. The road was dangerous, she knew. But they'd never to make it to Paris on foot.

A Frenchman. He had a cigarette in his mouth, a jacket over a turtleneck. He was slumped low in his seat, his head tilted down as if he were barely watching the road.

Claire climbed onto the asphalt as he approached. She waved her arms in front of her, a welcoming smile. The brakes squealed as the car stopped.

"Madame, what is wrong?" Voice concerned, his hands gripped the wheel.

As she walked up to the window, her gaze slid over a permit hung from the front window bearing a swastika stamp. "Well, Monsieur—" She pointed the pistol in his face. "We need a ride." She loaded the girls into the backseat and slid into the front seat next to him, the gun trained on his chest.

His gaze fell on Anna's bruised face. "I'm a doctor." When Claire didn't respond, he pointed to the permit on his windshield. "That is why I am allowed to drive. I'm a doctor and need to see my patients."

"You *need* to drive." Claire glanced at the permit. "Docteur Lagarde."

He clenched his mouth and pulled onto the road. Claire curled up in the seat so she could face him, rested the Luger on her knee and tried to ignore how much it hurt her shoulder.

He glanced at Anna in the rearview mirror then at the pistol in Claire's hand. "It is not impossible to guess how you might have acquired a German officer's pistol. But I must tell you it is not necessary to point it at me. I would like to help you."

"No. It's better this way. If you are a good man, a patriot, then you will willingly drive and won't have anything to worry about if you are questioned. If not, well, that is what the bullets are for."

He sighed, turning his eyes to the road. "*D'accord.*"

The girls curled up asleep on the seat behind her. The exhaustion she refused to feel all day submerged her. Claire rested her head on her palm, elbow propped on the seat, Luger pointed forward.

Claire jolted alert when the car stopped, lights out, off the side of the road in the trees. The doctor said nothing, lit a cigarette and inhaled as if it were his last. He glanced at her then at the gun.

"We are outside of Vernonnett in le Forêt de Vernon. The checkpoint is over the next hill." He pointed past her into the forest. "Just out of sight, there is a small path, like an animal trail. It leads to the river. That is where the smugglers work, where they load cargo on barges for Paris they don't want regulated by the Germans."

Claire squinted into the forest. "How will I find them?"

"They'll find you. They are well armed. The pistol will do you no good. But perhaps with the gun you can buy passage." He looked back at the sleeping girls. In the dim light, his face was etched with exhaustion and sadness. Like a man who has found his limits and was haunted by how insurmountable they were.

Claire knew how he felt. "Thank you." She reached back to wake Marta.

Claire led the way down the trail with Anna sleeping in her arms. Marta trudged behind with the bags. Guided by the sliver of a moon, feet testing the forest floor before each step, they inched through the darkness.

The moon dipped from view. Their strides faltered. Claire bunched fallen leaves together to make a small bed between trees. Marta was too tired to do more than pull Anna in tight and wrap her coat around her. They huddled close, Claire leaning against the tree, gun in her hand, head resting on arms crossed in front of her. She closed her eyes and fell into a dreamless sleep.

Snapping branches awoke her. A boy stood over her carrying an old-fashioned hunting shotgun slung in the crick of his elbow. As Claire straightened, she stretched her arm so the pistol was in view.

"Docteur Lagarde sent us. We are looking for a barge," she said.

He was tall, his face thin, features boyish under a coat of dirt. He glanced at her, then at Marta, who woke up and stared at him.

"This way," he said.

They followed him until the sun rose well above the trees and lit small clearings in bright light. He walked with one eye on the trail ahead and the other scanning the trees around them. Still, that didn't keep him from exchanging looks with Marta. They are miraculous, Claire thought as she adjusted Anna resting on a hip. The young in the world will always be the same. She turned to share a smile with Grey, then remembered she was alone. Fear and loneliness pricked at her chest before she forced the throbbing away. One foot in front of the other. Just keep moving and it will be alright.

She heard a low-pitched gurgle but the river remained hidden. The forest opened up onto a clearing surrounding a shack. As they approached, a man appeared out of the trees with a rifle casually pointed at Claire's chest. In his twenties, she guessed, muscles earned the hard way, his eyes cold and his face showing his distrust. She forced herself to keep walking.

An older man stepped out of the shack. A dingy white beard bristled over a thick collar. His face was dissected in lines from too many hours under a blazing sun, but his features matched the boy's.

Claire steeled herself as she faced the old man. She set Anna on the ground behind her and offered her warmest smile. "*Bonjour, Monsieur.*"

"I found them on the trail, Papa," the boy said.

"Who sent you?" the rifleman said, keeping the barrel fixed on Claire.

"Docteur Lagarde."

They exchanged a look.

Claire set the Luger on a knotted wooden table at her side and tossed the reichsmarks next to it. "The pistol and money for transport to Paris."

Flicking the gun across the worn surface to the rifleman, the father flipped through the bills like a banker. He examined Claire with respect in his eyes.

"*Bof!*" The rifleman exhaled in a burst. "That's not enough. Not for all three."

The father nodded, though his voice was quiet when he spoke to Claire. "The danger is greater with three. Not easy to hide. And the young one may scream out and jeopardize everyone. No good."

"But, Monsieur." Claire stopped. She had nothing to say. Nothing more to offer. She stared at the packed dirt beneath her feet, unable to argue or meet Marta's eyes.

"There is more," Marta said.

Everyone turned to stare. Marta's skin was chalky and her forehead had picked up a welt along the trail. Two bright spots of color appeared on her cheeks, and her lips pressed together in a hard line. She stepped forward with the monogrammed leather case, unlocked the latches and swung it open.

Two canvasses were rolled up inside. Marta reached for the first. "These were painted by Tamara Decler." She opened the canvas against the scarred wood. "This is called *Adam and Eve* and was commissioned by the Duchess du Boucard."

The man and woman stood, unclothed, twisted around each other like tree trunks. The lines were refined, the colors luminous. Claire was awed at the artistry revealed in every brush stroke.

Marta unrolled the second canvas. "This one was not commissioned. These two paintings were worth over four hundred thousand francs. There are people who will pay. A list of their names and addresses is in this case."

Tears sprang to Claire's eyes. On the second canvas a dark-haired girl slept with her head on a table. The thin fabric of her nightgown was tight against a lean hip. Thoughtful, even in sleep. It was Marta, painted with a loving hand.

"There will be a boat tonight," the man said.

"But we can't trust girls not to talk," the younger man protested.

"They have more to fear than we do, Jean. Show our guests where they may wait, Luc." The father gestured toward the trees. He reverently rolled up the canvasses and dropped them in the case with the money. "Tonight."

The boy led Claire and the girls to the edge of the clearing. They settled in the grass under the trees, the river a presence only by its low-pitched murmur. Claire reached into her bag and handed apples to Marta and Anna. Marta offered the boy, Luc, an apple, but he shook his head and lit a cigarette.

They ate a quiet meal. Claire's gaze kept finding the shack, thinking of the paintings inside, the woman who painted them and the girl who just gave them up.

"She painted you beautifully," Claire said.

Marta didn't meet her eyes, she shrugged. "Mother denied she had a daughter until she was pregnant with Anna. The name of the painting was *Girl Waiting*."

The pain in Marta's voice was clear. "The man who arranged for us to meet Monsieur Grey did it for those paintings. That was the price for our freedom."

Anna dragged an apple core through the leaves. "I miss Monsieur Grey. How will he find us here?"

"He won't, Anna. He left us." The words burst from Marta's mouth, then she clamped her lips shut, looking away.

"No. That's not true," Claire said, louder than she intended.

Anna listened with round eyes. Marta looked up through her hair.

"Grey will find us." She held the gaze of each girl. "He promised."

"Good," Anna said, as though it were settled, and tossed the core into the bushes.

Claire hugged her arms to her side and closed her eyes. She remembered the feel of Grey's fingers on her cheek before he drove away. If only it were true.

As night fell, the father reappeared from the shack with a gas lantern in his hand. He and Jean led them, Luc trailing behind. They followed a winding trail through the trees, the smell and the sound of moving water intensifying at each bend.

The river still murmuring out of sight, the trees opened up onto a small canal the width of a truck. They stopped at a pile of debris and leaves at the canal edge. The men each grabbed a branch at the edge of the heap and lifted. A cover of matted branches and leaves came off in a single form, revealing a motorboat stacked high with wooden crates.

The men climbed aboard and started the engine, stoking it to a low rumble. The father reached for Marta, then Anna and Claire. A low whistle sounded in the distance. Luc pushed the boat off the side and leapt aboard. The engine caught and the boat slid down the small channel like a cork coming out of a bottle.

The Seine opened up in front of them. A tugboat chugged into view, smoke boiling out its long smokestack. As it approached, Claire saw the line of three barges trailing along behind it. The father steered the motorboat on an intersecting course. Jean watched the shore, rifle butt snugged tight against his shoulder. Even in the darkness, Claire felt exposed on the open water. She motioned for Marta to slide lower.

The boat maneuvered up next to the tugboat. Luc threw a line up and grabbed another line slung down. In a moment they were docked with the tug, the motor silenced, and the men climbed aboard.

Two crew members swung down to the motorboat and maneuvered the craft back to the first barge. With a practiced ease, a crew tied heavy lines around the crates and wrenched them aboard. Once the crates were stowed on the barge, the men motioned for Claire and the girls. A crate stacked on the top row was popped open with a crowbar. A crewman pointed to the opening with an apologetic shrug.

"Your passage, *Mesdames*," he said.

A last look back at the open night sky and Claire went inside. Even with slits between the wooden slats, the crate was stuffy and smelled of burned diesel and old onions. Anna tried to yank free but Marta scolded with a stern voice and pulled her in.

The crewman handed Claire a small iron bar. "This crate will be unloaded on a dock. Wait until you hear a whistle, then free yourselves. The Quai Saint-Exupéry is on the other side of the warehouses and will take you into the heart of Paris."

The small space rang with the percussion of driving nails as they were sealed inside. Claire's ears echoed as she listened to the footsteps of the crew fade, then the engine of the motorboat rumble to nothing. Anna began to whimper.

"Quiet, Anna," Marta said, her own voice tight with anxiety.

Claire leaned back in an attempt to get comfortable. She thought of an afternoon long ago, dim lights flickering against a giant screen, the soft cushions of red velvet seats.

"Once upon a time," she said, reaching for each girl's hand in the darkness, "there was a handsome paleontologist, Docteur Grant, who was obsessed with a dinosaur bone. A beautiful socialite named Mademoiselle Hepburn met the paleontologist and fell in love with him, but he was engaged to marry another woman. A very boring, unkind woman. But, you see, the social-ite had a pet leopard named *Bébé*."

"A pet leopard?" Anna snuggled into Claire's side. "*Vraiment mystérieux!*"

They slipped off the barge at dawn and made their way into Paris and to rue du Colisée. The blue awning of the flower shop was a beacon in the bright morning sunlight. The girls stowed in the alley behind the shop, Claire strolled past the windows of La Vie en Fleurs. A glance inside. The florist stood at the counter, helping a soldier, his back to the window. Madame's eyes tracked Claire.

Claire and the girls circled the block, then slipped down the alley. The florist waited at the back door. Claire enveloped her in a tight embrace, feeling the emotion and strength in her taut frame.

A soft whispering caught Madame's attention. She looked over Claire's shoulder. "What do we have here?"

A deep curtsy from each girl and a quiet introduction.

The florist examined Claire, a question in her eyes. After a moment, she smiled and extended her arms. "I am Madame Palain. Please come in."

"I'm sorry," Claire said.

Madame met Claire's gaze, her eyes serious. "Don't worry, my dear. We are women. We will make do."

Madame pulled out the china. They ate a breakfast of apples and thin-sliced bread, speaking of weather and flowers, sitting on stools amongst greenery in the back room. No questions were asked.

Afterward, the florist led them upstairs into Claire's room. It was the same as Claire left it; a fresh rose in the crystal vase. Madame saw Claire's glance, a small nod.

"We will have Georges bring up a mattress. It will be perfect," the florist said.

"It will be fine, Madame, thank you. But we can't tell Georges," Claire said. "No one can know. No one can talk."

The woman turned to Claire, her eyes sparking anger. "Just because Georges is not fast doesn't mean he isn't a good boy. He never said anything about *you*, did he?"

Claire glimpsed a trace of the pain her deception caused. "No. He didn't."

"*Bon.*" Madame turned toward the girls. "We will get started on your new room before Georges comes over."

Claire watched as the girls arranged the room with the florist's oversight. Madame told them *elegance is in the details.* Marta and Anna listened with rapt eyes. Claire knew they would settle in nicely. A look of gratitude to her friend and she reached for her paper and pen.

That afternoon, Claire slipped a note into the slot of the dentist's office as she walked by, her quick eyes on the street around her. A young couple strolling, a white-haired man bent over a cane, a boy with worn oversized clothes belted around his thin frame. No one watched her, none trailed too close behind. She got as far as the corner before she turned back. She couldn't make herself hide at Madame's and wait.

There was an empty sidewalk table at Café Raphael. Claire claimed a chair and sat down facing the dentist's office. She ordered a coffee to give her hands something to do. Even with the girls tucked away in the shop, it felt as though a vise were tightening around her, and her body fidgeted for action.

She shifted on her seat, her eyes searching. It was a beautiful fall afternoon, but the street looked shabby in the golden light. The structures seemed to hunch together and the pedestrians stooped from the oppression blanketing the city.

A man emerged from the office. He had the nonchalance of a patient leaving his dentist, but at the end of the block, his eyes flicked over his shoulder to the street behind him before he abruptly descended the stairs to the Métro.

He was the man who had handed her the package on the way to the Gestapo. Dropping coins on the table, Claire hurried across the street and down the steps. She kept his head in view along the long tunnel to the platform. He slipped on the train as the whistle blew.

Claire jumped into the nearest car as the train began to move. She saw him exit the train at Europe station. She shoved her way out onto the platform and scanned the crowd. Not seeing him, she chose the nearest of three possible exits. She hurried through the tunnel, up the steps to rue de Madrid.

A busy street, but the man was not there. She had lost him.

"What a coincidence, running into you here."

Odette was at her side. Her smile did not make it up to her eyes. She shoved her arm through Claire's. "Let's talk."

Claire pulled her arm free. She was done being intimidated. "I'll talk. You listen."

They walked on rue Portalis toward the dome of Église Saint-Augustin de Paris. Passing the statue of Joan of Arc, they entered the church doors and sat. Claire faced straight ahead and spoke about the farm, the messenger who came for Grey and the pilot, the soldiers and her escape with Anna and Marta.

Finally, Claire turned to Odette. "I need two things. One, to know where Grey is now. Second, Anna and Marta need safe passage out of France."

Odette stared into Claire's eyes. From her somber face, Odette appeared to read more there than Claire wanted to reveal. "I knew it wasn't you that betrayed us. I can do nothing for the girls. I am sorry. About Grey, I will do what I can."

Odette nodded at a figure by the door as she left. The man Claire followed from the train slipped a pistol in his jacket as he followed Odette outside.

Sunlight through the stained-glass rosette window painted the church in blues. As the priest moved to the front of the church, Claire stood and walked out.

# Chapter 10

## THE CHÂTEAU

52, rue du Colisée, Paris. October 30, 1943.

Claire turned up the lapel of her coat as she locked the shop's front door two mornings later. The light was soft grey, an unseen sun hid behind a heavy mist that blanketed the street. The buildings were faint outlines; her steps muffled in the heavy air. Head down, eyes darting from side to side, Claire hurried toward parc Monceau.

She slid through the side gate from avenue Hoch and took the center path. The apartments surrounding the park were invisible except for soft light from a single window, several stories up. Trees and sculptures seemed to come out of nowhere as she hurried down the passage. The ache in her head, the mist itself, tamped down any fear for her own safety.

She fingered the note in her pocket that had been tucked under the door after closing last night. *Meet at the Roman pond in the park at 6 tomorrow morning.* She struggled to keep her pace natural. The wait felt far too long for this meeting.

A tall man faced the pond, face half-hidden in a scarf, hat pulled low. "Evelyn?"

"Yes."

"Danielle sent me. As you thought, you were betrayed. The one you asked about was captured." He handed her a slip of paper. "Memorize this address. Outside Paris. It's near Noisiel."

Her eyes skimmed over the crisp letters. *31, rue de Jardin, Champs-sur-Marne.* It was an address she didn't recognize. Captured. The word chilled her. "Is Grey alive?"

"For now. But you must go today to this address and search for materials that might incriminate anyone. Names, locations, dates, photos. Destroy anything you find."

Claire gripped the paper. "How would the Gestapo know to go there?"

"It was his home. We must expect him to break. Everyone does."

"Show some respect." She slapped him hard across the face.

His eyes narrowed. A red splotch marked his freshly shaved cheek. "This is our life, Madame. He got caught, well, then he will break. If he is lucky, he will die first."

He fished a cigarette from his pocket, brought it to his lips and lit it with a match pinched between his thumb and the side of his first finger of his other hand. Her eyes were drawn to his fingers. They'd been shattered, four twisted digits curled under his palm.

He took a deep draw from the cigarette and peeled back his lips in a bitter smile. "Everyone breaks a little." He shoved his ruined hand back into his coat pocket. With the other, he pulled the cigarette from his mouth and pointed toward the note. "Go today."

\* \* \*

Claire caught the eastern train from Gare du Montparnasse out of the city at midday. The sunlight was brittle on the bleached countryside and scattered villages that passed outside the window. The Marne River snaked back and forth beneath the tracks; small boats loaded down with cargo sailed along their route.

The rhythmic chugging of the train's wheels on the tracks sounded like a heartbeat. She remembered a warm afternoon, the sunlight on her skin, she and Grey lying tangled on their castoff clothes in a small grassy hollow. Her head rested on his chest, her eyes closed. She felt his heart beating against her cheek, strong and calm.

"Madame?"

Claire opened her eyes.

A French policeman stood in front of her. *"Vos papiers, s'il vous plaît?"*

Skin prickling, she pulled the card from her purse.

"Reason for travel?"

"A friend in Noisiel is very sick. I am going to visit her." Chin down, a sad sigh.

*"Il est regrettable."* He handed her the card.

Her gaze returned to the window as his footsteps faded. Who could have betrayed them? She knew so few people. That was how the Resistance worked. Small cells that didn't know each other, so one leak couldn't bring them all down. Grey was apparently high enough that he knew more. She would damn well look through everything he had. If there were documents to be found, perhaps they would lead to the traitor.

The train reached Noisiel station in less than an hour. Claire exited with a small crowd. Even here, a patrol awaited on the platform, guns ready.

It took nearly an hour of asking in shops in Noisel to find Champs-sur-Marne. In the end, she paid a little boy to draw a map in the dirt to rue de Jardin. *You will see it,* he promised her. Another hour of walking along a picturesque lane before she found an ornate wrought-iron gate.

Gripping the curling bars, Claire peered in. A long straight gravel lane led to a château in the distance. On each side, cut green lawn was bound by tall hedges formed into curving parterre. Three rows of high windows marked the stone building. A grand portcullis was set out in the center. A second-story balcony overlooked the path and entrance.

A push and the gate opened with a creak. Claire slipped inside and started down the path, her mind racing. The challenge of carrying out her mission began to dawn on her. Near the house, the path split into two and circled a large fountain, with some sort of sea god crashing through limestone waves. She ran a hand over the marble edge. It looked like something at Versailles, designed by Le Nôtre. How did she know this? She sighed. An afternoon's walk at jardin du Luxembourg. Grey had told her.

The massive stone portcullis shaded intricately carved wood doors at the château's entrance. Claire gripped the gilded lion door knocker and rapped.

The heavy door swung open with a wheeze against wood parquet flooring. A woman stood before her, her face guarded but friendly. She was in her fifties with the polished look of aristocracy, strong bones, luminous eyes, firm mouth. "Yes?"

"Grey—Thomas Grey asked me to come by. I am Claire Badeau. A friend."

The woman's expression clouded. She looked in the distance behind Claire as if Grey might be there. "Where is he? He hasn't called—"

"No, he can't call, not now. He can't come. That is why he sent me here." Claire tried a reassuring smile.

The woman studied her a moment. "Your accent. You are *l'Américaine?*"

*The* American? Claire nodded.

"I am Yvette Wyles." She squeezed Claire's hand and led her inside the door. "If you are a friend of Thomas, you are welcome to our home."

Yvette led her to an intimate salon filled with paintings and books. On one wall, a row of oversized windows overlooked an estate that stretched into the distance. In the corner, against the windows, a table was set for two. A man sat hunched on a chair, blankets bunched about his shoulders, slender hand clutching a cup. Thinning blond hair was combed carefully back. His face was chalky and drawn, as if aged by sickness.

Yvette stepped over to his side and rested a hand on his shoulder. "This is my husband, Peter Wyles."

With a shaking hand he set a tea cup on the table. He tipped his head forward. *"Enchante,"* he said, a clipped British accent bleeding through the French.

"I am Claire Badeau."

"A friend of Thomas. *L'Américaine,*" the woman completed.

Claire was shown into a seat with a cup of tea set in front of her. Yvette disappeared then returned with a cup, pulled up another chair and sat next to her.

"You know our Thomas? Wonderful. How is he doing?" Peter asked.

Their kindness cut into her. She took a sip to give herself

a moment before answering. She looked at Peter and formed a casual smile. "I was with Grey about a week ago. Outside of Paris. He asked me to check up on you."

Peter turned to Yvette and smiled, as if to say *I told you he was fine.* Yvette played with her cup. She didn't look convinced.

"Grey's home is much grander than he spoke of," Claire said.

Peter laughed, the sound died into a wheeze. "He can be rather circumspect. Can't he, Yvette?"

Yvette only arched an eyebrow, sipping her tea.

Claire leaned forward in her chair. "You said *the* American. What did you mean?"

Peter chuckled, he glanced to Yvette.

She returned the smile. "Forgive my rudeness, Madame Badeau. Thomas has not remarked upon many Americans."

"What did he say?"

The couple shared a glance and a small smile.

"Very little, actually," Peter said. "Like I said. Circumspect."

"I noticed your accent. Is Thomas your son?"

He chortled. "Oh goodness, no. Thomas is solid upper-crust British merchant wealth. My father was a tailor. I was a gentleman's gentleman."

Claire examined the room, her eyes seeking out open doorways, counting rooms in her mind. It was going to take a while to find Grey's room or rooms, before she could even hope to search them. She noticed their stares. "This is an amazing house."

Yvette smiled. "You are kind to say."

Peter coughed and wiped his mouth. "This château was in Yvette's family since it was built in the sixteen hundreds. Marie Antoinette walked these dusty halls."

Yvette glanced around the room, her expression fond. "This place has seen better days."

Claire looked around at the furniture. Obviously well cared for, it was a bit worn and faded. "Haven't we all."

Peter coughed, his thin form twisting in the chair.

Yvette stood. "Peter must retire to his room to rest. If you'd like, afterward, I will offer you a tour and we might speak."

"That would be wonderful," Claire said with a warmth she didn't feel.

Yvette sturdied Peter as he pushed himself off the chair, said his good-byes and shuffled on her arm from the room.

"Please, finish your tea," Yvette said. "I will only be a moment. I need to get him settled. He had a difficult summer."

The sound of shuffling feet faded down a corridor. At the click of a door lock, Claire stood and peered down the long hall. She crept down the corridor, silently opening and closing doors. The rooms were musty with high ceilings, lightly furnished, the walls heavy with old paintings of landscapes and portraits. She heard voices and hurried back to the salon, returning to face the windows. Yvette joined her a moment later.

The estate was laid out like a dramatic painting framed by the château's windows. They overlooked a grand parterre, coiling evergreen hedges inside two basins on either side of an extended central axis that led the eye all the way to the Marne River.

Yvette looked over to Claire. "You are interested in the gardens. You share Thomas' passion?"

At Claire's questioning glance, she continued. "For gardens?"

Claire remembered the long walks lost in Luxembourg garden. "Of course. I do. I am a florist myself."

"How appropriate."

Claire nodded, but her face must have shown her confusion.

"You don't know what he does?" Yvette looked doubtful.

"Well." Claire smiled. "It seems Grey learned everything

about me, but you know how secretive he can be when it suits him."

"Yes, he can be maddening." She turned to the window. "Thomas is a noted landscape architect. He has been commissioned to create gardens in Britain, New York and here in France. His expertise is in French gardens of a certain era."

"Le Nôtre," said Claire, without thinking.

Yvette smiled. "Yes, gardens based on André Le Nôtre's designs in the eighteenth century. He has told you more than you thought."

Claire turned away from Yvette and stared out over the landscape. Her chest ached. No wonder he loved meeting her in the Parisian gardens. It was the Paris he loved and he had shared it with her.

Yvette gestured toward the gardens. "It's a bit overgrown now, with Thomas traveling."

Claire's mind churned, her heart anxious. She had to search the place. If there was evidence, and she did not find it, people, including herself, would be captured, tortured and likely killed. Yvette and Peter may be in great danger. But she ached to know what this place was to Grey. What he had said about the American. She turned to Yvette. "I can't imagine growing up in a place like this. It must have been like living in a fairy tale."

"I had a privileged youth, although I didn't realize it at the time."

"How did Grey—Thomas—come to live here?"

Yvette gazed over the landscape, her attention far away. "My family was once considered important. As befitted my status, I was sent to the finest schools, traveled across Europe, associated with the best families. Then my grandfather, the Baron de Langon died. We learned, as did all of France, that the family was completely impoverished. The servants were sent away. I was sixteen and brought home from school. All that was left to the de Langon name was this château. Nothing more."

"What did you do?" Claire asked.

"I became a governess, employed by a family in England. An upper-class family with a young boy. The parents were cold, but Thomas—he was kind, warmhearted and so curious. When he turned nine, I got permission to bring him and his family's gentleman on a trip to the château for the summer. His gentleman was Peter." Yvette stopped, lost in the memories.

Claire stared at Yvette. A boy of a priggish family, destined to be more of the same. Into his young life saunters a beautiful, sophisticated Frenchwoman. Of course he was enchanted. Of course he changed his life. She was suddenly grateful to old de Langon for losing the family's wealth.

"These gardens were designed by Claude Desgotz, the nephew and pupil of Le Nôtre. But for years, this looked nothing like what you see today. My parents, then myself, hadn't the means to keep this up. By the time Thomas was grown, the château had fallen rather badly into disrepair."

Claire shrugged. "It looks amazing now."

"Thomas restored much of the gardens to their original state. He also created his own private gardens near the château. I believe Le Nôtre himself would enjoy this view." She turned to Claire, her schooled voice charged. "Of course, the last couple of years Thomas has been gone. To Paris. Other places. Perhaps, you know more about that than I?" Yvette's expression was polite, but her eyes searched Claire's.

"A bit," Claire said, her mind working.

"I would enjoy hearing about Thomas' life away from here." Yvette smiled, but Claire saw the worry in her eyes.

"I think Grey should tell you that."

Yvette sighed; she turned back toward the window. "It is impossible to get back to Noisiel this evening. There will be no train until morning. You will stay tonight."

"You are so kind," Claire said.

Claire helped Yvette prepare a simple dinner. Potatoes, a piece of beef from a neighbor down the road. For Peter, a broth. They ate in the salon; the small table pulled close to the fire crackling in the hearth. Yvette and Peter regaled her with stories about Thomas when he was a boy. The summer he decided to be a farmer and secretly bought a goat from a boy down the road. He kept it hidden and fed it grass and apples for nearly a month. His secret was discovered when they woke up one morning with the goat standing in the fountain on Neptune's head.

Claire soaked up the gentle stories and laughed alongside the pair. The warmth of their affection was like a fire on a cold night. "Grey was lucky to have you," Claire said as she mopped up the last bite of potato with a slice of bread.

Peter gazed at his wife, a smile in his eyes. "Yvette certainly did brighten up a number of lives. Before that, well, the Greys were cold fish. Then his father died and left Thomas to deal with the finances and help raise his baby sister."

"Mary Jane," Yvette said. "She was born when Tommy was nine."

"Did she come to France?"

Yvette stood. Stepping behind Peter, she repositioned the blanket wrapped around his waist. She squeezed his shoulders, her face tender. "No. Peter and I married in '21. Mrs. Grey didn't approve. We came back to live here year-round. Mary Jane was still too young to know us."

"And how is Mary Jane now?"

"She is well, we understand. She and her daughter, Abigail, have a nice home now outside of London. Away from the bulk of the bombing," Yvette said.

Abigail. A burst of warmth flowed up Claire's body. Grey's silence had been discretion for his sister's sake. The conversation flowed around her as she soaked up the information. A wartime indiscretion wasn't unheard of. But in that sort of family, it just might take a protective older brother across the channel to help.

He hadn't been untrue. The glow in her chest turned into an ache.

After dinner, Claire followed Yvette up the grand staircase to a small room, simple and spare. A bed and nightstand were tucked next to a compact marble hearth set with logs.

Yvette kneeled and coaxed the fire to life. "I apologize for the simple quarters. Thomas stays mostly in Paris now. Except for his rooms, we closed up this floor last winter. Heating . . ." She shrugged.

"I understand. Your home is magnificent. Thank you for letting me stay."

Yvette moved to leave then stopped. "It is Thomas who lets *us* stay. We couldn't pay; we would've lost this place. Thomas bought it. He couldn't bear to let it go." Yvette faced Claire. "He did mention *un femme américaine*. Not by name and without details. But when he spoke of her, he could not help but smile. He said her eyes were blue, like the ocean. Made to be drowned in. I know you are more than a friend." She reached for Claire, laid a warm hand on her arm. "Please, I must know. Where is he?"

"I'm sorry. I can't say."

Yvette's expression hardened. "Thomas is a good man. Whatever he is doing, it is because it is the right thing to do for us. For France. Tell me, do you do the right thing for Thomas? Will you?"

Claire held her gaze and forced herself to nod. But inside she felt her chest begin to throb.

Yvette exited the room. Claire leaned against the door, listening as the woman descended the stairs. After a moment, the faint light shining under her door faded to black and the only sounds were the creaks of the ancient house settling in for the night. She took the lit candle from her bedside and crept outside.

The hallway was black. Claire could see no more than the faint area surrounding the flickering flame. She remembered doors evenly spaced along the wall; hers was closest to the stairs. She felt her way along. A few steps later, her hand connected with the cold metal of a doorknob. The hinges squeaked as she peered in with the candle brandished high in front of her. Dust. A near-empty room. The furniture sold or burned for warmth. The next three doors opened more easily, but the contents were the same.

She found Grey's study behind the fourth door. Heavy velvet curtains thrown open, a full moon lit the room. It was a man's library. A leather chair waited behind a heavy wooden desk. Stacks of books lined the shelves that extended well above Claire's head. She walked over to his desk. On top, a silver-framed photo of woman. Blond, pretty in a perky way. She had Grey's steel-colored eyes but her sunny smile promised fun. She was hugging a soldier in uniform. Mary Jane, Claire presumed.

Claire searched through the contents of each drawer then slid her fingertips underneath the wooden frames. On the shelf there was a stack of thumbed-over volumes of the *Journal of Garden History*. She picked up a thick book, its pages stuffed with neatly written notes. She read the title, *Architecture de Jardins*. Nothing more than the normal everyday sort of clutter a cultured landscape architect might have in his library.

Claire padded to an oversized table near the window. Large sheets of vellum paper half the size of the tabletop were stacked on the hardwood surface. Ink pens stuck out from the top of a silver cup. Straight and arced rulers were shoved against the back corner. The bright moonlight illuminated garden layouts that had been painstakingly hand drawn with black ink. Large swoops and swirls, long straight lines, Claire imagined the gardens dreamed on these pages were beautiful but she couldn't make any sense of them. She needed her dreams to be flesh and blood, leaf and stone.

She walked through the door separating his study from his bedroom. His wardrobe was sparse with worn work clothes and a few conservative wool suits. Muddy work boots slumped on the wardrobe floor.

A large four-poster bed. She pictured him in it, with her in his arms. It would feel so luxurious after their stolen moments on the farm, soft sheets pulled up over them. She sat on the bed, ran her hand over the blankets.

"Tell me your secrets, Grey," she whispered and willed her mind to clear. Facing the room, she dropped to her knees, candle in hand. The small flame next to her face, she searched an inch at a time across the bedroom to the study.

She found the box an hour later. It was under loose bricks in the floor of the fireplace, beneath a coating of cinders. She blew ashes from the top and cracked open the lid as she settled back on the wood floor.

Sitting on top was a thin paper with three columns. Holding it close to the flame, Claire saw it was names of officers, ranks, the date they got to Paris, where they worked, and where they stayed. Most were in hotels, some had street addresses. Her eyes skimmed the page to the bottom. Von Richter—Sturmbannführer—SD—13.02.43—84, avenue Foch/Paris Ritz.

Her stomach churned as she realized the near misses she must have had with von Richter in the Ritz. Rolling the paper into a tube, Claire held it over the candle until it caught, tossed it in the fireplace and watched it burn.

The rest were snapshots. Claire riffled through, examining each in the candlelight. A worn photo of Laurent and Grey in graduation robes. They had serious, reserved mouths, but their young faces beamed. A later photo of Grey with a grin, his arm slung over a woman's shoulder, her face turned away from the camera. Claire felt a stab of jealousy, then recognized Odette's profile. Jacques, Odette and a dark-haired boy sat on a fountain's low limestone wall.

These were photos taken before the war. Too dangerous to expose but too precious for Grey to lose. She sat back and held the photos to her chest. These were a part of who Grey really was. The same as this house and the couple sleeping below.

She dropped the photos back in the container and, box gripped in her hands, sat heavily in his desk chair. What if Grey was gone forever? Her eyes were drawn out the window. The dark outlines in the landscape showed up against the moonlit sky like paper cutouts. Her gaze followed a line of hedges to a small open garden room with vine-covered stone walls. The glint of light marble revealed a statue of a woman against one wall. In the corner, an apple tree filled the sky.

Claire froze.

The garden from the photo. She would know it anywhere. Box in hand, Claire hurried down the stairs and slipped out of the house. She traced her way through the hedge maze until it opened up to a tall stone wall. She stepped through the opening.

Her eyes flicked around her. The statue. The tree. The roses that rambled up the hedge, pink and white. The stone bench, sitting in the shadow of an ivy-covered wall. She sank into the bench, taking in the garden with each breath. She had dreamed of this garden since that evening at Laurent's gallery show in New York. It led her to Laurent; it led her to Paris. She shut her eyes.

The garden delivered her to Grey.

The garden slept around her, like an enchanted maiden from a fairy tale. Grey's garden. His mind, his heart, was in every stone, every branch. Her voice, strong and clear, startled her in the night air. "I love him."

The flush of warmth was replaced by a fierce stab in her heart. The first time she'd said it and understood what it meant. But Grey was gone.

Her body began to shake and she slid off the bench. She clawed at the grass with her hands, sinking her fingers deep into the dirt until she'd dug a hole. Pain cramping her chest, she nestled the box into the earth and covered it with dirt. Leaning against the bench, she watched the garden wake as the moon arced over the horizon and the stars faded to an indigo sky.

The house was quiet as she climbed the stairs to her simple room. She stared at the bed, still made, and wondered at the alertness she felt. She looked into the small mirror over the dresser. Her cheeks were flushed, her eyes overly bright.

She found a slip of paper and a pen in the desk. *I will do the right thing for Thomas.* She signed it, *La femme américaine.*

* * *

Turning onto rue du Colisée later that morning, Claire's eyes lit on the blue awning of the flower shop. In the distance, the windows were dark, as though they didn't reflect the morning sun. Her pace quickened as she crossed the street.

The window panes were broken. The door hung off its hinges and leaned drunkenly against the frame. Claire gripped the knob, the metal felt cool in her hand. The blood pounded so loud in her ears she felt but couldn't hear the glass crunch beneath her shoes. She nudged the door aside and entered.

The sun lit the front half of the shop; the back lay in shadows. Trampled flowers and dented tin buckets were strewn everywhere. Claire's breath caught as she saw a dark shape on the floor behind the counter. She forced herself forward.

The shape she found was a heavy clay urn broken on its side, on top of a pile of broken roses. Relief made her lightheaded. Then she saw a large dark pool underneath the blossoms. Her gaze followed dark brown flecks splattered up the grey wall. About chest height, she saw them. Two small circles in the wall. She pushed herself off the floor, her fingers reached out and pressed into the broken plaster.

Bullet holes.

Claire pounded up the stairs and pushed through the broken bedroom door. Clothes and papers were scattered across the floor. The dresser facedown, the back cracked open. Mirror shards glinted crazily throughout the room.

Claire sagged against the wall, her eyes on Marta's suitcase open upside down on the floor. A small pink sock with ruffled edge stretched from under the broken latch.

"Claire. Come with me now." Dupré stood in the doorway.

His expression grim, he jerked his head toward the stairs and disappeared.

Claire pushed off the wall and stumbled after him down the stairs. At the back door, he peered each way then slipped out. She followed, her mind numb.

At the end of the alley, he saw her expression and reached for her arm. "For God's sake, Claire, be strong now."

They walked into the street as a strolling couple. Claire concentrated on keeping on her feet, only vaguely aware of where they were going. Another alley and then a dark squat building backed up to a passage, the heavy door covered in locks.

Dupré fiddled with a massive key and, one by one, the locks snapped open. He motioned her inside and closed the door behind them. "My warehouse."

The building was littered with crates, lit by a string of bulbs dangling from the low ceiling. Dupré slid through the space between a crate and the wall. On the other side, a small storeroom. Short empty crates were pulled up to a table. Three forms huddled together.

Georges saw Claire first, his face red and wet from tears. At his yelp, Marta turned. Her face was white, her lips pale. Anna was clutched to her, head buried in Marta's dress.

Dupré spoke first. "Yesterday afternoon, I sent Georges to the warehouse to retrieve boxes. He was barely gone when I heard shouting. Shots. I ran into the street. The police were in Madame Palain's shop." His mouth worked to spit out the words. "That *flic bâtard* who'd been hanging around held the pistol in his hand. Madame was—"

"He must have seen us, somehow. But we weren't there," Marta whispered.

"*Pape* didn't know I took Marta and Anna to see our

warehouse. It's not far. Madame said it was alright. But I wasn't there. I couldn't stop them," Georges said.

Claire put her hand on Georges' shoulder as Madame would have done. "If you were there, my Georges, you couldn't have helped. They would have hurt you too." She squeezed the girls against her. "Thank you, Georges. You saved Marta and Anna." She turned to Dupré. "What about Madame Palain?"

He shook his head.

"Did they take her?"

"*Non.*"

"Can I see her?"

He gritted his teeth, his face wrinkled in pain. "She is gone."

Her eyes held Dupré. He had been right, what he told her long ago. Her friend had paid the price for her trust. Pain stabbed deep in her chest. "I am so sorry," Claire said, but the words felt meaningless.

He turned toward Georges. "We will do what we can. You must take the girls and leave."

A fire raged inside Claire, burning hot and leaving ice in its wake. Her mind raced, clear and sharp; her eyes recorded every detail. Georges' breath. Anna's sobs. The pulse in Dupré's neck. "Stay here. We will leave after dark. I am going back to the shop."

"They are watching the street." Dupré caught her arm as she opened the door; his eyes sought hers. "I went in as soon as they left. She was holding on to life to speak. She said one thing. She said to tell you La Vie en Fleurs must go on."

In his eyes, Claire saw only pain, no recrimination. "How can I—"

"Madame's flower shop must survive."

Claire could not meet his gaze as she pulled her arm free and slipped out the door.

* * *

A block away, Claire found the man watching the shop. He leaned against a doorway three buildings down. She backtracked up an alley and slipped into the back door. He had seen her go in the front door an hour before. He would see her leave that way.

Claire raced upstairs, grabbed Marta's case and threw in all the girls' clothes she could find. Moving to the window, she peered out at the man below. He glanced up and she slid out of view. Cursing, she turned to the clothes piled on the closet floor and tossed a few in a bag.

At the rumble of a diesel engine, Claire rushed to the window. A heavy delivery truck rolled up the street. As it passed below in front of the shop, the man disappeared from view. Claire pushed open the window, reached out and grabbed the brick in the windowsill. She dropped to her knees against the wall as the truck moved forward, jewelry roll and bills clenched in her hand.

Glass crunched under her feet as Claire walked to the door. A corner of the garden photo stuck out among the mirror shards. Claire stared at it a long moment before she dusted off the glass and picked it up. The picture was scratched and torn nearly in two. She slipped it in her jacket pocket and stepped over the flattened blush rose in its shattered crystal vase.

For Grey. For the girls. She would find Albrecht von Richter.


Three shadows slipped through the darkened city. They crossed the Seine at pont Alexander III. Claire carried Anna; Marta gripped her suitcase as they moved south through back streets and alleys.

In the 14th arrondissement, at 12, rue Brézin, Claire motioned the girls inside a large apartment building. Up four floors in a cage elevator to number 42. A low knock and moments later the door opened a crack.

"It is Claire Badeau," Claire said, her voice low. "I'm sorry, but . . ."

The door swung open; wide eyes stared from the darkness. "Come in, quickly."

Two tired but frightened faces greeted them as they entered. Martin Oberon locked the door behind them, while Adele tied her robe and flicked on a small light.

Claire tried a smile but failed. "Monsieur, Madame Oberon, I am so sorry to come to you like this, but—"

Adele took one look at the girls. "*Mesdemoiselles*, give me your coats. Put down your bag. You look so tired, sit here on the sofa."

Marta nodded gratefully and Anna offered a tentative smile as they complied.

"Have you any toast?" Anna said.

"Anna," Marta scolded.

"I do have toast. You rest while we get you some." Adele looked meaningfully at Martin and Claire, who followed her into the kitchen.

Claire gestured to the girls in the next room. "I ask you a favor that is too great to ask, but I don't have a choice. They are Jewish and on the run. I am trying to get them out of France to a safe place."

"Their parents?" Adele said.

Claire shook her head in response. She glanced around at the simple kitchen, spare yet welcoming. "You can tell me to leave right now and we will go. I won't think any less of you. But I thought you might . . ."

A look between Martin and Adele. A conversation in a glance.

"Of course," Adele said. "They can stay with us, until . . ."

Martin nodded. "Until."

Claire let out a breath she hadn't realized she was holding. She felt nothing, she couldn't, but somewhere inside a piece of her pulled back from the abyss. "I will give you what I can." She reached for her purse.

"*Non,*" Martin said.

Claire pulled out all the money and ration cards in her wallet and handed them to Adele. "Girls need things."

Adele nodded and slipped the money in a robe pocket.

"Thank you," Claire said. "I will find a way to get them out. I will do what I can to help you until then."

"They will be cared for here." Martin grasped Adele's hand in his.

Claire hugged each girl tight on her way to the door, trying to show in her arms and her eyes what she couldn't say.

"Don't promise." Marta squeezed Claire tight. "Just come back."

The street was dark and silent as Claire stepped out of the building. Gulping in the cool air, she turned north. Toward the Ritz.

# Chapter 11

## THE NAZI'S MISTRESS

Place Vendôme. November 1, 1943.

A chill settled over the city as the shrouded sun dropped behind the horizon. A cold breeze that smelled of rain whipped fallen leaves across the open square in the Place Vendôme. Claire pulled her coat tight and glanced up at the mottled sky as the wind ripped at yesterday's issue of *Le Temps*, open on her lap.

She sat on the curb at the Place's north entrance on rue de la Paix, her gaze on the Ritz's front doors at the northwestern corner of the square. She made a show of stretching her legs and pressing the fluttering pages flat as the soldiers guarding the hotel's entry watched impassively.

After Claire left the Oberons' last night, she'd slipped through the darkened streets until curfew was lifted then checked into a small hotel in Saint-Germain. The place lacked charm, but it was cheap and also lacked an inquisitive front-desk staff. She paid for two nights then crawled up the stairs to her room. Rolling up in her coat on the rickety bed, Claire stared at a crack in the wall's plaster until the street outside came alive. Giving up on sleep, she splashed water on her face and stared into the clouded mirror over the sink.

She was alone, without a plan or resources. But she had a certain way with von Richter, and she knew how to find him. And, no matter the risk, she wasn't about to walk away from Grey or the girls.

Claire suppressed a shiver as she glanced back to the Ritz, scanning the street for cars. Von Richter had stepped out of a black sedan and entered the hotel nearly an hour before. From what he'd told her in New York about his vacations spent in Parisian cabarets, she knew he would soon be seeking the dark side of Paris' beauty as the weekend began. And she would make sure he found what he sought—and then some.

A gust of wind ripped the paper from her hands as sleet began to pepper her face. Claire shivered, pulling her knees close to her stomach and wrapping her arms around her legs. The tall colon-nade in the center of the square offered shelter, perhaps, beneath its elaborate verdigris surface, but she wasn't about to parade across the open pavement to get there. Another glance back at the hotel and Claire cursed. The soldiers at the hotel's entry eyed her with cool interest.

Claire stood stiffly and turned away from the square. Her face tucked into her collar, she hurried down the sidewalk. Icy wet pellets drummed against her bare head. An opportunity lost. Another night spent in that dank hotel staring at the cracked wall. She wanted to scream; instead she concentrated on the slick pavement beneath her feet.

"*Fraulein.*"

Claire froze, then turned to stare over her upturned lapel at two black sedans idling at to the curb. The driver's window in the first car was cracked open; he waved her closer with two fingers. SS skull-and-crossbones insignia were visible through streaks in the car's steamed windows. Claire shrugged her coat collar up higher.

"What is the way to Le Boeuf sur le Toit?" the driver said in halting French.

Claire stepped up to the car door, her eyes scanned the interior. The party inside the vehicle had already started. A bottle was being passed around, cigar smoke billowed through the window opening. One man faced the others, his back toward her. He was in the middle of a joke, it seemed; ashes fell from his waving cigar as he paused dramatically at their laughter. He turned toward the driver as he laughed, the visor of his cap hid his eyes, but a thin scar traced a line under his lip. Claire feigned a cough, her voice hoarse. "Avenue des Champs-Elysées to rue du Colisée."

The window rolled up as the first car pulled onto the street, the second car trailed behind. Claire let out a breath as they accelerated away. When the cars turned off the street, she began to run.

She remembered the feel of that scar under her fingers. *A duel,* von Richter had told her with some pride. She charged down the Métro stairs and ran toward the platform. It was 17:00, she would just have time to get to the hotel, change, and make an appearance at a certain Nazi-favored brasserie.

Blocks from La Vie en Fleurs, from a dark corner across rue Colisée, Claire watched a crowd of soldiers lounging in front of the entrance to the brasserie. The building was a modern jewel with sleek, hard lines, and Le Boeuf sur le Toit capitalized in Art Deco letters over the entry. A mass of officers crowded around a small table tucked beneath the overhang. The sleet had stopped. Heavy traffic trampled the icy pellets into dark patches of wet cigarette butts and trash.

A doorman in a white jacket held the coveted list, his haughty expression visible at a distance. You couldn't keep the Germans out of Paris, Claire thought with a grim smile, but you could keep a few of them out of your brasserie.

Claire shifted the heavy vase brimming with crimson ranunculus in her hands. She couldn't risk going to the shop so she'd purchased the flowers at a ridiculous price from the window of a jewelry shop on les Champs. Based on the doorman's sour expression, she'd made the right decision. Crossing the street, she backtracked and turned into an alley behind the restaurant. She steeled herself and marched up to the soldier guarding the back entrance.

He grimaced at the wind that ruffled the papers clutched in his hand. A glance at a worn tablet hanging on the wall next to him. "Badeau is not on the list."

"But you see right here I have a pass for flowers. The arrangements for tonight were made," Claire said, concern building in her voice.

He shook his head and motioned toward the alley with the flick of his thumb.

Claire pushed the flowers at him. "An SS kommandant paid 275 reichsmarks for this. A special party for his mistress. What will happen when he calls tomorrow and wants his money back? Shall I tell him to charge you?"

After a moment, he scowled and pushed the flowers back at her. "If you are lying, I will shoot you myself."

Claire bowed her head in a display of humility. *"Merci,"* she murmured as she hurried past. At this point a bullet was not an unexpected outcome. But she had higher aspirations tonight.

In the restroom off the back hall, Claire set the vase on a counter and inspected herself in the mirror. She looked like hell. Soaking wet, her hair was slicked against her head and her coat hung off her like a wet blanket. If the guard came searching for her tonight, he would be looking for a drowned rat. Not this, she thought slipping off her coat.

The diamonds at her neck caught the light like a thousand candles. Claire released the clip at her waist and the full volume of her creamy silk gown spilled over her legs, circling her feet. She pulled a pair of delicate grey pumps from her coat pocket and slipped them on her feet. A towel for her hair, a little brushing, a coat of red lipstick.

Claire examined the identification card in her hand. Claire Badeau stared back at her. *Parisienne.* Knowing. A spark of drama in her eyes. She slipped the card into her décolleté. Inspecting herself in the mirror, she willed her heart to numbness and arranged a smile. She broke the stem from a ranunculus blossom and threaded it behind her hair.

The card read Badeau, but Claire Harris Stone was back.

She dumped her coat and shoes in the trash. White-vested servers loaded with trays bustled past her as she paused at the doorway of the main dining room. Clusters of drinking officers, men in tuxedos and women in evening gowns stood at the mahogany bar and sat around tables. A pianist played from a glittering alcove. The room smelled of a decadent blend of roasting meats overlaid by tobacco.

She stroked the cool stones around her neck with the tips of her fingers. It was the kind of party she expected when she came to Paris. Before Madame Palain, before Grey.

The music was brisk, some sort of complicated waltz. She slowed herself down to half-time as she sauntered through the tables. A ripple of silence followed her to the bar.

The bartender leaned on his elbows, hands mechanically wiping a glass with white linen. His lined eyes were focused on the distance like a man who preferred to think he was someplace entirely different. He glanced at Claire, his gaze rested on her necklace for a second before returning to her face. "*Bonsoir, Madame. Bienvenue.*"

Claire bellied up to an open space at the bar. "*Merci. Ça va?*"

"Not too bad. What can I get you?"

"Champagne, please."

He nodded and reached below the bar. "A strange place tonight for *une Américaine*," he said, voice soft.

Claire smiled. "It is a strange place tonight for all of us, no?"

He smothered a grin as he poured. "*Oui*, Madame."

The champagne tingled all the way to her empty stomach. She turned to face the room, cocking her hip and slinging one bare arm on the bar. She inspected the men present. All were Wehrmacht, regular army. Von Richter wasn't in the room.

A towering captain stood at the end of the bar. His massive shoulders were shaped like a battering ram, his face red from drink. She caught his eye and let a pleased smile grow on her face.

There was a lot she didn't know about von Richter. His favorite drink, his favorite club. She sure as hell didn't know how that party boy ended up in the SD. But she did know that when it came to women, von Richter wanted what he couldn't easily have.

* * *

It was her second glass of champagne, the captain's second bottle, when von Richter's party finally arrived. Their drunken shouts and giggles drowned out the pianist as they swept into the mezzanine next to the bar. The group had grown; dancing girls had joined the officers. The women were wrapped in coats for the weather but still wore sparkling headdresses and heels.

Claire and the captain leaned against the bar, the better to be seen. He'd been a good choice. He spoke no French and didn't care that she didn't understand German. His face so flushed that his blue eyes stood out like beacons, he continued a story he had started thirty minutes ago. She didn't follow a word, but at von Richter's entrance, Claire laughed loud enough to be heard over the roar and stroked the soldier's brawny biceps.

Out of the corner of her eye, she noticed von Richter's approach. She slid closer to the captain, one hip pressed against his muscled thigh.

"Madame Stone," a voice said behind her shoulder.

Claire didn't respond. After a moment, the soldier's story trailed off into silence. She watched the scowl grow on his face before she turned around.

Von Richter faced her. "A long way from home, aren't you?" he said in English.

Claire responded in French. "I'm sorry, Monsieur, but you have mistaken me for someone else."

Von Richter replied in smooth French. "There are some things I don't forget."

"I am flattered to be considered so memorable, but I am not who you think I am."

The soldier looked between them. He frowned but didn't

speak, his eyes on von Richter's rank and SD insignia. A blonde, no more than sixteen, stumbled up behind von Richter.

She giggled as she slung an arm over his shoulder. "*Venez, mon beau gosse.*"

"Your little friend is lonely," Claire said.

The girl glared at Claire and burrowed against von Richter's back.

Claire traced the line of the captain's biceps, her eyes on von Richter. "We were just on our way out, weren't we, Kapitän? Someplace a little more . . . confidential."

Von Richter's eyes hardened as he glanced at the soldier.

"They're going inside without us." The girl tugged on von Richter's arm as the party filed down the hallway.

He shrugged, a small intrigued smile. "Forgive my mistake, Madame." He turned on his heel.

Claire watched him disappear behind a heavy wooden door, disappointment flaring inside her. Her mind worked as she finished her drink. Had she overestimated his interest in New York? No, she decided, remembering the hardness she felt dancing next to him that night.

The captain finished his third bottle in a swig and straightened up to his full height. He motioned toward the door and spoke. It didn't sound like a question, but she got the idea. She forced a smile and walked toward the exit.

A pale, hard-faced SD Lieutenant stopped them in the lobby. He spoke a few words to the soldier then turned to Claire. "Would the lady accompany me to the back room?"

The Wehrmacht captain spit out a curse and stomped into the darkness.

The lieutenant smirked and turned to Claire. He leads you to a room full of snakes, she thought, her palms sweating. She gave him a smile and walked, hips swaying, before him down the hallway.

The smoke-filled back room was swinging. A waiter with an armful of bottles ducked between drunken couples entwined on chairs, tables and the floor. Three women had shucked their coats and stood on a table, diamond-patterned panties glittering in the faint light. They clicked a rhythm with their dancing shoes while an officer sitting in a chair below stared up at them, his eyes half slits.

Von Richter inspected Claire from across the room. The blonde sat on his lap, wearing only ruffled pink panties and a garter belt, her arms wrapped around his shoulders, fingers in his hair.

Claire walked up to face him. "I feel overdressed," she said, her eyes on the girl.

"Then take off your clothes," he said with a smirk.

She didn't reply.

"What is the point of this game, Claire? You play with fire. I thought you were smarter." He absentmindedly stroked the girl's leg. She nuzzled his neck.

Claire inspected him. First she needed to get rid of that damn girl. She shrugged. "Ah, Alby darling, if you insist on pulling skeletons out of closets, at least pour me something."

He shoved the girl off his lap and stood. "Champagne, then," he shouted to the waiter. "And a private table."

A table against the wall was cleared; two chairs placed side by side. Claire and von Richter sat as the waiter placed a bottle and two glasses between them. Von Richter turned his chair to face hers, his eyes on her as he played with an unlit cigar.

Claire ran her hand over his insignia on his uniform sleeve. "My, Alby darling, haven't you become important."

He smiled and pulled the cork. "When I last saw you, you were in New York."

"The last time I saw you there was plenty of scotch involved. I saw at least two of you. And you were all very grabby."

"We are known for that." He lit his cigar.

"It's your fault I'm here. Your stories of Paris lured me."

"You hadn't heard?" He gestured with his cigar at the room full of soldiers.

"This is Paris. The good times don't change."

He nodded, his eyes on a woman who walked by, nude except for a man's leering face painted on one butt cheek. "Only who enjoys them." He looked back at Claire, his eyes hardened. "So, what about the name?"

"What name?"

"Stone. Why the deception?"

Claire ran a hand over her diamonds; let her fingers rest lightly against the curve of a breast. "No deception. A fresh start, I call it."

He sat back and puffed on his cigar. "Giving a false name to a German soldier is a crime."

Claire forced a smile. "I've learned certain skills in Paris. I can give the *right* German soldier a few things that would be considered criminal—in more civilized countries." Claire drained her glass. "I don't think he'd mind."

He reached out and gripped her necklace, tugging her toward him. "So what should I call you?"

"Claire Badeau."

"French?" He looked surprised.

Claire shrugged, let herself drift closer. "A husband—briefly. French."

"Another husband? You move quickly."

"You did business with Russell. How easy do you think it was to get away from him? With the name Stone, I get on a list and *poof*, I am back in New York."

Von Richter laughed.

Claire started. "What is it?"

"You don't know, do you?"

"Know what?"

He smiled. "Russell Stone is dead. I would offer you my condolences, but I don't think you need them."

Russell was dead? Claire struggled to find an emotion for her husband. She felt nothing. His face was fuzzy, indistinct, like a faded photo. "How do you know?"

"Our steel contract was severed. I inquired as to why." He smiled and refilled her glass. "Stupid of you not to stay with him longer. You'd be a wealthy woman today."

Claire shrugged. "I got what I wanted and I moved on."

"To Badeau?"

"Badeau was handsome, French; he knew people. He was a fresh start."

Von Richter's eyes remained suspicious, but he looked intrigued. "Was?"

"The war. He didn't last long." Claire drank, allowing for a suggestion of sadness. She leaned back in her chair, letting her legs rub against von Richter's. A broad smile. "But I find there are perks to being a widow. What do I care about a man's war? I am a woman, Alby darling. I make do."

"You certainly do."

A waiter brought another bottle of champagne.

Claire slid in close and traced her fingers down his uniform buttons. "Have you conquered those clubs you once told me about?"

"I am working on it. It takes time and"—he grinned—"utmost concentration."

She had to get him out of this brasserie, not just to the back-seat of one of those black sedans, but inside—deep inside—the Ritz. Licking her lips, she leaned in close. "I am sure you are an unrelenting conqueror." She pressed her mouth to his ear, her mind flashed to a flower arrangement that Madame Palain had taught her. "You have experienced *Le Lis Enchaîné*?"

"No." His brow furrowed.

She laughed as if she were shocked he would miss something so delicious. She ran her fingers over her necklace, let them rest against her breasts, as her mind raced. "You will need two silk scarves, a fine cigar, three bottles of champagne and a very knowledgeable, willing woman."

He faced her, his eyes burning. "Just one woman?"

"You must learn to walk before you run," she said.

He captured her hands and pulled her close. His hand slid down her leg. A sigh. "No stockings to remove. Sad."

Claire placed her hand over his and moved it to the warm inside of her thigh. "We will have to think of something else for you to do with your teeth."

Von Richter gestured to the lieutenant who had retrieved Claire from the lobby. "*Mein auto,*" he said, gesturing toward the door.

The lieutenant smothered a frown and disappeared. He re-appeared a moment later. Claire and von Richter followed him into the brasserie lobby.

"Sturmbannführer von Richter." A stout officer stepped up to them, a thin woman at his side. "You are leaving?"

Von Richter nodded. "An important matter calls for my attention."

The man examined Claire's body in the thin silk, his gaze caught in the curve of her breasts. His lips turned up in a thin smile.

Claire stared at the woman next to him. Mean eyes, small mouth. They recognized each other at the same moment.

"Madame Sylvie Olivier," Claire said, before she could speak. "How enchanting to see you again."

Sylvie stared at Claire's necklace. "How did you get in here?"

Claire felt her face go hot. Forcing a smile, she snuggled tight against von Richter. "Perhaps you can ask to review the guest list next time."

"Goodnight, Kapitän." Von Richter pulled her against him as they stepped out into the cold night air. "Interesting acquaintance you have, Claire."

"Mmm," Claire agreed, her attention on von Richter's hand sliding below the curve of her back.


Von Richter tasted Claire from her lips to the vee of her dress before the car pulled up in front of the Ritz. The soldiers that had stared at Claire earlier that day offered sharp salutes as the couple stepped through the arched stone doorway into the hotel.

He steered Claire toward tall golden columns at the bottom of a staircase. The soldier standing guard saluted von Richter, his eyes moving discreetly to the floor as Claire passed. At the top of the stairs, von Richter glanced over his shoulder then looked to her with some pride. "Only officers of the Reich may occupy the Vendôme building of the Ritz. The decomposing remains of Parisian high society are stuck in the back against the Cambon."

Claire thought of the parade of jackboots down this long

hallway and swallowed the bad taste in her mouth. The walls seemed to narrow as they walked. Von Richter's hand slid lower.

He stopped in front of the third door, one hand fumbling with the keys, the other hand on Claire. The door opened and he pulled her inside the foyer. A phone rang.

He released her with a sigh. "One moment."

Claire stepped into the salon, her eyes taking in every detail. She passed an antique desk and chair in Louis XVI style and walked toward the windows. The skyline of Opéra Garnier was visible in the distance. She glanced at a stack of papers on the desk; the top sheet dated that day. A list of names followed by numbers, then in the last column, initials. *Ml, MV, Fs, Verkehr.* A signature line at the bottom awaited von Richter's hand. Could those initials be the prisons, Montluc, Mont-Valérien, Fresnes? What was *Verkehr*? Hope bubbled inside her. A trail to find Grey.

Von Richter hung up the phone behind her and met her at the window, sliding his hands down her sides to the slit of her dress. He kissed the side of her neck. "Nice view, isn't it?"

Her resolve hardened. "Hmm," Claire said, allowing herself a small smile.

"Tell me about this *Le Lis Enchaîné*," Von Richter said.

Claire lifted her dress. "Step one."


The room was black, heavy shades drawn tight. Claire slid from the bed and crawled on all fours to the salon. She felt her way to the door, slipped inside then pushed it shut behind her. Sitting on the desk chair, she felt for the matches she'd seen earlier, found one and lit it.

The diamonds she wore glittered in the light against her bare skin. She moved the flame until she saw the pile of papers.

Lighting a candle, she peeled open the stack of forms, scanning each one. A week of what she thought might be prisoner transports, memos in German. But no mention of Thomas Grey. She sat back and closed her eyes, shouted at the ache in her groin. She knew Grey had to be alive. And she'd find him.

In the meantime, she'd be a good spy.

Claire pulled out a pen and hotel stationery. She began to write in clear small letters. She had completed the page when she heard von Richter stir. In one movement, she blew out the match, grabbed the notepad and replaced the paper on the stack. On her knees, she found her dress thrown over the sofa and slipped the page beneath it. A moment later, she slid back in bed, heart racing, as she listened to von Richter's slow breath.

The next morning before light, Claire pulled on her dress, tucked the paper inside the lining and, shoes in hand, headed for the door.

"Where are you going?" Von Richter sat up in bed, his mouth petulant.

Claire went back and kissed him long and hard on the lips. "Miss me already?"

He wrenched her to him and jerked the dress over her head. Claire palmed the paper as it slipped free. Her free hand reached down beneath the covers, grasping him tight, as she slid the note between the mattresses.

He smacked her on her buttocks then threw her on her back on the pillows. "I didn't say you could leave yet." He reached between her legs.

His roughness made it easy to shut down, to arrange her body as she would a doll. Her goading whispers in his ear hurried him. She had a delivery to make.

Afterward, von Richter smoked a cigarette from bed as he watched her dress. "I know your type, Claire. Your French husband may have left you a few centimes, but a woman like you doesn't stay alone."

She gave her best enigmatic smile, body tensing for his next words.

"He is married isn't he? He keeps you on the side, an apartment near a Métro station. He comes by in the afternoon on his way home from work."

Claire sat on the bed, bent over to slip on her shoes and slide the paper back into her dress. He had Claire Harris Stone pegged alright. Once upon a time that man might have been Laurent, the Comte, anyone. "You got a better offer, Alby darling? What would your Führer say?" She turned toward the door. "We had a night. A very, very good one. That's all it can be."

Von Richter caught up with her in the foyer. He pulled her against him, spoke into her hair. "I am a Sturmbannführer. I can have whatever or whoever I want. Don't forget that." He pressed his lips hard against hers until she softened in his arms. "Bring your things this afternoon. Lieutenant Schneider will take you to your room—on the Cambon side." He reached for the phone. "The lieutenant will escort you to the door."

The sky was scrubbed to a clear blue and the air smelled fresh, with just a hint of last night's storm. Claire forced herself to take a leisurely route to the dentist's office to drop off the note, keeping an eye behind her and doubling back twice. She made a show of considering the play in the theater next door before she slipped the note in the dentist's box without stopping.

In her mind, she was cataloguing what she'd seen in von Richter's study the night before. She knew she'd be able to find something of value. Grey's voice, wry and low, came from the recesses of her mind. *Don't get greedy, my little spy.*

Her heart ached. She paused in front of a store window. Her reflection stared back at her. *Haunted* was what she would call that face. She willed her features to smooth, her eyes turned to glass. They see weakness and you're dead, she told herself. And so is Grey. She took one last look behind her and boarded the Métro for her hotel. It was time to move up.


Lieutenant Schneider met her at the Ritz concierge desk off rue Cambon, his face impassive, eyes cold. Without a word, he took her bag and led her down the corridor. An elevator to the third floor, at the end of a hallway. He opened the door, set her bag inside and handed her the key. "The Sturmbannführer asked you to notify me should you need anything." He turned on his heel and left.

Her breath caught in her throat as she stepped inside her room. Ceiling-to-floor windows overlooked the gardens below with leafy trees shading a long grass *alleé*. A delicate chandelier hung over the bed, a gilded mirror rested over a white vanity. Claire dropped her bag and slid onto the four-poster bed that seemed to welcome her. Suddenly feeling her lack of sleep, she examined the pale butter walls through half-closed eyes. Blue curtains were gathered with silk rope; the floor was carpeted in flowers the color of sky. Her eyes closed and her head sank into the pillow. She couldn't help it.

She felt Grey's arms around her. She couldn't help that either.

* * *

Von Richter didn't come that night. *A major operation,* Schneider told her when he called. Claire spent the night staring at the dark outline of buildings and the street below. A major operation against who, she wondered. She woke the next morning with a churning stomach. Throwing off her blankets, she dressed and left the hotel.

On the watch for Odette, Claire took a long walk that ended at parc Monceau. A heavy-set man in a long coat trailed her the whole distance. He moved like a bull, confident, his attention focused ahead, and tossed a half-smoked cigarette onto the ground without a thought. Only Gestapo would waste precious tobacco that way. She threw bread crumbs to the birds and went back to her room to brood.

Schneider knocked on her door that afternoon. Averting his eyes from her thin silk robe, he spoke. "The Sturmbannführer will take you to the opera tonight. He asked if there was anything you needed."

Claire could feel the disdain radiating from the lieutenant. She let her robe slip open an inch. "Please give the Sturmbannführer my thanks. I require a new opera dress. And hat. And gloves."

The afternoon was spent on les Champs. Schneider bought the dress, midnight blue with a nipped waist and a thin deep vee with gathers over the breast. A matching hat tipped forward on her forehead, topped with a silver feather. She decided against gloves but *required* a fur stole.

If von Richter was going to make her wait, he should know he would pay.

Schneider doled out the money, but his eyes burned. Claire slid her hand down his arm and smiled as he picked up the wrapped boxes. He walked two paces in front of her back to the hotel.

That evening, a driver dropped von Richter and Claire in front of the Opéra Garnier next to a wooden pole bristling with German signs. Von Richter took her arm, cutting through the crowd toward the theater entrance.

He examined the women hanging on to milling officers, then glanced down at Claire's dress. "You did well today."

"All for you." She ran her fingers over the diamonds. "Consider it a gift for you to unwrap."

They passed beneath stone arches and entered the foyer. An usher led them up a glittering marble staircase. Claire stared as they stepped into a box overlooking the auditorium. They were on the second level; there was one more above to the high-domed ceiling. The walls were covered in gold, the stage impossibly far away.

"You like it?" von Richter said as they settled into red velvet seats in the front.

"It's spectacular." The awe in her voice was real.

He touched the diamonds nestled between her breasts and let his fingers slide down to her thighs. "Tell me this is why you came to Paris."

The smile froze on her face. She would have come here with Grey. She'd have worn a flower in her dress lapel, something simple and refined, chosen by Madame Palain. It felt as though the world had split in two. The Paris she dreamed of. And what was. She pressed against von Richter. "This is why I came to Paris."

The seats filled in around them, then the floor below. German men in uniforms and business suits. The suits weren't less dangerous, just more discreet. Some of the women were French, judging by their look. A few sturdier women, their expressions all business, Claire pegged to be German.

The room dimmed, lit only by a giant chandelier hanging from a painted dome and a circle of glowing lights. A burst of sound, with the trill of violins crashing over a low rolling bass. The curtain rose, revealing the dark timbers of a building, a woman tending the fire burning inside. A warrior limped in and began to sing in German to the woman.

"What is happening?" Claire asked von Richter.

He turned from his survey of the crowd and ran his hand over her thigh. "Siegmund. Kinky fellow. Full of brotherly love."

At intermission, they joined the crowd from the upper boxes in the Grand Foyer, a long hall with glossy marble floors, painted ceilings and heavy chandeliers.

"Sturmbannführer von Richter," a voice called out and a group of officers approached.

A server in a white coat offered glasses of champagne on a silver tray. He leaned into Claire as he handed her a flute. "A friend awaits you."

"Where?" Claire said under her breath.

He tilted his head toward a side door. "Go left."

"I need to powder my nose. Don't forget me," Claire said to von Richter with a wink. He nodded and turned to the officers.

The door opened into a long hall. Claire passed by two servers loaded down with trays, then paused, a glance back, then descended a long set of stairs. The air turned chill and damp. The walls were heavy stone, marked with writing, and cold under her hand. She shivered as the stairs ended at a small room, the far side shrouded in darkness.

"*Bonsoir*, Evelyn." Odette stepped from the gloom.

"You took your sweet time to contact me, Danielle."

"You must leave Paris," Odette said. "While you still can."

"Didn't you look at my message? You have to figure out those codes, what they mean."

Odette shook her head impatiently. "Information is being leaked to the SS. We will find and plug that leak. But right now, we cannot risk your knowledge of us getting to the Nazis. You must go."

"I'm inside the Ritz, Odette. Where you wanted me to be. What I passed to you is just a taste."

"Your Nazi, von Richter, is *Sicherheitsdienst*. Nazi intelligence. He points, the Gestapo kills. You will be forced to choose between Grey and a man who holds your life in his hand. You will compromise us all with him."

"Grey could be on a list. Or others. I have to take the chance."

"Christophe won't allow you to proceed," Odette said.

"Grey needs your help. I am offering you a real chance. You are going to walk away from that and turn your fight against me?" Claire fought the urge to shake her.

"They will stop you."

Claire turned back toward the stairs.

Odette's voice echoed off the stone walls. "You endanger everyone you know, everyone you touch. This is your warning. Your only warning. If you don't leave now, you are on your own, you understand?"

The sheets tangled around Claire's legs as she traced lines on von Richter's bare back with the soft tip of her silk stocking. He leaned off the side of his bed, pouring a glass of scotch from a half-empty bottle.

Claire felt as though she were made from glass. Her heartache bled through to her skin. It was good von Richter was damn drunk.

"You've gone too quiet. Entertain me," he said.

Claire crawled onto his back, wrapping the stocking around them both. "I was wondering, Alby, how you got to be here."

He took a long drink and wiped his mouth with the back of his hand. "I told you long ago. There is a thing about this town and the women."

Claire took the glass from his hand and drank. "You're too handsome to need a uniform, Alby. And rich. They would spread their legs for you anyway. Why this?" She gestured at his uniform crumpled on the floor.

He frowned, took back the glass, refilled and drank again. "I cared nothing for Hitler's party. They are too serious, too sacrificing. But what could I do? I was going to get pulled in one way or another. In Germany, one must participate." With an arm, he swept her off his back and rolled over to face her. He raised his glass to her. "This way I came to Paris. My dirty factories are chugging along in Saxony and churning out money, without me." He leaned in to kiss her. "Like you, I came here for pleasure."

"What happened to your partner, Merkel? Is he stuck in the factories?"

He shrugged and dropped the empty glass. The heavy crystal thudded as it hit the carpet. "Come to find out, his grandfather was a Jew."

Claire's stomach turned. She forced a smile and pushed him onto his back, straddling him, then reached for the bottle. She welcomed the burn that slid down her throat like a flaming bomb. Better to feel that than the chill that cramped her chest.

You don't get to kill Grey too, she told him silently. She slid her hand between his legs.

When the empty bottle lay abandoned on the floor and von Richter's heavy snore filled the room, Çlaire slipped from the bed and padded silently toward his study. Closing the door softly behind her, she lit a candle and moved toward the desk. The night outside was black, the moon a sliver. She had time.

The night passed with Claire examining every paper in the study for any indication of Grey. She gave up as traffic began to flow outside the window. Every honk, every rumble, made her heart race. She crawled in bed, her nerves brittle.

The ring of the phone jangled too loud in the sunlit room. Von Richter moaned and rolled over beside her. A mumbled German curse and he reached for the receiver. "Of course. Come by at 9:00. We will talk." Dropping the receiver in place, he rolled from bed. "Duty calls. Get out now, my luscious *schlampe*."

Claire only stretched, curving her body toward him. She wasn't going anywhere without seeing what this was about. "You smell like a dead bum, *mein Sturmbannführer*. Let me bathe you."

He threw her dress at her and jerked on his pants. "You are leaving. Dressed or not. Your decision."

A theatrical sigh and Claire reached for a stocking. She was dressed and at the entry when the door reverberated with a light knock. Glancing back, she saw von Richter bent over the bed slipping on his boots. He hadn't heard.

"Go." He strode into the bathroom. Water splashed in the sink.

Claire reached for the knob.

The Comte de Vogüé stood in the doorway, his eyes flicked open wide.

A gasp escaped her mouth. She heard von Richter walk in the room. *"Entrez,"* she said.

He examined her, a soft smile, and he entered.

Von Richter offered the Comte a tight smile. "Good morning."

"We haven't been introduced," the Comte said, his eyes boring into Claire.

"Comte de Vogüé, this is Madame Badeau." Von Richter opened the door wide for her to leave.

Her gaze was glued to the Comte's face.

*"Enchante."* He reached for her hand and held it tight as he brushed his lips against her skin.

"Madame Badeau is just leaving," von Richter said and turned to his desk.

The Comte pulled Claire toward him. "You play with fire," he whispered in her ear then kissed her cheek. *"Au revoir,* Madame. I hope to see you again. Soon."

"Madame Badeau," von Richter said, the impatience clear in his tone.

*"Au revoir."* Claire sucked in a deep breath as she stepped into the hall. She didn't know if she should run for the exit or dress for lunch. She pressed her ear to the wood.

*Américaine?* the Comte said.

*They should start getting used to real men between their legs,* von Richter said with a laugh.

She slid from the door as she heard the creak of hobnailed boots in the hallway. *Soon,* the Comte said. She didn't know his game, but she would play along, if that was what it took. If not, then she just had to make sure he died first. She strolled past the soldiers toward the stairs. Her olive skirt and jacket for lunch, then.

### Place Vendôme. July 12, 1944.

A soft rain tapped the awning in front of the Ritz. Claire pulled her coat tight as she stepped out onto the sidewalk, nodding at the soldiers positioned on each side of door. The sun had dipped behind the rooftops, leaving the square in misty blue-toned shadow.

Claire waited for von Richter's car. Another evening hung up at the SD office on avenue Foch, he was already an hour late for the dinner and show at Le Bal des Etoiles. The breeze was perfumed with blooming chestnut trees. *It smells of summer, Claire. No army can stop that,* Madame Palain told her last year when the trees blossomed on their street. It had been a beautiful day, the shop windows glowing with a golden light. Madame's arms had been full of jasmine. The memory dug into Claire's chest. She sighed and tugged on the waistband of her yellow silk dress, reflexively checking the seams of her silk stockings.

She needed a drink.

Last night she'd dreamed of Marta and Anna again. Claire never saw their faces, only heard them. Sobbing. Keening. She awoke sweating in her sheets, her eyes swollen. She was dressed and in her coat before she convinced herself not to go see them. *You endanger everyone you know, everyone you touch,* Odette had said. Now on the street she thought of Madame and her eyes ached. I just need to get out, a little music, she scolded herself.

Her body tensed as she watched a burly dark-haired man striding on the opposite sidewalk. A resemblance to Jacques, but when he turned onto the street, she saw a long thin face she didn't know. She released her held breath.

Claire saw Jacques once last winter after Odette's warning, as she walked along the Champs-Elysées. He was waiting for her in a doorway. He made sure she saw him but said nothing, his face hard. She understood the message, and on ration day before Christmas, Claire rode the Métro to the 14th arrondissement and found Adele Oberon in the ration line on rue Brézin. Claire said nothing but slipped one last message and a pile of francs and reichsmarks in Adele's shopping bag before she walked away. Then the dreams began.

Claire watched the rain drip from the leaves of chestnut trees and puddle onto the cobblestones. Bullets couldn't stop summer's sweet offering. But the sky wept for Madame Palain.

"He's put some meat back on your bones."

Sylvie shrugged on a jacket as she scrutinized Claire from silk dress to strappy heel. Claire stared at the street. She wasn't in the mood to trade jabs today. Together they watched von Richter's car approach.

Sylvie leaned into Claire's ear. "Enjoy it while it lasts."

The car door opened. Claire slipped in next to von Richter.

He scowled at Sylvie as they accelerated into traffic. "What was that foolish woman talking about?"

Claire watched Sylvie out of the rear window until she disappeared from sight. She smiled at von Richter, slid over onto his lap. "She said you were making me fat."

He raised his eyebrows. "At Le Bal des Etoiles, I will be the judge." He squeezed her thigh.

The cabaret had already started when they were shown to their table. On the stage, women in garters, hats and little else rode carousel animals to a jaunty circus tune. The smoke-filled room was packed with German soldiers on their *Tour Paris*. Claire drank deep at her scotch as von Richter rested a hand on her leg. She blew him a kiss.

Three hours and too many drinks later, the music ended. The soldiers in front called for more and pounded empty bottles on their tables. Von Richter laughed at them, finished a desultory cigarette and pulled Claire to her feet. The couple joined the crowd emptying the theater and teetered toward the exit.

Claire leaned against von Richter, her body pleasantly numb, her mind fully occupied with staying upright. Still, she noticed the soldiers watching her, the yellow silk cut tight and low against her skin. Whispers, gazes like wolves, but von Richter's uniform earned a wide berth.

Their car waited out front, headlights nearly invisible through the pounding rain. The driver waited at the entrance with an umbrella. Claire's dress was soaked when she stumbled into the backseat.

They pulled onto rue Victor Massé and von Richter gave the driver an order in German. The driver glanced at Claire in the mirror. A quick nod. Passing headlights spun around her. The air was thick with cigarette smoke, and the drink churned in her stomach. She wished she could roll down the window. She closed her eyes.

The driver pulled into a dark alley and killed the engine. Claire opened her eyes as the driver unbuttoned his uniform jacket. He lit a cigarette.

Von Richter leaned into her, gripped her shoulder strap with one hand then yanked. The thin fabric tore away.

"Alby," Claire said, trying to shove him back. "I just bought this."

He pushed her down onto the seat, gripped the bodice and ripped.

"*Merde*, Alby," Claire said through gritted teeth, pushing against him.

His face spun above her. She heard his zipper. Her legs were forced open. He was clumsy, too drunk. He whispered hoarsely in German as he entered her.

She leaned her head back, trying to keep her dinner down. Upside down, she watched rivulets of water run up the rear window. The driver's eyes watched in the rearview mirror. A surge of anger and she swung her arms. He deflected her with an elbow, and her knuckles smacked something under the seat. A briefcase. Her heart began to pound.

Von Richter finished, grunted and pulled away. He sat back in the seat, his pants half-open. Another command to the driver. *Zigaretten und alkohol.* The driver started the car and pulled back onto the street. A few blocks later, they stopped in front of a brasserie. The driver pounded on the door until it opened. He disappeared inside.

Claire pulled at the shreds of her dress around her, her eyes out the window. She had seen the briefcase twice before on his desk. And both times found it empty. But tonight, here it was. Straight from his office.

Von Richter closed his eyes. His voice trailed off to a snore. Another breath, Claire watched the brasserie. The driver was still inside. She plucked a matchbook off the seat and slid onto her knees on the floorboards. She glanced back at von Richter. His eyes were closed, head tipped back. She flipped open the case's leather flap and slid out the contents. Von Richter's boot moved next to her. She froze. Another snore. She lit a match.

The top of the pile was *Signal*, the Nazis' version of *Life* magazine. Beneath, a typed form with a column of items and a column of numbers, with lines for signatures. A request form. She struggled to make out the words. *Opel Blitz. Quantity 11.* Heavy transport trucks, she'd seen them hauling soldiers. *Division der SS.* Soldiers then, too. But it was the words written across the bottom that caught her eye. *Fort Montluc zu Compiègne. 23/07/44.* She knew those places. Both prisons. A convoy then, prison transport.

Her hands shook as she flipped the page. A list of names. Another match lit and she skimmed the print. *Kinsel, Raymond.* They had captured Christophe? She got to the bottom of the page. That was all.

Von Richter shifted and exhaled. Claire shoved the papers into the briefcase. No, she protested silently. Another match flamed. She pulled the pages out and reread the names, one by one. The match burned her fingers as she flipped the page over. Five more names were listed. *Grey, Thomas Harding* was the last.

Outside, a door slammed. She shoved the papers into the case and slid onto the seat as the driver opened the door.

Von Richter opened his eyes and sat up, zipping his pants. *"Zigaretten."* He lit a cigarette then reached for the bottle. "Drink?" He tipped the bottle toward Claire.

She shook her head and slid her trembling hands beneath her. Grey was alive. The engine started, they pulled into the street. Von Richter drank, she turned to stare out into the rain. In eleven days, Grey would be outside prison walls. He could be rescued.

The bottle was half-empty when they pulled up in front of the Ritz. Von Richter leaned on her shoulder through the lobby, his briefcase swinging loosely in one hand. At the base of the stairs, he pushed Claire against the wall and ran a finger down bare skin. Claire forced herself to look up into his eyes and smile. He pressed his lips against hers.

"Duty," he said regretfully, thumping the case. He smirked at the soldier standing guard then laboriously worked his way up the stairs.

The sentry stared at the skin revealed by Claire's ripped dress. She spun and hurried down the long corridor to her room. Turning on the water in the bath and stripping down, she climbed in and began to scrub.

She stared at a small round burn on her shoulder. Von Richter's cigarette. She hadn't felt it. She laid back in the bath, submerged up to her face. It was worth it. Grey was alive.

She remembered Odette's words. *You are on your own.* Her body tremored. What if the Resistance wouldn't help?

They will help, she said silently. Water drained off her as she stepped out of the tub. Still dripping, she walked into the bedroom and over to her desk. She pulled out a pad of stationery; a crown decorated the top.

*I found Christophe. Noon in front of the pool by the temple to discuss price.*

*Evelyn*

The Resistance had turned away from her. But they wouldn't abandon Kinsel. Or Grey.

Claire made the drop at first light. Café Raphael across from the dentist was closed. She didn't wait and turned back toward her hotel. She had been counting on this news for the last few months. Grey was alive.

Lost in thought, she turned off Faubourg Saint-Honoré onto rue du Colisée, her feet making their way to their old home. Claire looked up to a tattered blue awning flapping in a brisk summer breeze over Madame Palain's flower shop. Claire froze, the image burned onto her mind. Only the words *La Vie* remained. The dark windows were boarded shut. Her chest aching, she turned and hurried back to the hotel.

In her room, Claire dressed carefully in a dark grey suit, matching pillbox hat and black heels. She stood in front of the mirror and tipped her hat forward over her curls. The woman staring back had the body and face men enjoyed. But her eyes were ice.

She took a long route, up boulevard Haussmann to rue de Monceau. Turning onto rue Rembrandt, she entered parc Monceau. The air was sweet with the smell of blooms. Lush greenery invited a stroll, a quiet picnic, more. She thought of Grey, of his body enveloping hers in the grass. She plucked a white rose blossom from a bush and tucked it into her lapel.

She turned onto a narrow curving lane. She paused, her gaze on the hedges surrounding the large oval pool. The skin on her neck began to prickle. No one to be seen, but she knew what it felt like to be watched.

Across the pool were the tall marble columns, wrapped in ivy. Claire's stomach churned as she stared into the murky pool, rubbed her clammy hands on her jacket.

"Bonjour, Claire."

She turned. Jacques leaned against a twisting tree trunk, cigarette in his hand.

"You mean Evelyn."

He shrugged. "It's a bit too late for that between us."

"Perhaps. But not for Kinsel. Or Grey."

He faced her in two fast strides, his body inches from hers. "Who?"

"You know where I've been," she said. "What I've been doing—"

"Who you've been fucking."

"It paid off. I know where your precious Kinsel is and I know where he is going."

"Why did you say Grey just now?"

"Because they are together. Kinsel and Grey," she said.

He looked over her shoulder and took a drag from his cigarette.

The fear in Claire snapped. "Don't you care? Grey is your friend. I've seen photos of him with your son." When she took a breath, she realized she had been yelling. Her cheeks were wet.

He pulled the cigarette from his mouth, started to speak then stopped.

She wiped her eyes. "I know you don't care about me. Not anymore. I did what I had to do. For Grey and for those girls. And I found him."

"In the note you said there was a price for Kinsel."

"Yeah. There is. Get Grey too."

"That all?"

"No."

He smirked.

"I want two transports on an escape line out of here."

"For you and who else? This German?" He dropped the cigarette on the ground and carefully snubbed it out with his boot. Finally he looked up at her. "Odette didn't come today because she refused to do what was necessary. What was ordered."

Claire's body went cold.

"You demanded payment to help the Resistance. You survived

unharmed when Grey was captured. You live like a queen with Nazi scum, you said to find Grey, but we were betrayed again. And this time, we lost Kinsel and seven good men. Maybe you are a traitor; maybe you are greedy. I cannot say. But you have become too great of a risk." He reached into his jacket pocket and pulled out a pistol. "I am here to end this."

She stared him straight in the eyes. "A prison transport. They are in Montluc. They are going to be transported to Compiègne on July twenty-third. There will be eleven transport trucks, at least sixty-five prisoners. I don't know how many soldiers. But that will be your chance. You have to do it." Her body tensed in anticipation of a bullet.

He held the gun steady, his finger against the trigger. But Claire saw uncertainty in his eyes.

"You're right. I'm not a good person. No one should do the things I've done. But someday this goddamn war will end. And it won't matter who we killed if we didn't save those we love." She stepped forward, felt the barrel press into her stomach. "Whatever you do, Jacques, save Grey."

He examined her, mouth turned down. "*Merde alors!* Odette was right. You do love him." He lowered the pistol. "If Grey lives, I would not let him rot in a *boche* prison."

"Convince them, Jacques."

"Impossible."

"I'm not going anywhere. If I am lying, you know where to find me."

He swore and slipped the gun back into his pocket. "I will do what I can."

When he was out of sight, Claire stumbled to a park bench and collapsed. She was back in her hotel room before she stopped trembling.

*  *  *

That night, Claire dined with von Richter and two officers at Le Boeuf sur le Toit. They sat at a dark table near the mahogany bar, the wall covered in photos and engraved mirrors. Claire watched herself play with a curl of hair in the reflection as the men spoke German. She sipped champagne, pointedly ignoring the looks they gave her. She didn't know what von Richter was telling them. Nor did she care.

In ten days, Grey would be transported to Compiègne prison. If the Resistance didn't believe her, if they didn't act, she knew what was next. Prisoners stayed at Compiègne only so long. Then they were shipped away to German camps. Those people never came back. She took a long drink, let the bubbles slide over her tongue. She couldn't drown the ache in her chest. She turned to the waiter in a starched white vest that hovered around their table.

"The bathroom?"

"This way, Madame." He led her to an oak-lined hallway.

As he pushed open a door he breathed into her ear. "Evelyn?"

She turned, her heart in her throat.

"They will try." He turned and walked away.

# Chapter 12

## THE ESCAPE

Place Vendôme. July 23, 1944.

Ten mornings later, Claire watched through her hotel room window as the sky brightened from deep violet to a saturated blue. In her mind, she saw Grey huddled in a prison cell, his eyes opening to darkness. It had been so long since he'd seen the sunrise over his garden. Did he still have hope?

A vibrant sapphire gleam and the sun broke free of the skyline. The tune of the Billie Holiday song echoed in her mind. *Just when you are near, when I hold you fast, then my dreams will whisper, you're too lovely to last.*

"A few more hours, Thomas." The whispered words brought a lightness inside her and propelled her away from the glass. A hot bath, hair set, a sweep of crimson lipstick and a spritz of perfume. From the closet, a simple smoky-blue dress, nipped at the waist. When she looked in the mirror, she was surprised at what she saw. A flush to her cheeks, a ghost of a real smile tugging at her lips. You look like woman in love, she thought.

She pulled a small key from beneath the lamp on the night-stand then perched on the seat facing her desk. Unlocking a deep drawer, she extracted a stack of postcards, her jewelry roll and a small wad of francs. She flipped through the cards, a tugboat under the elaborate pont Alexandre, the Eiffel Tower, the Concorde. Not something she'd send—who the hell would she send them to?—but a shuffling of order was a good indicator her drawer had been searched yet again. She didn't mind. The important thing is they found what they expected. Nothing more.

Dropping the roll and francs in her purse, she walked over to the bed and wedged herself behind the headboard. Bracing her back against the wall, she pushed the heavy frame toward the center of the room. On her knees, she slid a fingertip underneath a thin slit in the exposed carpet. A moment later, she pulled out an envelope.

One last look at her room. A forlorn rose floated in water in a highball glass on the empty desk, an unmade bed, and a row of dresses and silk gowns in the closet. The gowns repulsed her like so many shed skins. She dropped the envelope into her purse.

Claire left the hotel and strolled along les Champs. Her eyes were on the shop displays, lèche-vitrine, window licking the French called it, alongside the handsome men in pressed suits, the striking women in gloves and hats, the German soldiers buying delectables to send home. She made a show of examining a deep red velvet jacket inside a shop window then ducked inside a busy café.

Pressing up to the counter, she ordered a madeleine and turned to watch the street. A flow of passing people, none glanced toward her, none paused too long to deliberate on a table before they moved on. Still, to be safe, she wrapped the pastry in a napkin and slipped out the café's side door into an alley. Paralleling the street for a block, she turned north toward parc Monceau.

The park was quiet. The carousel was empty, its brightly colored cars suspended in midair. She walked along the gravel to the pool then settled on the shaded bench beneath a gnarled oak.

By now, the transport would have left. Grey would be on the road between Fort Montluc and Compiègne. Where would Jacques' group attack? An empty stretch of road? A bridge? With her fingers, she ripped a piece from the small scallop-shaped cake and chewed without tasting.

Afterward they would have to hide out somewhere. A farmhouse perhaps. Not Paris. But still, if Grey was close, this is where Jacques would find her. And then nothing would stop her from reaching Grey. She tore at the pastry and hurled pieces to the birds pecking in the grass around the pool's edge. She would be ready.

A blond woman and small girl walked by at lunch. The girl tossed pebbles into the mossy water. After a moment, her mother pulled her away. She protested, her voice echoing. *Pas plus, Marie*, no more, the mother told her. In the afternoon, an elderly couple rambled past. The woman's diaphanous snow-white hair glinted in the sun; she gripped the man's elbow with frail hands.

Claire pulled the envelope from her purse. She stroked the paper, felt the texture of the gold engraved Ritz Paris crown and seal under her fingers. But she couldn't bring herself to open it. Not yet. The sun disappeared below the buildings and the light faded.

"Madame?" A slender man in glasses and a thick scarf faced the bench.

"Yes?" Her voice quivered. A message from Grey?

"You have been sitting here so long; are you unwell?"

She flushed, suddenly mortified. "*Non, merci.* I lost track of time. I must be going." She hurried away without looking back.

Claire forced a confident stroll as she stepped onto boulevard Haussmann, but her insides ached. She paused a moment before she turned onto boulevard Malesherbes. Of course it wouldn't have worked this way. But damn. She had so wanted it to.

The concierge stopped her in the lobby. A note. Sturmbann-führer von Richter was expecting her in his study. Directly.

"*Komme,*" Von Richter barked when she tapped on his door.

She steeled herself as she paused in the threshold. Give Grey time.

Von Richter leaned over his desk, his briefcase opened and empty in front of him. "Ah. So you decided to grace me with your presence." His faced was flushed with excitement but his eyes sparked with anger.

A white-coated server pushed a cart through the door behind her. Two bottles of champagne jutted from an ice bucket. Silver trays brimmed with cheeses, chocolates, pastries and fruit.

Von Richter glared at the man. "I called a half hour ago. Are you purposefully wasting my time?"

The server blanched. "No, Sturmbannführer. We had to retrieve the chocolates from a shop that was raided—"

"On the table. Now. And go." Von Richter turned to Claire, waved his hand toward the offering. "What do you think?"

She forced a smile and stepped into von Richter's arms. "Alby, darling. Is it your birthday or mine?"

He smirked, his eyes sparkled. "Better." He reached for the champagne.

\* \* \*

The table led to the bed. One bottle was empty and the sheets between them stained with crushed berries when von Richter finally answered Claire's questions.

"A coup. And a promotion." He pulled the sheets up to his waist and reached for a crystal glass.

"How did you manage all that?"

"You know how it is, Claire. The world favors some. It is merely for us to reach out and pick up the spoils."

Claire leaned against his back, felt the heat from his skin soak through her thin silk slip. She massaged his shoulders as she kissed his neck. "The spoils?"

"Today was an important prisoner transport. But a Resistance bomb took out the bridge in front of the convoy. Fighters swarmed from the trees. Gunfire, more bombs. Quite chaotic, I understand. It was a major offensive for those criminals."

"Oh?" Claire forced her hands to continue kneading the muscles of his neck.

"But, Claire, I am Nazi intelligence. And the escape attempt was not unexpected."

Fear clawed at her stomach.

"I almost wish I could have seen the looks on their faces when our tanks rolled out of the forest behind them." He laughed, shook his head in wonder at the imagined sight.

"So, what happened?"

"As you would expect. The criminals fought for their lives. Most were mowed down by our soldiers."

"And the prisoners?"

He shrugged. "Most died chained in the trucks. An unfortunate result of the heavy fighting. A few managed to run into the forest."

"And then what?"

"Our dogs made short work of them." He emptied the glass. "My superiors are understandably pleased with the convenient execution of a number of notorious criminals in custody, as well as the destruction of a dangerous insurgency cell. It will make a fine news item in the papers tomorrow. With a list of the executed criminals, of course."

Her fingers trembled. She pushed harder against his skin and forced her words around the expanding pain in her chest. "How exciting. Would I know their names?"

"Beauchamp. Murrell. Kinsel. The man called himself a patriot. Loyal to a dead world, sanctimonious fool." He rolled his shoulders and let out a long, satisfied sigh. "And a British spy. Would have made it out, but for the dogs, I'm told. He was shot out of a tree. Grey was his name. Appropriate for a damn Englishman, isn't it? Grey."

The room dimmed around her. Von Richter kept talking. More names flowed by. Blackness pressed against her and crept into the edges of her vision. She rose like a specter.

"Where are you going?"

"I need a bath," she said over her shoulder as she pulled the bathroom door shut behind her.

Claire turned the faucet then collapsed to her knees on the marble floor. She leaned against the tub, her face pressed against the cool porcelain. When the bath was full, she climbed in and sat. At the touch of water against her skin, she began to shake violently. Her breath came in small, quiet gasps and she felt her chest rip apart. She slid backward until her face was submerged.

She lay under the water, her eyes shut as if she could stop time. The burning in her lungs grew.

She imagined Grey, the line of his jaw, his serious eyes. The smell of him next to her, their bodies melded together in a hollow of grass. Gunned down. As lights began to pop in her eyes, she choked and sat up. She dragged herself from the tub, reached for a towel and stood, dripping in front of the mirror.

"What are you doing in there?" von Richter said.

She stared at her reflection, transfixed. In spite of herself, wheels turned inside her head. Von Richter had expected something. The Resistance would think she had set them up.

In the end, her choice was simple, really. She toweled off and ran a comb through her hair. The door swung open and she stepped out, letting the towel drop to the floor. She picked up the phone, *A bottle of your best scotch. Room 527.*

She pushed von Richter back on the bed as she dropped the phone into the cradle. "Reach out, Sturmbannführer, and pick up your spoils."

He pulled her against him.

Claire slipped from beneath the silk sheets and felt her way across the darkened room, heavy curtains drawn against the glimmer of early morning sun. She found her dress crumpled up on the floor by the foot of the bed, shook it out and slipped it over her head. Von Richter's snores rumbling in the background, she crawled around the floor and found one then the other shoe. Climbing to her feet, she tiptoed into the study.

She pulled the door shut behind her, wincing at the click of the lock snapping into place. Von Richter's drunken snores continued. Out cold.

In the faint predawn light, outlines of chairs and desk were barely visible. Hands held in front of her, bare feet sliding over the carpet, she shuffled to the heavy oak desk. Grabbing the desk chair, she hurried back to the door, wedging the chair back against the handle. It took all her strength to push the sofa against the door leading to the hall.

With the room as secure as Claire could make it, she clicked on the lamp and surveyed the room. She was done fumbling around with a candle in the darkness. Von Richter had most of a bottle of scotch on top of two bottles of champagne in him. And she was going to tear apart every inch of this damn room. She had to know what had happened.

First the briefcase. She used a letter opener to split open the seams one by one. In the end, an expensive pile of leather scraps at her feet. Nothing. Starting on one corner of the desk she worked her way through. Drawers pulled out and pried apart. Cubbies examined. The lamp shining up from underneath, first a visual examination, then by touch. After that the chair, silk cushion ripped open, the sofa, the paintings off the walls and frames pulled away. The table. Dresser. Nothing. She forced her mind to focus and dropped to her knees. From one corner, she worked across the carpet, her fingers probing each inch for a slit, a bulge.

She sat back underneath the window; the rising sun broke free of the buildings to illuminate the far side of the room. Her head fell back against the cool glass. She listened to the growing rumble of car engines on the street below, the noise merging with von Richter's snores.

There was nothing. No proof it was her fault. But nothing to show it wasn't. Claire climbed to her feet. It wasn't enough. She pulled the chair away and pushed open the bedroom door.

The room was still dark, curtains pulled. The lump of blankets that was von Richter smelled of sour alcohol. She walked over to stare at the back of his head showing above the covers. How to exorcise the secrets from inside there?

She sighed and sat heavily on the floor, her head in her hands. It didn't make sense that she found nothing today. Not even a loose paper, a receipt. He had to keep it all hidden someplace. A safe, perhaps, but she'd looked behind the paintings on the bedroom walls before.

Sighing, she examined the carpet beneath her and ran her fingers across the heavy grey-green wool. The faded swirls showed the wear of years of scuffling feet. A rug rested in the corner beneath a reading chair and table. Claire crawled over to the corner to get a closer look. The rug's green didn't quite match the carpet's.

She gently pushed the chair and table away, then rolled back the rug. Beneath, a ragged square was cut in the carpet. She peeled that back. The floorboards had been sawed away. A square metal safe sat inside the opening. She ran her hands over the metal, felt the sharp corners of the keyhole.

She'd seen von Richter's keys before. A quick trip to the closet, his uniform jacket pocket. She squeezed the key ring tight in her palm to keep it from jiggling as she crept back. The third key turned; the click made her flinch.

Claire gripped the metal handle and pulled the heavy door open. A holstered Walther rested incongruously on a pile of folders. She set the pistol gently on the floor next to her then reached for the papers.

On the top, a thick envelope with the emblem of the SS. Claire stuck a finger under the flap and peeled it open. Squinting in the dim light, she unfolded the pink pages inside. *Ausweis. Laissez-Passer.* Four blank travel permits. Better than gold. Tucking the papers back inside, she slipped the envelope inside her dress against her skin.

The first folder she opened appeared to be a pile of invoices. She set it aside and picked up the next. *Obere Sicherheit. Sicherheitsdienst.* The SS insignia. She flipped open the cover and her heart stopped. She grabbed the entire pile beneath the open folder and tore into the study. The files spilled onto the desk beneath the glow of the lamp. Her hands began to shake.

Top left of the page, a photo of Grey. The photo was taken surprisingly close, his gaze off to the left. His eyes were dark squints, forehead lined in a frown, hands stuffed deep into the pockets of his worn jacket. The text under the photo was written in German. Claire couldn't make out any of the neatly typed, single-spaced lines. She flipped the page. A photo of Grey and Jacques. They walked shoulder to shoulder, deep in conversation. The next page, Grey and Laurent. Grey had the same scowl; Laurent was smoking a cigarette, one hand on Grey's shoulder.

Claire took a deep breath and flipped the page. Claire and Grey. It was taken the day they met in jardin du Luxembourg. The photo was taken at the end of the long *allée* of squared-off plane trees. They stood in front of a statue of a couple embracing. Grey was smiling, his face open, boyish almost. She was speaking, the edges of her mouth curving into a grin. Her fingers rested on his forearm. We look like lovers, she thought.

Her fingers trembled as she turned the pages. More photos of her and Grey, photos of her walking alone, photos of her leaving the flower shop. A photo of Claire and Madame Palain in front of the shop, drinking real coffee, the day Claire splurged on her ration cards. The bottom of the photo under Madame's image was stamped in heavy blue ink, *Geabschaffen.* In von Richter's hand, the date of Madame's death and initials, *AvR.*

Her heart pounded so loudly in her chest that all noise faded into static. Her gaze went to the bedroom, to the dark shape of the pistol still resting on the floor. The phone rang on the desk. A quick jump and Claire hit the receiver. It stopped, mid-ring.

It was too late. In the bedroom, von Richter cursed, the bed creaked.

Claire jumped toward the safe. Her fingers closed on the holster as her knees hit the carpet. She came up with the Walther, pointed at von Richter.

He sat up blinking, still half-drunk. "What the fuck are you doing?"

Her finger was pressed tight against the trigger. "You knew."

"Knew what?"

"Grey. The flower shop. Me." She shook the barrel at him. "Who gave you this information?"

He glanced down at the open safe and shrugged, his lips twisted into a hard smile. "The world favors some of us, Claire. It is only that you are currently operating for the wrong side."

Her finger tightened against the trigger. She saw Grey's slate eyes. *I promise,* he told her. He promised he would be back for her and the girls.

The ringing phone jarred her attention. She and von Richter stared at each other as they listened to the phone.

"Schneider," he said. "An appointment. He will be here momentarily."

Claire could take Schneider too before the guards got her. But she felt the passes pressed against her skin. And she had promised Marta. She slammed the metal gun butt across von Richter's head. He slumped sideways across the bed.

Von Richter's suit jacket hung by the door. She slit a hole along a seam of the lining and slipped in the folder. She shrugged on the jacket and dropped the Luger in a deep front pocket. Her shoes, her purse, and she caught her reflection in the mirror as she walked out the door. Face pale, her eyes dark burning circles.

Claire crept down the hallway, jacket pulled tight, the folder pressed stiffly against her through the thin fabric of her dress. She glided down the stairs, her head erect, chin out. Soldiers stood guard below her on each side of the stairwell. She'd passed them hundreds of times tucked in von Richter's side or on her way back to the room. Now, in a rumpled dress and man's jacket, her eyes wild, they watched her approach with hard stares.

The sharp corners of the folder bit into her rib cage. She felt perspiration break out under her arms and run down her back.

Schneider met her at the bottom rung. He took in von Richter's jacket, her face. His eyes widened. "Where is the Sturmbann-führer?"

"Sleeping one off."

He examined her. His mouth tightened. "You will come with me to see him."

"*Non, merci.*" Her hand slid inside the jacket pocket, reaching for the gun.

He spoke a sharp command to the guards. The soldier at her side grabbed her above the elbow. "Come with us, *Fräulein.*"

She went cold, her finger slid over the trigger.

"Madame Badeau, what seems to be the problem?" The Comte stopped in front of the soldiers. "Lieutenant," he said to Schneider in a cool greeting then looked back to Claire. "Sturmbannführer von Richter will be upset if you're late with his breakfast, no?"

Claire painted a smile on her face and shrugged her shoulders as if it was something that couldn't be helped.

Schneider glared. "I just phoned. He didn't answer."

The Comte's lips turned up in a smile that didn't reach his eyes. "He didn't answer you, you mean."

Schneider flushed. "You spoke to the Sturmbannführer?"

The Comte didn't answer, dismissed Schneider with his eyes. He turned to the soldiers. "Perhaps I should take your names so I can let the Sturmbannführer know who held up his breakfast and his mistress?"

They looked at each other, to Schneider, then back to the Comte. Claire felt the grip release on her arm.

The Comte let a smile creep into the corner of his mouth, he extended an elbow for her. They walked arm-in-arm through the salon toward rue Cambon.

"It is a good thing, I think, my assistant was not able to retrieve *Le Monde* for me this morning, no?"

Claire nodded, still unable to loosen her grip on his arm. In her mind, she counted the seconds before Schneider found von Richter. Before they would be after her.

She found her voice as they approached the front doors. "You told me to be careful when you saw me with von Richter. What did you know?"

"Not enough. Never enough." He reached down and pulled his arm free of her, patted her hand gently. "This I do know. It has been a long night for France. Leave her now or you won't live to see the dawn."

"How long did you know about me?"

He examined her as if deciding what she could hear. "About you? A long while."

Images clicked in her brain. The dinner long ago. Had he left her the note about the Resistance leader in his trash? Had he given her a chance to save Christophe? She looked up at him. His eyes were sad. She recognized the weariness she saw. Of someone who had played the game too long and lost too much to get there.

"Are you a good man?"

He looked genuinely surprised, like no one had ever considered it. He shook his head, a sad smile. "Not yet." He turned to the concierge.

Claire took a breath and marched purposefully through the double doors. She could almost hear Schneider's voice ring out, feel the impact of bullets tearing into her back. A glance back inside. The Comte leaned against the concierge's desk; a newspaper folded under one arm. He smiled at her as the door closed.

She turned to face the street, wrapping von Richter's jacket closer about her. Soldiers positioned on each side of the door watched the hem of her dress fluttering around her pale thighs in the soft summer breeze. She pasted on a flirty smile and started walking. She fought the urge to look back, kept her pace measured, her hips swinging.

A yell echoed from inside the hotel and Claire burst into a run. A whistle blew as she rounded the corner onto rue Saint-Honoré. A quick turn onto rue Duphot and she ducked into the dark space between two buildings. Pressing herself against the bricks, she peeked toward the intersection. Pedestrians on rue Saint-Honoré scattered off the sidewalk, spilling into the street as an invisible wave crested the corner. She jerked her head back in as troops pounded into view. A long whistle echoed off the buildings. Claire looked behind her.

Ten feet farther and the opening ended at an oversized iron gate, bound with an enormous medieval-looking lock. Sloping pavement behind the iron bars descended into darkness beneath a tall building. She ran to the gate, peering into an underground garage. Voices called out from the street, a whistle shrilled, and heavy footsteps pounded closer. Her heart skittered but she forced the panic down. Head tilted back, she noticed a slender opening between the closed gate and the iron crosspieces above.

Her body trembling, she clenched her purse in her teeth, gripped the bars, wedged a foot against a rung and lifted herself in the air. Another breath, another step. The edges cut into her palms; she wedged her knees between two bars to climb higher. She gripped the horizontal bar above the gate, got herself sideways, shoved one foot through, a leg, then another leg. The air wheezed from her chest as she pulled her torso through. Her elbows smacked against metal and she slid. The weight of her falling body jerked her grip loose, and she was in the air.

Claire hit the cobble floor with a thud and rolled like a ragdoll down the steep slope to the parking lot floor. She lay gasping in the darkness, listening to shouts as soldiers ran past the alley. She pushed herself up to her elbows and froze. Two soldiers faced the gate, their forms outlined against the sunlight. She held her breath and closed her eyes. The gate rattled and they were gone.

Forcing herself to her feet, she found her purse and felt her way across the dark empty space. A dim corridor led to a heavy wooden door that opened up onto rue Saint-Florentin. Claire blinked in the sunlight and merged into the flow of pedestrians. She ducked onto the first side street. Tracing her way south, she slipped through private courtyards and twice backtracked out of blind alleyways until she was walking along the Seine, her slim heels clicking on the cobblestone path.

The chalk-grey pont Royal stretched over the dark river. Claire stopped on the bridge midway across. She sagged against the railing, leaning her elbows over the edge. She felt brittle,

like too-hot glass that would explode at a touch. Grey, Madame
Palain—how many other people had died because of her? Igno-
rant little dirt farmer—you should have stayed back home. It
would be so easy to slip over the barrier, to ride the churning
ripples and eddies to the sea. She squeezed her arms close. The
folder corners bit into her stomach. No. There was still time. Not
everyone had to die.

O n rue Bezin, Claire paused in the doorway of a small neighborhood charcuterie, the cases nearly empty of meat. The
*boucher* sat in the corner at a table reading the paper. He glanced
up at her, shrugged apologetically toward the empty cases and
went back to his paper. Claire looked back down the boulevard,
scrutinizing people walking past. She thought she could spot a
Nazi tailing her, but a *Resistánt*? Odette, Jacques, Laurent; they
looked Parisian, nothing more. How could she tell who was sent
to kill her?

Claire hurried across the street. She entered the Oberons'
apartment building and pressed the button for the fourth floor
inside the cage elevator. As the elevator edged upward, Claire
pulled the envelope holding the passes from her décolleté.

At the fourth floor, Claire knocked on number 42. A low
call, Martin cracked the door open. After a quick check, his lips
twisted into a warm smile.

He waved her through the slim opening. "Bonjour, Claire.
This is a surprise."

A quick peck on each cheek, her eyes scanned the room.
"Where are Madame Oberon and the girls?"

Martin pointed to the closed door off the salon. He took in

her clothes, her expression. His face paled. "To be safe, Adele hid the girls in the closet when we heard the door."

The apartment was even homier than when she'd been there before. The scent of simmering broth. A photo of their son on the mantel, surrounded by half-burnt candles. A storybook left open on the arm of the couch. Martin must have been reading with Anna before Claire knocked.

"Tell Adele they don't need to hide, but I must speak with you both, alone."

Adele hurried out at Martin's call. Her expression went from happy surprise to pinched fright. Her eyes lingered on Claire's face as they embraced.

Claire pressed the envelope into Martin's hands and walked to the window. He stared at the seal. *Totenkopf.* The SS skull and bones. Slipping on his eyeglasses, he unfolded the papers. "What exactly is this?"

"Freedom," Claire said, peering through the drawn lace curtains to the street below.

"What do you mean?" Adele slipped to Martin's side. Her hand found his arm.

"She means these are transit papers. Legitimate, I think," he said. "They would allow the bearer to pass into unoccupied territory, even out of the country."

The street below was clear. No soldiers. No black sedans gathering out front. Yet. Claire spoke without looking away. "Spain to Portugal, most likely. From there, one could go anywhere." She turned to face them. "For the girls. For you."

A clock ticked loudly in the silence. Adele looked to Martin, then to Claire. "You are asking us to take them."

"There is no one else, no other way," Claire said.

Martin pulled off his glasses. "There's more, isn't there?"

"I've been compromised. People around me, good people, are dead. Executed. I don't know if you have been identified yet. But you will be found."

Adele paled, her wide eyes dark against her face. Martin patted her softly. The papers held his gaze.

Adele looked at Claire. "We knew this could happen, when we took the girls in." Her eyes locked on her husband. Her voice lowered to near whisper. "We gladly accepted that risk, Martin."

"How much time?" he said.

"Not long. This afternoon. When they realize these papers are gone, they will be watching the stations."

"You said you were compromised." Martin slipped the papers into the envelope, thumping it with a finger. "Why offer these to us?"

The image of Anna on Grey's shoulders, Marta at Claire's side dissolved into an ache deep inside. She shook her head. "Marta and Anna need a chance at a real life. They need parents. I need to settle some debts."

"I'll tell Marta to pack her suitcase. We'll need a few things, not much. Martin, you get the money we set aside. It will have to do." Adele hurried to the closed door and ducked inside.

Martin tucked the envelope into his shirt pocket. He stared around the room as if he were fixing it in his mind.

"I'm sorry, Martin." Claire didn't know how many more people she could lose.

He took her hands and cupped them between his. He looked over at the photograph on the mantel. "You can't imagine what it's like to lose your only child. We didn't know how we could go on. You gave us two reasons to live. More than that, to make a new life." He released her hands and turned toward their bedroom. He paused in the doorway and looked back. "No matter what happens, we are forever grateful to you."

Adele hurried from the girl's room clutching Anna in her arms. The girl had grown; her lithe legs hung past Adele's waist, long little fingers interlaced in Adele's collar. Her face pale, eyes wide, she was trying to be brave. She kissed Claire's cheek with trembling lips, then sniffled as Claire hugged her tight. Adele murmured a piece of song into Anna's ear, holding the girl close, and followed Martin into their bedroom. Claire knocked softly on Marta's door and entered.

The room was small, neat, a narrow bed pressed against the wall. A lace curtain fluttered in a window in the warm summer air. The scent of fresh flowers came from a small posy on the sill. The old suitcase was thrown open on the bed as Marta tossed in clothing from an open drawer. A small yellow dress fluttered to the floor. She didn't turn around.

Claire damn well couldn't blame the girl for being upset. She sat at the foot of the bed and patted the spot next to her. Marta stuffed another wad of clothes in the case.

"You and Anna are leaving France. You are going to be safe," Claire said.

Marta stared at the floor. "Okay."

Claire almost smiled at Captain Walker's *slang américain.* "The Oberons are good people. They'll take care of you."

"Adele said you won't come with us." Marta abruptly sat at Claire's side.

"I have to do something for Grey."

"Monsieur Grey?" Marta looked up. "You found him?"

"Yes." The word hurt, but Claire forced a smile. "But there is still more to do."

Marta nodded that she understood; her dark eyes focused on Claire's face. "You can find us too. Afterward."

"I will try." Claire wrapped an arm around Marta's shoulders. "I want to show you something." She pulled out the jewelry roll from her purse and set it on her lap.

Marta couldn't help herself, her eyes sparkled with curiosity. "What is it?"

Claire untied the silk ribbon and slowly unrolled the fabric. The necklace and earrings were jumbled like a pile of broken glass. The diamonds caught the faint afternoon sun streaming in the window and sparkled like embers.

Marta gasped. Claire picked up the necklace and handed it to the girl, sunburst in her palm.

Marta cradled the pendant, looking up at Claire. "My mother would have loved it. This must be worth so much. It's beautiful."

"Beautiful? Yes." Claire nudged the dangling gems. As they swayed, white facets danced on Marta's skin. "But I find many things more beautiful. Like, the light in your eyes when you smile."

Marta smiled back. "And roses. You love roses."

"Yes."

"And Monsieur Grey. You think he is beautiful."

The words cut into Claire. She forced in a breath. "Yes. He is." She examined the necklace, remembered the night she got it from Russell, the lying that preceded it and all the lies that followed. The woman who loved that necklace was gone. Buried. "You must always see the difference between what the world says is beautiful and what your heart says is beautiful. Do you understand?"

"You sound like Madame Palain," Marta said.

"Thank you. And I am also right." Claire laughed softly. "The jewelry is expensive, true. But its worth—you will decide that in its use."

"Me? I can't take it." Marta pushed the necklace back at Claire.

The diamonds were warm in her palm as Claire nestled the jewelry on the silk. Rolling up the fabric and tying it carefully, she turned to Marta. "Stand up in front of me." Claire slipped the roll into the waistband of the girl's skirt. "This is where you hide it, where they won't look for it. Use the strings, like this, and tie them to your slip, where it can't be seen."

"It is too much."

"Keep it hidden, always. If you need it—when you need it—you will know what to do."

Marta's lips trembled. She flung herself against Claire and rested her head on her shoulder.

Claire leaned her cheek against the top of the girl's head. "You and Anna are going to have such wondrous lives."

Marta looked up at her, the trace of hope turning up the edges of her mouth, even as tears clung to her dark lashes. "*Vraiment?*"

"Truly." Claire smiled. "You have courage, Marta. I've seen it with my own eyes. The strength not just to survive but to be true to yourself—true to what matters."

"I don't know."

"I do. Promise me you won't ever forget that."

"I won't forget anything. I promise." Marta wrapped her thin arms around Claire, clenching her tight.


Claire left their apartment building with her head down; she had the purposeful stride of someone with a place to go. She inspected herself in the reflection of the windows as she walked. A light wool jacket thrown over a sky blue dress. From Adele, both a touch too long, they covered the scrapes on her knees. The jacket had an inner seam, just opened for the folder; the pistol nestled in an inner pocket. Von Richter's jacket and her ripped dress were ashes in the fireplace. She looked back once as she turned off rue Brezin, her gaze on the fourth floor, her eyes searching for fluttering white curtains. Another promise. She prayed Marta could live to keep it.

The afternoon turned blustery, the branches swayed overhead, leaves shaking. Claire's coat whipped around her legs, slapping the raw skin. She stepped inside a doorway as rain began to fall. Sagging against the bricks, she shifted her weight back and forth on her aching feet as she watched the avenue behind her. She was tired. She needed to be vigilant.

Claire glanced at the sign across the street. *Hôtel Jasmine.* A worn four-story façade, the namesake vine clinging to crumbling bricks. She peered in the door. A dark lobby, tattered but clean. The kind of discreet place a woman would go to meet a man for the afternoon.

Another glance at the street, no soldiers in sight. Claire walked into the pharmacy next door. A moment later, she came out with a bag in her hand and crossed the street to the hotel. No identification necessary, 270 francs for the night, she signed in as Madame Martin.

"I assume Monsieur Martin will be joining you later?" the clerk asked with a knowing smile.

"Of course."

Claire climbed two flights of stairs to number 17. The room was small, faded pink carpet and curtains, a badly patched porcelain washbasin in the corner.

Behind the high window, Claire watched the street below. She gripped the gun as a black sedan rolled up the block. She exhaled and pulled the curtains closed as the car accelerated past. She set the pistol on the nightstand and peeled the folder from her jacket lining.

The photo of Claire with Madame Palain in front of La Vie en Fleurs was taken in the fall of '42, more than a year and a half ago. The photo of Claire with Grey in jardin du Luxembourg was taken in spring of the last year. It was impossible to say when the other photos were taken. Von Richter knew about her; he knew about them all. And had for months. She went word by word through each line of text in the reports, sifting for a name, a location. Nothing.

Claire rolled back onto the bed, wincing against her scrapes and bruises. Someone had betrayed them long ago. She stared through the cracked window at the deepening sky. The clouds let loose and a torrent of rain pelted the glass. She closed her eyes and smelled the jasmine's perfume. She slept.

She woke to darkness, her body protesting. Shivering in front of a wash basin, she stared in the small mirror. Her eyes were dark, her face drawn. She reached for the pharmacy bag.

An hour later, she stood in front of the window. Ashes from the shredded box made dirty trails in the sink basin behind her. Light from the blanketed sun cast a chalky pall over her skin. The pallor accentuated the darkness of her short brunette hair, curled around her face. Claire stared at the folder open on the bed and then peeled a photo of Grey and Jacques from the paper. She flipped the photo over and scribbled a note on the back, then reached for her jacket.

She closed the door behind her. A man stepped in the hall from the next room. He glanced at her, then looked again, longer, from head to toe. She reached into her pocket, gripping the Walther.

His shadowed face melted into a small grin. "A shame I did not see you before. Join me for a smoke?" He pulled a hand-rolled cigarette from a pocket, gesturing toward his room with the flick of his head. He was weaving, the hand holding the cigarette unsteady.

Claire released her grip on the gun. She descended the stairs quickly. His footsteps thumped unevenly behind her. As she reached the final flight of stairs, the lobby came into view. Her heart stopped. Two Germans in black suits faced the clerk. Gestapo. One was pointing to a photograph in the clerk's hands.

She pulled her jacket close and felt the folder pressed against her. She reached into her pocket. The thumping behind her stopped. Claire turned.

The man stared quizzically at Claire from above. "Change your mind already?"

Claire smiled, a slight nod. "How about breakfast first? And a drink?"

He shrugged, stepped down beside her, one hand slid down her backside. *"Pourquoi pas?"*

She slipped her free hand around him, her other hand still clenching the pistol. He cupped her hip and pulled her close. She smelled alcohol mixed with stale tobacco. Together they went down the last stairs to the lobby, the man between her and the Gestapo. A cold sweat pricked at her neck. She giggled softly, staggered as if she were drunk, ran a hand through her short brunette hair. One of the Gestapo glanced at the couple once, frowned and turned back to the clerk. *If you see her,* she heard, and then they were out the door.

A half block later, the street opened up to an alley. Claire pulled them around the corner. The man reached for her, she pushed his hand back. "*Merci*, monsieur. But I don't smoke."

She turned and ran.


Cold rain dripped down Claire's neck as she turned off rue de Tocqueville. The street was nearly empty in the early morning rain. No tables were pulled out onto the sidewalk at Café Raphael. Across the street, the theater was dark, the dentist's building looked closed.

Gusts of wind tore at yesterday's *Le Figaro* Claire held over her head. She clenched the message in her pocket, took a deep breath and walked toward the drop. A moment spent below the theater marquee to examine the poster, a woman planning her evening, then she walked past the dentist's window. Her hand slipped into her pocket, the paper palmed in her hand. A glance at the dentist's door, her hand moved toward the mail slot.

The door was boarded shut. The dentist was gone.

She forced herself to keep moving. A few more steps and she paused, as if to adjust her shoe. She glanced back for a better view. The heavy wooden door had been shattered, twisted hinges dangled from the broken doorjamb.

Claire let the newspaper fall to the pavement as she strode away. She didn't notice the rain running down her face. Who could she turn to? She broke into a trot as she turned the corner. She didn't slow down until she stood across from 22, rue d'Artois.

The lights were on in Laurent's apartment, the curtains pulled. She remembered standing out here when she first got to

Paris a lifetime ago. Claire wiped the rain from her face. She knew she looked like hell, but Laurent had to understand.

Her heels clicked against the cobbles as she crossed the street. Inside the lobby, she stopped and stared at the mailboxes. Laurent's name had been scratched off the plate.

A harried-looking maid passed, barely more than a girl, her arms full of boxes.

"Who lives in number 4?" Claire asked.

"Kommandant Klein," the maid said and turned to climb the stairs.

Claire's legs were shaking as she hurried down the street. It wasn't possible. They couldn't all be gone. There was only one person left who might know. Claire had to talk to her without getting killed first.

The city was dark under the heavy clouds, with the street-lights blued out. Rats scurried in the darkness of the alley behind La Vie en Fleurs. Claire had watched and waited until the streets emptied after curfew. Now she picked her way through the trash to the doorway she knew so well. Her searching hands found the key still hidden beneath a rusty iron flowerpot. The door opened with a familiar squeak.

The shop interior was inky black. The air was musty, the rains had leaked through boarded windows. Claire moved carefully. The floor was slippery in a layer of dust. The broken glass, scattered flowers and tins were gone.

She felt her way to the counter, pulled open a drawer and reached in for a box. *He buys the best flowers he can afford for his women. He has spent a great deal of money here,* Madame

Palain said of Laurent so long ago. Claire had never looked through the receipts. Now she needed to know.

A match flared, Claire bent low over the open box. *Olivier, Sylvie.*

Sixty-seven, rue de Lisbonne. A tall grey building, ornate stone façade, not far from parc Monceau. Oversized wooden doors with an archaic lock. Claire reached for a hairpin. A quick flick into the lock and she was inside. Climbing the grand staircase, she stepped out into a dimly lit hallway and paused in front of Sylvie's entry.

Her ear pressed to the door, she heard nothing inside. What were the odds, Claire wondered, Sylvie was home, much less alone? Gripping the Walther in her pocket with one hand, Claire took a deep breath and knocked.

The door opened a crack. Eyes flashed wide with surprise and the door swung open another inch. Sylvie frowned at Claire. As good of a reception as Claire could hope for.

"Are you alone?" Claire said.

"Yes, why?"

"We need to talk."

"About what?"

"Not in the hallway."

Sylvie scanned the corridor behind Claire. "Come in, then." She wore a luminous green silk robe, an immense emerald cocktail ring. She eyed Claire's hair.

Claire fought the urge to smooth her curls. She met Sylvie's gaze. "The Nazis have taken over Laurent's apartment. Where is he?"

Sylvie turned away. She shook her head as she lit a cigarette.

"Bold of the mistress to ask his wife, isn't it? Just like *une Améri-caine. Gauche*."

Claire stared at Sylvie. Of all the reactions Claire expected, how could Sylvie be so cavalier? "Your husband is missing. You can find out where he is, what happened to him. Ask your Kapitän."

Sylvie turned to Claire. Her thin lips stretched into a smile. "Why? What have you done, lost your Sturmbannführer?"

"Yes."

"So you want my husband back, eh?"

"I want to know where he is. I would think a loving wife would be the least bit curious. What do you know, Sylvie?"

Sylvie frowned, seeming to mull over her words. "We'll find out together. I will make a call." She reached for her phone.

Claire crossed the room to the window and stared out at the street. Nothing moved in the darkness. She moved away from the window and looked at the painting over the mantel. Children picking over a harvested field. The same painting she'd seen in Laurent's apartment.

Her skin prickled as she heard Sylvie's smooth voice. "Claire Harris is in my apartment. Of course. Tell them to hurry, won't you?" The phone clicked against the cradle as she hung up.

Claire whirled around. Sylvie held a pistol in her hand.

"Beautiful, isn't it? Pearl handled," Sylvie said. "A present from *my* Nazi. My grateful Kapitän."

Heat blossomed in Claire's body as she put it all together. "It was you? You're the traitor?"

"Laurent thought I couldn't see what his little gang was up to. They thought they were so smart. They weren't."

"Why, Sylvie?"

"There is a new world order now. I intend to enjoy it."

Claire stared at Sylvie's mouth, her hard eyes, the perfect hair, the silk robe, the emerald on her finger. My God—how Laurent had underestimated her. Laurent and Grey had thought they were using her. Sylvie had destroyed them all. Claire jerked the Walther from her pocket. They faced each other, guns drawn.

"Ah, you truly are a *Resistánt*, aren't you? *Liberté* and vengeance and all that," Sylvie said.

Engines roared on the street below. Doors slammed and voices shouted.

"They must really want you." Sylvie sneered. "I knew you were gutter trash the moment I saw you. So common. My husband had you. The Englishman? How many others?"

"Better that than a whore to the Reich's gold."

Sylvie's mouth twisted. She fired. A bullet burned Claire's cheek as her ears recorded the shot. The Walther jerked twice in her hands. Two bullets tore through Sylvie's chest. The fabric of Sylvie's silk robe turned dark as blood flowed through her grasping fingers. She gaped at Claire, her face slack with shock, then crumpled to the floor.

Claire examined the body slumped at her feet. Sylvie's face was blank; the set of the mouth and the discreet canniness in the eyes bled out on the rug. All that deception and greed wrapped up in silk and jewels. Paid for with the lives of everyone Claire loved. The heat inside Claire died away to ashes.

Heavy boots thumped up the stairs. Claire rushed for the door. She yanked the handle open. A rifle butt met her in the face. The world went black.

# Chapter 13

## THE CHOICE

11, rue des Saussaies, Paris. August 19, 1944.

Soft keening woke her. Her eyes closed, she didn't move, trying to find her way back to the formless darkness and a reprieve from pain.

A sob echoed from across the cell. The girl was crying again. Maybe she was still crying. Claire couldn't be sure; she had drifted between sleep and unconsciousness throughout the night. Her breath hissed between clenched teeth as she pushed herself to a seated position against the cold stone wall. Hot pokers pierced her ribs and stomach. After a couple of tries, she managed to open her eyes. In the dim morning light, the girl was just a lump across the cell.

A faint rumble caught her ears. "Did you hear that?" She winced as she sat forward, her ear cocked to the high barred window. "Quiet," she said, toward the sobbing.

Weeks had passed, how many she couldn't say. She had heard

a shout one morning, when was it? It had come from down the hall, amidst the noise of a scuffle. *The Allies are coming for you, boche. They are coming soon.* It ended in a scream, then silence. Claire prayed it was true. She turned to scratch a line on the wall behind her to mark the day, to track it. *Soon.* Her hand dropped as she stared at the wall, to the right of the words she had read countless times, *I, Francois, die tomorrow.* Her nine short vertical scratches.

She knew that wasn't right. The days she spent in a cold sweat, waiting to be taken to the room where they bored into her mind, scouring for details about the Resistance. She forced herself to forget the names she knew they wanted. Beatings, countless days lost afterward when she didn't know where she was, her mind floating above the pain. Two or three trips to a makeshift doctor's exam room one floor up. A ten-by-ten room with a long metal table, a room to shower next door. A female Nazi stripped her down. Claire was pushed beneath a cold shower, then on the table to be poked and prodded. She watched as the doctor made notes, then she was handed another dress and led back to her cell.

Marks on the stone meant nothing. Time meant nothing. Life only existed out there. The rumbling in the distance stopped. Now there was only silence.

The door swung open and banged against the wall. Claire squinted at the light spilling in from the hall.

"*Sie kommen.*" The guard yanked her to her feet.

Claire bit her lip against the pain as he pushed her into the hallway. The walls spun around her as she was marched down a long corridor. She stifled a shudder as they passed the heavy locked doors, the occupants the source of the moans that drifted the hallways at night.

The guard was in a black mood today. Not bothering to speak, he ground the point of his baton into her ribs every few steps. At the end of the hall, he shoved her down another dim corridor.

More doors lined this hallway. The scent of antiseptic, urine and fear assailed her. She nearly stumbled as she realized she was going back to the interrogation room. Her stomach churned like it was being stirred from within. She felt cold sweat run down her back, her dress stuck against her crawling skin.

Two guards dragged a man out of a door. His head lolled to the side at an impossible angle. She turned to catch a glimpse as he passed. Though battered and swollen, his face was long and thin, his mustache neatly trimmed. He wore a worn wool suit, a conservative cut. His hands, dangling in front of him, were covered in ink. He was a backroom academic, she thought, who got caught publishing what he knew. And then died for it. His guards glanced at Claire, their faces bored.

She swallowed the bile rising in her throat, pulled her shoulders back and straightened. She wasn't going to leave rue des Saussaies alive, but she would hold out another day.

The guard opened a door and pushed Claire inside. A bathtub sat against the wall with a wooden slat on top. She shook with relief when she saw the water had been drained, the lungripping choke of repeated drowning had been escaped today. She was shoved toward the single wooden chair in the middle of the room. A lightbulb dangled from a broken ceramic fixture over the chair, creating a spotlight, as if a show was about to begin. Claire knew it was.

An officer stood in the far corner, his face hidden. He barked a short dismissive command. The guard turned on his heel and left. The officer stepped under the bulb's glare, gripped the back of the chair.

"May I offer you a seat, Claire," von Richter said, in English.

The rush of adrenaline kept Claire upright. She pursed her lips, sighed and arranged the expression of a bored socialite. "Hello, Alby darling. I think I'll stand, if you don't mind."

"Suit yourself." He examined her, a disappointed shake of his head. "I must say I am displeased with how things have turned out."

"No more than I, I'm sure."

He let go of the chair. "But you only have yourself to blame."

Her body tensed, her fists closed. He likely ordered Madame's death. He certainly arranged for Grey to die. Claire imagined leaping at him, ripping that smirk off his face. But she could hardly stand and wasn't about to fall at this bastard's feet. She shrugged.

Von Richter walked around the chair and planted himself in front of her. "Really, Claire. You are no more of a patriot than I. Your naive rebellion accomplished nothing."

"Really?" Claire raised an eyebrow. The Oberons and girls had left Paris and were, she prayed, safe. Sylvie was dead.

"The Kapitän's woman, you mean?" He snorted. "The shrew's usefulness had come to an end. You saved us the trouble of dealing with her. We have moved on to fry the bigger fish." He smiled at the term. "I believe you know the Comte de Vogüé?"

Claire kept the bored expression. Inside she crumbled a little bit more. Hold on another day.

The room rattled. It was an explosion outside. The lightbulb swung lazily overhead; the spotlight traced a circle over the worn, bloodstained bricks. The same noise she had heard earlier. She smiled. "The Allies are coming."

"Just overeager patriots with very misplaced expectations. All the little poodles out there who have decided to nip at our heels are, in fact, going to face a harsh reality."

"I don't believe you."

"It doesn't matter." His face was inches from hers. "I own you either way."

Claire stared into his eyes. His perpetual sneer was gone, his gaze serious.

He pressed her against the wall. "End the charade, tell me what you know. Paris is my oyster. It can belong to us, together." He stroked her cheek, let his fingers trail down over her breasts to her hip. "You and I are the same. I've known that since we met in New York. We are cut from the same cloth. When others fall, we succeed, we thrive."

Claire sighed. She was so damn tired of loss and despair. What he offered was all she had once dreamed of. Claire traced the scar on his chin with her fingertips. Couldn't she go back to being that woman, if it meant the pain stopped, if it meant a real life?

He dug his fingers into her hip, a triumphant smirk on his lips. "You're a smart woman, Claire."

She closed her eyes, let herself sag against him. "Smart," she whispered.

Sylvie's cold eyes flashed in her mind. That was what smart was, the price of accepting his offer.

"We were the same when we met," Claire said, her gaze met his. "But not anymore. All that Paris offers someone like you means nothing to me. Its beauty can't touch you, Alby. You aren't thriving. You aren't even really alive." Claire pulled herself up straight, chin up. "I chose to live. Truly. Deeply. At least for a while."

Von Richter's palm cracked across her face. Her head snapped back against the wall and she slid to the floor. He closed his fist, cocked it to strike. Claire stared up at him, her face expressionless.

The muscles in his jaw bulged as he bit out his reply. "You chose to die, my darling. We are making a strong statement about traitors. At noon, the guards are going to line up all the criminals here and shoot them." He tapped the crystal of his gold watch. "You have about two hours left. Try to savor the beauty of your Paris with Lieutenant Holtz."

He shouted out a command. The door opened and he stalked from the room.

Claire let out a long breath. It felt like she'd been holding it for months. She rested a hand on the cold floor. There it was, then. Not so surprising, after all.

A soldier walked in flanked by two guards. He took up half the room with his wide shoulders and barrel chest; the guards at his side barely reached his shoulder badge. It held the designation of a specialist. It wasn't hard to guess his specialty.

The guards lifted Claire and pushed her into the chair, binding her arms and legs. He dismissed them with a word, his meaty hands carefully rolled up each sleeve, showing corded arms crisscrossed in scars. He looked up and spoke in grammar-school French. "I am Lieutenant Holtz. You must have made Sturmbann-führer von Richter angry. He made a special request for you."

Claire glared at him, straightened against the chair. "I won't talk."

He rolled his massive shoulders and clenched his fists. "I won't listen."

Claire's heart charged like a frightened horse.

The first blow lifted the front feet of the chair off the ground and snapped her head back. Bright lights splintered inside her closed eyes. Her mind curled inside her like fingers closing into a fist as the chair teetered back. She floated away, only dimly aware of her body shaking from the blows, the chair sliding backward across the uneven bricks. She puzzled at the howling of the wind in the distance. Is winter here already? As the velvety gloom closed in around her, she recognized the cries of her own raw voice.

It was the scent of roses that called her. She felt the cool breeze on her neck, the sun warming her face. She opened her eyes. Behind her was pain; in front of her was spring. Grey's garden bloomed around her in deep greens and soft pastels. The apple tree showered blossoms onto the statue. Palest pink roses tumbled down a stone wall.

Claire flinched, the garden shook. Darkness grabbed her and she was in the room. Holz stood over her, blocking out the bulb's light. The taste of blood filled her mouth. The smell of his sweat burned her nose. She saw his fist driving at her stomach.

Claire gasped, then blinked in the sunshine. She perched on the garden bench, sucking in deep breaths of fresh air, hands gripping the cool stone. Deep inside she heard the wind, stark fingers clawed at her, dragging her back into the blackness. She fought against it and savored the sweet tea scent of the roses, the rich deep smell of fresh earth.

"They look good, don't they?"

Grey slid onto the bench next to her. He pointed a finger at the roses. "I knew they just needed to feel a lovely spring day." Grey smiled, his eyes dancing. He wore the clothes she'd last seen him in. His worn leather boots were coated in farmyard mud. "That is all anything really needs."

Claire tried to reach out to touch his face. She felt a flash of cold. In the darkness, her lungs burned, a part of her knew she was being slowly choked. Lights popped behind her eyes. Her body screamed for air.

Claire dropped her hand to her side, kept her eyes on Grey. She shuddered in the sun. "Thank you, Grey, for this place."

"This isn't real."

A pulse of pain stole Claire's breath. She fought as pain's icy fingers tried to draw her back in. The burning lightened. Holz had let go. Far away, her lungs sucked in great gulps of air. "You're here," she said.

The firmness of his voice nearly startled her. "No. Neither of us is here. Not yet." He cupped her face with a hand, enunciating every word. "You have to fight, Claire."

Claire looked down at his hand, covered in smudges. She couldn't tell if it was bruises or dirt. She closed her eyes, concentrated on the smell, the sound, the feeling, etched it in her soul.

Pain welcomed her. Claire slid forward as her hands and ankles were cut loose. She half caught herself as she hit the brick floor. There were more voices than before. A hand with bloodied knuckles grabbed the front of her dress and pulled her to her feet. She squinted against the glare of the bulb's light. Her eyes focused on Holz.

He bared his teeth in a grin, the tendons in his neck bulged out around his collar. "Too bad. You should thank your luck. They are going to shoot you early."

The words sank in as she was pushed from the room and carried down another long corridor. She heard scattered rifle shots in the distance as she stumbled down stairs and through a doorway in the courtyard.

Claire shielded her eyes against the sun's blinding glare. The guard behind her shoved and she fell into a crowd of prisoners. Hands, bloodied and torn, helped her to her feet. Head swimming, she examined her surroundings. Soldiers pressed the battered prisoners up against the doorway. Before them stretched an open brick courtyard. Over the high stone walls, she saw rooftops and light blue sky. On the far wall, a line of heavy posts had been sunk into the ground; the stone behind them pockmarked by bullets.

"*Américaine*," a gruff voice rumbled.

Claire stumbled toward the edge of the crowd. Jacques leaned against the wall, his side covered in bloody bandages up his chest.

Tears crept into her eyes as she faced him. "Jacques." She reached out a hand.

He looked her over, didn't reply.

Claire dropped her hand, stung. She didn't know what to say. To apologize, to confess, to explain. Nothing seemed adequate.

He grimaced from pain as he examined her. "You look like *merde*."

Claire looked down; her aching hands unconsciously smoothed the soiled wrinkles of her dress. With shaking fingers she traced a trail of blood up her front, gingerly felt her raw neck, touched her swollen mouth and nose, both sticky with blood. She felt an oozing over a cheekbone where the gash from Sophie's bullet had been reopened. Her hand came away crimson.

She looked back at Jacques. The slightest smile tugged at the edges of her mouth. "You are not so beautiful yourself."

He nodded, chewed his lip, as if he were taking that into account.

The guard shouted a command, pointed his rifle toward the man standing in front of Jacques. "You there. First group." He counted off. Jacques was seven, Claire eight. "Come now." A group of soldiers broke them off from the rest.

Claire flinched, lost her breath, as she put her arm around Jacques.

He muttered as they staggered forward. "We join an esteemed group of patriots, today. The next group is going to have to load our bodies onto trucks before they die."

Her body screamed at the effort. She forced her legs to stay straight, her eyes on Jacques. She couldn't look at the posts or she might collapse. "Aren't we lucky to go first and miss that chore."

Jacques chuckled, it sounded more like a groan. "Grey was right about you."

"No, Jacques. I don't think he was."

Jacques pulled her to stop. "You did what you had to do. It's nobody's fault except for those *boche* we didn't get Grey out."

A guard barked out a command and shoved his rifle barrel into Claire's side.

Claire stumbled, hauling Jacques forward. She spoke under her breath, her voice shaking. "Did you see him die?"

Jacques turned to her, his face twisted. "Grey?"

"He was chased down by their dogs. Shot."

He shook his head. "No. I was hit. And he was at my side, the last I remember. I'm sorry."

Jacques was yanked from her arms. They were lined up each in front of a post. Claire closed her eyes as a soldier looped a rope around her, pulling her tight against the wood. She looked down the line of people. Young and old. Male and female. Aristocrats, schoolteachers, communists, farmers. The firing squad leveled their rifles.

Claire trained her gaze on the sky. Felt the sun on her skin, the breeze in her hair.

A deafening blast wrenched the pole from the earth and tossed Claire with it to the ground, knocking the air from her lungs. She laid there dazed, then took in a breath of air and dirt. The rope came free beneath the pole. Claire rolled over, gasping and choking.

She opened her eyes to the courtyard filled with smoke,

bodies and running legs. Stone and wood splinters rained down; their impact kicked up dirt whorls in front of her face. Claire looked down. She wasn't shot. She wasn't dead. A crater the size of a car smoldered between her and what was moments ago the firing squad.

A pair of legs ran up to her; a hand pulled her to her feet. A French policeman, half his uniform cast off, pointed toward a large opening in the wall to the street. Her ears ringing from the blast, it took a moment before Claire realized he was yelling.

Fighters swarmed in through the opening, a mix of men in business suits, worker's coveralls, and uniforms of firefighters and police. They carried pistols, rifles and machine guns. The citizens of Paris were around her. By God—Paris was armed and fighting.

Claire grabbed the policeman's arm and pulled. Crouching, they picked their way over bodies and rubble. She dropped to her knees in front of Jacques' crumpled form and rolled him over onto his back. Leaning over his face, she felt his warm breath on her cheek. A bullet tore into the dirt next to her hand.

Jacques' eyelids fluttered. Claire grabbed his arm, the policeman grabbed the other. Dragging Jacques between them, they fell over a splintered post and around a sprawled man tangled in slack rope. His dead eyes stared toward the sky. They joined another freed prisoner crouched behind a fallen wall. Claire watched the bullets kick away bits of stone and dirt around them.

The policeman pointed back toward the prison. He spoke, she heard nothing. He tapped his white armband. The letters FFI and a double-hashed cross of Lorraine were drawn in black. He squeezed her arm, his eyes shining. *Vive la France,* he mouthed, then rushed back toward the center of the courtyard.

Claire watched him join a group of fighters charging through the yard toward the doors. They were met by a surge of Waffen-SS with machine guns that poured from the building. The German soldiers mowed down everything standing then advanced toward the opening, toward Claire and Jacques.

She felt Jacques stir next to her. She clenched his hand. "Jacques, we have to go. Now."

His eyes slowly focused on her as she tucked her shoulder under his arm. Her legs nearly buckled. "Help me, Jacques. I can't do this alone."

He gritted his teeth and pushed himself off the ground. She straightened and hefted him to his feet. Bullets whipped by them as they stumbled toward the opening.

More fighters scrambled by, coming, going, bloodied or whole, their faces were ferocious, shining. Half dragging Jacques, Claire stumbled onto the sidewalk. Bodies littered the cobbles. Overhead, rifle barrels jutted from windows.

They crouched behind a burning car. "We have to run," Claire said.

He nodded, his face ashen. Arm in arm, crouched low, they half ran, half staggered up the street. An explosion roared behind them, and they turned onto rue de Surène.

Claire saw the imposing Greek temple façade of L'Eglise de la Madeleine ahead. "The church."

He nodded, but his face was pinched and his shirt dark with blood. She took a step, his legs gave out, and they toppled to the ground. Gunfire sputtered as a truck gunned up the street toward them. FFI and the cross of Lorraine were drawn on the side of the truck in white paint.

"Jacques." Claire pulled at his arm. She heard the brakes scrape as the truck stopped next to them.

"Hurry," a low voice called. A teenaged boy leapt out, followed by a woman holding a rifle. *"Forces Françaises de l'Intérieur,"* the boy shouted out as he muscled Jacques into the back of the truck.

Claire crawled up behind them and the engine gunned. Two blocks later, when the truck roared past a burning German tank, Claire understood. The Allies were coming.


The FFI dropped them off a few blocks from the fighting. They holed up in a Resistance apartment in Saint-Germain. Jacques on the bed, Claire on the floor; she collapsed into sleep where she fell. A day and a night later, she woke to find him delirious and burning with fever; the bullet in his side infected. Amidst sporadic gunfire, patrolling tanks and milling crowds, Claire staggered with Jacques through the wounded into the Hospital Hôtel-Dieu next to Notre Dame Cathedral.

Two medics took Jacques; a nurse led Claire to a women's room. After her cheek was flushed with a mixture that made her spit out farmyard curses, she was bandaged and ordered to rest.

When the nurse left the room, Claire located a small shaving mirror. Her face was swollen; a heavy bandage covered her cheek. Her eyes were puffy and black, her nose inflated, the bridge bruised. She stared for a few minutes, ran her hands lightly over the bandage on her cheek, imagining the wound below. Well, she decided, living had to count for something.

Tossing the mirror on the bed, Claire went looking for Jacques. She found him in a large room lined with wounded; his cot was next to a window overlooking the cathedral. Unconscious and fevered, he mumbled under his breath. The bullet had been taken out, the nurse told Claire, but he was very weak. Too weak, her tired eyes said. The nurse gave him an injection for the pain, muttered a prayer and moved on to the next cot. Claire curled up on the windowsill next to his bed. If he was going to die that night, he shouldn't die alone. If he lived, well, even better she was nearby.

The next morning Claire woke with the warmth of the sun heating the bandage on her cheek. Stretching stiff muscles, she stood, a hand unconsciously feeling her face. She winced as she touched her cheek. But her nose, at least, felt less swollen.

"Claire?"

Laurent strode toward her, a white band on his arm and a pistol holstered on his hip. He enveloped her in a hug that made her gasp.

He released her, a smile radiating from his stubbled face. "I heard this morning about a wounded fighter and American woman who escaped rue de Saussaies. I had to know if it was you."

She slid her hands into his. "It's so good to see you. Your apartment—I didn't know what had happened to you."

"I am like a fox, *ma chérie*. They could not catch me." His smile faded as he turned to face Jacques. "How is he?"

"He was shot, the wound is infected. The doctors don't know if—"

"They don't know him," Laurent said. "He is too stubborn to die. Not now."

Her gaze on Laurent's holstered pistol, Claire spoke. "What is happening out there?"

"War," he said simply. "War has finally come to Paris. And we fight."

"Tell me, Laurent. Please."

"*Forces Françaises de l'Intérieur*." He pointed to his white armband with FFI and the blue cross of Lorraine. "The Allies are battling their way toward us. We fight the Nazis and Milice however we can. We are outgunned, but we continue to capture weapons and trucks, and are building barricades across the city. My unit controls the Sorbonne. We will hold out."

Jacques called out feverishly, then his voice trailed away.

Laurent kneeled, resting a hand above the bandages that swathed Jacques' side. "I can't get word to Odette. She and Gerard are hidden in the countryside."

"Odette is alive?"

He nodded. "The morning Jacques and his group were to attack Grey's transport, my apartment was raided. I escaped through the window, down a drainpipe. I found Odette and warned her we had been betrayed. She took Gerard and fled. It was too late to contact Jacques. We couldn't get to you, to warn you."

"You knew I was not a traitor?" Relief flooded Claire.

His mouth tightened. "Sylvie called me just a few minutes before the raid. My dear wife worked to keep me on the phone as they came inside the building."

Claire reached for Laurent's hand. "She's dead. I shot her."

His mouth twisted like he wanted to spit. "I would have killed her myself if I got there first. She deserved much worse than a bullet." A deep breath and his voice softened. "And Grey?"

"They said he was killed with Kinsel."

His eyes crimped shut. A long moment and he sighed. "I'd heard about Kinsel. But Thomas. *Merde.* I am sorry. I had hoped for better news."

Gunfire rumbled in the distance.

Laurent embraced her gently. "I'm sorry I asked you to come to Paris."

She smiled, though the effort made her eyes tear. "I regret many things. But not coming here. Never that."

He nodded, his eyes on hers. "If we survive this, my offer still remains, *ma chérie.*"

A soft kiss on his sculpted face. She shook her head.

Laurent kissed her unbandaged cheek then released her. He lit the stub of a Gauloises. A shrug and he moved toward the door.

"*Au revoir*, Laurent. Be safe," Claire said.

"*D'accord.*" A lopsided smile as he took a drag on his cigarette. "If you change your mind, *ma chérie*, you have my address. After, of course, we clear out the scum." He stepped out the door.

Claire watched through the window until Laurent disappeared at the corner. Jacques moaned behind her. She wrung out a wet towel and pressed it against his burning forehead. "Odette and Gerard need you, Jacques. Fight."

Three nights later, a sliver of a moon hung in the sky over Notre Dame Cathedral. From her seat on the window ledge, Claire could see the outline of the northern tower and a few of the grand dame's buttresses. The Seine was a shining black ribbon, churning alone in its banks, beyond the deserted cathedral's square. The flicker of burning cigarettes and the flash of the moonlight on metal on the street corner were the only hints of the armed men guarding the barricade below.

Jacques fought for his life, cursing and muttering at her side. On the street below, Paris did the same. Claire watched men in Resistance armbands walk openly with captured Nazi guns in their hands. They tore up the street below, building a barricade with bricks, felled trees, twisted metal and stone.

She hadn't seen skirmishes, yet, but she'd heard them. Resistance fighters defended barricades across the city; battled with German tanks and heavy arms burrowed in strongholds. A dangerous time for the soldiers without uniform, as they had become known. She'd seen them carried in, patched up when possible and laid out on cots down the line.

Jacques stirred and sighed. It was only in the last few hours he slept, though every once in a while he thrashed and moaned. The room beyond him was filled with wounded. In the dim light, men huddled together, their heads close over Resistance papers, published openly now, or around a crackling radio reporting the BBC.

Outside, Paris was quiet, as if the city itself held its breath. Beyond distant gunfire, the only sound was the faint splash of the Seine testing its banks, a muffled cough from the fighters below. It was just before midnight and balmy. Claire welcomed the faint breeze that cooled her aching cheek.

The radio crackled. *Allied troops moving into Paris. Heavy fighting in the region around Rambouillent and d'Arpajon. General von Choltitz threatens to attack the public buildings with heavy arms. It was reported Hitler ordered the maximum destruction of Paris.* That was no surprise. She'd seen the smoke rise from Grand Palais as it burned yesterday.

Claire watched the moon trail across the sky, rubbed her burning eyes. She was ungodly tired but couldn't sleep. No one in Paris would sleep that night. Everyone knew Allied soldiers were in the outskirts of Paris. And that Choltitz might destroy the city before they arrived. Claire shut her eyes and breathed deep.

Across the square, the bells of nearby Notre Dame began to ring. Another church took up the refrain and then another. A cascade of sound washed over her. Her body vibrated to the chimes. She gripped the ledge to keep from floating away.

"Claire?" Jacques spoke.

Claire turned to him. His eyes were shining in the dimness.

"Yes, Jacques?"

"What is it? What has happened?" His first coherent words in days.

The bells of the churches could mean only one thing.

"The Allies are here, *mon ami*. Paris is free."

The faintest smile touched his face then he let out a long breath, closed his eyes and fell asleep.

Tears flowed down her cheeks as Claire gazed back out at that radiant moon, her arms pressed tight about her. As she watched, darkness faded and the first rays of sun lit the stones of Notre Dame. The church doors were flung open as a crowd filled the courtyard. A liberated Paris came to give thanks.

The Seine flowed on.

# Chapter 14

## LA VIE EN FLEURS

La Vie en Fleurs. May 15, 1945.

La Vie en Fleurs was as alive as the Parisian streets that bustled outside. Plaster walls pockmarked from the spray of bullets were adorned once again with lines of blossoms. Claire, in a simple grey skirt and white shirt, sleeves rolled up to her elbows, stared up at two framed photos on the scarred wall next to the counter. The images were small, intimate, in plain silver frames. As she studied the photos, she unconsciously slid her fingers over the thin white scar lining one cheekbone. She frowned as she caught the gesture, and dropped her hand to her side.

Madam Palain smiled from the left frame. She was seated, her hands in a rare restful place on her lap.

"*Bonjour*, Madame," Claire said, under her breath.

On the right, the photo of a simple garden; the jagged rip visible from the Nazi raid that killed Madame. She reached up her hand and stroked the edge of the frame.

The newly replaced door squeaked open behind her. Claire turned to see Jacques and Gerard enter. Jacques nodded hello, still holding his side a bit gingerly. Dusky hair curling about his ears, Gerard beamed at Claire with his mother's laughing eyes as he wrestled with a bundle that threatened to overcome him.

Claire hid a smile. She had met him eight months ago, the day of the liberation, when he and Odette had found Jacques in the hospital. Since then, Gerard had sprouted.

"Good day, Miss Badeau," he said, in English, carefully enunciating the words she knew he had practiced with his father all the way down the block.

"Good day, Gerard."

Gerard plopped his package down on the counter; a large blue cloth rolled tightly and secured with twine. Proudly, with great show, he unrolled the fabric across the entire counter. In fine script, it read *La Vie en Fleurs*. Below was an exquisitely painted pale pink rose, so real it seemed to have its own fragrance.

Claire shut her eyes, her head bowed. The shop was hers. The full weight of the gift that was this simple shop made her heart stir in her chest. Now Jacques, who had become so dear to her, had scrounged a bolt of heavy canvas and created a new sign with the men and ink at his liberated presses.

Gerard watched her, concern written in the wrinkles on his forehead. This was not the reaction he was looking for. "Is something not correct?"

"I love it, Gerard." She swallowed the emotion and regained the poise Madame Palain would have expected. She smiled at him fully. "It is beautiful. *Magnifique*." She looked up to Jacques, tears sparkling in the corners of her eyes.

He nodded, hands in pockets. He indicated the bare framework outside the door with the tilt of his head. "I will come back with helpers tomorrow. Odette too. We will hang it, if you approve."

"I approve. I wholeheartedly approve. *Merci*, Jacques." She kissed Gerard then Jacques on both cheeks. "You are good men."

Gerard beamed.

Jacques shrugged. "Good." He reached for Gerard's shoulder. Side by side, father and son stepped from the shop and disappeared down the street.

Claire turned back toward the sign. She ran her fingers over the fabric, memorizing the feel of the rough texture of these threads, burning the image in her mind. Proof that Madame's elegance and beauty lived. And someday, somehow, Marta and Anna would be welcomed back to Claire's arms by this symbol.

The door creaked again behind her. A husky male voice said, "Have you any lilies today, Madame?"

Claire froze, breath stranded in her chest. Strength left her; she clenched the countertop. Her elbow glanced off a pail of flowers that clattered to the floor. She held perfectly still, afraid any movement would break the spell and end this dream she'd woken from so often.

"Claire, look at me."

Reaching for a rose, she cupped the blossom under her nose. She spoke toward the photo in front of her. "There was a marble statue of a woman in that garden. The roses there smelled of honeyed tea and sunshine. And their color was—"

"Like the pearl of a shell," he said.

The air was freed from her chest and she breathed deeply.

"Did they please you?" he said.

Claire snapped the cane from the rose and tucked it behind an ear. A smile played at her lips. "The garden pleased me very much." She turned.

Thomas Grey sagged against the doorway. His heavy beard covered a face made sharp by hunger. His clothes hung in tatters; a dirty bandage covered a knee.

Claire held the smile on her face. She moved to the door and faced him. "You're late," she said.

"The road was long." His slate eyes penetrated her soul. He pulled her against him. "But I'm here now."

She exhaled his name as she softened into the warmth of his embrace. This dream was real. Her damn Englishman must have walked all the way from a liberated German prison. She gazed into his face, ran her fingers over his cheek. "The first thing you're going to do, Grey, is shave that beard."

He smiled. "No. That is the second thing." With two fingers, he tilted her chin up.

With both hands, she grabbed the man she loved and pressed her lips against his.

# READERS GUIDE FOR

*The Last Time I Saw Paris*

# DISCUSSION QUESTIONS

1. Claire's most prized possession when she left Manhattan was her Cartier jewelry. How did the importance of this jewelry change for Claire throughout the book? Do you have a piece of jewelry that holds meaning for you? Is its worth measured in monetary or sentimental value? Have you inherited an antique or valued treasure from a loved one that carries important memories for you?

2. The book described the elaborate floral displays that Claire and Madame Palain created for the Nazi-occupied hotels, as well as flowers tumbling down a garden wall and a bucketful of simple stems that Claire loved. What did these different flowers represent in the book? What did they mean personally to Claire? Do certain flowers hold meaning for you?

3. Did you find elegance in Claire's expensive Manhattan brownstone, or in the simple wine and bread dinners Madame Palain served, or both? Give other examples of elegance from the book. How do these different examples each represent elegance? In today's society, do you believe people define elegance based on material things, or is it an attitude and an approach to life?

4. Madame Palain told Claire that "elegance is in the details" the first night they met. How did Madame demonstrate this belief in her daily life and in the way she ran La Vie en Fleurs? Did Claire embrace this way of living? How did it shape her actions and beliefs? Have you had a similar mentor in your life?

5. Claire went to Paris to change her life. She did, but was it in the way she'd expected? Where in the story did you see a dramatic shift in Claire? How many people were touched by Claire's character growth? Have you had an experience that transformed your life in unexpected ways?

6. How did Claire's changing perception of Grey mirror her own shifting consciousness? Did your opinion of Grey change along with Claire's? How was he different from other men whom Claire had known? What was it about Grey that drew her in?

7. Why did Claire assume that the Oberons would take in Marta and Anna? Would you risk your safety and open your home to children in peril?

8. Odette pressed Claire to put her life in danger to save the Resistance leader Kinsel, and justified it by saying, "We are in a war, Claire. I must sometimes act as a soldier, not as a friend." Could you ask your friends to risk their lives in an attempt to fight a great evil?

9. What historical details of life under the Occupation were most surprising or moving for you? In what ways do novels provide a means for understanding history?